"Keep mo   ld
still   ...ose lasers!"

Dolby and Jessop were down. Fitzgerald was down. Three other gun walkers scattered across the Temple platform all were struggling with overwhelming numbers of hostile machines. The Marines had now given up trying to provide cover for the walkers; there were so many alien fliers that every Marine had more than enough to handle just with the alien machines swarming around him or her.

A flight of black machines tumbled through the air toward Courtland. He snapped off three bursts from his laser, burning down two of the attackers but missing the third, which swooped suddenly, then slammed into his chest and exploded in a splash of black goo.

The impact staggered him back a step. He waved his arms wildly, uselessly, trying to shake or scrape off the liquid adhering to him.

Warning, his armor told him, the voice hammering in his head. *Suit integrity compromised.*

He was bleeding atmosphere. The good news was that the atmospheric pressure at Heimdall's surface was less than half of what he carried in his armor, so his air mix was leaking out, and the ammonia and sulfur dioxide outside was not leaking in . . . yet.

By Ian Douglas

Star Carrier
EARTH STRIKE
CENTER OF GRAVITY
SINGULARITY
DEEP SPACE
DARK MATTER
DEEP TIME
DARK MIND

Andromedan Dark
ALTERED STARSCAPE

Star Corpsman
BLOODSTAR
ABYSS DEEP

The Galactic Marines Saga

The Heritage Trilogy
SEMPER MARS
LUNA MARINE
EUROPA STRIKE

The Legacy Trilogy
STAR CORPS
BATTLESPACE
STAR MARINES

The Inheritance Trilogy
STAR STRIKE
GALACTIC CORPS
SEMPER HUMAN

DARK MIND
STAR CARRIER
BOOK SEVEN

IAN DOUGLAS

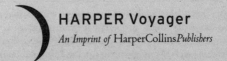

HARPER Voyager
An Imprint of HarperCollins Publishers

HarperCollins
PUBLISHERS
Since 1817

DARK MIND. Copyright © 2017 by William H. Keith, Jr. All rights reserved. Printed in the United States of America. No part of this book may be used or reproduced in any manner whatsoever without written permission except in the case of brief quotations embodied in critical articles and reviews. For information, address HarperCollins Publishers, 195 Broadway, New York, NY 10007.

First Harper Voyager mass market printing: May 2017

ISBN 978-0-06-236898-0

Cover art by Gregory Bridges

Harper Voyager and) are trademarks of HCP LLC.

17 18 19 20 21   QGM   10 9 8 7 6 5 4 3 2 1

*For Deb and for Brea,
bright lights illuminating my
dark mind . . .*

DARK MIND

Prologue

It thought of itself as the "Consciousness," and it was very, *very* old.

How old? There was no way even it could know the answer. Billions of years, certainly, as certain organic life-forms measured time . . . and possibly older than that, through an eternity spanning trillions of years and several universes.

Only recently had the Consciousness emerged into this latest, young and vital, universe, following the tug of gravity across the dimensional walls of the metaverse, seeking the siren call of Mind. Indeed, advanced intelligence had left numerous traces in this universe, and the Consciousness intended to find and merge with that intelligence . . . and assimilate it, molding it to the Consciousness's will.

They'd entered the universe through a patently artificial gateway, a rapidly spinning rosette of black holes that served to tear multiple openings through the fabric of spacetime. That artifact itself was the most obvious evidence of local advanced intelligence and technology. The so-called Black Rosette was located at the center of what appeared to be a giant globular cluster of 10 million stars, but which in fact was the stripped-bare core of an ancient dwarf galaxy cannibalized by the far larger barred spiral known to a few of its inhabitants as the Milky Way.

A billion years before, that dwarf galaxy had been oc-cupied by a consortium of intelligent species, a bewildering mélange of alien bioforms. Most had . . . passed on—there was no better term for it—entering their version of a techno-logical singularity that had removed them from the mundane cosmos of matter. A few individuals had remained behind, survivors of the singularity that had reorganized themselves into a new civilization calling itself *Sh'daar*.

Kapteyn's Star had been just one of the suns of that lost dwarf galaxy, the home of a race that had chosen to convert itself wholly into digital format, uploading some trillions of individuals into a series of circuits and metallic channels etched into the very rocks of their home planet. There, they passed the eons at a vastly reduced pace, experiencing a second or two for every thousand years that flickered past on the outside, in effect traveling swiftly into their own remote future. Within their digitized universe, they experienced near-infinite virtual vistas, worlds far richer, more detailed, and more rewarding than anything the natural cosmos had to offer.

Or they had until now.

Because the Consciousness was enveloping their entire cosmos, slowing a part of itself down to more easily inter-face with the digitized natives, and beginning the process of relentlessly drawing them into itself.

Chapter One

Approaching Heimdall
Kapteyn's Star
0840 hours, GMT

A quintet of sleek, Pan-European KRG-17 fighters fell past
Bifrost, the sullen, red-banded, ice-ringed gas giant named
for the Rainbow Bridge of Norse mythology. Kapitanleutnant
Martin Schmidt tried boosting the gain on the incoming
scanner data, but the receivers were already maxed out.
Static crackled and hissed in his in-head feed. Radiation
effects from the planet? Possibly. Bifrost's field storms could
get pretty bad sometimes.

But Schmidt was pretty sure that the interference was
from something else. Not the random, natural hiss of
charged particles accelerated by Bifrost's magnetic fields,
but something *deliberate* . . .

"*Adler Eins Zu* Himmelschloss," he called. "*Adler Eins
Zu* Himmelschloss."

Static shrieked in reply.

He tried again. "Eagle One to Skycastle, Eagle One to
Skycastle, please respond. What is the tacsit at Heimdall
now? We're blind out here. Over."

Still nothing.

"What's going on back there, Kapitanleutnant?" Leutnant Andrea Weidman, Eagle Five, called to him. "Ghosts?"

Ghosts referred to the unidentified craft that had been appearing in this star system for the past month or so, first singly, but then in ever-increasing numbers. That they were spacecraft of some sort was undeniable . . . as was the fact that they represented an unimaginably advanced technology. All attempts to make direct contact with them, however, had failed so far.

"Possibly," Schmidt replied. "That's what we're here to find out. Adler Flight . . . shift to stealth mode and arm weapons."

The black surfaces of the fighters rippled and shifted as the craft adjusted their outer shapes from winged to teardrops. While not optically invisible, their hull nanoflage absorbed nearly every whisper of incoming radar pulse, every bit of light. Their environmental systems shifted into high gear as well, storing the rising internal heat rather than radiating it as infrared.

The five Pan-European fighters skimmed in beneath Bifrost's system of broad, brilliant rings, each circle eerily reminiscent of the concentric grooves of an old-fashioned twentieth-century phonograph record. Kapteyn's Star, the local red dwarf sun, was a bright red pinpoint shining through the rings, wan and distant. Three and a half astronomical units from the giant Bifrost, it contributed little light and less heat.

"*Himmelschloss*," Schmidt called. "Do you copy?" The message was tight beamed and shielded, but Schmidt knew they would have to switch to radio silence soon.

Still nothing but static. *Himmelschloss*—"Sky Castle"— was the Pan-European monitor that had brought them here, to the Kapteyn's system, now following a few hundred thousand kilometers astern and shielded from Heimdall by the vast, sullen, and storm-shrouded bulk of Bifrost.

"If it's ghosts, Marty," Leutnant Herko Dobrindt said over a private com channel, "we're not going to be able to fight them. Not with these antiques."

Schmidt had just been thinking the same thing. KRG-17 Raschadler fighters were a Franco-German design twenty years out of date and well past their prime. They were still effective space fighters—not as maneuverable as the latest North-American fighters, perhaps, but they carried the latest weaponry. Schmidt doubted, however, that even the most up-to-date KRG-40 Raumsturm would have a chance against those . . .

Whatever those flying *things* were.

An orange crescent appeared ahead, beyond the broad plane of the giant's rings. The world was Heimdall, a moon the size of Earth, kept warm this far from its diminutive sun by tidal stresses with Bifrost. The surface temperature now was a few degrees below the freezing point of water. At one time, though, a billion years earlier—so the scientists had told them—Heimdall had been warm and Earthlike. . . .

Heimdall, like its sun, was *very* old.

"I'm picking up ghosts up there," Leutnant Gerd Heller announced. "My God, *look* at them all!"

"Record everything," Schmidt ordered. "*Everything.*"

Bifrost appeared to be enveloped in a hazy, filmy light. At first, Schmidt assumed he was seeing the world's aurorae—Heimdall's strong magnetic field interacted wildly with the charged-particle storms swirling about Bifrost, and the world's icy surface often was bathed in a lambent, electric glow—but a closer inspection showed that the glow was in fact caused by planet-girdling clouds: a haze of apparent dust motes at this range, but consisting of some trillions of discrete objects ranging from millimeters wide up to several meters or more across.

And . . . there was something more. A *lot* more. Dimly glimpsed, so faint that Schmidt thought that they must be a trick of his eyes, there were shapes. Huge shapes dwarfing Heimdall, dwarfing even massive Bifrost. From his vantage point, skimming along beneath Bifrost's rings, it seemed as though Heimdall was suspended within a vast and far-flung web so insubstantial, so gossamer, it was difficult to tell if it was there at all.

And yet it was filling all of space ahead. . . .

"Kapteyn Orbital," Dobrindt said. "It's *gone*!"

"We knew that," Schmidt said.

"I mean there's not even any trace of wreckage or debris. Something that big couldn't have just vanished!"

No it couldn't, Schmidt thought.

The station, a Stanford Torus housing more than 12,000 people, had been the principal base of the Kapteyn's research colony, a Confederation facility built to study the enigmatic ruins on the moon it circled. Shortly after the arrival of the Rosette Aliens, six months ago, the base had been destroyed.

Or, at least, it had disappeared without a trace. Some still hoped it had simply been transported elsewhere.

Which meant the hopes for finding 12,000 Confederation personnel alive were fast dwindling. The heavy monitor *Himmelschloss* had deployed to the Kapteyn system to investigate.

Schmidt's fighter jolted hard. His instrumentation showed what seemed to be ripples in spacetime, moving out from Bifrost. The static was growing stronger, too, as were the bizarre light effects, like aurorae engulfing all five fighters.

"Okay, Adler Flight," Schmidt called. "This is where we part company. Maintain radio silence. I'll . . . see you on the other side."

"Good luck, Marty," Dobrindt replied. "Going silent . . ."

The other four craft, nearly invisible even at this range, slowed, then dropped astern. Schmidt's fighter continued drifting ahead, everything shut down now except for life support—struggling to control the fast-rising onboard temperatures—and passive scanners. No one knew if the alien ghosts would be able to track the fighter or not . . . or if they even cared. They appeared to be completely aloof to mere humans. But better safe than sorry.

Schmidt had volunteered for this, back on board the *Himmelschloss* during their voyage out from Earth. His chances seemed a lot more slender now, here in the blackness as he hurtled toward the light-enveloped moon ahead. The vast bulk of Bifrost dwindled steadily astern and he emerged from the shadow of the rings into wan, reddish starlight. His sensors could no longer detect the other Adler Flight ships, lost now in the radiation and magnetic fields encompassing the gas giant.

Schmidt felt alone—alone and lost in a way he'd never felt before, even when his partner of twenty-some years had left him a decade before.

I'm not going to survive this, he thought. But it was no good dwelling on *that*. Quickly, he thoughtclicked a series of in-head icons, compressing all of the data he'd acquired so far into a nanosecond burst. Fired in a tightly coherent pulse aft toward the other fighters, it might not be picked up or recognized by the aliens ahead . . . but who the hell knew what they were capable of?

Time passed. Once each minute he dispatched another nanosecond radio burst. All the while, the array of shifting lights, the weirdly interpenetrating patterns, the mysterious structures and shapes all spread until they filled the sky, with the moon at the glowing heart of the phenomenon. He magnified the images, zeroing in on the activity both on the surface and in orbit. Kapteyn Orbital was definitely gone; not even dust remained.

Twelve thousand researchers . . .

As the dark and silent teardrop streaked across Heimdall's sky, the ghosts appeared to have taken notice. Schmidt was first aware of them as a stream of glowing motes rising from Heimdall's surface, and he thought of a cloud of fireflies.

And there was something else moving out from the light-shrouded moon. Something *huge*.

"Mein Gott . . ."

He heard the cloud pelting the external hull of his ship, felt the jolt as they began dissolving the nanomatrix.

He was screaming as the hull of his fighter began to dissolve under the swarming assault.

26 October 2425
Watergate Convention Center
Washington, D.C.
United States of North America
2015 hours, EST

The diplomatic reception was in full swing, with well over a thousand physical attendees standing about in knots of color and formal dress. Others were present virtually, their holographs showing only a faint translucency to give away the fact that they were projections of people from all across the Earth and, in many cases, beyond.

Alexander Koenig, the current president of the United States of North America, stood in the Watergate's Grand Gallery, with its floor-to-ceiling curving transparencies slowly rotating through 360 degrees across D.C.'s nighttime cityscape. The Grand Gallery, enclosed beneath a stadium-sized dome nearly two hundred meters across atop its forty-story tower, was crowded with dignitaries—politicians and military officers and social luminaries from around the globe, all of them gathered here to celebrate the simultaneous reopenings of the Pan-European embassy here in D.C. and the USNA embassy in Geneva.

And—just incidentally—they were here to celebrate, at long last, *peace*.

The throng dazzled in light and color. Costumes ran from military full-dress to liquid light to quite fashionable nudity, and nearly everything in between. President Koenig wore a rather severe two-tone gray dress jumpsuit with the presidential seal just above the formidable holographic display of his military ribbons. His personal security detail hovered close by, anonymous in black utilities and opaque helmets. Koenig smiled as those helmets turned to closely scan Generalleutnant Reinhardt Kurz as he approached the president. Evidently the Pan-European officer passed inspection, because the detail let him through.

Here it comes, Koenig thought, turning to greet the general.

"Mr. President?" the man said quietly, speaking English rather than through a translator. "I have . . . news."

A half dozen journalism drones hovered nearby, reminding Koenig that he needed to watch what he said. Hell, he *always* needed to watch what he said . . . one of the antiperks of political office. But something about Kurz's tone made it clear this *needed* to be private.

Koenig glanced again at the drones, then thoughtclicked a command on his in-head security menu. It alerted his security team that the current conversation was private and that nearby news drones should be blocked.

President Koenig already knew most of what the Pan-European general was about to tell him, but when it came to international politics, it always paid to be careful about revealing the depth of your knowledge . . . and the accuracy of your intelligence sources.

A confirmation light winked within Koenig's consciousness, and he nodded at Kurz. "Go ahead, General. We can speak freely." The drones were already drifting in different directions, looking for other news bytes to record and transmit. He knew that a few would be hovering at the periphery of his awareness, though, watching for the opportunity to record again.

Kurz drew a deep breath. "Sir, Kapteyn Orbital has been destroyed. We have confirmation. There is nothing left."

"Son of a bitch," Alexander Koenig replied with what he hoped was a convincing demeanor.

"At least ten Americans were on the orbital when it . . . vanished," Kurz added. "Their names have been turned over to your state department."

"Thank you, General."

The man shrugged. "The least we could do, Mr. President."

They stood side by side for a moment next to that part of the gallery's transparency that currently overlooked the Potomac River and Roosevelt Island to the west. Beyond, a few lights showed against the darkness . . . but much of Northern Virginia was still mangrove swamp and tidal flat. Until quite recently, the entire D.C. area had been a part of the Periphery, lost to the United States of North America, most of it flooded by rising sea levels centuries earlier. Soon, though, nanufactories would be working out there, growing new arcologies from rock, dirt, and rubble.

Once a historic hotel complex on the river's eastern shore, the original Watergate buildings had long ago collapsed into the rising tidewaters that had swallowed much of old Washington. That had been during the dark years of the late twenty-first century, when large stretches of the coastline of the then United States had been abandoned to rising sea levels and storm surges. Under Koenig's administration, however, many of the abandoned Periphery regions at last were being reclaimed. The D.C. mangrove swamps had been drained, and a system of levees and dams had been constructed to keep the city from flooding again. The buildings were being regrown by nanotechnic agents programmed and released into the freshly revealed mud and rubble. Where possible, historic monuments and edifices had been renovated or rebuilt, but most of the buildings were completely new, as was the city's overall layout. Whereas the original city had been drafted by Pierre Charles L'Enfant, the new plans were the work of Frank Lloyd WrAIght, an artificial intelligence already well known for its restoration work on Columbus and in the Manhatt Ruins.

As the dome smoothly rotated, new vistas slid into view. To the south and east, the newly regrown city soared and gleamed, ablaze with lights. The population was still small—fewer than fifty thousand had moved back so far— but Koenig was more than confident that it would grow.

If anything, there are always those who want to be as close to the seat of power as possible. He shook his head at the cynical thought.

No—this is a time for optimism. A fresh start after the Confederation destroyed Columbus.

We're literally creating a new world for ourselves. He looked over at the man who should have been his enemy, and prayed his hopes were not unfounded.

After a long moment's silence, Kurz looked uncomfortable. "Herr Koenig, I'm not sure how to ask this . . ."

Koenig had been fully briefed on the Confederation request. Since the massive cyber attack on the Genevan computer net months before, there were precious few Pan-European secrets to which USNA Intelligence was not privy. "I find the direct approach is generally the best," he said. "Whatever it is, I'm sure I won't find it *that* shocking."

"It is our intent," Kurz said carefully in his heavily accented English, "as soon as may be possible, to send an expeditionary force to Kapteyn's Star. We want to look for survivors, if any. We have reason to believe there may be such . . . on one of the inner planets of that system."

"I see. . . ."

"We also want to establish contact, if possible, with the Rosette entity."

Koenig smiled. His advisors had told him that when the Pan-Europeans made their request, he should put them off, that he should say that he would have to consult with his staff.

"Of course, Herr Generalleutnant," he said instead. "We would be most happy to take part in your expedition."

Kurz looked at him sharply. "I'm surprised, Mr. President. Gratified, but surprised! Don't you need time to discuss this with your people?"

"Not really. I was already aware of much of what you've just told me. I'm sure you knew this already."

"Well . . . yes. . . ."

"And you will also know that I don't like games, political or otherwise."

"I can appreciate that, Mr. President."

Koenig glanced around, then pulled up a finder map on his in-head feed. He was in this throng somewhere . . . *ah! There.*

Gene? Koenig called, sending a mind-to-mind call. *Get your ass over here.*

On my way, Mr. President.

Admiral Gene Armitage separated himself from a small mob on the other side of the huge room and made his way toward Koenig and the Pan-European general. Head of Koenig's Joint Chiefs of Staff, Armitage was his principle military advisor and the man who would get the ball rolling in the planning of any new military operation.

"Herr Generalleutnant Kurz . . . head of the Joint Chiefs of Staff, Admiral Armitage."

"We've met. Admiral? Good to see you again."

"At Geneva last month," Armitage said, nodding. "A pleasure, sir."

"We're going to be sending a contingent with the Confederation to Kapteyn's Star, Gene," Koenig said. "Discuss the details with the general, please, and then make it happen."

"Aye, aye, sir." Armitage's expression remained shuttered, giving nothing away. Which was commendable, seeing as he'd been the one who'd recommended that Koenig not give the Pan-Europeans an immediate answer.

The biggest problem, Koenig thought, turning away and leaving the two to talk in private, was the fact that few in the USNA military trusted the Confederation yet. The Brits were okay; their defection during the war had accelerated the enemy's disintegration as a coherent fighting force. The Russians, the North Indians . . . the USNA could work with them well enough. But the Pan-European destruction of the city of Columbus the previous year had left the USNA with a bitter taste in its mouth, and the fact that the attack apparently had been carried out by renegade elements within the Genevan government hadn't made the bitterness easier to swallow. There were still many within the former United States who wanted to charge the Pan-Europeans, in particular, with crimes against Humankind.

That, Koenig reflected, *isn't going to happen.* Behind-the-scenes deals cut by his administration before the public negotiations had guaranteed the Confederation immunity from war-crimes charges if they would agree to the peace talks. That strategy had been strongly urged by Konstantin, the powerful AI located on the far side of Earth's moon. The USNA was clearly winning the short, sharp war against the Confederation, but they *needed* peace. They were in very nearly as bad a shape as the Pan-Europeans—worse, possibly, after major strikes against American soil—and with the looming advance of the Rosette Aliens, Humankind needed to come together in a united front *now*, at any cost.

Koenig didn't always understand Konstantin's logic, but this time it seemed straightforward enough. It still wasn't clear that the Rosette Aliens were overtly hostile, but they had destroyed human ships and bases, and Humanity had to come before any petty geopolitical squabbles.

Especially since, in the background, the alien Sh'daar, time-travelers from the remote past determined to block Humankind from its approaching technological singularity, always lurked in ambiguous mystery. They'd agreed to a cease-fire with Earth . . . but for how long? Their long-term motives were still far from clear.

Shadowed by his four bodyguards, Koenig made his way to one of several bars set up on the slowly turning floor. They moved with a fluidity that betrayed an essential fact: presidential security was now handled by *robots*—in this case a quartet of human-looking androgynoids far faster, stronger, and smarter than anything modeled in flesh and blood. They could pass as human—very nearly—though the deliberate blurring of sexual characteristics gave them a touch of the uncanny valley effect. Like the old United States Secret Service, you could tell what they were by the fact that they constantly watched *everyone* in the room except for the person they were protecting.

Koenig ordered a jovian from the robotic bartender. One of the security bots closely scanned both the botender and the mirror-polished globe it passed to Koenig.

"Thank you," he told the robot behind the bar. He glanced at the security machine and cocked an eyebrow. "Don't worry. He's one of yours."

"Of course, Mr. President." But it completed the scan anyway. Security was a lot tighter—and far more automated— since the Confederation strike at Columbus.

He wasn't actually complaining.

"Mr. President," a woman said behind him. "I haven't had a chance to welcome you to D.C."

Koenig turned to face Shay Ashton—*Governor* Shay Ashton, rather. Once a crack USNA fighter pilot, she'd retired to her home in the D.C. swamps, and ended up leading the defense of the ruins when the Confederation tried to claim some of the supposedly abandoned USNA Peripheries for themselves. She'd gone on to become interim governor for D.C. as it was formally reintegrated into the country, and was titular head of the territory now. There were rumors that she was going to be drafted as one of the D.C. representatives to

Congress in next year's general elections, though she'd not formally announced her candidacy.

He smiled. "Madam Governor! It's good to see you again."

Two of the security 'bots were giving her a *very* close scan, checking for weapons, explosives imbedded inside her body, anything at all that might be a threat. It was hard to see how she could be hiding much; she was wearing a holographic sheath of rippling light in greens and blues, with the image of the Freedom's Star ribbon glowing above her left breast. An animated tattoo of a bright green butterfly opened and closed its wings on her right cheek.

She smiled sweetly at one of the machines. "See anything you like?"

"That *will* do," Koenig told the machines. "I've known Ms. Ashton for a long time, and if she's a threat, it's definitely to the other guys."

"Of course, Mr. President," one said . . . but, as with the 'botender, they completed their scans.

"Machines," she said. "I still can't get used to them."

"I know what you mean." Actually, Koenig thought, he *didn't* know what she meant . . . he couldn't. Shay had been born and raised outside of the USNA's comfortable high-tech envelope, where the locals had to farm and fish just to survive. She'd been exposed to advanced technologies, certainly—from robots to genetic prostheses to AIs to nano-grown cerebral implants during her tour in the Navy—but you really needed to have grown up with that sort of technology to get the most out of it. Even now, millions of people all over the country were *Prims*—Primitives—people brought up in the Peripheries, who didn't have access to high tech, or who'd come to it later in life.

The expression on her face told him she'd caught him out, and he shrugged. "Sorry."

"That's okay, Mr. President." Her right forefinger touched her forehead, her left the center of her sternum. "You're almost there . . . thirty centimeters."

He chuckled and nodded. Thirty centimeters—the distance

between brain and heart. Knowing a fact was different from *feeling* it.

Koenig lightly squeezed the silver jovian in his hand, and the upper surface slid open, releasing a small, thick puff of greenish vapor. He inhaled, savoring the tingling rush channeling directly to his brain.

He smiled at Ashton. "Can I get you one of these? They're good. . . ."

"Thank you, no, sir. Prims have trouble with brainstimming, sometimes. I can't handle the stuff."

The green vapor consisted of clouds of nanotechnic units programmed to send waves of pleasurable sensations directly into the brain via the olfactory bulb. The sense of smell was the only one hardwired directly into the brain rather than through a long chain of nerves, and brainstimming gave a socially acceptable euphoric buzz without impairment or hangover. People who'd received their cerebral implants later in life, however, rather than as small children, could have trouble handling the storm of sensations, could become disoriented and might even pass out. Such, apparently, was the case with Ashton.

"Of course."

"So we're really going to go through with this, Mr. President? The new alliance, I mean?"

"It seems to be the best course for us. For Earth, I mean."

"That's assuming we can trust *them*." She nodded toward General Kurz, now deep in conversation with Armitage.

"Well . . . yes."

"Some of them wanted to sell out to the Sh'daar."

"I know, Ms. Ashton. And to a certain extent I agree with you. But Konstantin says that we won't survive another encounter with the Sh'daar if we don't work with the Confederation . . . to say nothing of the Rosette Aliens. We unite, or we die. There is no middle ground."

"Konstantin." She made a face. "Another machine."

"A machine some thousands of times smarter—and millions of times faster—than any organic brain we've encountered."

"That's right. Smarter . . . *so* smart we don't know what it's really thinking. Or what it's planning for the future."

He smiled. "Perhaps you'd like to sit in on the next meeting of my cabinet."

She looked shocked. "Oh! I'm sorry! I didn't mean to suggest—"

He waved her down with a gentle motion of his hand. "No, no. That's okay. I was just picturing you tearing into Sarah Taylor, the secretary of Alien Affairs. Or Phil Caldwell. It might be fun."

A USNA admiral in full dress approached them. "Do you need rescuing, Mr. President?"

"Not at all, Vince. The governor was just . . . questioning certain affairs of state."

Admiral Vincent Lodge smiled at Ashton. "Maybe you need rescuing from him."

"I think I can watch out for myself, Admiral."

"Good." He looked at Koenig, and some of the humor drained from his eyes. "Mr. President? A word, if I could?"

"Excuse us, Ms. Ashton?"

"Of course."

They stepped aside. "What's the word?"

"Mr. President . . . we've received a Konstantin intercept."

Konstantin had intelligence connections imbedded all over Earth, and well beyond. Admiral Lodge was the head of Naval Intelligence . . . the *human* head, rather, since in many ways Konstantin was the true director of cyberintelligence. A Konstantin intercept meant that the AI had picked up a transmission of some sort, probably classified and definitely important, if Lodge was interrupting him at a party about it.

"Tell me."

"A courier just dropped into normal space outside Neptune's orbit and began transmitting. It's from Kapteyn's Star . . . from the Pan-European monitor they sent out there."

"Go on. . . ." Couriers were high-speed interstellar vessels, usually unmanned, that could make the Alcubierre passage between the stars much more quickly than larger, more cumbersome star-faring vessels. They wouldn't have sent one if things weren't critical.

"We know what the Rosettes are doing at Heimdall, sir. They're waking up the Kapteyns. They *may* be assimilating them."

"The Kapteyns!"

"Yes, sir. And for the first time, we just may have gotten a glimpse of what the Rosette Aliens are after."

"You have my full attention," Koenig told him.

Chapter Two

TC/USNA CVS America
Admiral's Quarters
0425 hours, TFT

Admiral Trevor "Sandy" Gray came awake in a darkened and empty room. Still half asleep, he clawed at the loneliness of the bed next to him. Where was she? It took him several moments to figure out where *he* was . . . his quarters on board the star carrier *America.*

Damn . . . it had seemed so *real.*

But then, it always did.

His partner in the erotincounter had been named Marie; for once she had *not* been Angela, his one-time wife, nor had it been his most recent partner, Laurie Taggart, who'd recently been transferred to the *Lexington.* Marie was pure fiction, created by one of *America*'s AIs, and very loosely based on a current sex-drama actress who went by the same name. In-head dramas, fed into people's internal hardware, were a major source of both entertainment and education. Gray preferred interacting with electronic avatars to address his sexual desires, rather than sexbots. The sensations and results were the same . . . but the relationship played out inside his brain rather than in his bed. So when the illusion dissolved, so did the partner. The feeling was precisely that of waking from a dream, and that could leave you feeling empty and a bit lonely.

"Admiral Gray," a voice whispered in his head. "Admiral Gray. Sorry to wake you, sir, but we're coming up on the triggah."

"Very well," he replied. The voice was that of Eric Conrad, his new chief of staff. He sat up, stretched, and thoughtclicked the room's lights to higher brightness.

Unlike a dream, the memory of his encounter with Marie hadn't evaporated upon waking. The memories were written directly to his long-term memory; the human brain literally could not tell the difference between what happened within its network of neurons and what happened in the real world outside.

Somehow, that made the loneliness worse.

But it kept his sex life uncomplicated.

"How close are we?" he asked over the open circuit. He took a small capsule from a dispenser and slapped it against his naked chest. The nanomaterial turned semi-liquid with the shock and flowed swiftly over his body from neck to feet, solidifying in seconds into closely woven shipboard utilities, complete with rank tabs at the throat.

"Twelve thousand kilometers, sir," Conrad replied. "We have battlespace drones out, and they're sending back some good images."

"Let me see."

The bulkheads of Gray's quarters went dark, then lit once more, showing a projection of surrounding deep space. Stars hung suspended in velvet blackness. Directly ahead, robot drones sent back images of the TRGA—the Texaghu Resch Gravitational Anomaly. From this aspect, it appeared to be a perfect circle, gray-rimmed, surrounded by a faint haze of dust and debris.

Properly known either as the Sh'daar Node or as the TRGA, the circle was in fact a hollow cylinder of ultra-dense matter twelve kilometers long and one wide, rotating about its long axis at close to the speed of light. Located over 200 light years from Sol, the TRGA—a "triggah" in Navy slang—was clearly artificial and clearly the product of an unimaginably advanced technology. There were others besides this one—tens of thousands, perhaps, scattered across the galaxy as a kind of spacetime transportation net. At one time, Earth Military Intelligence had believed that the alien Sh'daar had created the things; certainly they *used* them, as did human star-farers. But no one knew for sure who'd actually built them in the first place, not even the information traders known to Humankind as the Agletsch. They worked, and for most people, that was enough.

This particular TRGA was the first one discovered by human explorers, thanks to information provided by Agletsch traders. Just recently, it had been given the code name Tipler, after twentieth-century physicist Frank Tipler, who had worked out the math for Tipler cylinders—titanic, ultra-massive constructs that might allow travel across vast areas of space and even through time. The TRGAs had turned out to be related to Tipler cylinders, but inside out—rotating hollow tubes rather than solid cylinders—though the effect was the same.

Perhaps a dozen TRGAs were now known, all of them named for important physicists and cosmologists from the past few centuries.

Sometimes Gray wondered if they'd have been surprised to see their theories become reality.

The circle slowly grew larger in size as *America* and her supporting fleet approached it. That cylinder, Gray knew, held the mass of a sun the size of Sol somehow compressed into something akin to neutron-star material. Inside that fast-rotating shell, Jupiter-sized masses rotated and counter-rotated, stretching local spacetime beyond the breaking point. That haze was in part dust, and in part gravitational distortions in the space within which the triggah was imbedded.

And they were about to go through it.

"Fighter status?" Gray asked.

"VFA-96 is ready for launch, Admiral," the staff officer replied. "Awaiting your word."

"Launch fighters," Gray replied. "And go to battle stations."

He was already on his way up to *America*'s bridge as the battle-station alarms sounded.

Lieutenant Donald Gregory
VFA-96, Black Demons
0440 hours, TFT

"It's too fucking *early* . . ." Don Gregory complained.

"There ain't no day or night in space, youngster," squadron commander Luther Mackey replied. "So no early or late. Deal with it."

"It's zero-dark thirty, Skipper," Gregory replied, "and I haven't had my damned coffee yet."

"My . . . *grouchy* first thing, aren't we?" Lieutenant Gerald Ruxton said over the tactical channel, laughing. He sounded . . . *awake*, Gregory thought. Disgustingly so. Bright, cheerful, and—considering the fact that he'd been in the ship's bar drinking with him about five hours ago and was, therefore, just as short on sleep as he—

"Ice it down, people," Mackey said. "Bearing one-seven-five by minus three-one. We're clear for launch. *America* has cut thrust and is drifting. Fifteen hundred kps . . ."

Gregory's SG-420 Starblade fighter absorbed the incoming data even as the skipper relayed it in staccato fashion. He could feel the flick and trickle of numbers downloading through his skull.

"Launch in three . . ." Mackey said, ". . . and two . . . and one . . . *release*!"

Mounted in the outer deck of the second rotating hab module, the fighters of Black Demon squadron, VFA-96, began sliding down their launch tubes, impelled by a half G's worth of centrifugal force. Gregory was third in the queue; together with Lieutenant Bruce Caswell's Starblade, he dropped into blackness, slowly drifting clear of the shadow of *America*'s massive forward shield cap, then rotated to align his craft parallel to the far larger star carrier. The ship was an immense mushroom shape nearly a kilometer long, its shield cap a hemispherical water reservoir four hundred meters across. Ahead, partially obscured by the shield cap, the perfect circle of the TRGA—blurred by rotation and by a fiercely twisted spacetime—hung suspended in the distance.

The remaining VFA-96 fighters dropped from the hab-module flight decks and took up station with the others, a flight of twelve Starblades already morphing into high-velocity teardrop shapes. Even in the vacuum of space, streamline counted for ships moving at close to *c*.

"*America* CIC, this is Point One," Commander Mackey said. "Handing off from PriFly. All Demons clear of the ship and formed up."

"Copy, Point One," a voice replied from *America*'s Combat Information Center. "Primary Flight Control confirms handoff to CIC. You are clear for maneuver. You may proceed."

"Okay, boys and girls," Commander Mackey said, addressing the squadron. "Time to thread the needle. Initiate program."

Tightly knotted gravitational singularities winked on just ahead of each fighter, dragging it forward as it flickered in and out of existence at thousands of times per second, accelerations building rapidly as *America* slid past the fighters, then began dwindling astern.

VFA-96 had drawn the short straw on this mission . . . flying point, leading *America* and her battle group into and through the huge, fast-spinning cylinder ahead. Gregory wasn't entirely sure he was ready for this. Three months ago—or 12 million years in the future, depending on how one counted things—his fighter had been damaged, and he'd briefly been marooned on the surface of Invictus, a frigid rogue planet wandering the darkness beyond the galaxy's rim. He'd lost his legs . . . and he'd lost Meg Connor, a woman he'd loved very much. The legs had grown back and he'd learned how to walk again.

But other wounds were a hell of a lot harder to heal.

He had to force his mind away from thoughts of Meg. The Black Demons had lost a lot of pilots at Invictus, and very, very nearly lost him as well.

Maybe, he thought, it would have been better if he *had* died.

TC/USNA CVS America
Flag Bridge
0451 hours, TFT

"Admiral on the bridge!"

"As you were." The call and the response were largely for tradition's sake, since coming to attention in zero-gravity was more or less pointless. In any case, it would have been bad form to interrupt personnel working their consoles and links.

Gray entered the flag bridge, giving a gentle tug to pull himself along one of the tethers that roped different parts of the double bridge complex together. Parts of *America*, those within the rotating hab module section—mostly personnel quarters and the fighter launch and recovery decks—were under spin gravity, but the flag bridge and the adjacent ship's bridge were located in a tower rising from the star carrier's spine forward of the hab sections, and therefore in zero-gravity.

He positioned himself in the command chair and let it tighten around his hips. He placed the palms of his hands on the seat's contact plates, letting them connect with his neural interfaces. Datastreams began flowing through his brain, opening in-head windows and connecting him with the AIs running both the ship and the fleet.

There was no up or down in zero-gravity, of course, but from the vantage point of his command chair, he was looking down onto the ship's bridge forward. The flag bridge formed a kind of gallery overlooking the ship's command center, where he could see about a dozen officers and enlisted personnel working at their consoles under the watchful electronic gaze of Captain Sara Gutierrez. On the large curving bulkhead above the bridge entrance glowed a projection of surrounding space, with the blurred and perfectly circular ring of the TRGA centered dead ahead. Dwindling numbers to the side gave range and closing velocity.

"The Demons are going in," the voice of Captain Connie Fletcher reported, whispering in his mind. She was *America*'s CAG, the officer commanding the various fighter and auxiliary squadrons.

"Tell them—" Gray stopped. He'd been about to wish them "Godspeed," but that would have been less than appropriate. There were those who thought the TRGAs had indeed been constructed, eons in the past, by godlike aliens, and the White Covenant discouraged statements that might be interpreted as religious sentiment by others. "Tell them good luck," he said. It might be a bit lame, but it shouldn't offend anyone.

"Aye, aye, Admiral."

Icons marking the twelve fighters of the Black Demon squadron appeared ahead, superimposed against the TRGA's maw. And then . . .

They were gone.

Let me see the fleet disposition, Gray thought. The viewpoint pulled back from *America*, so that the star carrier could be seen from the side, in the distance. Other icons appeared strung out behind her. *America* was followed in line-ahead by the railgun cruiser *Leland* . . . and behind her came the alien *Nameless*. The Glothr, it seemed, didn't name their ships, so the humans on the expedition had given the vessel a name of their own.

Not quite the most clever name, but there you go.

The fighters were through. Data began pulsing back . . . but broken and static-blasted. Communication across a TRGA gateway tended to be intermittent and unsatisfactory, requiring precisely positioned transmitters and receivers, as well as a great deal of power. There was enough to tell the battle group that the fighters had emerged, however, and apparently in the right epoch.

Fighter pilots called it threading a needle . . . a reasonable analogy. The interior opening of a TRGA was only slightly wider than *America* was long. Still, within the TRGA's lumen, minute variations in position and velocity created wildly different pathways through space and time. The ships of the *America* battlegroup were following a carefully programmed and precise series of maneuvers as they entered the spinning maw.

"Okay, people," Gray said softly. "All nav systems to automatic. Let the AIs take us through."

The warning was unnecessary—more nervous reassurance than anything else. All twelve ships of Battlegroup *America* were being guided now by powerful artificial intelligences. Presumably, the additional ship, the Glothr *Nameless*, was guided by non-organic systems as well. Jellyware brains—even enhanced by AI implants—simply weren't precise enough or fast enough to handle the variables successfully.

For a breathless moment, the star carrier *America* hung on the verge between one space and another . . .

And then unimaginable energies seized the vessel and dragged her in.

Lieutenant Donald Gregory
VFA-96, Black Demons
0458 hours, TFT

Something strange was happening to time.

The TRGA was just twelve kilometers long. Traveling at some twenty kilometers per second relative to the alien portal, Gregory should have been through and out the other side in six tenths of a second. It *felt*, however, like ten or fifteen seconds, an impossibly long time as the blurred gray walls of the tube swept past his ship, terrifyingly close. The slightest miscalculation, and his fighter would be shredded by contact with a wall moving at very close to *c*. Even if he didn't hit that motion-smeared surface, a ten-meter drift in any direction would put him on a different spacetime trajectory . . . and the gods alone knew where he would emerge . . . or when.

Then the TRGA's walls vanished, whisked away at twenty kps as Gregory's fighter emerged into open space once more.

And this new space was extraordinarily crowded with stars.

"My God . . ." he breathed, awed. The White Covenant be damned—the phrase spoke to how he felt.

The Black Demons were moving through the central core of the N'gai star cluster . . . a dwarf galaxy just above the plane of the vast spiral of the Milky Way. The TRGA had brought them back through time as well—some 876 million years into their remote past. In this epoch, life on Earth was still confined to the planet's seas and was only just then discovering that sex and genetic diversity were useful evolutionary ideas.

"Commsat away," Mackey reported. The satellite would drift in front of the TRGA, recording all transmissions from the squadron. If anything happened to the fighters . . .

Gregory didn't allow himself to think about that.

"We have company, Skipper," he reported. "Bearing zero-zero-five, minus two-one, range three-zero-thousand."

"Got it, Greg. All Demons, shift vector to zero-zero-five, minus two-one. Do not, repeat do *not* initiate hostilities. . . ."

"Not unless they freakin' initiate first," Kemper added.

Gregory could see the oncoming alien spacecraft in an in-head display, picked up by his fighter's long-range optics, magnified, and streamed through the craft's AI into his brain. They were small, each only a meter or two across. They were oddly shaped, too, no two precisely alike. Perhaps more important, there were *thousands* of them in an onrushing cloud.

It did *not* look like a friendly reception.

And something was happening within that cloud of oncoming craft. Individual ships were shifting position, orienting themselves as though seeking to form some larger structure. Within his in-head, Gregory could see a series of rings, perfectly aligned, each a hundred meters across.

What the hell?

"Thirty thousand kilometers," Mackey said. "We need to get . . ."

"*Hostile incoming!*" Lieutenant Cynthia DeHaviland yelled over the tactical link. "*The bastards are firing!*"

A tightly coherent bolt of energy struck Demon Six—Lieutenant Voight's ship. The Starblade vanished in a cloud of white-hot vapor.

"Spread out and accelerate!" Mackey ordered. "Boost to five hundred Gs! Let's close the gap!"

The eleven surviving Starblades hurtled forward, their velocity increasing by five kilometers per second each second. Ahead, the cloud of silvery objects continued to maneuver to organize themselves into a huge, indistinct structure. The energy bolt had come through those closely aligned rings, and Gregory's long-range scanners were picking up evidence of a fast-building magnetic charge. . . .

"It's a particle cannon!" Gregory called as understanding gelled. "It's a fucking particle cannon five kilometers long!"

Gregory wondered how they'd managed that trick . . . positioning individual spacecraft like pieces in a titanic puzzle, not touching physically, but apparently locked together by magnetic fields. He didn't ponder it long, as another pulse of energy surged up through the floating rings and very nearly caught Lieutenant Caswell, who rolled clear just as the particle beam passed him.

"Spread out, damn it, *spread out*!" Mackey yelled. "Arm Kraits! Target the dense parts of that cloud!"

Each Starblade carried a full complement of thirty-two VG-92 Krait space-to-space missiles, plus six of the massive and more powerful VG-120 Boomslangs. Still, a total of 418 missiles of varying megatonnage, Gregory reflected, was not going to go very far against that vast and sprawling cloud of diminutive alien vessels.

They would have to make each shot count, taking great care in the placement of every one. By targeting the thickest regions of the alien spacecraft cloud, they would do the greatest damage with what they had available.

I hope.

"Fire!"

Gregory had already brought up the control icons for the first two Kraits in his magazine, arming both and setting their yields to a hundred megatons each. The alien swarm dominated an in-head window; he zoomed in on a dense knot of alien vessels—a part of the open architecture of the enemy's immense particle cannon.

"Demon Four, Fox One!" he yelled over the tactical channel. "Times two!"

Centuries before, the "Fox One" radio call had meant the launch of a heat-seeking missile. Now it meant a smart missile like the VG-92 Krait shipkiller, the Boomslang, or Fer-de-lance . . . or even the old-style Kraits, the VG-10s, now obsolete and considerably less competent in the AI department.

With his first two shots away, Gregory shifted targets, brought two more Kraits on-line, and loosed them. His primary tactical display was fast becoming an indecipherable mass of fighters, targets, and the slow-crawling contrails of missiles in flight. All of those contrails swung wide before angling in toward their targets, and their onboard AIs had them dodging and twisting to avoid enemy defensive fire, turning the display into a classic dogfighting furball. His AI could read the mess though, even if he could not. This allowed Gregory to focus his attention on maneuvering the Starblade, trying to make sure that it was *not* where the enemy was aiming and firing that colossal particle gun—

—which fired again, an instant before the first Kraits detonated in silent blossoms of white light . . . one blast after another, each equivalent to 100 million tons of high explosive.

Alien ships evaporated by the hundreds, caught between multiple expanding plasma shock waves and by intense bursts of electromagnetic radiation. Nuclear explosions were not nearly as effective in the vacuum of space as they were in an atmosphere, but the temperature at the heart of each blast still measured well over 100 million degrees. As the fireballs faded, large bubbles of emptiness were stitched through the mass of silvery spacecraft. The precise organization of the particle gun appeared to have been disrupted, and the remaining fragments of the structure dissolved as alien spacecraft abandoned it.

And then the Black Demon squadron was plunging into and through the cloud of alien ships. Bright red icons representing hostile targets filled his mental view of the surrounding starscape. Gregory lined up on one of the enemy vessels and triggered his own particle weapon, sending a beam lancing into the target with savage precision.

"Watch it, Demon Four!" Caswell called to him. "You've got two coming in fast behind you!"

"I see 'em."

The two aliens dropped onto his six and he flipped his Starblade end-for-end, hurtling backward as he snapped off one burst of electric flame . . . then a second . . . and a third when one target evaded his attack and kept coming.

The Sh'daar fighters had teeth. A beam caught Demon Eight, a newbie named Romero, and ripped her Starblade in half. Gregory eased his fighter around and teamed with DeHaviland. Together, they vaporized another Sh'daar fighter.

"How long before the fleet comes through?" DeHaviland called.

"Don't know, Cyn," Gregory replied. "Should be any sec now!"

That wasn't just wishful thinking. Fighter point missions weren't intended to engage in long-term combat. The point element was intended to go ahead of the battlegroup, find out if there were hostiles ahead, and engage them until the capitals could come up.

At least, that was the idea. If the battlegroup didn't come through the TRGA for some reason, there were ten Starblade fighters on this side that would be in a hell of a lonely situation.

Worse would be what might happen if the local hostiles proved too much for the entire battlegroup. *America* and her escorts might die here, on this side of the TRGA.

Which would mean that the Black Demons would have already been wiped out.

An enemy particle beam grazed his fighter, jolting him hard. He bit off a curse and tumbled to the left, targeting an alien that was close—*too* close—and firing. The plasma shock wave jolted him a second time.

Damn it, don't think so much. Angry, now, at allowing himself to be distracted, he focused all of his attention on the data cascading through his link with his fighter.

Where was Cyn? He'd lost her in that last exchange. An icon flashed against the dazzling backdrop of thickly crowded stars. *There* . . .

The red icons were drawing together, bunching up.

What the hell are they up to?

TC/USNA CVS America
Flag Bridge
N'gai Cluster, T.$_{-0.876gy}$
0503 hours, TFT

Emergence. . . .

Gray leaned forward in his seat, staring out into the throng of crowded suns, the central heart of a pocket-sized galaxy almost 900 million years lost in the remote past. At least, that was the idea. . . .

"*America*," he said, addressing the ship's primary AI. "Do you have the temp-nav data yet?"

"Affirmative, Admiral," the ship's mind replied, more as a mental impression than as distinct words. "Downloading to Navigation now."

"Got it, Admiral," Commander Victor Blakeslee reported. "Looks like we're spot-on. According to the positions of three hundred key stars, we're at the same spot as the Koenig Expedition, plus twenty years."

"Looks like we arrived after the armistice," Commander Dean Mallory, the chief tactical officer, observed. "*That's* good news."

Gray nodded. "Time seems to pass at the same rate on both sides of a triggah," he said. "Good to know. I wasn't looking forward to fighting the sons of bitches again."

"No, *sir.*"

Around *America*, other ships of Task Force 1 were gathering as, in ones and twos and threes, they slipped through from their present to their remote past.

"Tactical! Do we have a fix on Point One?"

"We have them!" Mallory replied. "Bearing zero-zero-five, minus two-one, range two-six-thousand. We have multiple nuke detonations and particle beam discharges."

"Captain Gutierrez . . ."

"Coming to new heading, Admiral," Gutierrez said. "Zero-zero-five, minus two-one."

"Punch it."

America glided forward, accelerating behind the thousand-times-per-second flicker of her gravitational singularity projected out ahead of her shield cap. The other eleven human ships of the battlegroup, plus the alien *Nameless*, edged into the new vector and accelerated in the star carrier's wake. Ideally, the destroyers *Diaz* or *Mattson* would have been in the battlegroup's van, along with a couple of frigates, clearing the way, but Gray didn't want to spend the extra time organizing his tiny fleet while one of the carrier's fighter squadrons was heavily engaged just 26,000 kilometers ahead. Judging from the swarm of alien fighters in the distance, by-the-book tactics weren't going to afford the carrier much protection in any case . . . if at all.

"CAG," Gray said, "you may loose the rest of the hounds."

Captain Connie Fletcher was *America*'s CAG, the commander of the star carrier's fighter group. "Launching fighters, aye, aye, sir."

"All ships," Gray continued. "Fire when you have a clear shot. . . ."

Chapter Three

TC/USNA CVS America
Flag Bridge/CIC
0507 hours, TFT

Admiral Gray dropped into *America*'s Combat Information Center, the CIC, located in the carrier's command tower just below the flag and ship bridge compartments. His physical body was still in the gentle grip of his command seat on the flag bridge, but the datastream feeding through his cerebral implants created the illusion—the perfect illusion—of standing one deck below, in CIC. Holographic projectors within the bulkheads gave him a realistic if insubstantial body.

Mallory looked up from the tank, a 3-D display area at the center of the compartment. "Virtual admiral on deck," he intoned.

Gray nodded to Mallory as he approached. "What do we have, Dean?"

"A very large number of Sh'daar fighters, Admiral. They were waiting when our fighters came through, and jumped them."

"Sh'daar fighters?"

"We assume so, sir. They're small—a couple of meters at the most. We're not sure, but we think they may not be piloted by organic intelligence."

"AIs, then."

"Or remotely controlled from a command ship we haven't spotted yet."

"That wouldn't be likely. Knock out the command ship and we'd take out all of the fighters."

"Yes, sir. Exactly. More likely they're acting as part of a massively parallel network."

"Meaning the whole swarm might be a single intelligence."

"Possibly, Admiral. Yes."

"Is there any chance that the swarm is part of some kind of sentry system?" Gray asked. "An automated defense network protecting this side of the triggah?"

"We're considering that possibility, Admiral," a woman floating upside down from Gray's perspective said. When he glanced at her, her ping data identified her as Lieutenant Commander Tonia Evans, and she was new to *America*'s personnel roster. "They act like an automated defense system."

He grinned. "And how would an alien defense net act?" he wondered. "What I want to know is why didn't they challenge us, why didn't they challenge the Demons when they first came through?"

She looked unhappy. "Unknown, sir."

"One way or another, the Sh'daar have some explaining to do," he said. "Attacking us for no reason at all was not in the armistice treaty."

Not that the Sh'daar necessarily understood that treaty, at least in the way humans did. Any agreement with such fundamentally different minds was going to be open to misunderstandings, misinterpretation, and outright confusion.

Still, "Don't attack us," should be pretty straightforward.

"We're certain we're in the right time?" Gray said.

"Navigation has double-checked the star positions, Admiral," Mallory said. "We're definitely in the double-T. Between eighteen and twenty-three years *after* we were here last."

Good. We hit double-T—the temporal target. So what the hell is going on?

Possibly, Gray thought, the attack on the battlegroup was simply the way the Sh'daar understood the treaty provisions: if the humans poked their noses into the N'gai Cluster of 876 million years in their past, they would get punched in the face.

If that was the case—if they didn't want humans hanging around in their epoch—they were going to *love* what the battlegroup had to offer them this time around.

Making this a very short-lived armistice.

"Targets within range," Mallory announced. "Firing . . ."

Beams lashed out from *America*'s main batteries, followed closely by beams and missiles from the battlegroup coming up astern. The enemy swarm began gathering, moving toward the fleet, even as 100-megaton blasts from Black Demon missiles continued to rip through the heaviest concentrations of Sh'daar ships. The carrier's other fighter squadrons were just beginning to engage the enemy as well: VFA-31, the Impactors, and VFA-215, the Black Knights.

A fourth fighter squadron, one brand new to *America*'s flight decks, hung back to provide close support for the battlegroup—VFA-190, the Ghost Riders.

Gray heard the chatter among pilots as the fighters attacked, in tones ranging from ice-cold professionalism to shrill excitement.

"Impactor Nine, moving in . . ."

"Target lock . . . Fox One!"

"Knight Three! Knight Three! You've got two on your six!"

"I can't shake them! I can't—"

America trembled as something struck the star carrier.

"Hit to the shield," Mallory reported. "We're bleeding. . . ."

According to damage control, however, the damage was minor, a few hundred thousand liters of water spilling into hard vacuum and freezing as glittering grains of ice. Self-

repair nano on the inner hull was already closing off the
hole.

"This is the *Mitchell*!" another voice called. "We're
taking heavy fire . . . damage to the main drive . . . damage
to primary power . . . —Damn it! Mayday! Mayday!"

A long stream of Sh'daar fighters had looped out and
around, coming in on the frigate *Mitchell* from astern. On
displays and within his own mind, Gray could see the ship,
her stern crumpling as the artificially conjured black holes
that plucked power from the vacuum spun out of control and
began devouring the ship from within.

Gray checked the tank to see which human ships were
closest.

"*Diaz! Young!*" he ordered. "Close in with the *Mitchell*!
See if you can hold those bogies off!"

It was too little, too late, though. The *Mitchell* died
quickly, collapsing into her own power tap singularity. . . .

"Too many of the bastards are getting through, Dean,"
Gray said. "Pull the fighters back."

"We can't go on the defensive, Admiral. We need to hit
them, hit them hard, away from the fleet!"

That was the conventional and established naval-fighter
doctrine.

But this wasn't a conventional fight.

"That won't help if the fleet is wiped out of the sky, damn
it. Pull in the fighters!"

"Aye, aye, sir."

It was becoming almost impossible to pull useful data
from the furball spreading out around the battlegroup. Thousands of alien craft continued to converge on the human
capital ships, while a scant forty or so human fighters tried
to hold them off. *America*'s AIs sifted through the mess
and extracted the most important info for human analysis,
but increasingly the fight was in the electronic hands of the
ship's combat system.

A bright flash snapped through the CIC. "What was
that?" Gray demanded.

"Checking sir . . ." Mallory adjusted the display field to

show the Glothr emissary ship *Nameless.* "It was the Glothr ship, Admiral. Looks like she has teeth."

"What the hell did they use?"

"Not sure . . . but I think they might've just time-twisted a laser into gamma ray frequencies."

Gray wasn't sure he understood what that meant, but that wasn't surprising, as Glothr technology embraced several concepts that most humans didn't yet understand. One of the more startling involved actually bending time. How they managed that trick was a mystery, but human xeno-technologists thought they might do it by using intense but short-ranged gravitational singularities tightly focused next to their hulls. By stretching time out—making an instant last seconds or longer—they could dissipate the energy of a thermonuclear explosion—a neat trick if you wanted to avoid getting fried by an incoming nuke.

Apparently, they could use the trick offensively as well. By turning a second into an instant, they could vastly increase the electromagnetic frequency of a laser, pumping it up to far more destructive energy levels.

Gray frowned. The extra energy had to come from *some-where*, but he wasn't sure he saw how it worked. Then he gave a mental shrug. Dozens of Sh'daar fighters had just evaporated in that beam. He would accept the gift-horse advantage of Glothr tech and worry about the details later. Maybe it was just the equivalent of firing a laser continuously for an hour, but compressing all of that energy into a single pulse.

At this point all he cared about was the fact that when the Glothr vessel fired again, more enemy ships flashed into hot plasma.

But there were simply too many of them. Each ship in the battlegroup now was surrounded by its own cloud of fighters, and they were pressing in close. Individually, they weren't that powerful, firing particle beams in the gigawatt-laser range of destructiveness. When fifty of them fired at once, however, aiming at the same target . . . or a hundred . . . or five hundred . . .

The railgun cruiser *Leland* was in trouble. The largest warship in the battlegroup after *America* herself—eight hundred meters long and massing a quarter of a billion tons—she was built around a magnetic accelerator tube nearly as long as she was, a mobile artillery piece designed for planetary bombardment or engaging large enemy vessels. Her primary weapon was useless against fighter swarms, however, and the elephant's point-defense batteries were swiftly being overwhelmed by clouds of Sh'daar mosquitos.

"*Verdun!*" Gray called. "*Deutschland!* Close in on the *Leland* and give her some support!"

The two ships were Pan-European heavy cruisers, former enemies now incorporated into the USNA battlegroup as a show of political will. Gray hoped their point defense weaponry would help keep the larger *Leland* from being mobbed.

But the European vessels were already fighting their own enemy swarms . . . and now the aliens attacking *America* herself were getting past the carrier's PDBs. The ship shuddered again, a vicious jolt, rolling heavily to starboard.

"We just lost Turret Five," Mallory reported. Damage control imagery showed that one of the big particle-beam turrets mounted on the carrier's central axis had been ripped away. For a moment, air vented into space from pressurized areas, mingled with clouds of debris and, horribly, several flailing human figures, made minute by the scale of their surroundings.

Then the open compartment was sealed off, and the escaping air—rapidly freezing into glittering flecks—dwindled away to nothing.

Gray knew he would remember those human figures—so tiny against the dark!—for the rest of his life.

A number of Sh'daar fighters slammed bodily into the long, lean hull of the French cruiser *Verdun*. They seemed to be eating their way in through the cruiser's hull . . . and then all of them detonated in a chain of white-hot flares that devoured the vessel's central spine. More explosions followed . . . with the wreckage crumpling in upon itself in a seething storm of radiation, heat, and light.

We're losing, Gray thought. *We're going under.*

"All ships," he ordered. "Come about and make for the TRGA."

There was no choice. They'd stuck their collective nose into this time and space and gotten it bitten off.

They had to retreat. If they were going to save even a few of the battlegroup's ships, they had to retreat *now*.

Lieutenant Donald Gregory
VFA-96, Black Demons
0516 hours, TFT

"Pull back and cover the *America*, people," Mackey ordered. "They're using fucking kamikaze tactics! We've got to stop them from getting through!"

Gregory had heard the order from the carrier's CIC already, and had witnessed both the destruction of the *Verdun* and the damage done to *America* herself.

It was a hopeless fight. So far, he'd run through about half of the missiles in his magazine, but as the fighting enveloped the carrier more and more tightly, he was having to shift to his Gatling cannon, firing high-velocity kinetic-kill rounds of depleted uranium. Nuclear detonations were tricky things to employ close to the hulls of friendly ships, and the USNA fighter pilots were being forced to use more surgical methods in their defensive tactics.

Surgical methods took longer—you couldn't yell "Fox One" and blow a dozen enemies away with a single high-yield detonation, and you had to be frustratingly precise in the placement of your warshots.

One alien fighter, gleaming silver and irregular in shape, came in across *America*'s stern and raced up the length of her spine, Gregory in close pursuit. He fired a burst of KK rounds, but the angle was bad and the rounds glanced off the hurtling spacecraft with minimal damage. The rounds that missed slammed into the underside of the carrier's shield cap forward . . . though with minimal damage as well, thank the gods. The carrier's hull shields absorbed or deflected much of the impact.

For a terrifying moment, he thought the enemy craft was trying for one of *America*'s three landing bays in the steadily rotating hab section . . . but the fighter slipped between two of the moving bays and plunged toward the blunt, forward-leaning tower between hab module and the underside of the shield cap.

Damn! They were trying for the bridge and CIC!

The alien vessel struck the bridge tower at its base, just above the main hull of the carrier's spine; Gregory's Star-blade flashed past an instant later, twisting around his grav singularity and angling out and away from the carrier. Braking hard, he reversed course and dropped toward the ship's spine again, gliding past the blurred hull metal of the bridge tower. His AI signaled a target lock on the alien, which was *melting* now into *America*'s hull, sinking through the low-level bending of space, just above the ship's outer hull, which deflected incoming energies. In another moment it would detonate, and the carrier might lose its bridge and combat information center all at once.

Gregory triggered his KK Gatling, sending a stream of high-velocity rounds slamming into and through the enemy craft. A particle-beam shot might do too much damage, though in fact he didn't have the time to give the decision any conscious thought. He aligned with the target and fired, watching white flares of heat and light and splashes of molten metal erupt from the partially sunken alien hull.

At the last instant, he pulled out, whipping around his drive singularity and using a tremendous burst of acceleration to shove his ship sideways to avoid becoming a kinetic-kill projectile himself.

He held his breath, waiting for the alien to explode.

It didn't.

"*America* CIC," he called, "this is Demon Four! You have an enemy bogie buried in the bridge tower!"

"We copy that, Demon Four. Acknowledged."

"Better send some Marines in case they're still alive." *And in case there's a loose black hole inside the wreckage*, he added to himself . . . but he didn't say so aloud. The shipboard response teams knew their business.

"Copy that, Four. Thanks for the assist."

"All part of our friendly Black Demon service," he replied, with a nonchalance that he definitely did not feel. That had been too damned close for sanity!

And they say the definition of insanity is doing the same thing over and over again and expecting different results. So here I go again. . . .

A group of eight alien fighters were inbound, a thousand kilometers out. He locked on and fired one of his dwindling number of Kraits. The detonation moments later took out seven of the eight; he nailed the survivor with another burst from his Gatling, watching the wreckage collapse in upon itself, folding up tighter and tighter until it vanished in a surprised pop of hard X-rays.

That was proof that the Sh'daar fighters had power taps similar to what the human ships were using—tiny black holes that skimmed energy from the frothing virtual energy at the base of reality and made it real. When a ship was destroyed, the black hole inside often ate much of the wreckage, then evaporated. Sometimes the singularity hung around long enough to become a menace to navigation, but luckily that wasn't the case this time.

Unluckily, there were more opportunities, because beyond those eight Sh'daar ships another ten were approaching at high speed.

"Damn it," Gregory snapped. "How many of these things are there?"

His Starblade's AI gave him an answer, though as an impression, an unspoken realization, rather than in words. More than six thousand, out of an original estimated nine thousand . . .

Too fucking many. They'd destroyed thousands of the things already . . . but thousands more remained.

"All ships, this is *America* CIC," a voice announced. "Be

aware . . . we have more Sh'daar vessels inbound, repeat, more Sh'daars inbound. Capital ships, this time . . ."

Great! he thought. *Just fucking great!*

TC/USNA CVS America
Flag Bridge/CIC
0535 hours, TFT

Admiral Gray stared into the mass of alien vessels headed for the battlegroup from dead ahead. *America*'s tactical AIs had counted over three hundred so far, including a couple of monsters that must have started out as planetoids, kilometers across and massing billions of tons.

There would be no escape from so powerful an alien force. . . .

He saw exactly three different tactical options—surrender, fight to the death, or order the fleet to scatter in the hope that a few of the battlegroup's ships, at least, might make it back through the TRGA and reach home. None of those choices was particularly appealing . . . and a fourth option emerged.

"Open a channel to that fleet," he told the communication officer on *America*'s bridge. "Use the Agletsch protocols. See if they're willing to talk."

"They are already willing to talk, Admiral." The voice was that of Konstantin—or, rather, of a clone of that powerful AI. "I am now in communication with them."

The Konstantin clone was resident within the TOAF module, a cylinder strapped to *America*'s spine aft of the rotating hab section, but was linked in through the carrier's electronic network to *America*'s resident AIs. It hadn't spoken before, and Gray had more or less forgotten that it was there, but he welcomed its input now.

"What do they say, Konstantin?"

There was a brief but agonizing pause.

"The force ahead is siding with us," the AI told him. "The small Sh'daar fighters appear to be . . . they are calling them counter-Refusers, which is confusing, but the word *rebels* may approximate the meaning."

"Counterrevolutionaries?" Gray suggested. He'd encountered the term once in a downloaded history of twentieth-century global politics.

"Indeed. The Sh'daar, remember, began as what they termed Refusers, rejecting the ur-Sh'daar *Schjaa Hok*."

"'The Transcending,'" Gray said, giving the alien term its closest English translation. "I remember."

They'd learned that bit of history twenty years ago, during the Koenig Expedition to this spacetime. Originally, the N'gai dwarf galaxy had been occupied by hundreds of mutually alien civilizations that humans now knew as the ur-Sh'daar . . . the *original* or *primal* Sh'daar. When that galactic culture had entered its own version of the technological singularity almost a billion years in Humankind's past, some, for various reasons, had rejected or somehow avoided the transformation, becoming known as "Refusers."

"Are you telling me that these fighter swarms are Sh'daar who *embrace* the ur-Sh'daar Transcending?"

"I do not yet have enough data on Sh'daar ideologies or political interactions to say with certainty," Konstantin replied. "However, that is certainly a valid possibility."

"So why the hell were they attacking us?"

"I do not have enough information as of yet to give you a meaningful reply," Konstantin told him. "But this rebel subgroup must feel threatened by our arrival in some way. Perhaps they wish to join the original ur-Sh'daar, and fear that we would threaten or delay their plans."

"Hell, if they want to go, let them," Gray said. "Attacking us without provocation isn't a rational act."

"Again, Admiral, I would caution you that we lack hard data as to their motives, needs, and aspirations. It's too early to speculate concerning their actions."

Damned machine. "Let me know when you have hard data."

"Of course."

"In the meantime, what about our new best buddies out there?"

The Sh'daar vessels ahead were spreading out. *America*'s long-range sensors were detecting bursts of gamma radiation—evidence of positron annihilation. The aliens were using antimatter weaponry.

"They appear to be attacking the rebels, Admiral."

"You're saying they're *rescuing* us?"

"So it would appear, Admiral."

"All ships," Gray said, using the battlegroup's tactical channel. "Disengage and pull back. The cavalry's just galloped in to the rescue. Stay clear and let them do their thing."

Sh'daar fighters continued to press their attack on the *America* battlegroup, trying to overwhelm the human defenses . . . but the fleet of capital ships was moving in swiftly, now, using precisely wielded bursts of antimatter particles to vaporize the minute alien ships.

And then the surviving alien fighters were breaking off and fleeing, scattering out and away and into the surrounding cloud of densely packed suns.

"Admiral, the Adjugredudhran commander of the Sh'daar flagship *Ancient Hope* gives you its greetings," Konstantin reported. "It hopes our force has not suffered serious loss . . . and regrets the counter-Refuser attack on our vessels. It suggests that we follow the Sh'daar fleet into the Core . . . to the vicinity of the Six Suns."

Gray let out a pent-up breath. He felt weak . . . shaky enough that he wondered if he would have been able to stand in a full gravity. *So close* . . .

"Please thank the Ad . . . thank the Sh'daar commander," he replied, "and tell it that we will comply."

"Well," Mallory said out loud. He'd obviously been listening in on the conversation with Konstantin. "Let the diplomacy games begin."

"Better with words than with particle cannon," Gray said with a shrug. "I guess it's a good thing we brought Konstantin-2 out here."

"It would've been nice if the good guys had been here to meet us," Mallory said. "I don't trust this."

"Neither do I, Dean. But let's see what they have to say."

And the battlegroup—the ten survivors, at any rate, plus

the Glothr liaison ship—fell into formation with the far more numerous locals.

Admiral Gray looked at the nearest of the Sh'daar vessels—a monster wedge five kilometers long, its hull gliding past a few kilometers away like a massive black cliff dotted with city lights . . .

. . . and felt very, very small.

Chapter Four

New White House
Washington, D.C.
United States of North America
0840 hours, EST

"So what's up on the docket for today?" President Koenig asked.

Marcus Whitney, Koenig's White House chief of staff, laid a secure data pad on the high-tech desk before him. "You had a nine-hundred with the Pan-Euro ambassador, sir, and an eleven-hundred with the Periphery reclamation council from Northern Virginia . . ."

"'Had?'"

"Yes, sir. I rescheduled. Konstantin wants to vir-meet with you."

"Konstantin? Wants to see *me*?" Generally, it was the other way around. "What about?"

"He has not divulged his agenda, Mr. President."

The powerful AI rarely mixed its affairs with those of humans. Even so, its effects on human culture, technology, and politics had been far reaching indeed. Its input had effectively ended the USNA's conflict with the Confederation government by employing memetic weaponry to turn civilian support against the war. It continually monitored news feeds and imagery from around the Earth, making suggestions that had averted famines, alleviated plagues, and blocked wars. It had guided presidents in both military and political exchanges both with other human states and with aliens.

Ever since Koenig had taken office as president, Konstantin had been an unofficial and highly secret special advisor. The strange thing was that the machine intelligence—not a human agency or department—seemed to have developed the idea.

And Koenig had no idea what the AI's true motivations might be.

"I guess," he said slowly, "I'd better find out what he wants. See that I'm not disturbed, Marcus."

"Yes, sir."

As his aide left the office, Koenig leaned back in his chair, which reshaped itself to more comfortably fit his frame. He placed the palm of his left hand on a smooth, glassy plate set into the chair's arm and on the desk, the datapad winked on. . . .

. . . and Koenig opened his eyes inside a small and dimly lit log cabin in Kaluga, Russia. An elderly man—white-haired, goateed, with wire-frame pince-nez and a sleepy expression—looked up from an old-fashioned book.

"Hello, Konstantin," Koenig said. "You wanted to see me?"

As always, Koenig had the feeling that the figure before him was studying him narrowly, with a superhuman intensity quite at odds with the sleepy expression on its very human face. Everything was an illusion, of course, created by the AI and downloaded into Koenig's mind through the virtual reality software running on his cerebral implants. The anachronistic touches demonstrated that—the real Konstantin Tsiolkovsky never had banks of high-definition monitors on the walls of his log house. Nor had the famous Russian pioneer of astronautic theory spoken English.

"Yes, Mr. President. It is time that you and I had a chat. I have some information that may be of interest."

"You haven't heard from your clone on the *America* yet. . . ."

"No. If our calculations are correct, they have only just arrived at the N'gai Cloud . . . if, indeed, the two different time frames can be meaningfully compared. But we have heard from the Agletsch. They have made available some information. *Gratis.*"

"They *gave* it to us?" Koenig was impressed. "That means it's either worthless . . . or of unbelievably high value."

"Agreed."

The Agletsch exchanged information from across a vast swath of the galaxy for other information, as well as for certain rare elements—notably isotopes of neptunium and californium. They never gave stuff away for free.

Not unless it very definitely benefited them as well.

"So what's the information?"

Koenig waited out the slight time delay. It took one and a quarter seconds for his words to reach Konstantin on Luna's far side, another second and a quarter for the answer to return. Every exchange had a built-in 2.5-second pause.

"They strongly suggest that we check out Tabby's Star," Konstantin told him.

"I don't know that one," Koenig said. "At least not by that name."

"Here is the download."

Information flooded through Koenig's implants and into his conscious awareness.

A mental window opened, filling with scrolling text.

Object: KIC 8462852
Alternate names: WTF Star, Tabby's Star
Type: Main-sequence star; **Spectral Type:** F3 V/IV
Coordinates: RA: 20ʰ 06ᵐ 15.457ˢ Dec: + 44° 27′ 24.61″
Constellation: Cygnus
Mass: ~ 1.43 SOL; **Radius:** 1.58 SOL;
  Rotation: 0.8797 DAYS
Temperature: 6750° K; **Luminosity:** 5 SOL

Apparent Magnitude: 11.7;
    Absolute Magnitude: 3.08
Distance: 1480 LY
Age: ~ 4 billion years
Notes: First noted in 2009–2015 as a part of the
    data collected by the Kepler space telescope. An
    extremely unusual pattern of light fluctuations
    proved difficult to explain as a natural phenomenon,
    and raised the possibility that intermittent dips in the
    star's light output were the result of occultations by
    intelligently designed alien megastructures.
KIC 8462852 received the unofficial name "Tabby's
    Star" after Tabetha S. Boyajian, head of the
    citizen scientist group that first called attention
    to the object. It was also called the "WTF star"—a
    humorous name drawn from the title of her paper:
    "Where's the Flux?" At that time, "WTF" was a
    slang expression of surprise or disbelief.
The Tabby's Star anomalies were eventually explained
    as a combination of an accretion disk and odd
    stellar geometry brought on by the star's high rate
    of spin and resultant gravitational darkening. . . .

There was a lot more information in the download, and
Koenig waded through it. He wasn't familiar with much of it.

In the early twenty-first century, the Kepler space telescope had continuously monitored the light coming from
some 150,000 stars in a small section of Cygnus; planets
orbiting those stars would periodically block a tiny percentage of the light, causing dips in the stars' brightness.

That period, from 2009 through 2015, was a heady one
of exploration and discovery, as thousands of exoplanets,
worlds outside of Sol's domain, were found, and Humankind
became aware of the fact that the Milky Way alone might
contain 40 billion worlds like Earth. Out of all of those
target stars, however, only one had showed a light curve as
bizarre as one sun at the very edge of the target area: KIC
8462852. Light dips were frequent, sharp, and aperiodic—

behaving like large numbers of huge objects orbiting their star "in tight formation," as one astronomer put it. One particular object did seem to have a regular period. The first time it was spotted, it obscured 15 percent of the star's light. The second time, 750 days later, it obscured 22 percent of the light.

Twenty-two percent? A super-Jupiter, the largest world possible, typically obscured about 1 percent of the light from its star as it passed in front of the star's disk. To cause that big of a drop in the light output of the star, the eclipsing object would have to be so large it covered nearly a quarter of the star's face. This could *not* be a planet, so what the hell was it?

Dozens of theories were fielded—possible natural explanations, including huge dust clouds, masses of perturbed comets, and colliding planets. None worked very well. The system was too old to have dust clouds or accretion disks, the chances of finding it just when planets had collided or comets descended were nil, and the amount of detectable infrared radiation was a bad fit for all of those possibilities.

Increasingly, astronomers were forced to consider the unthinkable—that the odd light curve of KIC 8462852 was due to some sort of alien megastructure, an intelligently designed and built structure or series of structures, such as a Dyson sphere under construction or, more likely, a Dyson swarm—thousands of objects absorbing energy from the star. The light curves seemed to suggest solid-edged, irregularly shaped structures with distinct boundaries rather than diffuse clouds of dust.

But the alien megastructure idea *had* to be the very last possibility to be considered. That was not because the astronomers didn't want to think about aliens, but because the alien hypothesis was not falsifiable by scientific testing . . . and so it could not be considered until *every* other possibility had been tested and ruled out.

And eventually, a natural explanation was found. Fast-spinning stars could suffer an effect called gravitational darkening while flattening from a sphere into an oblate spheroid; several large planets transiting across different parts of the star's surface, plus an accretion disk of dust, could cause greater or lesser dips in the light curve.

There were problems with that theory, though. The star *did* spin quickly—at the equator it rotated once in 21 hours and a few minutes as opposed to 25 days for Sol—but not fast enough to cause severe distortion of the sphere. And, again, the star just wasn't young enough to have an orbiting cloud or accretion disk of dust.

But by that time, the twenty-first century had been in free fall toward utter chaos. Stunning and widespread political corruption, quickly rising sea levels, economic collapse, global war with Islam, the First Sino-Western War, and the ravages of the Blood Death . . . it was a wonder, frankly, that Humankind had survived. The hanging of the first space elevator, in the twenty-second century, had helped reverse the collapse, bringing in the raw materials, cheap energy, and improved technologies that ultimately transformed the planet.

But as Humankind began to establish a firm foothold in the solar system, the excitement over KIC 8462852 was largely forgotten. It became an interesting anomaly, quickly explained and as quickly filed away and ignored.

"Okay," Koenig said after several minutes reviewing the material. "An interesting observation, but it says here they explained it. Why are the Agletsch interested in the thing? Or, maybe I should say . . . why do they want *us* to be interested?"

"They did not discuss that," Konstantin replied. "But they seem to believe that our explanation was wrong. That Tabby's Star is in fact the location of an advanced alien civilization."

"But not an ally of the Sh'daar, I take it."

"Correct."

Humankind now understood that the Sh'daar were interlopers from the remote past, from $T_{-0.876gy}$ . . . a term usually abbreviated as "Tee-sub-minus," or, in other words, from 876 million years in the past. They appeared to have recruited a number of alien civilizations in T_{prime} (meaning time *now*, the twenty-fifth century): the Turusch, the H'rulka, the Nungiirtok, the Slan, and quite a few others. That alliance, called the Sh'daar Collective, had been deployed against Humankind in an effort to force them to give up tech-singularity-inducing technologies. The Collective apparently extended into the future as well; the Glothr, from a rogue planet millions of years in the future, might well have been working with the Sh'daar, though the nature of that relationship was still uncertain.

The only reason Humankind had survived against that alliance as long as it had was the fact that the different members of the Sh'daar Collective had as much trouble communicating with one another as they did with humans. Organizing a joint military campaign across millions of years and with dozens of space-faring species with wildly diverse means of communicating turned out to be damned near impossible.

"Huh," Koenig said, thoughtful. "If the Tabby's Star aliens haven't been pressured by the Sh'daar, they might turn out to be useful allies for us."

"Exactly. Assuming, of course, that they care to involve themselves with humans."

"What . . . they might not because we're so primitive? Or would they be put off by our body odor?"

"Whatever terrestrial astronomers observed at Tabby's Star in the year 2015," Konstantin reminded Koenig, "would have happened 1480 years earlier . . . in the year 535 C.E., to be precise. If they were actually building a Dyson sphere when Europe's Dark Ages were just getting started, where are they, and what are they building *now*? Such beings might seem like gods compared to humans."

"The Stargods . . ." It was an old idea, one suggesting a source for unexplained technological artifacts like the TRGAs scattered across the galaxy . . . or the Black Rosette at the heart of Omega Centauri. Laurie Taggart had been a passionate devotee of that idea, a member of the Ancient Alien Creationist Church.

But it was also an idea that explained nothing.

"What people enamored of the Stargods tend to forget," Konstantin said, "is that such beings very likely have absolutely nothing in common with us. Would *you* stop to communicate with an anthill?"

"I don't know," Koenig replied with a virtual shrug. "It depends on whether I could understand what the little buggers were saying. And there are entomologists who *would* be interested in finding a common language, if there was one."

"It is possible to push such metaphors too far, Mr. President. The point is that the Tabby's Star aliens may have nothing whatsoever in common with humans, and no wish to communicate with them . . . or to help them against the Sh'daar."

"I could also imagine them having reached their own technological singularity," Koenig said. "They might have built the thing, whatever it is . . . and then left. They're not around any longer."

"True. Still, the fact that the Agletsch have suggested that a human ship explore Tabby's Star outweighs, somewhat, the low probability of finding useful allies there."

"Well, if anyone in the galaxy knows about such allies, it would be them. I just wish we knew a bit more about the Aggie agenda. What the hell do they get out of all of this?"

"You will need to treat this . . . *gift* of information with caution," Konstantin said. "The Agletsch *are* Sh'daar agents, members of the Sh'daar Collective. We must assume the Agletsch have an agenda of their own, a reason to share this information freely. It is unlikely that they would actively help us against the Collective."

"Maybe they're tired of sticking to the Collective's party line. Maybe they're trying to rebel."

The idea had been explored before. In the past, some Agletsch had seemed to be working outside of any Sh'daar influence. Others definitely worked within. There'd been . . . hints that they would prefer that their entire civilization be free of Sh'daar influence. And, indeed, the information they had traded to humans in the past concerning various Sh'daar client races had again and again proven to be priceless.

But what was their angle this time?

And can we risk ignoring their advice while we try to figure that out?

"I would like to send our best out there," Koenig told the AI, coming to a decision.

"The star carrier *America*," Konstantin replied. "Admiral Gray."

"You know, Konstantin, we *do* have other star carriers. Not enough, maybe . . . but we have others."

"Most currently undergoing repairs."

"There are the *Declaration* and the *Lexington*."

"Both untried as yet. And the *Declaration* is still undergoing space trials. I recommend using *America* when she returns from the N'gai Cluster."

"We were going to deploy *America* out to the Black Rosette. Operation Omega."

"But to explore what might well be an entire Dyson sphere," Konstantin pointed out, "it would be best to have several fighter wings available. Star carriers offer certain specific tactical advantages not possible with cruisers or even light carriers."

"Point," Koenig conceded, reluctantly. "But we've taken some heavy casualties. We may not have the luxury of using our first choice."

TC/USNA CVS America
Flag Bridge/CIC
N'gai Cluster
1640 hours, TFT

Admiral Gray floated in the CIC, gazing into a tangled jungle of suns ahead, against which even the biggest Sh'daar warships appeared to be toys. He remembered this vista from his last deployment here, back when he'd been a fighter driver under the command of Admiral Koenig.

Now *he* was admiral . . . but the view was the same.

Local space was crowded with suns, including hundreds

more brilliant than Venus at its brightest in the skies of Earth. Six stars, in particular, outshone all others—a perfect hexagram of dazzlingly brilliant blue suns gleaming almost directly ahead. The Six Suns were the hub of the N'gai Cluster, a kind of central, focal monument for the Cluster's star-faring civilization. Each giant star was forty times the mass of distant Sol, orbiting with the others around a central gravitational balance point in a perfect Klemperer rosette. Obviously they'd been engineered that way, probably nudged in from elsewhere in the galaxy and dropped into position. Quite possible those blue-white giant suns themselves were artificial, engineered by some highly advanced science. The stellar arrangement suggested an astonishing degree of technological prowess and skill, one millions of years in advance of current human capabilities.

Eight hundred and some million years in the future, in the time Gray thought of as the present, those suns had long since gone supernova, reducing themselves to black holes—the enigmatic Black Rosette at the center of Omega Centauri. The N'gai Cluster—a dwarf galaxy—had been devoured by the gravitational hunger of the much larger Milky Way. The Omega Centauri star cluster itself was now known to be the remnant nucleus of this, the N'gai Cluster, 872 million years later.

Gray stared into the brilliance of the Six Suns, and wondered . . .

What were the Rosette Aliens?

All he knew was that they were enigmatic and highly advanced beings of unknown capabilities and unknown origin who'd appeared at the Black Rosette and begun building . . . *something*, a structure vast and utterly mysterious.

Were the Rosette Aliens somehow related to the Sh'daar?

Maybe we're going to find out at last, Gray thought.

Numerous other artifacts also hung against that dazzling starscape, all indicating an advanced civilization far more technically proficient, far more ancient than anything merely human, such as the TRGA cylinders and artificial planets, not to mention strange structures, vast and incomprehensible. There were enormous tube-shaped habitats hundreds of kilometers across, rotating to provide artificial gravity and displaying terrain across their curving inner surfaces spread out like maps. Black holes ringed by artificial structures were obvious sources of high-tech energy, and starships the size of sprawling cities made their way across the crowded backdrop of the dwarf galaxy's core.

A number of Sh'daar vessels, many considerably larger than *America*, by now had gathered around the human fleet, bending space briefly, and bringing the battlegroup across several light years to the dwarf galaxy's heart. Now those ships were guiding *America* and the other vessels to their final destination, an entire world larger than Earth, covered over completely with black metal and the tangled, blazing knots of what could only be urban centers and vast industrial facilities. More of that planet's surface appeared to be roofed over in artificial, light-drinking ebon materials than was open to the sky.

It was a single city the size of a planet.

The metallic world did not appear to have a sun, but was wandering among the densely packed stars of the cluster's core, bathed in their light.

"The Adjugredudhran commander of the Sh'daar flagship reports that this is their capital world," Konstantin-2 reported. "Daar N'gah."

"Very well," Gray replied. "Thank you. Do we have their permission to approach the consulate?"

There was a long pause. "Affirmative, Admiral. Deep Time currently is in an extended orbit, about half a million kilometers farther on. They request that we give Daar N'gah wide clearance due to local traffic."

Which might, Gray reflected, be the full truth, or it might reflect Sh'daar concerns about more rebels appearing and the potential for collateral damage to the planet if another firefight began. Either way, it made sense to him from a tactical standpoint if he were in their position.

"Tell them we will comply."

America, under her own power now, swung wide of the

black metal world and decelerated into the indicated orbit. The consulate station unofficially known as Deep Time gleamed ahead in the harsh, reflected light from the Six Suns, a silvery, glittering torus rotating to provide those aboard with artificial gravity.

Deep Time had started out eight months earlier as a small USNA deep space military base constructed in the N'gai Cloud to keep an eye on the Sh'daar, a concession by the Collective possible only with the base's near-total demilitarization. No lasers or particle cannon, no high-velocity KK weaponry, nothing that might upset the unknowable currents and eddies of time itself. The men and women stationed here *were* permitted sidearms, but the posting was strictly made on a volunteer basis. Hand lasers and man-portable pee-beeps were no match for five-kilometer flying mountains.

A couple of months earlier, while *America* had been deployed to the far future, the Deep Time station in the far past had been designated as a kind of semiofficial consulate, Humankind's ambassadorial presence in the N'gai Cluster . . . though, again, no one knew what the Sh'daar themselves thought of the arrangement. The consulate staff, including almost a hundred xenosophontologists, had been studying the Sh'daar and their civilization, at least as it had existed in the remote past, the epoch known as Tee-sub-minus.

Humans now knew that the ancient Sh'daar had timetraveled to Earth's galaxy in the twenty-sixth century, the epoch they called Tee-sub-prime, and made contact with the various star-faring civilizations that had been fighting their on-again, off-again war with Earth. On Earth, it begged the question were the Sh'daar of the twenty-sixth century under the control of the ancient N'gai civilization? No one knew for sure, and attempts to query the ancient Sh'daar had so far been frustrating and inconclusive.

With the civil war on Earth concluded at last, however, it was time to find out the truth . . . and also for the humans to warn the ancient Sh'daar about what they had learned even further into the remote future. The *America* battlegroup had been dispatched as an escort for the Glothr emissary—an opportunity to show the flag, and to back up the Glothr representatives with firepower if necessary.

Gray desperately hoped that firepower would not be necessary. The Sh'daar were so far in advance of Earth technology that it was difficult to even compare the two. Human tacticians still weren't sure what it was that the Sh'daar had feared about *America* and her escorts twenty years ago . . . or why they'd given in so easily.

Or if they had truly given in at all, Gray thought.

"Range to Deep Time One now four thousand kilometers," Mallory reported. "We're slowing our approach."

"We're receiving telemetry from DT-1," Pam Wilson, the communications officer added. "They report everything quiet and normal."

"Very well." *So far, so good. . . .*

The attack as they'd emerged from the TRGA had shaken Gray more than he cared to admit.

Gray no longer needed image enhancement and magnification to see DT-1. It was visible in CIC's forward view, just a kilometer away, now.

"Konstantin?" Gray asked. "Are you ready?"

"Of course, Admiral. You may release me at your discretion."

"Captain Gutierrez," Gray said. "If you will . . ."

"Aye, aye, Admiral. Releasing the baby in three . . . two . . . one . . . *launch.*"

The Tsiolkovsky Orbital Computer Assembly—TOCA, for short—was a ten-meter cylindrical habitat that had made the voyage out from Earth strapped to *America*'s spine aft of the landing bays. It carried the computer hardware that was housing the sub-clone downloaded from the original Konstantin AI.

Gray wasn't certain the Sh'daar understood the concept of "ambassador," but they'd given permission for the TOCA cylinder to be brought to N'gai, and for it—and Konstantin-2—to be linked to the Deep Time facility. The fact that the AI had already been in touch with the Adjugredudhran commander said they at least accepted Konstantin-2 as someone they could talk to.

Something, Gray thought, definitely had changed in Sh'daar attitudes. Twenty years earlier, they'd been terrified that a human battlegroup had penetrated both space and time to reach this cluster. The Sh'daar had been willing to do almost anything—like end a war—to make the humans leave. Speculation and scuttlebutt had played with the idea that they were afraid human activity here in the past would rewrite the future—a future in which they had a vested interest.

Now, however, they seemed to be welcoming contact.

Gray suspected that they feared something else more than they feared humans . . . even humans playing in their own temporal backyard.

The cylinder carrying Konstantin's sub-clone passed *America*'s shield cap and dwindled toward the gleaming silver torus.

And Gray couldn't help wondering if even a super-AI was going to have trouble figuring out just what made the Sh'daar tick.

Chapter Five

Deep Time Orbital Facility-1
N'gai Cluster
1020 hours, TFT

Gray was seated in what appeared to be a large classroom or lecture hall. Concentric rings of comfortable benches overlooked a central well a dozen meters across. A dome overhead looked out into the heart of the N'gai Cluster, filled with stars, with artificial worlds, with the enigmatic gleam of the Six Suns. McKennon, the lead xenosophontologist of the Deep Time facility, was seated next to him . . . or *seemed* to be. In fact, Gray was back in his office on board *America*, while McKennon was in a communications chamber on board DT-1. AI software created the illusion—the virtual reality—of their conversation within their cerebral implants.

Other conference attendees—all human, so far—were scattered through the room, waiting for the start of what promised to be a *very* interesting meeting.

"Yes," Gray said, "but we weren't sure of that. All we knew was that if we were just a hair off course during the passage through the TRGA cylinder, it could screw both with where and when we emerged . . . possibly by quite a lot." Gray chuckled. "You have no idea how terrified I was that we might emerge *before* Koenig arrived here . . . twenty years ago. *That* would have done a job on causality, let me tell you!"

"Twenty years out of eight hundred seventy-six million?" McKennon said, and nodded. "You would need a degree of precision good to within one part in forty-three point eight million. You're right. That's pretty tight! Fortunately, it looks like there's some leeway built into the thing."

"We suspected as much when we took our initial temporal navigation readings," Gray told her. "But it's good to hear it from someone who knows what she's doing."

"Who, me?" She laughed. "Just about everything we've done since we got here has been pure guesswork!"

Gray looked up at the apparent dome covering the virtual classroom. Beyond, high in the sky and made tiny by distance, those six brilliant, blue-white suns locked together in a hexagram served to mock mere human science, math, and technology. They represented an obviously artificial engineering on an interstellar scale, one that utterly dwarfed human ideas of what was possible . . . human ideas of scale and scope and sanity.

"I'd say your team has done a pretty good job so far," Gray said slowly, "given that you're working with ideas and capabilities that we can't even begin to understand."

She followed his gaze up, up and out into the distance to the tightly ordered gleam of the Six Suns. "Every time I see that . . . *thing*," she admitted, "I wonder how it's even possible that we've survived as long as we have. The Sh'daar could have wiped us out easily, at any point since our first encounter with them. Instead, we've fought their proxies piecemeal. It doesn't make sense."

"Did the Sh'daar build it?" Gray asked. "I thought there was some question about that."

"Well, if it wasn't them, it was the ur-Sh'daar. Before they transcended. Same thing, really. The Sh'daar are the ur-Sh'daar . . . leftovers?"

"Maybe," Gray replied. "Or maybe there was a still earlier civilization."

"*Please*, Admiral," McKennon said, raising her hands in mock pain. "We don't need to complicate things by imagining whole pantheons of mystic ancient Stargods!"

Gray laughed. "Of course not. But still . . . the universe started thirteen point eight billion years ago . . ."

"Thirteen point eight *two*," she said, correcting him.

"Thirteen point eight *two* billion years," he agreed. "Subtract four and a half billion years, which is how long it took to evolve a tool-using, spaceship-building species on Earth. That leaves well over nine billion years to play with. How many species can evolve; develop spaceflight, computers, and nanotechnology; and reach the point where they . . ." He stopped, looked up, gestured at the alien sky. ". . . where they can move stars around just to create a titanic *objet d'art*?"

"The Six Suns are probably a transportation system, like the TRGAs," McKennon said. "Those rotating stellar masses twist spacetime, and open a gate to . . . I guess to somewhere else. Maybe some*when* else, too. We have no idea what it does. But I know what you're saying. Whoever built the thing did it so . . . so *casually*. Like it was nothing for them to set six stars orbiting around a common center of gravity."

"Uh-oh," Gray said. "Looks like the Glothr just linked in."

The image of one of the Glothr, presumably their equivalent of an ambassador, had just materialized off to the right side of the virtual classroom. Three meters tall and very roughly resembling a terrestrial jellyfish, the being stood on a writhing mass of tentacles, with a filmy mantle at the top, like a parasol. Much of the being was transparent or translucent; you could *see* the brain within a circle of twenty-four jet-black eyes. Its body, a column intermittently glimpsed behind the tentacle mass, was transparent, encasing its translucent internal organs.

Gray was glad that the writhing tangle of tentacles usually hid the being's interior from view. Those tentacles—the thicker ones used for locomotion, the thinner ones for manipulation—tended to be translucent near their bases, but shaded into opaque grays and browns. The translucent parts shimmered with rainbow colors, like a shifting, oily sheen, and clusters of blue and green lights gleamed and winked within the glassy depths of the body. The Glothr, Gray knew, communicated with others of its kind by changing color. Translation to a spoken language could be a real bear . . . but one of the numerous Agletsch trade languages had been designed for beings that communicated visually. You just needed a computer to handle the actual color-to-speech part.

"That's a *Glothr*?" McKennon asked. She seemed intrigued. But then, in her line of work, she would be.

"Yeah. That's the Agletsch name for them, anyway. We ran into them something like twelve million years in the future."

"You mean twelve million years after 2425?"

"That's right."

"We need a special grammar to handle time travel."

"We certainly will need one."

She laughed. "Okay. I downloaded one preliminary report, but I haven't had a chance to follow through on them, yet," McKennon said. "What are they like?"

He thought about the Glothr.

Twelve million years in the future—counting Gray's home time as the present—a rogue world had given rise to a spectacularly advanced technic civilization. Sunless—adrift in emptiness with no star to call its own—the world named Invictus by humans was frigidly cold, at least on the surface, and eternally dark. Five times the mass of Earth, its surface chemistry was similar to that of Titan, based on liquid methane and ethane; a radioactive core kept a vast and lightless ocean liquid beneath many kilometers of ice as hard and as solid as rock.

And that's pretty much all they knew. They were still a complete enigma, so far as Gray was concerned. They were apparently connected, in some way not yet understood, to the Sh'daar of Earth T_{prime}, though they'd come from 12 million years further up the line. When Gray had managed to make peaceful contact with the Glothr out beyond the edge of the galaxy in future deep time, there'd been hope that perhaps the Glothr could communicate with the Sh'daar of the remote past, and end their attempts to tame and assimilate Humankind. The oddly shaped ship that had brought this Glothr to the Sh'daar capital, the *Nameless*, was a Glothr time-bender ship, brought back across the eons to attempt just that. Gray didn't know for sure, but he was pretty sure that Konstantin had been the one who'd thought of the idea.

"Hard to understand," was all Gray could say at last. "They're not at all like us. They're actually colonial beings, kind of like the Portuguese man-of-war in Earth's tropics. Lots of different organisms working together. And whatever they have for emotion . . . well, it doesn't come through the translators very well."

"The report I saw said they're from a Steppenwolf."

Steppenwolf world was a slang term for a rogue planet, one without a star . . . a lone wolf wandering the galactic steppes.

"That's right. Invictus. It must have been flung out of its original star system billions of years ago, and has been wandering on its own ever since."

"Huh. Daar N'gah is a rogue."

"I saw when we entered orbit. I understand the Sh'daar— well, we would say *terraformed*—basically created it. They made the planet habitable using quantum power taps, or something like them."

"That's right. I don't see a direct connection between the two, though. Daar N'gah was dead and frozen until the Sh'daar—or possibly the ur-Sh'daar—reworked it."

"Well, they would have had lots to choose from." Gray chuckled. "They're estimating that there are more Steppenwolf worlds floating around in the galaxy than there are stars."

"Yup. Four hundred billion plus. Apparently, every planetary system spits out a bunch of rogues early on, when the planets are starting to settle down into neat orbits. Most rogues are frozen and dead, of course. . . ."

"But given the right conditions," Gray said, "with enough internal warmth to allow liquid oceans and carbon chemistry for a few billion years, some of those billions are certain to evolve life, like Invictus."

She nodded. "Or permit large-scale colonization, like Daar N'gah."

Their conversation moved on to other things as more and more attendees, both human and not, appeared within the simulation. Newly arrived humans materialized on the benches. Others stood on flat areas between the benches . . . or the imagery was rewritten to eliminate sections of the benches entirely.

Gray and McKennon began discussing the Sh'daar of T_{prime} as compared with those of $T_{-0.876gy}$ . . . what President Koenig had once called *late Sh'daar* as opposed to *early Sh'daar*. After fifty-eight years of intermittent warfare, humans still weren't sure if the various species arrayed against them—the Turusch and the H'rulka and the Slan and all the rest—were themselves Sh'daar or were merely *manipulated* by the Sh'daar. It seemed a small distinction, but it was a damned important one. How committed were, say, the Turusch to forcing Humankind to give up their beloved advanced technologies? Could they be convinced to turn against their alien masters from out of deep time?

And as they talked, Gray studied the woman with growing interest . . . and felt a pang of . . . what? Loneliness? Wistfulness? Possibly . . . guilt?

For a couple of years, now, Gray had enjoyed a close relationship with Laurie Taggart, *America*'s weapons officer . . . but Laurie had been offered a chance to advance her career, as exec on board the new battle carrier *Lexington*. It was an excellent opportunity for her; in a couple more years, she might have a chance at her own command.

But it left Gray missing her—and Angela—more than ever. Damn, damn, *damn* . . .

He considered asking if McKennon wanted to come over to *America* for dinner later . . . then sharply cut the thought off. He would be returning to T_{prime} soon, while she stayed here, 876 million years in the past. That was a hell of a burden to put on any relationship.

An Agletsch materialized in the room just a few meters from where Gray and McKennon were sitting, intruding on Gray's increasingly unhappy thoughts. Her ID tag, which popped up in Gray's mind alongside her image, identified her as Aar'mithdisch, one of the spidery, four-eyed Agletsch liaisons who'd come in on board the Glothr vessel. He knew it was a *her*; Agletsch males were small, leechlike creatures that adhered to the female's body, like male anglerfish on Earth. After a time, they actually became a part of the female's body, and eventually were absorbed completely.

At least, he thought, they didn't have to worry about courtship and dating.

"Admiral Gray!" the translated voice of the being said when she swiveled an eyestalk in his direction and saw him. "The great moment is upon us, yes-no?"

The Agletsch had been the first nonhuman civilization encountered by humans as they spread out into interstellar space, an encounter in 2312 in the Zeta Doradus system, just 38 light years from Sol. Zeta Doradus was not their homeworld. No human knew where they'd come from originally; the price the Aggies put on that piece of information was literally astronomical. Called spiders or bugs by many humans, their oval sixteen-legged bodies vaguely resembled some terrestrial arthropods . . . in a bad light, perhaps, or after too many drinks.

Few humans trusted them. Some of that was due to their phobia-triggering looks, true, but for most Navy men, it was the fact that many carried nanotechnic storage and communications devices called seeds planted by the Sh'daar, which made them little better than spies. Gray had worked with them on numerous occasions, and didn't *think* they would *willingly* betray their human clients, but he also knew that understanding nonhuman motives and mores was a tricky bit of guesswork at best. For a time, human warships had stopped carrying Agletsch advisors despite their obvious usefulness as translators and as sources of Sh'daar insight and galactography.

But Gray had insisted that Agletsch be brought along

on this mission to assist in translating for the Sh'daar. The Joint Chiefs and President Koenig had agreed, but only if the beings were restricted to the Glothr vessel. That suited Gray just fine. He'd wanted someone over there that he could trust handling translations between humans and the Glothr anyway.

"The great moment is indeed here, Aar'mithdisch," Gray replied. "I'd like to stress that it is vitally important that we have accurate translations of both sides of the negotiations. This may be the most important bit of diplomacy in my world's history." He grinned. "No pressure."

"We do not understand this last comment," the alien said. "The gas-filled portions of the Glothr vessel maintain an internal pressure of—"

"Never mind, never mind," Gray said. "It was just a humorous expression."

The Agletsch's four weirdly stalked eyes twitched in complicated patterns, a rapid semaphore of sorts. Gray still couldn't read the emotional overtones that eye movements conveyed to other Agletsch. No doubt, they had the same difficulty understanding human facial expressions, like the grin he'd just tossed into the conversation when he'd said "no pressure." The Agletsch built very good electronic translators, but no translation system or artificial language could possibly take into account all of the subtle differences among cultures, biologies, and worldviews.

Considering how truly alien different species were when compared to one another, it was a wonder anyone could understand *anything* that another species was trying to say.

"We translate, Admiral Gray. Accurately . . . though we note that humans sometimes have trouble understanding other humans even when they share the same terrestrial language."

"You understand us disturbingly well," Gray said.

The being responded with a dip in two of its eyestalks—a gesture, Gray assumed, of agreement or, possibly, one simply of acknowledgement. Two more Agletsch materialized alongside the first, and the three of them appeared to be in close conversation among themselves.

"Look what just dropped in," McKennon said, nodding toward the front of the room. The image of another being had just materialized. It looked like a stack of starfish three meters tall, smaller at the top, larger—almost a meter across—at the bottom. Several skinny arms with multiple branchings, like the branches of a tree, emerged from different points along and around that body, while eyes gleamed at the tips of myriad highly animated tendrils.

"Well, well," Gray said, his eyes widening. "My software is flagging it as Ghresthrepni . . . one of the Adjugredudhra."

"One of the senior spokesbeings for the Sh'daar," McKennon said, nodding slowly. "And commander of the *Ancient Hope*."

"Ah. That's the ship that warped us in here. *Big* sucker."

Like so much about this mission, not a great deal was known about the Adjugredudhra. They'd been prominent, Gray knew, among the ur-Sh'daar before the Transcendence . . . a species that had delved deeply into advanced nanotechnology. From what few records he'd seen, acquired during *America*'s visit to the N'gai Cluster twenty years before, the original Adjugredudhrans had developed nanotech to an astonishing degree, building smaller and smaller machines of greater and greater power, machines that allowed them to transform their own bodies molecule by molecule, to literally remake those bodies into any shape or form they desired.

But very few galactic cultures, it seemed, were completely monolithic. Some species organized along the lines of ant or bee colonies, perhaps, could maintain a laser-sharp focus in the way they saw themselves and the universe . . . but for most, sapient cultures usually contained diversity and variability, subcultures and factions, even misfits and renegades, *refusers* who did not drink too deeply of the background culture of their civilization. When the Transcendence came . . . the *Schjaa Hok*, the Time of Change, there were millions of refusers left behind. Their civilization collapsed, technologies were lost, and wars—survivor remnants squabbling in the ruins of a galactic civilization—destroyed what was left.

Over the course of thousands of years, however, those who remained pulled together and rebuilt much of what had been lost, including worldviews, traditions, and imperial ambitions . . . until the Sh'daar rose anew from the wreckage that the vanished ur-Sh'daar had left behind.

Another nonhuman being had appeared alongside the first . . . a huge squid standing on its head was Gray's first thought, its tentacles spread across the floor holding semi-upright a two-and-a-half-meter brown-mottled body curled at the end. A single saucer-sized eye—plus other sensory organs of more dubious uses—peered out from the base of the tentacle mass. Those tentacles flashed and shifted in their color patterns and textures; like the Glothr, they communicated with color and light in vivid visual displays.

Gray's in-head database filled in the Agletsch name of the species: *Groth Hoj.* According to what humans had learned with the Koenig Expedition, the Groth Hoj had been masters of robotics, manufacturing massive robotic bodies for themselves . . . imitations of their natural bodies, at first, but then more and more outlandish machine designs.

Not all Groth Hoj had followed that route, which many apparently thought to be an evolutionary dead end. The refusers had stayed behind. And that must be who was here, today.

Another nonhuman appeared . . . but with this entity Gray drew a complete blank. He'd never seen anything remotely like it in any downloaded report or description of the N'gai civilizations.

His first impression was that it was a dinosaur—a long-necked sauropod—but it was held off the ground by six legs, not four. No tail, either, and the extra legs were unusual, set along the being's center line, one behind, and one ahead; its walking pattern, Gray thought, would be . . . odd.

The hide looked like broken rock, the flanks like the side of a cliff, the neck like a cantilevered crane.

Most of all, the image he saw before him looked like it must be of a creature absolutely titanic in size, hundreds of meters long, perhaps, and massing tens of millions of tons. The head, broad, flattened, and wide, like the head of a hammerhead shark, swung ponderously at the end of that massive neck. Eyes—Gray *thought* they were eyes—glittered within the shadows underneath the head. A forest of what might have been a tangle of hair hung from the head's underside like an unkempt beard. As the hairs twitched and writhed, Gray realized that they were manipulatory appendages. They almost hid a pulsing, V-shaped orifice that *might* be a mouth. . . .

No. Not a mouth. A breathing orifice, perhaps? A creature that huge would have to eat continuously to feed that ponderous bulk, and a mouth that small just wouldn't be up to the task. So how *did* the thing eat? And what?

For some reason, he really didn't want to find out.

"What," Gray said, "is *that*?"

"The Agletsch call it a Drerd," a voice in his head said, and Gray realized it was Konstantin speaking to him through his implants, not McKennon.

"Hello, Konstantin," he transmitted. "Getting settled into your new base of operations okay?"

"Everything is most satisfactory, Admiral," the AI replied in its maddeningly calm and precise voice. "I have managed to interface with the Sh'daar systems of data storage and begun downloading information on their civilization. There are a number of species here in the files which we have not previously encountered."

"I suppose that's to be expected," Gray replied. "When *America* paid her last visit here, we didn't hang around for very long."

"No. There are some hundreds of mutually alien species that evolved within the N'gai Cloud over the course of some billions of years. We knew of only a handful."

Gray looked at the gathering aliens in the virtual meeting space and wondered why *they* had been chosen, as opposed to, say, the F'heen-F'haav symbiote pairs, or the sluglike Sjhlurrr.

It begged the question: who the hell was calling the shots for the Sh'daar?

Before he could figure that out, he realized the Drerd appeared to be speaking:

We give formal greeting to our visitors from the future. . . .

The voice was a deep baritone and clearly human, or more likely an AI human avatar. According to data now appearing in side windows in Gray's consciousness, the huge being was rumbling at infrasound frequencies, producing sound waves down around 8 or 10 Hertz, well below the 20 Hz limit of human hearing.

Ghresthrepni, the Adjugredudhran ship captain, responded, in a smoothly blended medley of clicks, chirps, trills, and tinkling bells.

We note, too, the being said in translation, *the presence of an associate from our Collective's future, whom the Agletsch name Glothr. We would know the reason for this conclave.*

Lights shimmered and pulsed within the Glothr. *We bring warning from your future,* ran the translation.

We would hear, rumbled the Drerd, *from the humans. It was they who requested this gathering of Mind.*

"You're up," McKennon said.

"I guess so." And Gray stood.

The virtual image around him shifted as he did so. Rather than in a classroom of some sort, he now stood on an endless flat plain. The sky remained the same—vast clots of stars, nebulae, and scattered artificial worlds. Now, however, a circle of beings stood on that plain, facing one another. The Drerd, Gray saw, was bigger than he'd even imagined—a ponderously mobile mountain, a mountain*scape* all in its own right. He was the only human, and the other species were represented by just one apiece. The Glothr, he saw, was standing a couple of meters to his right, an Agletsch just to his left, while the Drerd towered above him perhaps fifty meters ahead, on the other side of the circle.

The others—Adjugredudhra, Groth Hoj, and perhaps thirty or forty others—gathered around. He saw here several that he recognized but he'd not seen in the classroom simulation: the Baondyeddi, like massive, many-legged pancakes ringed about with eyes; the monstrous but beautiful Sjhlurrr, eight meters long and mottled gold and red; and a swarm of silvery spheres hovering together in midair, the intelligent component of the F'heen-F'haav hive-mind symbiosis.

So they are *here. Interesting.* Most—not all, but *most*—of the beings in that circle towered over Gray: the Groth Hoj by a meter or so, the Drerd by literally hundreds of meters. Individual F'heen were a few centimeters across, but that flashing, shifting sphere of hundreds of closely packed individuals was easily ten meters across. The Agletsch was smaller than a human, perhaps half of Gray's height, and there was something to his right that looked at first glance like a glistening and flaccid pile of internal organs a couple of meters long and half a meter deep. Those few smaller beings, however, didn't lessen at all the impact of standing with so many giants. Gray felt dwarfed, less than insignificant. It didn't help that every single entity there belonged to a civilization more mature, more technologically advanced, than Earth's. He felt like a child in a roomful of very tall, very *old* adults.

And how could it have been otherwise? Humankind had emerged from pre-technological darkness only the blink of an eye ago. It had been ten millennia since the invention of the plow, a mere six hundred and some years since the discovery of radio, and half that long since the first human faster-than-light voyage. The chance that any star-faring aliens encountered would be younger than humans was nil.

He thought of the assembly as the Sh'daar Council, though how accurate a description of the group that might be he had no idea.

"I have information for this Council," Gray said, speaking through his cerebral implants. "Information acquired from the remote future—from a time twelve million years beyond my own epoch, and about eight hundred eighty-eight million years from this time we're in now. We learned this from the Glothr, on the sunless world we call Invictus.

"And I think all of you, the Sh'daar Collective Council, need to know this. . . ."

Chapter Six

Virtual Reality
N'gai Cluster
1212 hours, TFT

Konstantin-2 fed recorded imagery to the Sh'daar Council as Gray continued to speak. The powerful AIs on board *America* had, 12 million years in Humankind's future, tapped into the vast and intricate web of Glothr information networks. The information and imagery found there had been returned to Konstantin in the year 2425, analyzed, and translated. Those records, now imbedded within Konstantin-2's memory, created a visual backdrop shared by all of the entities present as Gray spoke.

"This," Gray said, "is the galaxy, *my* galaxy—we call it the Milky Way. This is what it looks like in my own time."

The plain and its looming circle of giant beings had vanished. In its place, the Milky Way hung in silent, glowing splendor against Night Absolute. The central hub showed a faint reddish tinge while the spiral arms around it glowed faintly blue. From this vantage point, it was easy to see that the galaxy was, in fact, a barred spiral, its hub elongated in its ponderous revolution about the super-massive black hole at its heart.

Four hundred billion stars . . . forty billion Earthlike worlds . . . some millions of intelligent species, many with star-faring civilizations—all within that single soft glow of tangled, nebulae-knotted, spiraling starlight.

"A wise human named Sun Tzu once said, 'Know your enemy,'" Gray told the others, "and so we humans have been learning as much as we can about the Sh'daar Collective. We know you evolved within this dwarf galaxy you call the N'gai Cluster, that your civilization was destroyed by the *Schjaa Hok*, the Transcendence, and that you rebuilt it from the ashes.

"We know that as the N'gai Cluster was devoured by the larger Milky Way, you spread out to create a new empire, one spanning both space and time . . . and that you were determined that the Transcendence would never again threaten your culture, or the cultures of other species that were interacting with you. We know that you found ways to travel from your epoch to mine, where you gathered many more species to your cause . . . the Turusch, the H'rulka, the Slan, and others. And when we humans refused what you offered—and what you demanded in return—you urged those species to attack us, either to force us into obedience, or to destroy us. . . ."

Thunder rumbled, deep and insistent—the Drerd interrupting. *You humans are balanced on the precipice*, the translation informed him. *You are closer to* Schjaa Hok *than you realize. If you fall, you threaten us all.*

"We have never understood your fears about this," Gray said. "If a single species in this entire, vast galaxy goes extinct—or if it enters its own transcendence and vanishes entirely—how does that threaten you?"

The spinning gateways give access not only to far expanses of space, another being—the one like a golden slug, the Sjhlurrr—reminded him, *but to the deeps of time as well. Causality can be broken. Whole universes of creativity and creation, of experience, of suffering and of ecstasy, of* Mind *can be made void in an instant. What thinking being could not fear such an eventuality?*

Spinning gateways. That must be what the Sh'daar called

the TRGA cylinders. He felt the Agletsch within his implant, confirming his guess.

"There may be," Gray said, "greater fears. We recently traveled twelve million years into our own future, and encountered the Glothr. We learned a great deal from them.

"And we learned about the end of galactic civilization . . . or at least of that aspect of civilization that includes the Sh'daar and Humankind."

And the virtual image of the Milky Way . . . changed.

That vast whirlpool of hundreds of billions of suns, young and bright and vital, its spiral arms picked out by the long, knotted battlements and parapets of black dust and by the piercing gleam of young, hot stars, faded away to shreds and tatters, to be replaced by . . . something else, a pale shell of its former beauty. The mathematical perfection of those spiral arms had been torn apart, the nebulae devoured, the myriad stars vanished or somehow dimmed—a handful of stars surviving of the myriads visible before. The galaxy had become a wan, dim shadow of its former light and strength.

And at the galactic core something *strange* was visible, nestled in among the remnant suns. Something shadowy, with just a hint of golden light. It was difficult to see, difficult to interpret, to *understand*, but it looked like an immense translucent sphere fully ten thousand light years across, forged, perhaps, out of the clotted clouds of suns that had been there before.

A scant handful of species, according to the Glothr records, and including the Glothr themselves, were in full flight from the ravaged galaxy behind them, fleeing to other galaxies across the empty gulfs of space. A number of dark and frigid worlds—a fleet, a *pack* of Steppenwolf worlds—were fleeing out into darkness.

"We think," Gray told the Council, "that what we're seeing in there engulfing the galaxy's central core is a full-blown Kardeshev III civilization . . . a galactic Dyson sphere."

As he said this, Konstantin-2 shared with the Council the background information to what must have been untranslatable terms to the alien species:

In the mid-twentieth century, the Soviet scientist Niko-lai Kardashev had lent his name to his proposed method of measuring an advanced civilization's level of technological development. A K-I civilization used all of the available energy of its home planet. A K-II used all of the energy from its star, and physicist Freeman Dyson had suggested how that might be possible: a hollow sphere, or, alternatively, a cloud of orbiting satellites, that collected all of the energy emitted by the civilization's star.

Which meant that a K-III civilization would use all of the energy available within an entire galaxy.

When Gray suggested the possibility of a galactic-scale Dyson sphere—and as they accepted the AI's data—he felt an uneasy stir move through his audience.

Why, the Groth Hoj asked him, *should we fear this? This . . . event lies nearly a billion years in our future. And it could well be our own remote descendents who do this. . . .*

The ephemeral is correct, the Adjugredudhran said. Its branching arms gestured sharply. *A mere four galactic rota-tions is a brief space of time for a truly mature civilization.*

The being's use of the word *ephemeral* almost jolted Gray out of the simulation. How long did the Adjugredudhra live?

And that question raised another. Presumably, they possessed long life spans—possibly even functional immortality—because they'd learned how to manipulate their own genome. But genetics was one of the proscribed technologies—the "G" in "GRIN," knowledge that could lead to the Tech Singularity. Supposedly, the Adju-gredudhra, like the rest of the Sh'daar, were doing every-thing in their power to avoid another one.

Were all of the members of the Sh'daar Collective hypo-crites on such an astronomical scale?

That thought disturbed him even as he answered their question. "Eight hundred seventy-six million years is more like *three* galactic rotations, not four," Gray said. "A mere instant!" He meant the statement as a joke, but sensed a kind of impact, an increasing sense of unease, among the alien listeners. Maybe they *did* casually think on a scale of hundreds of millions of years. "And in my time, my epoch, we might be seeing the first arrival of the galactic Dyson sphere makers. We believe them to be the Rosette Aliens."

At Gray's mental signal, Konstantin-2 loaded another set of images into the collective, virtual consciousness— images originally returned to Earth from the heart of the Omega Centauri star cluster. "A lot of ephemeral lives were lost," he said, "getting this information."

Konstantin was showing the gathered beings images collected by *America*, and by various survey ships and probes sent into the cluster's heart. The six black holes the Council were seeing—cosmologists were now certain—were the far-future embers of the Six Suns of the remote past.

The beings gathered about the virtual circle stared up, with wildly different sensory organs, into utter strangeness. Not all of them had eyes . . . but the imagery had been made available in a wide range of formats.

The Six Suns all were hot, young stars, each some forty times the mass of Earth's sun. Such large stars were profligate and short-lived. They burned through their stores of nuclear fuel in just tens of millions of years before ending their relatively brief lives as Type II supernovae and collapsing into black holes. The various star-faring beings around him had to know what these images implied, but he said it aloud anyway.

"This is the ultimate fate of your Six Suns," Gray told them. "Six black holes spinning in a rosette. Those masses, rotating that quickly, distort spacetime in the same way as the TRGAs . . . what you call the Spinning Gateways."

Gray knew, though, that the most intriguing part of the images humans had recorded weren't the black holes themselves, but what was within the central opening at the Rosette's heart: starscapes.

Different starscapes.

They changed with the changing angle of the recording sensors as they passed the opening, and Gray thought about how a slight change in the angle of approach through a TRGA cylinder could change your destination in both time and space. Here, one view of a sparseness of stars—a stellar desert—gave way to the teeming myriads of suns at the heart of a cluster or a galaxy, which in turn gave way to tangled, knotted curtains of nebulae . . . to the emptiness of intergalactic space . . . to a view of a binary star from relatively close . . . to a view of a spiral galaxy—quite possibly the Milky Way—seen in all of its spectacular beauty from Outside.

Some of those different views, those different *realities*, were alien in the extreme. One appeared to be a realm of searing, white-hot energy . . . the core of a sun, perhaps . . . or the chaotic incandescence of an instant after the big bang . . . or even a cosmos of completely different laws and makeup.

Cosmologists studying the changing scenes had concluded that each different starscape was looking into a different universe—alternate, parallel realities, some very like this one, some completely *other*.

"We believe the Rosette Aliens came through this gateway," Gray told the assembly. "They might be from the remote future. More likely they're from an alternative universe, a different reality. Some of our cosmologists have speculated that they're from a universe that is nearing the end of its lifetime, a universe in the final eons of cold, entropic decay. If so, the Rosette Aliens might be seeking a younger, healthier universe. They would be migrating here to escape their dying cosmos.

"But we don't know. We haven't been able to establish communications with them. We don't know what they are, what they're thinking, where they're from. They may be so far advanced that they literally do not, *can*not notice us.

"Some human xenosophontologists have begun speculating," Gray went on, "about the galactic Dyson sphere we glimpsed in the far future . . . eight hundred eighty-eight million years after this epoch you inhabit here. It seems statistically unlikely that we're dealing with *two* Kardashev-III species here—one entering my time as the Rosette Aliens, and a different one building a galaxy-sized Dyson sphere just twelve million years later. If these two . . . *manifestations* are in fact the same species, we need to confront them before they become well-established and begin cannibalizing the entire galaxy. This is completely beyond the scope and capabilities of Humankind. But if it is of interest to the Sh'daar, perhaps an alliance between humans and the Sh'daar is a possibility after all."

Gray hated saying that, hated the necessity of stating it. He'd spent most of his adult life fighting the Sh'daar. He'd started off as a fighter pilot off the *America*, then gone on to flying a console at Navy HQ Command. He'd served as CAG on board the *Republic*, as skipper of the *Nassau* and then as XO back on board the *America* once more, before eventually moving up to becoming *America*'s CO.

And now he was a fleet admiral in command of the *America* battlegroup, with orders from the president himself to forge an alliance with the federation of alien cultures he'd been fighting now for twenty . . . no, twenty-*four* years.

No . . . he didn't like that one damned bit.

Hell, the whole point of the war had been to maintain Earth's sovereignty against a coalition of beings determined to incorporate Humankind into their own order. But now here he was, with orders from President Koenig to explore the possibility of recruiting those same beings into an alliance with Earth. Could the Sh'daar be trusted? Could they even be understood?

Were humans going to lose their independence after all, after nearly sixty years of bitter and bloody conflict?

It tore at him, knowing so many of his soldiers—so many of his *friends*—had died because of these beings, and now he was essentially here, begging for their help.

He'd stopped speaking, his message delivered, and he realized that all of the gathered aliens were discussing it now with considerable animation. Gray found that he was unable to follow more than a fraction of what was being said. It was like being in a conversation where everyone was talking at once, and hearing only a word here and there.

He found the Agletsch's channel. "Aar'mithdisch? I'm not following the translation."

"The human brain has limitations," she replied. "It is unable to follow multiple threads, it seems."

"Are you telling me these beings can?"

"To an extent. All have been enhanced to one extent or another. You will be able to use the translation software to pick out separate threads and hear them in isolation, perhaps at a later time."

Which didn't help him understand what was going on *now*. He tried to tune in on different threads.

We do not know if these images represent non-Sh'daar manipulation of the galaxy. . . .

We do not know that these images represent reality. . . .

If the Glothr flee . . .

The ephemerals distort the truth. . . .

. . . has nothing to do with us . . .

. . . ephemerals do not . . .

. . . a billion years . . .

. . . afraid . . .

"What are they saying?" McKennon asked on a private channel, and for the first time, Gray realized that she had been experiencing this virtual reality as well, even though he didn't see her avatar here.

"I don't know," he replied. "Our translation expert says human brains aren't good enough for us to join in."

"Some Sh'daar brains and nervous systems have been artificially enhanced," she told him. "The Adjugredudhra . . . the Zhalleg . . ."

"I thought these species were all Refusers?" Gray replied, a petulant edge to his mental voice. "No GRIN technologies, no genetics, no robotics—"

"As far as we've been able to determine," McKennon told him, "that was almost never an absolute for them. If humans gave up all technology, that would include fire, sharpened sticks, and the hand ax. The most virulent Luddite wouldn't demand *that*."

"I suppose not. It just seems . . . I don't know . . . *hypocritical*,

I guess, for them to demand we give up certain technologies while they continue using them."

"They're also *alien*, Admiral. By definition, that means they don't see things the same way we do."

"I've heard that one before." He laughed. "And I still think that's a piss-poor excuse that explains nothing."

"Well, excuse *me* . . ."

"Oh, I wasn't picking on *you*. They have different world-views, a different context. I *get* that. But if this were a virdrama, having the villains do something weird just because they're alien wouldn't cut it."

"Maybe the problem is that this isn't a virdrama," she told him. "Real life is *never* as neatly ordered—or as explicable—as fiction."

. . . the Six Suns of the future . . .

. . . the Spinning Gateways . . .

. . . if the ephemerals upset the balance of . . .

. . . we must not . . .

. . . they must not . . .

"Are you recording all of this?" Gray asked McKennon.

"Of course. Aren't you?"

"I am. It's good to have a backup, though. You may be picking up pieces that my hardware misses."

"Good thought."

"Konstantin should be able to untangle it all later. But I *do* wish we knew what the argument was about *now*."

"Ask the Agletsch."

"Damn it. Of course. . . ." He shifted channels. "Aar'mithdisch? What are they arguing about? Explain it for my poor, underdeveloped human brain."

"They do not argue . . . not precisely. There is doubt that the imagery you bring from the remote future represents what is really happening. Two—the Adjugredudhra and the Baondyeddi—think it likely that the galactic Dyson sphere you've imaged here is in fact something built by the far-future descendents of the Sh'daar Collective. If that is true, of course, there is nothing about which they need to be concerned . . . yes-no?"

"The Glothr records show Sh'daar species fleeing the galaxy."

"The term 'Sh'daar' may have no meaning—or pertinence—in another four Galactic rotations.

"Too, others continue to insist that a billion years is too long an expanse of time for anyone to worry about what lies beyond. Those inhabited worlds fleeing into intergalactic space could be the future equivalent of Refusers, for example, or a defeated faction . . . or almost anything else at all. Nearly a billion years is a very long period of time, in which cultures will likely evolve and change out of all recognition."

"How . . . ephemeral of them. . . ."

"Some Sh'daar species are extremely long-lived," the Agletsch said. "They tend to take what you humans call the long view . . . and with good reason. But most feel the problems of today are more than enough to occupy their full attention . . . yes-no?"

"Time travel rather puts a different spin on things, though," Gray pointed out. "What the Sh'daar do here, in the N'gai Cluster, has spread to my own time."

"Of course. But of greater moment . . . the technically advanced species of the remote future may be able to travel back in time and affect what happens here. The Glothr, clearly, can do this. You humans have done it, by means of the TRGA cylinders. What terrifies the decision makers of the Collective is the possibility that someone . . . you, the Glothr . . . the Rosette Aliens will come back to this time *or before* and wipe out all that they have built here."

"Why? What are they building that is so damned important?" He meant the words lightly, a kind of joke.

The Agletsch liaison answered him, though. "They seek to undo the Technological Singularity, which destroyed their former *totsch.*"

The Agletsch word was not easily translated. According to Konstantin-2's database, though, it carried elements of the words "glory," "reputation," and "effectiveness." Gray decided that a good fit might be the Asian concept of *face*.

Could that be the answer? The Sh'daar had set out on

their anti-singularity jihad because they were *embarrassed*? Because they felt they'd lost *face*?

It didn't seem reasonable. And yet, knowing the human causes for so much of their own history, maybe that shouldn't be surprising.

"The war itself may be an emergent phenomenon," Konstantin-2 whispered in Gray's thoughts, almost as though reading them.

"What do you mean?"

"The Collective consists of several diverse species, each with its own agenda . . . and with numerous individual members of each species with their own goals and desires, all interacting with one another in essentially unpredictable ways. The pro-singularity Sh'daar who attacked us upon our arrival are a case in point."

"So?"

"Emergent behavior is defined as a larger pattern or behavior arising from interactions among smaller or simpler entities which may not, themselves, display that behavior. Mind arising from trillions of neural synaptic connections would be one such. Life itself, emerging from the associated cells of an organism, is another."

"Okay, okay. I get it. But *war*?"

"It seems evident that no one of the Sh'daar species rules or dominates the others. All do fear a repeat of their singularity event, however, and seek to prevent this. Their interaction with one another, however, might have led to a social acceptance of warfare as a means to an end, and the attitudes of other species would reinforce the emerging group ethic."

"Like a lynch mob," Gray said slowly.

"Precisely. One human alone might be unwilling to execute another human, but a large group, with the members exciting one another, would not hesitate. Humans have demonstrated this principle time and time again, in Nazi Germany, in Soviet Russia, in the Chinese Hegemony . . ."

"So what do we do about it?"

"Unknown. Improved lines of communication will help."

"Of course it would. The problem is we can't even understand them *now*."

The ephemerals try to deceive us. . . .
The ephemerals are of no consequence. . . .
We should investigate the Rosette intelligence. . . .

Who'd said that? Gray checked the datastream, and had Konstantin-2 tease out the tagline on the statement. It was the Sjhlurrr.

The Sjhlurrr posed an interesting problem for those studying the Sh'daar Collective of species, Gray thought. According to the data acquired twenty years ago, the red-golden slugs appeared to be less psychologically attached to a particular body image than were humans. Evidently, they'd used advanced genetic techniques to alter their ponderous and often inconvenient forms, transferring their considerable intellects into other, smaller and more mobile organic bodies in myriad shapes and sizes.

"I wonder," McKennon said, "if that's the Sjhlurrr's real shape."

She seemed to be reading his thoughts. "I thought the Refusers rejected the idea of genetic manipulation."

"Some did. But just as not all of the ur-Sh'daar went along with the technologies that kicked off their singularity, not all members of a species buy into a single ideology or meme. Think of how diverse human beliefs are."

"I guess so. It's easy to see all aliens as alike. . . ."

"There are some. One F'heen is pretty much identical to every other F'heen in its swarm, both genetically and in its worldview. They form telepathic group minds, so they kind of have to all look at the world the same way, not only within their home swarm, but among *all* swarms. But for most other species? No, they're as much individuals within their own groups as are humans."

Gray thought about that statement for a moment. While he agreed in principle, he was not completely convinced. For a long time, humans had assumed that the near-mythic Sh'daar were a single alien species, the monolithic power behind an alliance of galactic species within the T_{prime} epoch that they'd set to attacking humans. When the *America* battlegroup had first traveled back in time to the N'gai Cluster, Humankind had discovered that the Sh'daar were, in fact, an assembly of several dozen star-faring species working together . . . an empire of sorts, spanning both space and time, united in the need to stop other species from entering their own technological singularities.

And something about that idea simply did not make sense. Gray felt like he was tantalizingly close to seeing a larger picture, a motive behind Sh'daar decisions and actions, something that humans had not yet grasped. It had to do with what McKennon had just said about diversity within the separate species . . . but he couldn't quite grasp it.

With a mental shrug, he decided to look at it later. Maybe Konstantin-2 would be able to help pin down what was bothering him.

The Sjhlurrr, meanwhile, appeared to have the floor. It was urging a consensus among the Sh'daar in the circle, a decision to send a major military force through to the future and there confront the mysterious beings of the Black Rosette.

Our course is clear, the being said, addressing all of the beings in the circle. *Some of us have already traveled to the remote future to work with star-faring species there . . . and to prosecute the recent war with the humans, so this is not an issue of feasibility. We need to dispatch a task force, one of considerable size and strength, and attempt to make direct contact with these Rosette Aliens the humans describe. We need information to know what this presence in the galaxy is and what its intentions are before we make any further decisions about Earth, and the human role in the Collective. . . .*

The human role in the Collective. Gray shook his virtual head.

No . . . he did not like this at *all*.

Chapter Seven

TC/USNA CVS America
Admiral's Quarters
2125 hours, TFT

"This is it," Gray said, stepping aside at the door. "Welcome to my humble abode, such as it is. . . ."

Harriet McKennon entered the room, which came alive as it detected her body heat and motion. "This is incredible!" she said, looking about with pleased surprise. "I didn't know Navy officers lived this well!"

"Well, junior officers bunk two to a room," he told her. "Sometimes four to a room, if things are tight, especially on smaller ships. But one thing a star carrier does have in abundance is *space*."

"Ha . . . ha . . ." she said with mocking deliberation, lightly punching his arm. "Very funny."

As the room came on, the domed overhead displayed a view of space outside—clotted masses of brilliant, close-packed stars; the brighter glare of the Six Suns; myriad orbital facilities, artificial worlds and deep-space habitats; industrial construction projects; the nearby globe of Daar N'gah, bright with cities sprawled across its surface.

"Nice view," she told him.

Gray had been surprised when McKennon had accepted his invitation to dinner on board *America*, and more surprised still when she'd come to his quarters. He'd almost not asked her . . . and had felt as shy and awkward as a first-year Downloader asking a girl for a first date.

"So . . . what do you think of Sh'daar motivations?" he asked her, cutting the tension just a bit. "You've been here . . . how long?"

"Eight months," she told him. "Deep Time One became operational in April. I was with the first science team deployment."

"Are they serious about peace with humans?"

"I think so," she said, giving the "I" the slightest of emphasis.

"You don't sound real sure."

"Well . . . it's really hard to be absolutely sure of what they're thinking, you know? It's not like they share human values, or think like us, or anything. . . ."

"I hear you."

Different human cultures could be wildly different, with differing worldviews, different attitudes, mutually alien religions, social structure, and ideologies . . . and those differences had more than once led to war.

How much worse was it when the two cultures in question were *literally* alien to one another, the products of completely different evolutionary paths, completely different psychologies and worldviews.

"Drink? Inhalant?"

"Love one."

"What's your poison?"

"Can you make a jovian?"

"I think the bar can manage that."

He busied himself at the compact bar in one corner of the room. He didn't indulge in nano-stim inhalants himself—he had trouble handling the feed from his implants—but the room's bar had a sophisticated and well-programmed replicator suite that could turn out a decent 'halant in fairly short order. He punched up a nada colada for himself. He didn't care for the falseness of values brought on by alcohol, and saw no point in getting buzzed only to have to immediately de-buzz with nanosoborifics.

Besides, he preferred a clear mind.

"Is bare okay?" she asked.

"Uh . . . sure. Be comfortable."

She touched a contact point on the shoulder of her civilian jumpsuit, and the fabric of her clothing evaporated. Casual social nudity was the norm in Western society, of course, but Gray still had some ingrained taboos from his upbringing in the Manhatt Ruins. He hesitated, then dissolved his uniform. Being dressed while she was nude felt more uncomfortable than the alternative.

A thoughtclick caused a comfortable sofa to grow out of the carpeted deck. They sat together, leaning back, watching the strangeness of the sky.

"I thought this part of your ship was under spin?" she said.

"It is." He tapped the deck with a bare foot. "Best gravity money can buy."

"Then how?"

"The image is from a set of cameras mounted on our shieldcap forward," he told her. "The room's AI delivers the image, and does it pretty seamlessly. It *could* run a simulated image instead, of course, but I like knowing I'm looking at the real thing."

"Of course. Stupid of me."

"Not stupid at all. Technology is such a pervasive part of our lives, it's impossible to grasp it all, or know how all of it works. We simply accept it . . . take it all for granted."

"I just wasn't thinking. I guess I just expected the view to be rotating all the time, like it usually does over on DT-1."

"I can have it spin if you prefer." Another thoughtclick, and the starfields began moving, matching the twice-per-minute rotation of *America*'s spin-gravity habitat modules.

"Actually, I liked it better the other way."

"Your wish is the AI's command." The rotation came to a halt. "Having it spin makes *me* dizzy."

"Can't have the admiral in command of Battlegroup *America* getting spacesick, now, can we?"

"That wouldn't do at all," he agreed. "Especially with such charming company. . . ."

Curious, though. Simulations and virtual realities were such a basic, intimate part of modern life that it seemed strange that she'd not picked up on the illusion displayed overhead. For a moment, he wondered if she, like he, was a Prim. Primitives from the cast-off Peripheries around the borders of the United States of North America weren't brought up with the myriad complexities of virtual reality, cerebral implants, and full-field holography that were the hallmark of modern technic life, and could easily miss something like that.

But not someone who'd grown up with it.

Well . . . it scarcely mattered. Maybe she'd just been making conversation . . . maybe with an eye toward appearing vulnerable to him. He put his arm on the back of the sofa behind her head. She responded by snuggling a bit closer.

She inhaled from the silver sphere in her hand. "Mmm. Good." She glanced up at him. "You didn't seem very happy this afternoon at the idea of a Sh'daar expeditionary force to Tee-sub-prime."

"Didn't I?" he asked her. "I was the one that gave them the invitation. . . ."

"I know, but I also know you were following orders. And I don't think you cared for those orders at all."

He sighed. "No. But it does seem to be the only way to make contact with the Rosette Aliens. They sure as hell aren't listening to us."

She nodded. "I know. I . . . had a lover, once. Sheri Hodgkins . . ."

He frowned. "That name is familiar." He ran a quick search through his implant RAM. "*Captain* Sheri Hodgkins?"

"Of the RSV *Endeavor*. Yes."

"Damn. I'm sorry. . . ."

Endeavor and her two military escorts, *Miller* and *Herrera*, had been lost just over a year ago while exploring the

Black Rosette at the heart of the Omega Centauri cluster. The data they'd collected—images of something astonishing emerging from the maw between the whirling black holes—had at first been interpreted as the Sh'daar entering the Milky Way Galaxy of Humankind from the remote past.

The *Endeavor* and her escorts, it was now believed, had been accidentally destroyed by a super-intelligence emerging from the Black Rosette, an intelligence that hadn't even realized that they were there.

Humanity's first encounter with the Rosette Aliens.

And Sheri Hodgkins had been *Endeavor*'s skipper.

"So, I guess you know about the Rosette Aliens not listening to us. . . ."

"Yeah. I do." She inhaled another whiff of her jovian. "'S'funny. I was almost on board the *Endeavor* myself. I'd been selected for a slot in her xenosoph department, and I'd been downloading contact protocols like crazy in preparation, y'know?"

He nodded. "What happened?"

"Sheri and I were married."

"So . . ."

"Monogamously."

Light dawned. "Ah . . ."

"Exactly. 'Ah.' I failed the psych exam."

Within the broad sweep of Western culture, casual sexual liaisons were almost universally accepted with no problem, as were most flavors of poly relationships—line marriages, group marriages, and the like. Monogamous marriage, while not forbidden, exactly, was generally deemed to be odd. *Monogies* were denizens of the Peripheries, where two people might bond with each other to watch each other's back. Gray knew. He'd been a monogie, been in a monogie marriage in the Manhatt Ruins until Angela's illness had forced him to enter the USNA proper to get her treatment.

That treatment had resulted in Angela leaving him and ultimately joining a line marriage in New York. And Gray had joined the Navy to pay for it.

The memory—he refused to have it edited—still burned like hell, but he'd gotten over it . . . mostly.

There was enough prejudice still within the USNA proper against monogie relationships to make things tough for them at times. Hexagon policy wasn't supposed to discriminate—it had accepted Gray, after all, despite his monogamous perversions—but every once in a while that old prejudice would rear its ugly head and try to make an example of someone. Failing the psych test probably meant that someone up the line had decided that it was a bad idea to have a married couple—McKennon and Hodgkins—on board the same ship, especially when one of them was the vessel's commanding officer. It would have been easier to replace a member of the survey vessel's science team than her CO, especially at short notice.

"Are you a Prim?" he asked.

"Hell, no. Born and raised in Harlan, Kentucky. I used to go hiking in the Appalachians."

"Sorry, Harriet. I didn't—"

"Hey, it's okay! Not a problem. But there *are* monogies who didn't grow up in the Peripheries, you know."

"I do now."

"You're from the Periphery, aren't you?"

He nodded. "That was a long time ago, though."

"I thought I'd seen something about it in your bio."

He wanted to change the subject, wanted it a *lot*.

"So . . . do you think the Sh'daar will succeed where we've failed?" he asked her.

She sighed. "Damned if I know. It's a long shot . . . just because the Sh'daar, almost by definition, are pre-singularity. The Rosette Aliens . . . well, we don't understand them, but that's probably because they're *post*-singularity."

"Huh. I hadn't thought about that."

She shrugged, which did delightful things to her exposed anatomy.

"Well, it kind of stands to reason, doesn't it? There was a lot of talk at first about how the Rosette Aliens might actually be the original ur-Sh'daar, the ones who transcended, coming forward into our time."

"I've heard that idea. It would explain why the Sh'daar are so afraid of them."

"Right. But the only link between the two—the Rosette Aliens and the Sh'daar—is the Rosette itself."

He nodded. "Most xenosoph people are discounting that now, though."

"What? Why?"

"To start with, the Sh'daar deny it."

"They could be lying."

"Maybe. But the Agletsch and the Slan both are pretty definite about that. The Rosette Aliens are *g'rev'netchjak*, but they claim they don't know who these guys are. And the Slan call them something that translates as 'sin,' meaning something that breaks all of the rules, that's unnatural. Again, though, they don't know who the black-hole aliens are."

The Agletsch word *g'rev'netchjak*, Gray knew, meant something so horrible that it could not even be described. "Usually when the Sh'daar get upset about something," Gray said, "it's because they're afraid of time travel. That seemed to be why they caved when *America* came to this epoch twenty years ago."

"That's right."

"I'm still not sure I understand why, though. They're terrified of temporal paradox? But if it happened, they wouldn't be aware of it, right?"

"Hard to say," McKennon replied. She pursed her lips, thoughtful. "Using the TRGA cylinders automatically implies travel through time as well as space. That's how we got back to the N'gai Cluster in the first place . . . and it's how the Sh'daar have been infiltrating our own time. It's built into the physics."

"So they ought to be aware of how it works," Gray said. "There's no grandfather paradox because of parallel branching."

For a long time, time travel—at least into the past—had been thought to be impossible, if only because of the problem of temporal paradox. Go back in time, kill your grandfather . . . but then how can you be born in order to do the deed?

The answer appeared to be that the multiverse—the totality of many, many parallel universes side by side within what cosmologists called *the bulk*—prevented that sort of embarrassing paradox by simply splitting off a whole new universe. Parallel branching: you go back and kill your grandfather . . . and when you return to the future you find yourself in a slightly different universe where you were never born in the first place . . . because years ago some stranger appeared out of nowhere and killed your grandfather. As for the friends and family you originally left behind: so far as they knew, you departed for the past and vanished forever.

"I think," McKennon said, "that they simply fear the whole idea of temporal warfare. That we might go back into the past before we ever met them and do something to make it so they never exist."

"Doesn't seem likely," Gray said. "The ur-Sh'daar were so far beyond us in technology . . ."

"A few hundred thousand years ago," she told him, "the ur-Sh'daar were gone, and the races that became the Sh'daar didn't even have space travel. When their civilization collapsed, some of them got knocked back to the stone age."

"Huh. I didn't realize things got that bad for them."

She nodded. "You can imagine how vulnerable they felt, how vulnerable they feel now. If we could get a line on an exact time within, oh, say a thousand years or so after their civilization's collapse, we could wipe them all out."

He shook his head. "I don't buy it, though. I don't think travel through the TRGAs can be that precise. We don't have a problem following a single known spacetime pathway back to here, but I can't begin to imagine how we would adjust things to open a gateway to a time a few thousand years earlier. And if that sort of thing is possible, why don't they go up to Tee-sub-prime, but just a few thousand years in *our* past? Wipe us out from orbit? Or take us over before we develop spaceflight ourselves?"

"As you say, I don't think it's possible to fine-tune things that much. Certainly it's not easy. Besides, they wouldn't be changing things. The original universe—with us going to the stars—would still be there. It would just be out of their reach."

"Which suggests that they have a use for us, even if we are too damned much trouble." He stopped as something new occurred to him. "Shit . . ."

"What?"

"I just realized . . . there's no way we could use time travel to wipe them out, or even change their history to any degree. Because their history is bound up with ours. Has been ever since 2367!"

"God, I didn't even think of that. You're right, though."

"If we do something to knock out the Sh'daar back here, then we can't go home . . . not to the home we came from. We'd find ourselves in a universe where the Sh'daar War never happened." He rubbed his forehead. "My head hurts. . . ."

"But that means . . ." Her eyes went wide. "God . . ."

He nodded, following her thoughts. "Right. Even coming back here and making peace-establishing nonaggression pacts and trade agreements—we're running the risk of changing our future. I don't know about you, but I'm kind of looking forward to getting back home. *Our* home."

"No . . . wait," she said. "That shouldn't make any difference. The war still happened. Admiral Koenig ended it twenty years ago—in this time *and* in our time—and things have gone on from there. It would just be a problem if we went back twenty-*one* years ago and changed something. Right?"

"I . . . I think so." He thought the logic through. "Man, I can understand why the Sh'daar don't care for the idea of time-traveling humans, though. We could really screw things up for *everybody*. Us included!"

"I wonder if we'll be able to convince them that we'll stick by our agreements. That we're not a threat."

Gray laughed. "I wonder if that's true!"

"What do you mean?"

"Humans aren't so good at keeping promises. Just ask the North American aborigines."

"Well, we'd better honor *these*. The Sh'daar intend to keep an outpost—a *military* outpost—in our spacetime. If we do something stupid . . ."

"They'll come down on us like a ten-kilometer dinosaur-killer asteroid. Maybe *with* a ten-kilometer asteroid. I know."

"We've assumed all along that the ancient Sh'daar had an outpost of some sort in our time," she told him.

"Of course. They would at least have some kind of presence with the various species they've established agreements with. They could build on that until they had a major presence . . . like our Deep Time base here."

"Maybe the Agletsch?"

"Possibly. They don't have much in the way of military capabilities, though. More likely it would be the Turusch or the Slan . . . one of those. Tough customers."

"You don't want the Sh'daar in our time."

"Is it that obvious?"

"In a word, yes."

He shrugged. "I don't trust them. I'd feel better if they stayed in their own time."

"Why?"

"They make no secret of wanting us to be part of their empire. That's been their goal since we met them, almost sixty years ago."

"Maybe. And maybe we just don't understand what it is they want."

He thought about this a moment. "Nope. Not buying that, either. They attacked us first, remember? They delivered their ultimatum, ordered us to join them and give up our GRIN technologies. When we rejected it, they attacked."

"Because they were afraid—"

"No! Not then! We didn't discover the TRGA cylinders for another . . . hell, almost forty years! We'd showed no sign of threatening them with time travel when they attacked us, okay?"

"We may have scared them just because we're so . . . aggressive. Argumentative . . . combative . . . quick to take offense . . ." She shrugged again. "They must have learned something about us from the Agletsch. We made first contact with them . . . when?"

"In 2312. At Zeta Doradus."

"Okay . . . that was over fifty years before they delivered their ultimatum."

"Fifty-five."

"Fifty-*five* years, fine. See," she said, smiling. "Argumentative." Gray rolled his eyes, but grinned himself as she went on. "Plenty of time to learn about us, about what we're like, about our *character* from the Agletsch. Maybe, so far as they were concerned, they figured we couldn't be trusted with GRIN tech."

"They're thousands of years ahead of us in their technology! What the hell are they afraid of?" Gray was shouting now.

"Ask the people of Columbus."

Right . . . Columbus. And that got Gray thinking. Three centuries before that, a Chinese Hegemony ship had steered a small asteroid into the North Atlantic, causing untold devastation as tsunamis slammed into the USNA East Coast and the western coast of Pan-Europe.

Search through Humankind's history, and it was possible to find dozens of similar examples, cases where the devastation and loss of life were limited only by the limits of the available technology. And, just maybe, *that* was what the Sh'daar in fact feared most: a star-faring species with factions and political subgroups and rogue states crazy enough to use such weaponry.

But there was more, Gray realized, and worse. It wasn't just the high-tech weaponry, but the cheerful willingness of humans to engage in wholesale slaughter, often on a colossal scale. How many times had humans engaged in genocide? There'd been the extermination of the Cathars by the Catholics, of the original native peoples of the Americas by Europeans and by Americans, of the Armenians by the Turks, of the European Jews by the Nazis, of Muslims by the Bosnian Serbs, of the Israelis by the Iranians . . .

The bloody list ran on and on and on.

It might be that the aspect of Humankind's character that most disturbed the Sh'daar was the human tendency to slaughter millions of their own kind simply because of minor differences in ideology, religion, or culture. For the first time in his life, Gray saw humans as the various alien species might see them . . . and the revelation was like a punch in the gut.

"I'm . . . sorry, Harriet," Gray said. "I didn't mean to yell. I wasn't yelling at *you*. I've been fighting the Sh'daar for a long time . . . I guess that I'm just not ready to trust them yet."

McKennon was silent for a long moment, then sighed. "It's okay, " she said, finally. "I don't agree with you . . . but I understand what you're feeling."

"Still, I shouldn't have lost my damned temper."

"Maybe you had reasons. I gather you were ordered to deliver your message to the Sh'daar? An invitation to come up to Tee-sub-prime and help us face the Rosette Aliens?"

He nodded. "That's right."

"If it's any consolation, the alien Sh'daar don't trust us, either."

"I was just realizing that. We don't trust what we don't understand. But . . . maybe the alien sons-of-bitches understand us all too well. And that means that they have their reasons to mistrust us. Shit . . ."

McKennon turned, rolling over until she was partly on top of him, her hands restlessly caressing him. They embraced.

They kissed. . . .

Later, Gray wondered why. He'd not exactly shown the woman his most endearing side. Yes, they'd flirted, but he was feeling thoroughly disreputable and awkward . . . definitely damaged goods. Sex with her in the hours that followed *did* seem to make it all better, leaving him relaxed and more self-possessed, more confident.

But the conversation with McKennon, he knew, had exposed a raw nerve.

Gray was going to have to do something about that if he was to work with the Sh'daar in the future.

Chapter Eight

TC/USNA CVS America
Admiral's Office
1512 hours, TFT

America and her battlegroup were on the final leg toward home—five days out from emergence into the Sol system.

And Gray was feeling ill.

It had started the day before with the symptoms of an oncoming cold: aching joints, headache, and a running nose. He'd linked in to *America*'s sick bay suite from his quarters and updated his biological virus protection. The medic program had recommended that he increase his consumption of fluids and wait for the upgrade to take effect.

Twenty-four hours later, it not only had not taken effect, but Gray had gotten distinctly worse. He was running a temp of 38 degrees—a low-grade fever—and the joint pains were worse. So was the headache, and the runny nose had turned into a sore throat and congestion in his chest.

He placed the palm of his hand onto the link pad at his office workstation and requested a full medical scan. Damn it, he shouldn't be feeling like this. . . .

One of the immediate benefits of the so-called Nanotech

Revolution in the late twenty-second century had been the development of ultra-small medical devices that could move through the human bloodstream or camp out among the body's cells. They could monitor the person's health, allow direct interfacing with external medical AIs, and download programming that could deliver treatment or even perform nanosurgery. Nanoscale medicine had resulted in the elimination of scores of diseases and conditions, and the various anagathic regimens had greatly extended the human life span. No one knew how far life extension could go, but there were some millions of people on Earth now in their third century and billions in their second, while showing no sign of aging or age-related disease.

But Gray felt like he was coming down with the flu. That shouldn't have been possible—the medical nano in his system would have detected any flu virus and eliminated it long before he could begin to show symptoms. "Connect me with the ship medical AI," he said.

"Ship's primary medicAI," a voice said in his head. "You are showing signs of a bacterial infection. Please wait while I conduct a complete scan."

There were human doctors on board the *America*, but they generally remained as backup for the extremely sophisticated medical AIs. *America*'s chief medicAI—the word was pronounced *medic-eye*—was nearly as powerful as Konstantin, was fully Turing-capable, and maintained a medical database far more extensive than any general AI like the one at Tsiolkovsky. Like Konstantin, it could communicate through speech as well as by impressions and background awareness.

And as with Konstantin, the Primitive in Gray sometimes wondered if humans could trust it. Its workings were far faster and far deeper than those of humans . . . so much so that its workings largely were incomprehensible. Gray had considered requesting one of the human physicians, but decided against it. *Trust*, he reasoned, was something you strengthened by using it.

He felt a sudden, sharp sting at the base of his thumb. The automed unit had just taken a sample of blood.

"Ow," Gray said. "Warn me next time, huh?"

"Normally I would use the nanobots already circulating through your system to identify the infectious agent," the AI told him. "I need a direct sample, however. One moment . . ."

"What do you mean, 'infectious agent?' I have a cold."

"You have what appear to be coldlike symptoms. A cold would have been automatically treated by the medical nano already in your body. This may be more serious. One moment . . ."

Gray waited as the silence dragged on. *More serious?* What the hell was the AI telling him?

Damn it, he hated waiting on test results like this, hated the uncertainty, the not knowing . . .

"You have been infected with an alien microorganism," the medicAI told him after a moment. Gray heard deep surprise in the inner voice . . . startling in an artificial intelligence.

"How? I haven't been to any alien planets . . . hell, I haven't been off the ship except through virtual reality."

"Indeed. Eight other personnel on board *America* have been infected as well."

"Wait . . . you said *alien*?"

"I did. And I do know how remarkable that statement is."

Remarkable? Well, yes. That might be one way of saying it. "Has there ever been a case of an alien microorganism infecting a human before?"

"No, Admiral. The TBB has held up since humans first ventured into space."

When the first astronauts to walk on Earth's moon had returned to Earth, they'd entered a three-week period of quarantine as soon as they returned. The chances of their picking up a pathogen on the moon were considered extremely remote . . . but the existential threat to the entire human species if they brought back pathogens to which humans had no natural immunity was considered serious enough to require the precaution. Quarantine procedures were enforced for

Apollo 11, 12, and 14; by Apollo 15, NASA biologists had decided that the lunar surface was sterile and the mandatory quarantine was dropped.

Throughout the coming century, special care had been taken both to avoid contaminating alien environments, and to avoid accidentally bringing back pathogens. By the early to mid twenty-first century, though, exobiologists had developed the concept of the Trans-Biospheric Barrier, or TBB. Microorganisms, it turned out, were highly specialized critters. Bacteria and viruses both had evolved over billions of years to infect certain specific life forms. Usually, a bug that made one species sick could not make the jump to another species. *Usually* . . .

Within a given biosphere—on Earth, for instance—things were not so cut and dried. Some pathogens could mutate and jump species—human immunodeficiency virus, or HIV, was a case in point—but were usually extremely specific in their preferred hosts. So it was possible.

However, cross-species infection became almost impossible when it came to life forms evolved on entirely different planets. Organisms that might mutate enough to cross species on the same world were blocked when the hosts were completely alien life forms, often with completely different types of proteins, sugars, and lipids.

All that meant that the chances humans might be infected by microbes from an alien biome dropped to virtually nil.

Medical AIs and human doctors kept watch against the possibility, of course, but in three centuries of spaceflight and encounters with dozens of alien species, alien bacteria or viruses capable of infecting humans had never been found. A human had a much better chance of catching a cold from a microbe found beneath the bark of a sequoia tree than of getting sick from anything encountered Out There.

"The chances of encountering a genuinely alien microbial life form that can infect humans are literally on the order of trillions to one," the AI told him as if reading his mind. "I would sooner suspect a human microbe that has mutated in an alien environment. However, I can find no genetic correlations between this organism and the terrestrial biome. Similarities, yes . . . but no direct genetic correlations. In fact, the mycoplasmid in question does not seem to be based on DNA."

He ignored what that might mean for a second. "Eight other members of the crew?"

"Here is the list, Admiral."

The names, ranks, and duty stations of six men and two women scrolled through an open window in Gray's mind. "Have you found any similarities here?"

"Yes. All of them had contact with members of the Deep Time One crew. Some invited members of that crew back to *America* during our layover at that station, while others requested liberty on board DT-1. It is likely that physical intimacy occurred in all cases."

Gray felt an inward jolt at that. "Good God! An STD?"

"A distinct possibility, Admiral."

A possibility . . . and a damned unpleasant one. While standard operational protocols were in place against casually inviting aliens on board, there'd been no prohibition against inviting humans over from the station. Each visitor would have been processed, of course, and given a standard medical scan at *America*'s quarterdeck. If any human passing through that checkpoint had been infected with something strange, something alien, the scan should have picked it up.

"Okay, so what you're saying," Gray ventured, "is that members of the DT-1 crew have already been infected. We showed up, and those of us who had physical encounters with them caught it, whatever it is." He had another thought. "How many members of *America*'s crew went on board the Deep Time station? A damned sight more than seven . . ."

"According to the records, over one hundred personnel from *America* crossed over to DT-1. Most of them were either engaged in offloading supplies for the station, or installing some updated electronics. Five appear to have picked up the infection there . . . all while on liberty. Three others, including yourself, Admiral, brought guests from the station on board this vessel."

He noted the names on the list: Chief Roger Drummond, from *America*'s electronics department, and Commander Dean Mallory, the ship's tactical officer. Chief Drummond, according to the visitor's log, had brought back a civilian electronicist named Paul Bremerton, ostensibly to look at one part of *America*'s electronics suite. Mallory had invited a Marine officer from DT-1's security detail, Major Sara Taylor.

And, of course, Gray had invited Harriet McKennon.

Had all of the people on the medicAI's list had sexual contact with personnel from Deep Time? That was an important question, and one they would need to investigate. A microorganism that spread through touch or by way of airborne particles would be a lot harder to stop than one that only spread through sexual activity.

"You'll need to question them about whether they had sex with DT-1 people," Gray said.

"I know. I began following the course of the disease as soon as the first personnel reported their symptoms. I have already begun questioning the others, seeking to build a comprehensive medical history. Two have not yet gotten back to me, but I should have at least a preliminary report for you in a few hours."

"We need answers right away," Gray warned. "They won't let us dock at SupraQuito if we report an unknown disease."

"Correct."

Another thought arose. "The other ships of the battle-fleet," he said. "Some of them had liberty parties ashore at Deep Time as well."

"Indeed. Three ships: *Bunker Hill*, *Deutschland*, and *Burke*, all of which are transitting to Sol with us. There are also the *Leland* and the *Verdun*, and the heavy monitor *Ceres*, which remained at DT-1. Altogether, I estimate a further forty-two hundred personnel are at risk besides our own crew. Of course, we won't know until emergence if any were infected."

Starships under Alcubierre Drive were for all intents and purposes isolated within their own tight little black-hole universe while surfing their gravitic spacetime waves at FTL velocities. They couldn't transmit and they couldn't receive until they were back in normal space.

"So . . . how bad do you think it is?"

"It's too early to say. However . . . at least so far, four weeks after the probable initial exposure, symptoms appear to have been confined to the original personnel. That argues for low virulence and a low rate of contagion. Symptoms appear no worse than a mild case of flu."

"Can you treat it?"

"Once I isolate the organism, it should be relatively simple to program a nanobiotic swarm to eliminate the infection. This does not appear to be a serious problem, and I would estimate that we can have the situation fully resolved by the time we return to Earth."

Gray nodded. "Keep me posted."

The USNA Navy was fairly relaxed when it came to sex. Centuries ago, the entire topic had been taboo; even in the wet-navy days of the late twentieth century, the subject had been avoided . . . or alluded to with juvenile snickers and salacious grins. Even in NASA, where the unspoken law of public relations had been "better to be dead than to look bad," the possibility of astronauts experimenting with sex in space was pointedly ignored . . . and married astronaut couples were never sent into space on the same mission. Even that much official disapproval had vanished with the first Mars missions, though, when married couples had been assigned to the first crews in the hope of maintaining a psychological balance over the months required for interplanetary flight in those days.

Nowadays, the assumption was that naval personnel were human, and that they would behave like humans when they were locked up together in mixed crews for long periods of time and under frequently stressful conditions. A second assumption went hand in hand with the first: naval personnel would act responsibly, and not allow human nature to get in the way of the mission.

And for the most part, those assumptions held out reasonably well.

There were some naval personnel who tried to live up to the mystique of the old wet navies, though . . . with wild liberties ashore whenever the vessel was in port, and attempts to find private time for coupling on board ship during long deployments. Fighter pilots, especially, (the male ones at least), seemed to be out to prove something in terms of their sexual prowess, as though a man's ability to maneuver a fighter was somehow enhanced by massive jolts of testosterone. That much had been a part of the breed since the days of canvas-winged biplanes.

Every now and then a directive would come down from on high warning personnel against fraternization . . . or against personal behavior that might degrade mission effectiveness. Navy HQ and the Hexagon frowned on more senior personnel having relationships with those of lower ranks simply because of the power imbalance and the potential for serious abuse. For the most part, though, the Navy command hierarchy simply didn't care. The two issues that had crippled the effectiveness of mixed-gender combat forces in the past—sexually transmitted diseases and pregnancies—were no longer problems. Medical nanobot swarms could be programmed to eliminate STD agents almost at the moment of infection, and effective contraceptives for both sexes had long since made pregnancy a matter of choice, not accident. So long as sex within military units was kept low key and didn't jeopardize good order and discipline, people could pretty much do as they pleased.

But something like this—an infectious disease that appeared to have an extraterrestrial origin and was spread by casual sex—that would almost certainly change everything. Military rules and regs might well snap back to the bad old days, when acting *human* was treated as a crime. Morale would suffer, discipline would suffer, and naval crews might again find themselves subjected to segregation and to intrusive monitoring of their every public and private moment. Hell, the ship AIs already monitored literally everything that happened on board Navy vessels. Privacy was not an issue because they simply kept the information to themselves.

It wouldn't be hard at all to eliminate privacy completely.

But then, it would be worse—*infinitely* worse—if *America*'s crew returned an extraterrestrial disease to Earth, and caused a wholesale biological catastrophe.

Gray was very much aware of the irony of the situation—a former Prim, a *monogie* for God's sake, conflicted—no, *angry* about the possibility that something so basic as casual, non-monogamous sex might become a thing of the past thanks to this incident.

Maybe, he thought, he'd managed to assimilate into North American culture more completely than he'd realized.

New White House
Washington, D.C.
United States of North America
1705 hours, EST

"Our assets, Mr. President," Lawrence Vandenberg said, "are stretched entirely too thin. There's no way we can cover everything that needs to be covered."

President Koenig scowled at his secretary of defense, then shook his head. "Not good enough, Larry. I know you've got a juggling act going, but we need to stay on top of all of this."

Koenig was closeted with a number of his closest advisors in a subbasement briefing room beneath the New White House. A holographic map floated in the air above the conference table, showing stars and the bright green icons marking ships, task forces, and battlegroups. The map showed the nearest star systems—those out to within a couple of hundred light years from Sol, though a window set off toward the general direction of the galactic center showed the teeming stellar swarm of Omega Centauri. Another peripheral window a third of the way around the table from the first showed the mysterious orange pinpoint known as Tabby's Star, which lay more than 1400 light years distant in the direction of the constellation Cygnus.

Among all of those stars gleaming above the table, only a handful had planets that were enough like Earth to allow humans to live there without extensive life support: Kore, Cerridwen, Osiris, New Earth, Chiron . . . a total of eighteen worlds where humans could walk unprotected in the open. Perhaps ten times that many worlds were sealed within airtight habitation modules, like those within Luna or on Mars, or—like the Pan-European base at Heimdall—were orbital facilities. Humankind was now an interstellar species . . . but its hold on the cosmos still was tenuous and thin. More than once, the various star-faring races of the far-flung Sh'daar Collective had taken some of those worlds and threatened to extinguish the human presence within its minute speck of the galactic disk.

Once, Koenig thought, looking down into the starglow, human philosophers arguing for reaching out into the cosmos had stressed the need to spread Humankind across a number of star systems in order to ensure the species' long-term survival. It was foolish, they'd argued, for humans to put all of their resources, assets, and hopes in a single planetary basket.

Establishing off-world colonies, however, had not markedly improved Humankind's position. The species would survive a cataclysm powerful enough to eliminate the home-world's biome . . . but they were learning that there were serious threats out there to *all* of humanity.

Hell, even the Sh'daar were terrified of one of those threats. . . .

"The war hurt us damned badly, Mr. President," Vandenberg reminded him. "*Very* badly. With the loss of the *Intrepid* out at 40 Eridani, we're down to just seven carrier battlegroups, and the *Saratoga*, the *Independence*, and the *Constellation* all are still undergoing repairs or refits in SupraQuito spacedock."

"True," Eva Morgottini pointed out. She was the current SecCol—the secretary of colonial development. "But on the other hand, *Constitution*'s repairs have been completed,

Declaration is wrapping up her space trials, and the *Lexington* is finally ready to launch, so that's something, at least."

Each battlegroup showed up on the map as a bright green icon, the *Constitution* and the *Lexington* at Sol—at Supra-Quito, actually—and the *Declaration* next door at Chiron, the colony at Alpha Centauri.

"And *America* is due back within a week or so," Admiral Armitage added. *America*'s battlegroup was not on the map, however. If they had been on sched, they should at least have returned to T$_{prime}$ by then, but they were still somewhere between Sol and the TRGA at Texaghu Resch, their exact position unknown.

Of course, all that hinged on whether they'd survived their visit to the remote past, and that remained to be seen. Koenig hoped they would arrive at Earth within the next few days, but he wouldn't know when that would be until they actually emerged from Alcubierre metaspace somewhere in the outer reaches of the Sol System.

"So . . . we need a battlegroup to cover Kapteyn's Star," Koenig said, trying to pull the disparate bits of data together, "and another one for this new mission out to Tabby's Star. *And* we need to build a task force to join the Sh'daar if they send ships. Operation Omega . . ."

That was the code name of the proposed probe of whatever the hell was out there at the core of Omega Centauri. The mission planners at Mars HQ had been assuming *America* would be a part of that, if only because *America*'s battlegroup was already—presumably—working with the Sh'daar.

"Sounds straightforward enough," the director of the National Security Council, Phillip Caldwell, said. "We have four available battlegroups and three missions, . . ."

"But we also desperately need a fleet—preferably a star-carrier battlegroup—to provide a deep-recon screen out here, in the outer Sol System, Mr. President," Armitage said, "*and* it would be nice to have another to cover near-Earth space, just in case the Confederation decides to take advantage of things."

Koenig gave the head of the USNA Joint Chiefs of Staff

a hard look. "Do we have any reason to suppose that they will, Gene? Phil?"

"The armistice is holding, Mr. President," Caldwell told him. "Things should stay quiet on that front, at least."

"I concur," Dr. Horace Lee added. He was a special advisor to the president, an expert in recombinant memetics, and part of the team that had finally brought the USNA's war with the Earth Confederation to a close. "The Pan-Europeans are wholeheartedly sick of war. Thanks to our memetic attack on the Geneva Net, they share a tremendous collective guilt for what happened at Columbus. There's always a potential for action by rogue groups, but for the moment, at least, the armistice is solid."

"I wish I felt your optimism, Dr. Lee," Armitage said.

"The biggest threat from the Confederation," Lee said, "is that they're *so* sick of war that they're willing to give away the farm when it comes to working with the Sh'daar. We might find that we've won the civil war with the Confederation . . . and surrendered to the Sh'daar."

"We won't know about that until we hear from the *America* battlegroup," Koenig said. "So we won't buy trouble . . . and we'll trust what Konstantin is telling us. The Russians, the Chinese, and the North Indians all are still pretty solidly with us. Pamela?"

"I agree, Mr. President," Pamela Sharpe, the secretary of state, replied.

"Okay," Koenig said, "carrier battlegroups. What do we need . . . and where?" He glanced at Armitage. "Not what would be nice. What do we *need*?"

"At *least* two carrier groups for Operation Omega," Vandenberg said. "Three would be better. That's going to be a big one. We were planning on *America*—because she's been working with the Sh'daar back in Tee-sub-minus, of course—plus the *Declaration* and the *Constitution*." He saw Koenig's expression and held up one hand. "I know, sir, I know. Just what's needed."

"The Pan-Europeans have been screaming for help out at Kapteyn's Star," Armitage said. "Heimdall—the orbital station out there, anyway—has been knocked out by something, almost certainly the Rosette Aliens. Putting a carrier group there is absolutely essential, partly because helping the Europeans will strengthen our new alliance with them, but mostly because Heimdall is twelve light years from Earth and that puts the Rosetters smack in our backyard, astronomically speaking."

"Geneva is saying the loss of their carriers in the civil war has left them vulnerable," Sharpe said, "and that we're going to have to pick up the slack."

"Exactly what are we supposed to do out there?" Koenig demanded. "If the Rosette Aliens are as powerful as we think, a carrier battlegroup isn't going to do diddly-squat."

"Maybe not, sir," Armitage told him. "But they need help looking for survivors—both from the orbital colony that's been lost, and from the ships they've sent to find out what happened to the monitor *Himmelschloss* and her escorts."

"Okay . . ."

"Ultimately, they want to mount a large expeditionary force that can grab the Rosette entity's attention and force them to talk with us."

"I can't get away from the fear that what we're going to do is force them to swat us like an insect."

"Maybe. But they're twelve and a half light years away, Mr. President. That is *entirely* too close for comfort."

"Agreed. What else?"

"We need a carrier group for Konstantin's suggested mission," Vandenberg said. He frowned. "Personally, I don't think that Tabby's Star is critical, or even relevant, but Konstantin seems to think it is."

"Konstantin is strongly suggesting that we send *America* out there," Koenig said.

"And maybe Konstantin can't always get what it wants," Armitage said. "My recommendation would be to send something small and unobtrusive out there . . . a frigate or a light cruiser, maybe. Let's see what we're dealing with before we commit a carrier battlegroup.

"And we need at least one carrier group for what we're

calling Operation Tripwire," Armitage said. He gestured, and an area of space around Sol glowed red. "Deep recon and perimeter defense."

"I didn't realize this was an actual operation," Koenig said. "Why is it necessary?"

"We are in an *extremely* vulnerable position with the Rosette Aliens, Mr. President," Vandenberg told him. "They appear to have dispatched a large force all the way from Omega Centauri to here," he said, pointing at the map, "Kapteyn's Star. From sixteen thousand light years away . . . to twelve."

"That's like going from the far side of the country all the way to our front porch in one step, sir," Neil Eskow, the secretary of science, added, "and it makes it *highly* likely that they will detect Earth, Earth's civilization, by picking up our stray RF leakage, if nothing else. We could be fairly confident that we were lost in the forest, invisible, before. Now, though . . . not so much."

"Exactly," Vandenberg said. "That's why we'd like to send at least *two* battlegroups to Heimdall, but we also want at least one more close in to Earth, serving as a tactical reserve. If they send another force toward us, either from the Black Rosette or from Heimdall, we need to know about it, and we need to have a force to block them."

In his head, Koenig tallied up the number of carrier battlegroups discussed so far. "Okay . . . so at this point we need five to six battlegroups . . . and we have four available. Am I understanding you people correctly?"

"That's about the size of it, sir," Armitage said.

"Okay. Why do we specifically need that many starcarrier battlegroups? We have Marine carriers, like the *Inchon* and the *Nassau*. And we have lots of naval task forces built around railgun cruisers or battleships. Why can't we use those?"

Armitage sighed, and spread his hands. "Mr. President, you of all people know that a star carrier is the single best naval asset we have for the widest range of missions, bar none. Showing the flag, projection of force, doing maximum damage to an enemy's system infrastructure, planetary bombardment, responding to the unexpected, the unknown . . . A carrier's fighter squadrons project force across an entire star system, and can do so at close to the speed of light. They can patrol, engage in deep recon, investigate deep-space RF leakage, protect the fleet. Simply put, no other warship can do the job as effectively.

"We do have Marine carriers, yes, but they only carry two or three squadrons, not six. They also carry at least a battalion of Marines for ground ops, and we don't like keeping them locked up in a tin can for months at a time. Railgun cruisers can pound a planet's surface infrastructure and operate against the enemy's large-scale space-based structures, but they're not as flexible when it comes to reconnaissance.

"Sir, we just don't have enough of the ships that count."

Koenig nodded. Normally, although the president was the commander in chief of the USNA's military, he or she refrained from direct involvement in the strategic planning. The president had other things to do besides micromanage the Navy.

But Armitage was an old friend and close confidant, and—as Armitage had just pointed out—Koenig himself had had years of experience commanding Navy ships. His experience counted for something. Counted far more than the mere fact of his office.

The hard part was resisting the urge to meddle. Standing here, looking down into the three-dimensional swirl of suns and fleet icons, it was easy to imagine himself back in *America*'s combat command center, giving orders to deploy the battlegroup.

He had to throttle the impulse, to hold himself back.

That didn't mean he didn't still have questions.

"So what are the currently scheduled deployments?" Koenig asked.

"*America* and *Declaration* were slated for Omega Centauri, Mr. President," Vandenberg said. "*Lexington* for Heimdall. *Constitution* . . . well, we could cancel her tour into Ophiuchi space—maybe replace her with a couple of heavy cruiser groups—and instead deploy her here in the

Sol System, both to keep an eye on the Confederation and to watch for the Rosetters coming toward us from Kapteyn's Star. I think my recommendation is to forget about Tabby's Star . . . at least for now. It's been there for over fifteen hundred years, it'll be there for a while longer."

"We *do* have several task forces available," Armitage added. "No more available carriers, but we have five ships organized around the railgun cruiser *Decatur* at Chiron. Seven with the *Porter* at Tau Ceti. Four ships with the *Jones* at Osiris. And five ships with the *Rogers* at Cerridwen. We might be able to pull one of them back for redeployment to Tabby's Star, and maybe use another to beef up our forces here at home."

"Konstantin strongly recommended a carrier group be deployed to Tabby's Star," Koenig said, thoughtful. "He was somewhat . . . insistent about it. And he suggested—again strongly—that we send *America*."

"We just don't have the naval assets to stretch that far, Mr. President," Armitage replied.

Almost . . . almost, Koenig took a breath to deliver a sharp and direct order: forget about watching the Pan-Europeans, send the *Lexington* to Heimdall, *Declaration* to Omega Centauri, deploy the *Constitution* as strategic reserve, and send *America* out to investigate Tabby's Star. That should work. . . .

But he would *not* micromanage his people. "Gentlemen . . . I appreciate you keeping me up-to-date. The decision is, of course, entirely yours. Just keep me up-to-date on your plans."

"Thank you, Mr. President," Armitage said, staring into the layers of holographic stars. "I *think* . . ."

But Koenig did wonder what he would tell Konstantin. The colossal machine intelligence would know what the decision would be almost as soon as it was made, but Koenig sometimes felt uncomfortable having to justify human decisions to an artificial intelligence.

He wondered, often, who was *really* in charge.

Chapter Nine

TC/USNA CVS America
Flag Bridge
1512 hours, TFT

Stardrive technology had improved tremendously in the past two decades. When Gray had been a young and uncertain lieutenant strapping on one of the old SG-92 Starhawk fighters, a capital ship like *America* could manage an Alcubierre rate of between 1.7 and 1.9 light years per day, and the 210 light-year voyage in from Texaghu Resch took between three and four months.

But drive engineers had continued their tinkering and, more important, powerful AIs had turned their artificial minds to the problem of increasing drive efficiency. Currently, the most powerful capital ships could manage fifteen light years per day, and could make the passage from Texaghu Resch to Sol in two weeks. Some smaller warships—the frigates and destroyers and gunboats—in a counter-intuitive reversal of ancient maritime technology—were a bit slower, the consequence of having smaller power plants and less available vacuum energy dragged from the Void.

Riding a gravity wave of her own making, then, *America*

swept into the outer Solar System fourteen days after her departure from the TRGA at Texaghu Resch. In a soundless nova of photons released from the tightly bunched space that held her, *America* dropped into normal space once again, emerging some eight astronomical units from Sol.

That was another engineering improvement, Gray thought as familiar stars became visible around a shrunken yellow sun. The Alcubierre Drive required what the engineers called a *flat metric*—space not warped by the gravity of nearby worlds or stars—in order to gather a closed pocket of spacetime about itself and accelerate. Two decades ago, forty AUs was pretty much the limit for emergence near a star of Sol's mass; now the limit was five AUs—about the distance of Jupiter from the sun. *America*'s navigation watch had emerged a hair early because Jupiter currently lay close to the straight-line course linking the TRGA with Earth, just thirty light-minutes ahead and slightly off to one side.

Only three of the original twelve ships of the battlegroup had accompanied *America* back to Sol—the heavy cruisers *Deutschland* and *Bunker Hill*; and the missile cruiser *Burke*. The badly damaged *Leland* and *Verdun*, plus the monitor *Ceres*, had remained at DT-1, while the slower destroyers *Diaz* and *Mattson* and the battlegroup's three frigates would be arriving in a few more days. Normally, the battlegroup's metaspace velocity would have been limited to the pace of its slowest vessel so that all could emerge together, but Gray's orders had been to get the star carrier back to Sol in as short a period as was possible. *America*, he knew, was scheduled to be taking part in the planned recon-in-force of Omega Centauri, and there was scuttlebutt that the star carrier would be given some upgrades first at SupraQuito.

And, of course, there was the minor epidemic on board to consider. Three more people had come down with cold symptoms, bringing the total number of those infected to eleven.

Eleven out of almost five thousand crew members was not terrifying in and of itself, but *America*'s medical AI had not yet been able to isolate the contagious element, and that most certainly was. *Paramycoplasmid*, the medical AI had said. Unfortunately, after that initial identification, the organisms had refused attempts to culture them.

It was almost as if the bacteria were in hiding. . . .

"Admiral?" Captain Gutierrez said, interrupting dark thoughts. She'd actually come aft to the flag bridge to speak with him personally, rather than using implant-to-implant electronic telepathy . . . a precaution against accidental eavesdropping. "The alert has been transmitted. Sixty-one minutes one-way."

"Good. Thank you, Sara." No one else was within earshot. He could drop some of the formality of rank and command.

"You realize that we're going to be quarantined . . . possibly for a long, long time."

"Yes, I do. But there's no alternative, really. Not until the medicAIs either decide this bug is harmless, or find the right nano to neutralize it."

America's medicAI might so far have failed to isolate the organism, but Gray was confident that once the full weight of Earth's medical infrastructure was brought to bear on the problem, it wouldn't be long before a solution was found.

It had better be found . . . or *America* and her crew would not be allowed to set foot on Earth—or any other human planet or colony—again.

Jupiter hung against the starfields ahead, a brilliant white star a few degrees to the left of the wan and diminished sun. *America*'s instruments announced the arrival of the *Deutschland* into normal space, and then, a moment later, the *Burke*.

"Make sure a complete report gets transmitted to the rest of the battlefleet, Sara."

"Already done, Admiral. As soon as we picked them up."

"Good."

"Orders?"

"Commence acceleration toward Earth . . . five hundred gravities. They'll come out and meet us before we get there, but I imagine they'll want us either in Earth orbit or at Mars."

"Will do." She hesitated. "Admiral?"

"Yeah?"

"Is it true the infection is alien?"

"That's what the medicAI thinks. It called it a paramy-coplasmid."

"What the hell is that?"

"I had to download the definition myself. It's in the ship's database if you're interested. The short story is that *Mycoplasma* is a genus of bacteria . . . Earth bacteria. It's characterized by no cell walls outside the cell membrane, which makes them resistant to drugs or nano designed to attack cell walls. Some are pathogens in humans; one type causes a kind of pneumonia. *Para*mycoplasmid just means it's *like* mycoplasmids. I gather from the medicAI that it doesn't have a cell wall either."

"So why can't they find it?"

"Good question." Gray opened a shared window . . . a view within a tube crowded with dark-hued wheel shapes—like doughnuts with flattened centers instead of holes. The inside of the tube itself was made up of distinct, roughly hexagonal shapes, like closely fitted brickwork. A scattering of tiny, translucent spheres raced ahead of the camera recording the scene, like minute bubbles each a fraction of the size of the larger shapes. They outran the reach of the camera's lights and vanished into shadows. "That was what *America*'s medicAI picked up in me during my physical," Gray said. "The big tire-shapes are red blood cells . . . each about five microns across. Those little spheres are each a tenth of a micron across . . . a fiftieth the size of a red cell."

"They're *tiny*."

"Roger that. They're cocci, which means they're spherical rather than rod-shaped. About the same size as terrestrial mycoplasmids . . . and those are the smallest true bacteria we know. Viruses and nanobacteria are smaller . . . but they're not really alive."

"And the medicAI couldn't find them again, after that one sighting?"

"Correct. I gather they've also been detected through some chemistries, but they haven't been able to culture them. And they'll need to, in order to find out what makes them tick."

"Sexually transmitted . . ."

"Um . . . yeah. Although one of the ship's docs told me they're assuming it spreads through any kind of contact . . . possibly within liquids. Saliva, skin secretions . . . If so, they could spread just by means of breathing in droplets in the air."

Gutierrez actually pulled back a bit at that . . . then relaxed. If the alien invaders spread by means of airborne droplets, every person on board the ship likely had already been infected. Air was screened for contagious organisms, of course, as it was recirculated through the ship, but the nanofilters had to know what they were looking for to block it.

It was a hell of a problem, and not one they could do much about. . . .

At least the illness itself wasn't bad . . . not yet, anyway. Gray still felt like he had a cold, with congestion, headache, and sore throat. Sick bay was treating the symptoms while they continued searching for the organism causing them.

But while researching mycoplasmids, he'd also seen an article about the Blood Death, a plague that had killed a billion and a half people in the turbulent last years of the twenty-first century.

That one had started off as a case of flu too. . . .

TC/USNA CVS Lexington
Approaching Heimdall
Kapteyn's Star
1710 hours, GMT

The star carrier *Lexington* emerged from its tightly warped sphere of metaspace five AUs out from the ruby-red pinpoint of Kapteyn's Star. Captain Terrance Bigelow was on the bridge. His second-in-command was Commander Laurie Taggart, newly assigned to the ship as executive officer.

The *Lady Lex* had only completed her shakedown cruise two weeks earlier, and had received her orders for her first active-duty deployment four days ago, on December 1. A full kilometer long, she was bigger and more massive than Taggart's last ship, *America*. Until the *Lexington* had launched, *America* had been the biggest warship in the USNA fleet.

Along with the heavy Pan-European cruiser *Valiant* and the USNA Marine transport *Marne*, she'd made the passage slowly—twelve light years in two days—to accommodate her slower escorts: the destroyers *Falk* and *Ramirez*, and the frigates *Gottlieb*, *Carruthers*, and *Ramaputra*. The other ships were dropping one by one into the reach of *Lexington*'s scanners as the light of their emergence reached the carrier.

"There," Bigelow said sharply. "*That's* the sucker. . . ."

"Yeah, but what the hell is it?" Lieutenant Donahue, jacked into the *Lex*'s helm, wanted to know.

"It's big," Taggart suggested. "Gods . . . it's *big*."

And is this *what you've been waiting for?* she asked herself.

The gas giant Bifrost hung suspended against the panorama of space ahead, a sharp crescent bisected by edge-on rings of silver-gold. Beyond the crescent's bow, Kapteyn's Star gleamed a deep ruby red, a star's pinpoint of light so small that the disk wasn't visible to unaugmented vision. Off to one side, a smaller crescent bowed away from the tiny sun, its poles aglow with ghostly auroras.

Space around gas giant, moon, and star was filled with something like mist, tenuous and translucent, all but invisible to the unaided eye. Within that mist, Taggart could make out complex shapes, alien geometries formed by the haze itself. Arcs and beams and more complex shapes appeared to interconnect the three, as the ship's sensors detected other, more solid forms adrift in the haze. As her eyes gained experience picking out the subtle details, she began to see something like a gossamer web stretching across space, lines and curves of light barely visible against the void.

"What do we have on the system?" Bigelow asked the *Lexington*'s AI.

KAPTEYN'S STAR

Star: Kapteyn's Star
Coordinates: RA: 05h 11m 40.58s Dec: -45° 01' 06.29" D 3.91p
Alternate names: VZ Pictoris, GJ 191, HD 33793, CD-45°1841
Type: sdM1
Mass: 0.274 SOL; **Radius:** 0.292 SOL; **Luminosity:** 0.012 SOL
Surface temperature: ~3570°K
Age: 11 billion years
Apparent magnitude (Sol): 8.85; **Absolute magnitude:** 10.89
Distance from Sol: 12.76 LY
Planetary system: 4 planets, including 1 Jovian and 1 sub-Jovian bodies, 2 rocky/terrestrial planets, plus numerous dwarf planets and known satellites, with numerous planetoids and cometary bodies . . .

KAPTEYN'S STAR PLANETARY SYSTEM

Kapteyn's Star I, Himinbjorg:
Planetary Type: Warm superterran
D: 0.168 AU; **e:** 0.21; **P:** 48.62D; **M:** 4.9 EARTH; **R:** 4.21 EARTH; **G:** 3.1 EARTH

Kapteyn's Star II, Fornsigtuna:
Planetary Type: Cold superterran
D: 0.311 AU; **e:** 0.16; **P:** 121.5D; **M:** 7 EARTH; **R:** 6.16 EARTH; **G:** 5.72 EARTH

Kapteyn's Star III, Bifrost:
Planetary Type: Superjovian gas giant
D: 5.1 AU; **e:** 0.13; **P:** 22Y; **M:** 2.3 JUPITER; **R:** 2.1 JUPITER; **G:** 3.73 EARTH
Moons: 67; One, Heimdall, is Earthlike.

Kapteyn's Star IV, Thrymheim:
Planetary Type: Neptunian ice giant
D: 8.9 AU; **e:** 0.46; **P:** 50.71Y; **M:** 0.65 JUPITER; **R:** 0.52 JUPITER; **G:** 1.73 EARTH Orbital artifacts include captive black hole of planetary mass.

There was a lot more, but Taggart focused on the largest moon of Bifrost, the glacier-haunted location of the enigmatic Etched Cliffs.

Kapteyn's Star III f; Bifrost f; Heimdall:

Planetary Type: Cold near-terrestrial gas giant satellite

D: 1,085,300 KM; **e:** 0.001; **P:** 7.8D; **M:** 0.97 EARTH; **R:** 1.12 EARTH; **G:** 0.94 EARTH; **ATM:** N_2, CO_2, NH_3, CO, SO_2 at 425.2 millibars; **T:** ~-50° to -5° C.

Notes: Kapteyn's Star was discovered to be an extremely old [c. 11 billion years] star that entered the galaxy approximately 800 million years ago when a dwarf galaxy, the N'gai Cluster, was cannabalized by the Milky Way. The core of that galaxy exists today as the globular cluster Omega Centauri. The first expedition to Heimdall discovered "the etched cliffs," natural rock formations covered by nano-etched circuitry forming the infrastructure of a powerful super-computer. Agletsch sources indicate that this planetary computer houses uncounted trillions of uploaded Sh'daar intellects, including members of the ancient ur-Sh'daar civilizations known as the Baondyeddi, the Adjugredudhra, and the Groth Hoj . . .

Taggart scanned through the cascade of downloading data, picking up the high points, skimming through the rest. She knew Heimdall by reputation, certainly; Sandy Gray had spoken of docuinteractives he'd experienced more than once, and told her about the Etched Cliffs. Here, the electronic ghosts of trillions of beings from the ur-Sh'daar resided in electronic slow motion, waiting out the eons. Xenosophontologists at the Heimdall orbital research facility believed that the planetary computer was ticking off time at the rate of something like a second per century . . . a kind of immortality in a way, at the cost of cutting themselves off from the rest of the cosmos.

She stared into the haze embracing Heimdall for a moment, wondering if the Rosette Aliens had come here because of the electronic ur-Sh'daar minds that existed within the planet-wide computer. Interesting thought. She filed it for later consideration. If it were true, then the cosmos had just come crashing in on the ur-Sh'daar afterlife.

Taggart heard the captain querying *Lexington*'s AI through the bridge links. The reply answered few questions. It raised more.

"The haze," *Lexington*'s AI told them, whispering in their minds, "consists of trillions upon trillions of small components, ranging in size from a few centimeters down to about a millimeter. The objects are not in orbit, but appear to be anchored somehow in space itself. . . ."

"But what's it *for*?" Bigelow demanded.

"That," the AI replied, "remains unknown."

"We can't fly through it," Taggart observed. "It would shred our hull . . . possibly vaporize us."

"Ablation," Bigelow said, nodding. "I know. But the two inner planets look clear."

"What does that buy us, Captain?"

"Time. And maybe some allies."

"What allies?"

"The Pan-Europeans had a major presence at Heimdall," Bigelow told her. "If there were survivors, if they couldn't flee the system, where would they go?"

"Ah . . ."

According to the *Lex*'s operational orders, the Confederation had dispatched a heavy monitor, the *Himmelschloss*, to Kapteyn's Star, along with a cruiser squadron in support. The flotilla appeared to have vanished, but there might yet be survivors in-system—fighters, perhaps, or capital ships damaged and unable to engage their Alcubierre Drives.

"Himinbjorg—Planet One—is in the star's habitable zone," Taggart said. "It's tidally locked, of course, but at least along the terminator there's liquid water. Surface gravity of three Gs. That won't be pleasant. . . ."

"The second planet out, Fornsigtuna, runs almost six Gs

at the surface," Commander Lee Yuan, the ship's xenoso-phontologist, pointed out. "*And* it's an icebox. Bad news all the way 'round."

"How about Planet Four?" Taggart asked, calling down additional data. "An orbital black hole . . ."

"We think someone used that to generate power once," Yuan said. "A *lot* of power, a very long time ago. But it's been dead for hundreds of millions of years, at least."

"Did they manufacture it?" Bigelow asked. "Or did they just find it somewhere and put it to use?"

"We don't know, sir," Yuan replied. "Thrymheim hasn't been well studied. All the attention has been on Heimdall and the Etched Cliffs."

"We'll concentrate on the inner planets, then," Bigelow said. "Comm . . . transmit to the other ships in the flotilla. Close with us and prepare for boost, low acceleration."

"Captain?" Taggart said, speaking aloud rather than using the electronic telepathy of the shipboard links. "A suggestion?"

"What is it, XO?"

"Send a fighter squadron out to the fourth planet, just to be sure."

"What makes you think the Confeds will have gone out there?"

"Camouflage, sir."

"Beg pardon?"

She indicated the electronic records. "According to this, there are a bunch of artifacts out there in orbit around the planet. Big ones. If the *Himmelschloss* was looking for a place to hide, it could do a lot worse than slip in among a bunch of dead alien hulks."

"Point. The Rosetters will probably know about those artifacts, though. They might be keeping an optical sensor on them."

"Which is why fighters might be able to sneak in, take a look around, and sneak out again without causing a fuss."

Bigelow considered this. "Okay, XO. Talk to Walt and set it up."

"Yes, sir." Captain Tom Walters was *Lexington*'s CAG, the CO of the star carrier's complement of fighters and auxiliary craft.

"You have ten minutes before we boost."

"Aye, aye, Captain."

Taggart passed on the skipper's orders, then turned her attention back to the enigmatic structures just visible in the haze.

So much of what they thought they knew so far was still guesswork. It wasn't certain that the haze and mysterious shapes were the product of the Rosette Aliens. After all, the Black Rosette was sixteen thousand light years away. And yet, those sweeping, vast shapes and geometries were uncannily similar to what had been glimpsed at the heart of Omega Centauri, and it was simpler by far—an expression from Occam's famous Razor—to assume that only one pack of godlike aliens was running around creating structures out of empty vacuum.

Godlike. She felt the stirrings of wonder, of awe. . . .

Angry, she shoved the thought away.

Laurie Taggart was—or *had* been until recently—a staunch Ancient Alien Creationist. Born and brought up in the Chicago metroplex, Taggart had joined the AAC Church when she'd entered a poly tetrad that included a couple of devotees. She'd not thought much about religion before her marriage—the laws of Earth's White Covenant blocked proselytism and kept all religion a more or less private affair. But one of her new husbands, Anton Brody, had been holding small meetings for years. The secrecy forced on all churches by the Covenant had allowed a group of formerly straitlaced Baptists to drift into new theological territory: God, they argued, had been aliens colonizing Earth hundreds of thousands of years ago, creating humans in their image and enlivening Earth's prehistory with the wild mix of mythology and misunderstanding known as the ancient astronaut hypothesis.

The idea had been around for a long time. *Le Matin des Magiciens* had been published by Louis Pauwels and Jacques

Bergier in 1960, long before popular writers like Van Daniken and Sitchin had grabbed hold of the idea. Many critics argued that Pauwels and Bergier had in fact gotten the concept from some of the fiction of H. P. Lovecraft from thirty years earlier. There was a lot of *At the Mountains of Madness* hidden within *The Dawn of the Magicians*.

Taggart had read them all. Had fallen deeply into the ideas.

Now she wondered if she still believed.

The problem was that the alien "gods" espoused by Van Daniken, Tsoukalos, Sitchin, and the other prophet voices of the AAC had turned out to be entirely too human. The first nonhumans Earth had encountered among the stars had looked like meter-long spiders with sixteen legs, four eyes, and mouths opening directly into their stomachs . . . and most of the species encountered over the next decades couldn't be described in terms of anything that had evolved on Earth. The most common habitat for alien life among the stars had turned out to be ice-covered oceans in the depths of gas giant moons, and among the species inhabiting Earth-like worlds in pleasant stellar habitable zones few were even remotely human in how they looked or, more important, in how they thought.

There were genuine mysteries among the myths and the archeological ruins on Earth, and in many cases alien intervention could not absolutely be ruled out, but neither could it be ruled *in*. There was no proof, and claims that early humans had been too stupid or too primitive or too unimaginative to dream or build big simply could not hold up.

Nowhere among the stars, at least so far, had there been a single suggestion that alien visitors had ever come to Earth, forged empires, built cities, or dumped their garbage.

None of that had bothered Taggart at the time, of course. Such beliefs, after all, were a matter of *faith*, not science. But Trevor Gray had kept asking questions and prodding the perimeters of her belief. He'd made her *think*.

And the more she'd thought, the more she'd questioned her church's central doctrine.

The final blow had come from her own experiences as *America*'s weapons officer. Again and again, human naval personnel had encountered artifacts, structures, and technologies that were stunning in their scale, awe-inspiring in their sheer depth of wonder, and utterly alien in their scope and psychology. There had been beings, ancient civilizations, colossi bestriding the galaxy far vaster and more powerful than any paltry deity of terrestrial mythology. Time and again, Taggart had felt the old stirrings of awe and wonder . . . and yet time and again, the civilizations stirring those emotions had proven to be fallible, mortal, or otherwise limited in their manifestations across the stars.

The aliens of the Black Rosette appeared to be the most awesomely and spectacularly advanced beings Humankind had encountered so far, with powers more akin to magic than to human technology . . . and yet even they seemed to have one flaw, at the very least. They were *so* advanced, *so* highly evolved, *so* utterly beyond merely human existence that they didn't even appear to notice human ships, technology, or attempts at communication. Xenosophontologists speculated that they were as far beyond humans as humans were beyond insects.

And yet, *surely* they must recognize starships and projected artificial singularities and quantum power taps as technology. Did they literally not notice human ships? Did they somehow assume that human ships were natural phenomenon? Or did they simply not care?

The thought that the Rosette Aliens were so advanced that they literally couldn't notice human technology was more than a blow to human pride. It begged the question were they so blind they overlooked clear indications of starfaring technology? Or, rather, were they so arrogant they *chose* not to see it?

Either possibility represented a significant blind spot in the Rosette Alien mindset.

And for Laurie Taggart, either possibility led inescapably to a single hard realization. Even beings as powerful as the Rosette Aliens had weaknesses . . . and fell short of Laurie's belief set regarding God.

The God of the Bible—the God of that original Chicagoan Baptist sect before they'd left their theological roots and wandered off in search of ancient aliens—was supposed to have been powerful enough to create the world, yet compassionate enough and observant enough to notice a sparrow's fall.

The universe, in so far as Taggart had been able to determine, possessed no being that versatile, that infinite . . .

. . . or that loving.

Chapter Ten

TC/USNA CVS America
Flag Bridge
2224 hours, TFT

"Didn't take them long to make a decision, did it?" Gray murmured, half to himself.

"There was a lot riding on that decision," Gutierrez replied. "Maybe the survival of the human species."

Gray was feeling worse, his head pounding and a nasty vertigo that tended to sneak up on him, especially when he was in microgravity. He was watching from the flag bridge as *America* decelerated into orbit . . . not at the SupraQuito naval base facilities, but in orbit around Luna, some 400,000 kilometers away. Gutierrez was below him on the ship's bridge, guiding the carrier in. They were carrying a second ship clinging to their spine, and maneuvering was awkward with the extra, off-balance mass.

Two hours after transmitting a message to Earth, including everything known so far about the possible alien infection, *America* had received new orders from Earth. She was to rendezvous with an escort now being assembled to bring her to quarantine . . . and to begin studying the mysterious and elusive microorganism.

That escort—three heavy cruisers and the medical support ship *Andreas Vesalius*—had matched course and speed with *America* and the ships with her an hour out from Earth.

The *Vesalius* was part hospital ship, part research vessel, and she carried some of the most powerful medicAI intellects outside of Earth itself. Five hundred meters long, she had come alongside *America* while the star carrier was still decelerating, clasped her spine with nanomophic grapples and snugged up beside her in a high-tech embrace. Multiple docking tubes connected the two ships, dissolving sections of *America*'s hull to form airtight seals rather than bothering with formal hatches and airlocks. Emergency techs were on board moments later, anonymous in full-coverage airtight suits indistinguishable from vacuum garb, and accompanied by humanoid medical robots. As *America*'s AIs took on the duties of human personnel, robots had the humans begin queueing up for nanomedical injection.

As one of the handful of infected personnel, Gray had been the first in line. The nano they were giving him, a human medic had told him, was more sophisticated than that available to *America*'s sick bay suite, highly flexible stuff that could take a wide variety of programs. It coursed through his circulatory system now, the ultra-tiny robots reproducing themselves from carbon and other elements extracted from his cells, their programming set to locate and identify invading microorganisms. Once they found the invader, they would begin eliminating it.

Hours later, the *America* had slipped into Lunar Orbit as techs and robots off the *Vesalius* continued to give out the injections.

"Admiral Gray?"

Gray turned to face Dr. William Hoffman, the human doctor in charge of the *Vesalius* medical team. Like the other new arrivals on board, he was wearing a hab suit to protect him from possible infection.

"Yes, Doctor. What's the word?"

"We've completed the injections for the entire crew. We finished on the other ships in your squadron a little while ago."

"How soon will we know something?"

"No way of telling, Admiral. You can't rush stuff like this."

"Whatever it is, it *is* spreading," Gray said. "I've had reports of additional cases just in the past few hours. The total number of cases just on the *America* is now up to twenty."

"I know, Admiral. There are more cases on the *Bunker Hill*, the *Burke*, and the *Deutschland* as well. Ninety-three total."

The spread of the disease was accelerating, then. *Not* good. The worst part, though, was that it might take a long time to isolate and identify the bacteriological agent.

And the crew of *America* and the rest of the ships with her would be prisoners at *least* until that happened. . . .

"I have given strict orders for all crews to avoid fraternization," Gray said. He was feeling . . . *guilty*, he decided. Not because of his tryst with McKennon, necessarily, but simply because everything that happened to and within the ships under his command were ultimately his responsibility. And somewhere along the line, he'd failed in that responsibility—failed . . . and raised the specter of introducing an alien plague to Earth.

Damn it, what else could he *do*? What else could he have done?

"Very wise, Admiral," Hoffman told him. "However, the evidence seems to suggest that transmission can be carried out by other means, not just through sex. This organism is the one epidimiologists dread. It spreads by means of *any* bodily contact, or by means of droplets floating in the air—from a sneeze, say."

"*America*'s medicAI already told us that."

"It also has a fairly long incubation period . . . and symptoms so minor that a lot of people don't report them. All of that means that once it gets a good foothold in the general population, it will spread like wildfire across Earth and every other human-inhabited planet. That's why we need to enforce isolation for your crews."

Gray nodded. "I understand that. And we don't yet know if it's dangerous."

"Exactly," Hoffman replied. "Which means we have to assume it's dangerous. The onset and the way it spreads . . ." He hesitated, shook his head, then added, "Admiral, it's suspiciously similar to the Blood Death."

That captured Gray's attention, because it was exactly what he had thought a few days back.

"It's not Blood Death, is it?"

"No. I wish it were, because we can identify and eradicate *Staphylococcus hemoragia*. Believe me, that was the first thing we checked." He hesitated. "And . . . there's something else."

"*Wonderful . . .*" Gray's voice dripped bitterness. The ache in his head and in his joints was worse, he realized, a *lot* worse. How long before he had to relieve himself of duty?

"Whatever it is, I think we can say with confidence that it *is* of alien origin. Almost certainly the Sh'daar, since you seem to have acquired this bug in the N'gai Cluster. That, and the fact that it's so damned hard to find now, after your medicAI first picked it up in a routine scan, suggests that it's not natural."

Gray's eyes widened at that. "Not . . . natural . . ."

"Admiral, the N'gai bug might be a deliberately bioengineered organism, or even a form of biological nanotechnology. In other words . . . a *weapon*."

Gray digested the implications of this. He almost said something more, but held back. Hoffman and his people were doing the best they could. Any useless exhortation he could make would be useless.

He would need to set up a long-distance conference with President Koenig, he decided. If they were facing an alien bioweapon, then the government had seriously misjudged the political situation, seriously misjudged the Sh'daar and their overtures of peace.

Seriously misjudged . . .

Gray's head was pounding, the pain a sudden flare of agony behind his eyes.

He twisted forward, adrift in the microgravity of the ship's flag bridge. Blood abruptly gushed from his nose, forming bright red spheres adrift in microgravity.

He felt Hoffman's gloved hand on his arm, heard Hoffman shouting, but couldn't make out the words through the pain.

Gods . . . he felt *sick*. . . .

6 December 2425
TC/USNA CVS Lexington
Command Bridge
0918 hours, TFT

"The planet is tidally locked," Lieutenant Carla Milton reported. She was *Lexington*'s chief navigation officer. "We expected that, of course. This close to the star, it would have to be."

"I've got the download data on the system here," Taggart replied. "Tell me stuff I *don't* know."

"Sorry, Commander." Milton sounded chastened.

Taggart started to say something sharp in response, then stifled it. She was in a foul mood. Being forced to re-examine her religion tended to do that to her. The White Covenant restrictions on talking to others about religious belief made it worse, and the sense of isolation left her angry and depressed.

"No, *I'm* sorry, Lieutenant," she said after a long moment. "You tell me whatever you think I need to know."

"Aye, aye, Commander." But she sounded hurt. *Damn* . . .

Strapped into the commander's chair, Taggart watched the bridge viewall screens ahead and above. The planet listed on the astrogational charts as Himinbjorg loomed vast on the bridge visuals, an immense black sphere edged by an orange-gold crescent. Patches of angry red showed on the world's night side, evidence of titanic lava flows and tidally induced volcanism. Beyond, Kapteyn's Star spanned .09 degrees of sky, just a bit less than twice the size of Sol as seen from Earth, and close enough that swarms of mottled black sunspots were clearly visible across the star's glowing red surface.

The name *Himinbjorg* came from the ancient Norse and meant "Heaven's Fortress" or possibly "Heaven's Mountain." According to myth, it was the home of Heimdall, the guardian of Bifrost, the Rainbow Bridge, which stretched between Earth and heaven. In the real world, it was a planet of extremes. It orbited within its star's habitable zone, where water remained liquid and the climate theoretically remained temperate. That would probably be the case but for the fact that one side remained anchored in place facing its sun, which meant that it was a baking desert with temperatures just below boiling, while the dark side was locked in glaciers with temperatures well below zero. Tidal stresses caused the volcanism, and continent-sized lava flows glowed eerily against the eternal night, helping free the water locked up in ice.

The twilight zone circled the planet, pole to pole, a narrow region where the sun seemed always to hover at the horizon, bobbing slowly up and down between dawn and sunrise with the planet's nodding libration. Temperatures here remained livable, though the lava flows boiled the seas, and so native life hung on by a thread. The atmosphere was predominantly nitrogen and oxygen, as on Earth, but was made poisonous by choking clouds of hydrogen sulfide and sulfur dioxide.

No human outpost or colony had been established on the hellish world, which wasn't suprising. They actually were counting on this fact, knowing that the Rosette Aliens would certainly have investigated Himinbjorg had there been a human presence there. The Pan-European ships in the system would have known this too . . . and might well be hiding there, either in orbit or somewhere down on the surface.

"Sensors," Taggart said. "Any sign of the Confeds?"

"Negative, Commander," Lieutenant Jorge Chavez replied. "There's nothing."

"How about the aliens? Have they noticed us?"

"How are we supposed to tell?" Bigelow's voice said behind her.

"Captain on the bridge," Taggart said, unsnapping her harness and floating clear of the command chair. "The ship is yours, sir."

"Thank you, Commander." With practiced ease, Bigelow slipped into the seat, which adjusted itself to his slightly more massive bulk, and snapped on the harness. "No sign of anyone home, huh?"

"No, sir. I'm beginning to wonder about the outer world. What's the name? Thrymheim."

"A distinct possibility. The Headhunters will find them if that's where they are."

"Yes, sir." VFA-211, the Headhunters, was one of the fighter squadrons operating off the *Lexington*. The *Lex* had launched them hours ago with orders to investigate Thrymheim . . . but quietly. Bigelow was concerned about attracting the Rosette Aliens' notice. The assumption was that they had such advanced technologies that they were aware of everything happening within the system. So far, at least, they'd not shown any sign that they knew the human flotilla was there.

Bigelow—and Taggart—hoped to keep it that way.

VFA-211
Approaching Thrymheim
1115 hours, TFT

Like the vast majority of gas and ice giants discovered so far, Thrymheim was a ringed world, though the particles were mostly coal black and the ring system was difficult to see, especially in the wan light of the local star almost nine AUs distant.

The name *Thrymheim* had been bestowed on the dark and icy world by the first human expedition to Kapteyn's Star late in the twenty-second century. In keeping with the Norse mythological theme of the system, the name meant "Crash Home" or "Thunder Home," or possibly "Power Home."

Power House worked too. . . .

Lieutenant Jason Meier didn't much care for the idea of a world called Crash Home, though the downloads he'd pulled off of *Lexington*'s computer before he'd launched suggested that the name referred to the crash of thunder rather than something—like an SG-420 Starblade, for instance— falling out of the sky.

Thunder was certainly in keeping with the idea of Thrymheim being located in Jotunheim, the world of the Norse ice giants. In fact, the members of the first Kapteyn's Star expedition had named it Power House because of Thrymheim's small and enigmatic companion.

The first interstellar expeditions out from Earth a couple of centuries earlier had found plenty of proof that humans were not alone among the stars. Long before they encountered the first living extraterrestrials—the Agletsch—human explorers had found alien ruins, the fragments and detritus and crumbled dreams of civilizations long passed into the Night.

And some of those fragments had been discovered here at Kapteyn's Star. The Etched Cliffs of Heimdall had not immediately been recognized as the product of a technological civilization, but the mysterious satellite Thrymheim was clearly artificial.

It was a black hole of roughly terrestrial mass, compressed into a knot of high-gravity strangeness a couple of centimeters wide. The accretion disk, the plane of dust orbiting the hole, was what tipped observers off as to its artificial nature. Spectroscopic scans of the accretion disk material showed a preponderance of the expected elements—iron, silicon, aluminum, carbon, and such—but there was also a surprisingly high percentage of rare earths and precious metals—gold, cobalt, neodymium, samarium, and holmium, especially.

The expedition xenotechnologists had assumed that the cloud of debris orbiting the miniature black hole was what was left of a large artificial structure that originally had enclosed a singularity at its heart—most likely as part of a power-generating complex. Human technology utilized artificially generated microsingularities both for propulsion and for power generation; a pair of resonating black holes orbiting each other could be used to extract almost unlimited amounts of vacuum energy. Someone had clearly been doing the same thing in orbit around Thrymheim, though whether the debris represented a large orbital power-generating plant or a *very* large spacecraft destroyed in orbit was still an open question. Those rare earths—the samarium, neodymium, and holmium, especially, as well as significant amounts of compounds like $SmCo_5$—samarium cobalt—suggested the use of ultra-powerful artificial magnets in the original structure. With all that background, an AI with an interest in Norse mythology had suggested the name for the planet: Power House.

The Earth Confederation had pumped a lot of resources into the orbital complex around Bifrost. Most of that research colony's attention, of course, had been directed at the moon Heimdall and its mysterious Etched Cliffs—in essence a planet-wide supercomputer housing trillions of uploaded minds—but their charter had also emphasized study of the high-tech wreckage out at Thrymheim.

Power House . . .

Lieutenant Jason Meier guided his SG-420 Starblade into a new vector, dropping toward the debris field. The bizarre object had been designated "AC-1"—AC for "Accretion Disk"—in his briefings, a term immediately morphed by the fighter pilots into "Ace." The thing was still invisible to the naked eye, but he could see it on his long-range sensors. From 250,000 kilometers out, the Neptune-sized world of Thrymheim showed as a huge, blue-green sphere blocking out much of the starfield ahead. A red computer graphic showed the position of Ace off to one side.

"So how come that accretion disk is still there?" Lieutenant Pamela Schaeffer asked, using a tightly confined directional comm channel. "It's been here for . . . what? Almost eight hundred million years, they say? Shouldn't the black hole have slurped all of that crap down by now?"

"It probably *did* eat most of . . . whatever was there," Meier replied. "But a lot of the stuff would have been far enough out to maintain stable orbits. Uh . . . we'd better maintain comm silence, Pam."

"Why? If the Rosetters are as advanced as everyone says, they *know* we're here."

She had a point. The squadron had not been ordered to maintain communications silence, if only because they needed to coordinate their maneuvers out here in the outer darkness. Besides, there was a blanket of interference from the interacting magnetic and radiation fields surrounding both Thrymheim and Ace; it should keep them safe enough.

Even so, it was impossible for Meier to escape the feeling that someone very large and very powerful was staring at him.

Staring as though undecided as yet what it was going to do about these mayfly intruders flitting about in its backyard.

"You're right," he said after a moment. "Hell, I think I'd feel better if the Rosetters *did* do something . . . just to let us know they care!"

"I hear you, brother." Schaeffer was silent for a moment, then added, "I'm starting to get a visual."

Meier checked his own optics, and found he could now make out the debris field—essentially a paper-thin ring twenty thousand kilometers across, but with a very wide, empty center.

At least it looked empty. At the exact center of that huge structure, he knew, was a marble-sized singularity. The gravity field, however, was identical to that of a planet with the mass of Earth; the accretion disk gap ended over thirty thousand kilometers out from the center.

"Look at the size of that thing!" he said. He could just make it out against the starfields beyond . . . a ring that looked like it was made of black powder with occasional glints of ice or diamonds or something more exotic mixed in. "The individual pieces of that disk have been grinding against each other for hundreds of millions of years and probably feeding the kitty all that time. But most of it stays stable now."

"We don't know it's that old," Schaeffer said. "The Sh'daar came forward through time, remember. Maybe this was a colony built in their future . . . but just a few centuries in our past."

"No, it's *old*," Meier replied. "Kapteyn's Star was a part of the N'gai dwarf galaxy, remember. The Milky Way slurped it down as a light snack . . . oh, what . . . half a billion years ago? We're not sure . . . but something like that."

"I heard seven hundred million years," Schaeffer said, "but what's a couple of hundred million years among friends, right?"

"Exactly. Anyway, Kapteyn's Star went walkabout when most of the dwarf galaxy was torn apart. And the xeno people think the Etched Cliffs on Heimdall are seven or eight hundred million years old too . . . probably going back to the ur-Sh'daar, before their Technological Singularity."

"I wonder what the rings were, originally."

"Who knows? There's enough mass in there for a small planet . . . not counting the black hole. Whatever it was, it was damned big."

"Cut the chatter, you two," the voice of Commander Victor Leystrom interrupted. He was the CO of the Head-hunters, call sign Hunter One. "We don't want the Rosetters picking us up."

Meier looked at the squadron formation, and noticed that Leystrom's ship had drifted in between Schaeffer's fighter and his own, close enough that he'd intercepted part of the laser beam carrying their communications channel. He grinned.

"Sorry, Skipper," he replied. "I didn't think they could hear us."

"We don't fucking know what they can hear, okay? So no talk except for what's absolutely necessary!"

"Aye, aye, Skipper."

"Roger that, Hunter One," Schaeffer added.

A pity, really. The laser-comm chitchat had helped cut back on the loneliness out here. With silence, the loneliness descended once again, a black and brooding emptiness that soaked through to your bones.

Strung out in a long line, the twelve fighters of VFA-211 fell toward the dimly visible ring in space. The Earth-sized gravity field was beginning to tug on their vector, pulling their fall into a gentle curve that would take them through the central opening of the ring but keep them well clear of the invisible singularity at the center.

Meier checked his instruments; the whole point of this operation was to try to find Confederation ships that might be hiding out here, and the assumption was that they would be carefully hidden . . . again, to escape the notice of the Rosette Aliens. One good possibility was that they were sheltering somewhere in that accretion dust cloud. A searching ship would have to get pretty close—a few tens of thousands of kilometers at most—to spot them.

"Hunter One, this is Hunter Five." Lieutenant Judith Kelly cut in over the squadron tactical channel. "I think I've got something here. . . ."

"Pass it to the rest of us, Five," Leystrom ordered.

"Transmitting."

Meier looked at the datastream coming in over the channel, and his eyes widened.

Jackpot . . .

TC/USNA CVS America
Sick Bay
1319 hours, TFT

Gray opened his eyes . . . then shut them tight once more. The glare from overhead was so bright as to be painful. He was soaking in sweat, as though a high fever had just broken. Somewhere nearby, medical equipment was going *peep* . . . and he heard voices nearby. Intense, *professional* voices . . .

A shadow blocked the light above. "Admiral Gray?"

He chanced opening his eyes again. The helmeted head of Dr. Hoffman leaned over him. Nearby, a medical robot made adjustments to the beeping machine. "Admiral Gray is awake," the robot said. "But I recommend keeping any conversation extremely short."

"How are you feeling, Admiral?" Hoffman said.

"Like I got hit head-on by a fighter pushing c," he replied. His voice cracked, and he felt terribly thirsty.

"You had us all pretty worried."

"I gather the disease turned nasty?"

"You could say that, Admiral. You're in *America*'s sick bay, by the way."

"I figured." Obviously he was on a hospital bed—the sort of high-tech foam support that encased his body and limbs and auto-inserted lines in various parts of his anatomy for nutrients and wastes. There was also *gravity*, about a half G, he guessed, which meant he'd been moved to the rotating hab section of the ship.

"There was talk of moving you to a containment facility on Luna," Hoffman told him, "but the orders from Earth are to keep everything isolated on the ships, at least for now."

"Makes sense . . ." He felt terribly tired, hovering on the thin, ragged edge of unconsciousness. "Anyone else?"

"Four others," Hoffman told him.

"Damn."

"Doctor Hoffman . . . Admiral Gray should rest. I would like to put him into medical stasis while we complete the treatment."

Hoffman glanced at the robot, then nodded. "Right. But before I go . . . we've got some good news for you."

"It's about fucking time. What?"

"We've isolated the bug. Apparently, it went into an intense period of growth, reproducing so quickly your immune system triggered, big-time. But now we know what we're dealing with . . . more or less. And we're trying to decide how to take the next step."

"What do you mean, 'more or less'?"

Hoffman shook his head behind the visor. "I'm not sure how to tell you this, Admiral. The alien microorganism?"

"Yeah . . ."

"It's *intelligent*."

Chapter Eleven

VFA-211
Thrymheim Orbit
1325 hours, TFT

The *Himmelschloss* was a flattened black spheroid spanning some five hundred meters—half the length of the
America, as big across as the star carrier's forward shield
cap was wide, but far more massive. The monster was a
heavy monitor, a highly specialized warship designed to
serve as a semimobile base within a target star system.
Heavy monitors stood guard close by several of the known
TRGA cylinders, and on the outskirts of the Solar System
back home. The monitor *Ceres* had been dispatched into
the remote past to protect Deep Time One, and another, the
Argus, was being prepared at the shipyards over Mars for
deployment into the far future. They were slow, they were
clumsy, but they were very heavily armed . . . and their
sensors could watch—could *monitor*—activity across an
entire star system.

The *Himmelschloss*, Meier noted, had been terribly damaged. She looked, for all the world, as though something had
taken a bite out of her. Fully a quarter of her hull was simply

missing, and perhaps another third was twisted, crushed, and misshapen.

God . . . what had *happened* to her?

"Hunter Flight," a voice called to the incoming fighters, "you are clear for trap."

"Copy that, *Himmelschloss*. We're coming in."

Lieutenant Meier rolled his fighter fifty degrees and morphed the outer hull into its landing configuration. Computer graphics unfolded in his head, marking the monitor's open landing bay and feeding him constantly updated numbers on his approach vector.

A second fighter squadron had been launched half an hour earlier, the aging KRG-17 Raschadler fighters of the Pan-European Eagle Squadron. A Kapitanleutnant Martin Schmidt was the squadron's CO—*kapitanleutnant* in the German rank system being equivalent to a USNA Navy lieutenant. The Pan-Euro squadron only had nine fighters; Meier wondered if they were flying with an abbreviated roster. He felt it more likely, though, that they'd taken some casualties earlier.

As the monitor loomed huge up ahead and Meier cut back sharply on his velocity, he glanced at the structural damage visible in the ship's hull. Fully half of the flattened sphere looked like it had been shredded, with gaping holes revealing deep internal structure, portions that appeared to have been melted, and twisted tails of wreckage dangling into space from massive impact scars. Most of the drive section, he noted, had been destroyed. These guys had been through the meat grinder, and no mistake.

The monitor had been parked on the inner edge of the Ace ring system, balanced in orbit against the tug of the invisible central singularity. The hull was taking hits as he watched, tiny sparks and flashes marking high-velocity impacts from the orbital debris. Enough of that, and the monitor would deorbit, falling down through the last twenty thousand kilometers into tidal destruction and oblivion—

Then there was no more time to think. The computer graphics opened around Meier's viewpoint, a brightly lit rectangle expanding directly ahead as his Starblade drifted in for a trap. Carrier landings in the USNA Navy were usually carried out on rotating flight decks, and were carefully choreographed to bring incoming fighters to relative rest in spin gravity. Landing—the term "trap" was from the old wet navy, when fighters touched down on the pitching decks of aircraft carriers with tailhooks and arresting cables—was simplicity itself by comparison. He reduced his fighter's speed to a handful of meters per second and a magnetic field inside the flight bay brought him to rest. Robot arms snagged his fighter and moved him forward, deeper into the bay, getting him out of the way of the next incoming fighter in line.

A boarding tube unfolded from a nearby bulkhead, growing into the side of his fighter. He released the hull integrity locks, and his Starblade opened into the *Himmelschloss*'s pressurized interior.

As he pulled himself hand over hand out of the boarding tube and into a large, open compartment, a young leutnant met him with a salute.

"Permission to come aboard," Meier said.

"Granted, sir," the leutnant replied, returning the salute. "We're glad to have you here!"

The compartment was a combination warehouse and dock facility, as large as a football field on Earth, but crowded with crates and containers of supplies, and a vast and intricate spiderweb of traverse lines designed to allow people to move freely through the space in microgravity. A number of other men and women in Pan-European uniforms were gathered there, floating in various up- and down-orientations, along with the other Headhunters who'd already trapped. A smattering of applause sounded from the Confederation personnel, and someone called out *"Ja, welkommen!"* Another yelled, *"Bienvenidos!"* over the applause, while still another shouted, "It's about bloody time!"

"We've been wondering if anyone would *ever* come find us, sir," the young officer told him. "I'm Leutnant Harald Mueller, by the way. Bay One officer of the watch."

"So where do we go now, Herr Mueller?"

"With me, sir . . . when the rest of your squadron is aboard. The captain wishes to speak with all of you."

Twenty minutes later, Meier and the other Headhunters found themselves in a lounge with gravity. The German-built monitor certainly didn't lack for room. At least a hundred of the ship's personnel were gathered there, and still the place did not feel particularly crowded. The dome overhead showed an electronic projection of the surrounding vista of space—the blue orb of Thrymheim on one side, the diamond-hard pinpoint of Kapteyn's Star on the other. The Ace ring was invisible, Meier saw, as might be expected. It was turned edge-on relative to their vantage point so that they were looking out through its thinnest aspect.

"You would like something to eat, sir?" the Leutnant asked as Meier took a seat at a round table with three other of his squadron mates.

"If you have enough to spare, yes," Meier replied. "I would have thought you guys were on rationing here, though." It had been, after all, almost two months since the *Himmel-schloss* had vanished.

"The ring outside," Mueller explained, gesturing at the overhead panorama, "has plenty of carbon, as well as various ices that provide the nitrogen, oxygen, and hydrogen for organics, and there are plenty of other raw elements available. We've been mining the ring with robotic harvesters."

"But you haven't been able to repair your ship?" Lieutenant Karen Lobieski asked.

"Unfortunately, no, ma'am," Mueller replied. "The damage was too extensive, and there weren't enough heavy metals available."

"What the hell happened to you?" Lieutenant Greg Malone asked.

"I . . . should let the captain explain," Mueller replied. "Ah! Here he is."

An older man in the dress-blue skintights of the Confederation Navy entered the lounge with a small contingent of aides and junior officers. "*Bonjour, mes amis americains,*" he said. "And welcome to the *Himmelschloss.* I am Kapitan zur Weltraum Jean-Yves Gilbert, and we are most grateful for your arrival here."

Though the *Himmelschloss* was German-built, her crew apparently had been drawn from across the Pan-European Union, and her skipper was French. Meier had thought the Pan-Europeans tried to segregate their crews by nation of origin, but obviously it didn't always work out that way.

"I must ask you, monsieurs," Gilbert continued, "how large a fleet you have brought to this system. I have over twelve hundred men and women on board this vessel who must be evacuated."

"That might be a problem, sir. We're here with a carrier battlegroup," Commander Leystrom said. "The *Lexington*... and two other vessels."

Gilbert's eyes widened. "And this is *all*?"

"I'm afraid that's all we have for now, sir, yes. The destroyers and other light escorts will be here in a day or two." He shrugged. "They're assembling a joint task force back home, but that will take time to put together."

"But you have had two months!"

"Sir, we're stretched so thin back home it's a miracle we got here at all. I suggest that you begin making preparations to leave. It'll be tight, but between them, the *Lady Lex*, the *Marne,* and the *Valiant* should be able to take all of your people on board."

"And when will these other two vessels arrive?"

"They're checking out the system's inner planets at the moment," Leystrom told him. "We need to tight-beam a message and let them know we've found you."

"In the meantime, sir," Meier added, "how about filling us in on what happened to your ship?"

Gilbert shook his head. "There is little to tell, Lieutenant. What happened is obvious. How it happened . . . we still have no idea."

Two months before, Gilbert explained, the small Confederation squadron had entered the Kapteyn's Star system with orders from Geneva to observe the powerful entities there, to confirm that the Heimdall orbital station had been destroyed, and—if possible—to make peaceful contact with the aliens. The situation was still murky, he explained. The entities were probably the Rosette Aliens, though that still needed to be confirmed. "Peaceful contact" might seem to be surrender . . . and yet the Rosette Aliens were so unimaginably powerful, with technologies so utterly beyond the ken of Humankind, that Geneva was convinced that a conciliatory approach—even all-out surrender, if need be—was absolutely necessary if Humankind was to survive this encounter.

Meier wondered if Geneva had consulted with Washington on that strategy . . . and what Washington thought of the idea. A large factor in the recent civil war between the USNA and the Confederation had been, in fact, the debate over conflicting strategies of dealing with the Sh'daar. The Confederation wanted to give in to the Sh'daar Ultimatum and accept their demands that humans limit their technologies. The USNA had insisted on fighting for sovereignty and for unfettered access to *all* technologies, including those forbidden by the Sh'daar.

Washington's stand-and-fight policy had worked, surprisingly enough, though there were still those who felt humans would have to cave in to the Sh'daar demands sooner or later. The question, Meier decided, was whether that strategy would work *again* . . . this time against an alien power far more advanced and technologically evolved than even the Sh'daar.

At Gilbert's electronic command, images began flowing into the Headhunters' minds, downloaded from the *Himmelschloss* data banks. In their minds, they saw the Confederation squadron drop out of metaspace far, far out in the cold and dark at the periphery of the Kapteyn's Star system. Eight ships—the *Himmelschloss*, the heavy cruiser *La Gravière*, the railgun cruiser *Lutzow*, two destroyers, and three frigates—had crept in toward Bifrost, spread out and moving slowly in hopes that they could manage to escape the notice of the aliens ahead. They heard orders flashing from ship to ship as the squadron organized itself and began a slow acceleration in toward the system's heart.

A five-ship fighter wing—the Eagles—had been dispatched as point. Meier watched as the entire squadron had approached the moon Heimdall while keeping Bifrost between them and the aliens. The Eagles had slipped past the gas giant, drifting along scant kilometers from the plane of the rings and shielded by the planet's far-flung radiation belts.

Ahead, in images transmitted by the squadron, lay impossible wonders constructed of liquid light.

"We call them 'ghosts,'" Gilbert told them. "They look like they're made of light, though clearly something else is going on. Our best guess is that what we're seeing are clouds—celestial *oceans* of tiny mechanisms that are somehow anchored in space."

"'Anchored'?" Leystrom repeated. "How is such a thing possible?"

"If we knew how to do it," Gilbert replied, "perhaps the alien technology would not offer such a challenge. We suspect it has to do with manipulating the vacuum energy of the Quantum Sea. . . ."

Meier gave a low whistle. Someone else in the room groaned. The Quantum Sea was the lowest base-state of the universe, so far as was currently known. Particles and antiparticles continually popped into and out of existence within the froth of the quantum foam, the vacuum energy that the tuned microsingularities of power taps could harvest, allowing them to extract the near-infinite energies necessary for star travel.

Theory held that matter and energy alike were the products of standing waves within the foam—the reason the base state had been called a sea. A continually repeating spike of vacuum energy *here*, literally popping in and out of existence billions of times per second, translated into Reality as an electron or a photon or a quark, giving them the properties both of particles and of waves. Three quarks together formed a hadron—protons and neutrons were the most stable examples. Variations on the theme created all of the other possible particles in the zoo of modern physics. When a standing wave moved, the particle it generated moved; enough of them close together bent space, creating gravity.

Gilbert was suggesting that the Rosette entities knew how to reach down into the quantum foam and manipulate the substrate directly.

Meier was stunned. If they could do *that*, they truly did possess godlike abilities: able to create matter out of nothing—which meant violating the ancient law of conservation of mass—or to anchor such mass in the infrastructure of the cosmos. They would be able to edit matter, to transmute any element, to bring any matter or energy in any desired form into existence.

Or to wipe it away as though it had never existed.

A civilization that could do *that* . . .

God, was there any limit, any limit at all to what they could accomplish?

Meier could feel the fighter pilot's sense of awe leaking through with the data, riding his own wonder. Trillions of dust motes, a haze of light, and within that haze . . .

Dimly glimpsed, so faint that Meier thought at first they must be a trick of his eyes, there were . . . shapes. Huge shapes dwarfing Heimdall, dwarfing even massive Bifrost. From his vantage point skimming along beneath Bifrost's rings with the fighters, it seemed as though Heimdall was suspended within a vast and far-flung web so insubstantial, so gossamer, it was difficult to tell if it was there at all.

Yet it was filling all of space ahead. . . .

And it was *moving*.

Reacting to the fighter wing's approach.

"One of those sheets," Gilbert explained, indicating a vast and rippling expanse of golden translucence looming ahead, "just folded over on itself . . . like a fishing net cast into the sea."

The five fighters in the lead seemed to dissolve as the sheet of light rolled over them. The squadron of capital ships, tens of thousands of kilometers away on the far side of Bifrost, saw what was happening on data feeds from the fighters and immediately began decelerating.

They reacted quickly . . . but not quickly enough. The translucent film of light swept over and past Bifrost, sliding past the planet and its ring system with no apparent effect, but it struck the Pan-European capital ships one after another, and with each strike a vessel flared in a dazzling burst of nova-hot radiance—flared . . . and vanished.

Himmelschloss alone escaped the sweeping light . . . but only just. The leading edge of the radiance swept over the monitor a couple of seconds after she completed an end-for-end skew flip and began accelerating as quickly as she could for open space. Her stern quarter seemed to ripple and fold, collapsing in upon itself as clouds of debris expanded into emptiness.

Tumbling helplessly, the *Himmelschloss* fell out-system. The aliens, as though they'd simply stretched out to brush away a worrisome insect, did not follow.

"We had maneuvering control," Gilbert explained. "And the power tap was still intact, thank God. We were able to change course enough to approach Thrymheim and to decelerate into orbit around the singularity. Almost eight hundred personnel were . . . *gone.* Folded out of existence by the sheet of light or spilled into hard vacuum. We still had manufacturing capabilities. We could nanufacture food, water, air. Our large-scale repair functions were totally trashed, however. We've been programming our exterior nanomatrix to fill in and cover the openings torn open when part of the hull dissolved, but we can't grow a new drive system, though, or grow new fighters, or do more than rough-patch the outer hull. We're helpless, *helpless* in the face of that kind of technology!"

And Jason Meier was forced to agree. Right now, the tiny USNA squadron was about as potent a military force against the Rosette entities as an obscene gesture.

Which meant they would be very lucky to get the *Lady Lex* and her consorts out of the inner system, load up the *Himmelschloss* survivors, and, as her Marines might put it, get the hell out of Dodge.

Judging by what he'd just seen, all of the combined military might of Earth brought together in a single fleet could no more than anger these beings.

If, in fact, a human fleet could have any effect on them at all.

TC/USNA CVS America
Sick Bay
1346 hours, TFT

"Explain that," Gray said. "You're not making sense!"

"The bacteria," Hoffman told him, "are intelligent. That is the only hypothesis that accounts for the facts."

"Intelligent *germs*?" Gray snapped. "That's ridiculous!"

"Actually," Hoffman told him, "we've known that it's possible for some time now. A number of terrestrial microorganisms show . . . indications of intelligence, at least of a sort. And now it looks like we've met some who might be as smart as we are."

"Look . . . that's just not possible!" Gray had the feeling that Hoffman was trying to play some sort of pointless, ridiculous joke on him. "Bacteria are single-cell organisms, for Chrissakes! By definition, that means they have at most a single brain cell! No synapses, no neural network, no way to store memory. They can't *think*!"

"Not as we use the word, no. But remember that even our kind of intelligence is an emergent property. A complex system arising out of a large collection of something much, much simpler."

"You're seriously telling me you've found intelligent bacteria. In *me* . . ."

"Not intelligent in the way you and I are, no," Hoffman told him. "And each colonial swarm must comprehend the universe in a very, *very* different way than we do. And there probably is no way to directly compare our minds to theirs. But everything we've observed shows that they do perceive, they plan, and they influence the actions of their hosts in unanticipated ways."

"That's just crazy!"

"No," Hoffman said calmly, "it just means that the universe is stranger than we've been giving it credit for."

Gray sagged back on the sick-bay bed. He felt dizzy. A bit weak. The headache was still there, though it had faded now into the background. He honestly couldn't tell if he was still feeling the effects of the bug he'd picked up in the N'gai Cluster, or simply feeling shock at what *America*'s senior human medical officer was telling him.

"I must insist," the medical robot said, interrupting, "that Admiral Gray rest. Your philosophical investigations into microbial intelligence can wait."

"Sorry, Admiral," Hoffman said. "I have to go anyway. Check out 'slime mold,' 'emergent intelligence,' and 'bacterial intelligence' in the ship's library . . . *if* your nanny here will let you. I'll be back later, and we can continue this. Suffice to say, we think we know where we stand with the controlling intelligence behind the Sh'daar now. And that's going to change *everything*."

He turned and walked away. "Wait!" Gray said, raising his voice, almost shouting. "You can't drop an orbital bomb like *that* and—"

But he was gone.

"I will, if necessary, administer a relaxant," the robot told him.

"Not necessary," Gray told the impassive machine. "I'll be good."

But once the robot glided away, Gray accessed *America*'s library, linked into the biological studies branch, and pulled down several thousand gigs of data on slime molds.

He'd heard of the things, but never seen one, nor had he paid any attention to them. The name was applied to several unrelated organisms, members of the domain Eukarya, which could live as single cells, very much like amoebae, but at times came together to form a unified mass. Unlike fungi or bacterial slimes or plants, but like amoebae, slime molds could *move*, crawling over the ground at a blistering pace of up to 1.3 millimeters per hour.

Their behavior, to say the least, was extraordinary. Plasmodial slime molds were essentially one very large, single cell—a supercell enclosing thousands of individual cell nuclei. Cellular slime molds, on the other hand, spent most of their existence as individual protists, like amoeba, but when conditions grew extreme or the organism needed to reproduce, the separate cells came together into a single mass that acted as one organism.

The trick was in how the slime mold "decided" to do anything. Clearly, chemical cues were involved . . . but somehow slime molds were able to all work together to move in a specific direction. They'd solved mazes in the lab, throwing out pseudopods to find food or light or moisture, and when they stopped to reproduce, different cells or cell components could change form and purpose to create spores and fruiting bodies. Perhaps strangest of all, each time the cell nuclei divided, they made numerous changes to the DNA, accurately and precisely, re-engineering the organism's genome on the fly.

They started off as amorphous cells like amoebae; when they came together, however, they could demonstrate something like genuine animal intelligence, *without* brains or nervous systems. Besides solving mazes, they could mimic human transportation networks, avoid toxic chemicals or dry conditions, and choose the healthiest food from a smorgasbord of options. In some experiments, they even seemed to *anticipate* changing conditions over time; when subjected to drying conditions every thirty, sixty, or ninety minutes, the slime molds would thereafter slow their movement to conserve energy . . . at thirty-, sixty-, or ninety-minute intervals.

Slime molds were not intelligent in the way humans were, of course, but they *did* show a kind of intelligence more akin to that of animals than of plants or fungi.

Fascinated, Gray moved from slime molds to emergent intelligence. There were many organisms known that joined together into so-called superorganisms: beehives, ant nests, termite mounds, and the odd little colonial mycomyrmidians of New Earth. A single termite had a brain smaller than the head of a pin and could not in any way be considered *intelligent* . . . not as humans used the term. A termite colony, however, functioned essentially like a single organism, the individual termites taking on the role of cells in an animal's body. Such a superorganism could monitor and control the temperature within the colony to within a fraction of a degree; could farm fungus in dank subterranean chambers; could perform astonishing feats of architecture, one bit of saliva-soaked dirt at a time; and could defend the nest with glue-squirting soldiers. Biologists referred to such feats as examples of *swarm intelligence.*

Indeed, individual human neurons were not intelligent and had no awareness of the big picture, no way of comprehending that they were part of a human organism. Yet millions of neurons working together generated their own form of swarm intelligence. Mind, intelligence, and society all were seen as *emergent phenomena* arising from the swarm.

All pretty standard stuff. But when Gray downloaded an article on bacterial intelligence, he was staggered by what was to him a completely new and unknown field of knowledge.

Just as a slime mold could exhibit what for all the world seemed to be an animal-like intelligence, just as a superorganism comprising millions of termites exhibited what seemed like truly intelligent behavior, bacteria and other microorganisms—protozoa and algae—showed remarkable abilities, including decision making, complex adaptive behavior, and even altruism. Amoebae built shells around themselves, showing manipulative skills and decision-making skills that seemed more in line with multicellular organisms than single-celled protozoa. The group known as Myxobacteria—"slime bacteria"—were unremarkable as individual cells, but, like slime molds, could come together in huge aggregates known as swarms or "wolf packs." They stayed together by means of molecular signaling between cells; as aggregates they were far more efficient in finding and digesting food.

But what really shocked Gray was information about the ways that bacteria seemed to influence their animal hosts. Evidently, a person's gut bacteria could influence how a person felt . . . and even what they wanted to eat.

Quite a lot of research had been carried out on the idea since the twentieth century. Only gradually did biologists come to see human beings not as a single, isolated organism, but as a swarm of trillions of cells working together. In fact, the human body was comprised of roughly ten trillion cells . . . and something like one hundred trillion bacteria. And the bacteria traveling with their human hosts, it turned out, had an astonishing degree of interaction, cooperation, even communication of a sort with those hosts. Imbalances in the microflora biome could result in autism, a condition that could be reversed by transplanting healthy proportions of gut bacteria. Certain bacteria reduced stress or depression, and others were intimately interconnected with the human immune system. Certain bacteria even appeared to signal the brain in ways that created cravings for certain food—chocolate, for instance. The bacteria decided what they needed to improve their environment . . . and signaled the host's brain for takeout.

The human organism, it turned out, was far more complex than anyone had imagined back in the closing years of the twentieth century. And an intimate part of that complexity turned out to be biochemical signals transmitted by the bacteria inhabiting the organism, bacteria literally outnumbering the cells of their hosts by a ratio of ten to one.

Bacteria that, through emergent behavior, acted in ways that could only be termed "intelligent."

What that might have to do with the Sh'daar, however, or with the paramycoplasmid infection Gray had picked up in the N'gai Cluster, was completely beyond him.

He found that he *very* much wanted to continue his conversation with Dr. Hoffman.

Chapter Twelve

TC/USNA CVS Lexington
Command Bridge
Thrymheim/Ace Orbit
1215 hours, TFT

"We are entering orbit around the singularity," Lieutenant Milton reported.

"And no sign that we're being tracked by the Rosetters," *Lexington*'s tactical officer, Commander Eric Gower, added, satisfaction enlivening his voice.

"Oh, they're tracking us, all right," Captain Bigelow said. "I can *feel* the bastards out there, watching, like cats at a mouse hole."

"There's the monitor," Taggart said, looking up. "Range eight hundred. Closing at five meters per second."

"Nice and easy . . ." Bigelow said. "Let's not screw things up now, at the very end."

The *Lexington* and her escorts had crept slowly across the nine AUs from Planet I to Planet IV at a comparative snail's pace and with a minimal expenditure of energy. They'd boosted at five thouand gravities for just a hundred seconds, skimming as close as they dared to Kapteyn's Star both to pick up some free velocity and to mask their movement, using the sun's glare, radiation, and magnetic fields. They'd drifted the rest of the way under zero-G, falling into Thrymheim's gravitational field and slowing with another five thousand-gravity burst.

It had taken them almost three full days to make the trip, but they should have been a lot less obvious in their passage than they would have been had they made the voyage under constant acceleration.

Even so, the skipper was right. The aliens *must* have seen them, must have been watching them the entire time. But so long as the squadron didn't make any threatening moves, the Rosette entities seemed content to continue their enigmatic activities with flowing, rippling light. What, she wondered, was the trigger? What line would the *Lexington* have to cross to provoke a response?

A final brief nudge, and *Lexington* came to a halt relative to the *Himmelschloss*. A few hundred meters to port, the Marine transport *Marne* took up station. On board were twelve hundred Marines who had a vital role to play in this deployment. . . .

If they could get past the Rosette Aliens.

TC/USNA CVS America
Sick Bay
1346 hours, TFT

"Are you ready to begin, Admiral?"

The voice was that of a fusion of medical AIs—of *America*'s medicAI integrated into Andre, the more powerful AI of the *Andreas Vesalius*.

"Yeah," Gray told the artificial mind. He steeled himself . . . for what, he had no idea. But it seemed like the right thing to do. "Go ahead."

He was lying on his back in a hospital bed, looking up into the glare of overhead lights. The light was partially blocked by heads—some human doctors, nurses, and technicians,

some humanoid robots. Nearby machines peeped and war-
bled; a mask over Gray's face fed him oxygen and smelled of
plastic.

The *internal* view, visible when he closed his eyes, was
more informative. In a window opened within his in-head
awareness, Gray could see a computer-graphic representa-
tion of his own body, rendered in translucent hues to give a
three-dimensional color-coded image: white for bone, dull
maroon for muscle, brighter pink for internal organs . . .
and sheets and knots of green for the bacterial infection he
was fighting. Hundreds of billions of nanotechnic medical
robots were moving throughout his body at this moment.
They'd started out as a few tens of thousands of devices injected three days earlier, when they'd entered Lunar Orbit,
but they'd been drawing elements—carbon, hydrogen,
oxygen, nitrogen, iron, phosphorous, even aluminum and
silica—from the food in his stomach and gut. He'd been
put on a special diet to provide specific amounts of raw material, in fact, and with those available resources the tiny
robots had doubled in number . . . then doubled again . . .
and again.

He now had very nearly as many robots inside him as
there were cells in his entire body. The robots were still out-
numbered by the hundred trillion or so bacterial cells shar-
ing him as host, but were roughly on a par with the numbers
of one specific organism: *Paramycoplasma subtilis*. Guided
by the medicAI minds, the nanobots had tracked down that
alien bacteria, found where they were hiding, and monitored their activity. The paramycoplasmids, it turned out,
had an affinity for the myelin sheaths around human nerve
fibers. Slipping between the epithelial cells lining the walls
of Gray's arteries, veins, and capillaries, they'd formed thin
sheets encapsulating various of his body cavities, but accu-
mulating in and around his major nerve trunks. There were
especially large knots within and around his brain, at his
heart, and around his solar plexus.

Besides those hiding in his nervous system, though, lots
of stray bacteria had been spotted in his circulatory system,

in his intestines, and elsewhere. The fleet of nanobots had dispersed throughout his body, tracking the germs down.

"It will take a few moments to reprogram the machines," a human technician told him.

"Sure." Gray was more than nervous; he was *terrified*. Born and raised a Prim, he'd never been comfortable with nanotechnic medicine . . . though when his wife had gotten sick, that hadn't stopped him from taking her across the USNA border to get her high-tech treatment.

And, after all, Angela's cure had been less than optimal. The stroke and the nanosurgery required to save her life had changed what she'd felt for him, had caused her to leave him.

The human body—more, the human *nervous system*— was incredibly complex. And that was putting it mildly. Modern technology could hardwire into it with cerebral implants, could treat its illnesses and even old age itself with robots smaller than a red blood cell, could create electronic access to the sum total of all human knowledge . . . treatments that literally conferred superhumanity on their creators. But for all of that, the human organism still displayed an astonishing and only partially comprehensible complexity, and the results of that kind of technological meddling—physical, emotional, and intellectual—were not always completely predictable, even yet.

Something Gray had known to be true his entire life.

This fear was exacerbated by the human doctors warning him that there were a number of unknowns in the process before they'd wheeled him in for the procedure. The fact that masses of the alien organisms were so intimately interwoven with Gray's brain and heart and nervous system meant that if something unexpected happened, the chances were good that Gray might suffer severe neurological damage.

Or he might die.

"We're here for you, Admiral," another voice said. "We're looking over your electronic shoulder, as it were."

"Who . . ." With a start, he recognized the voice. "Mr. *President*?"

Gray was aware of the briefest of hesitations—the two-

and-a-half-second time lag for the round trip between Earth and Luna. "The same. They told us about your condition. How are you feeling?"

"Not too bad, sir." Which was the truth, at least in physical terms. The nano they'd loaded him with had been treating his symptoms, and he was actually feeling pretty good. The headache was a faint echo of its former self, and they'd brought a sudden spike in his blood pressure under control. What was left were vague complaints—body and joint aches, numbness, tingling, dizziness—and all of those were a lot better than they'd been.

"I've seen Hoffman's report," Koenig told him. "You appear to have encountered yet another new alien species. An intelligent bacterial slime."

"Yeah, well . . . it's the glamour of this job that keeps me at it," Gray replied. "That and the exotic and interesting people you meet."

Koenig chuckled in his thoughts. "The doctors tell me they expect to nail this thing pretty fast. You just hang tight, and know that a lot of us are here, pulling for you."

"Thank you, Mr. President. Uh . . . who's 'us'?"

"My staff, of course. The Joint Chiefs. Although, interestingly, the one who is really interested in your situation is Konstantin."

"I am on this channel as well, Admiral," another voice added.

"Your, uh, kids have been really helpful, Konstantin."

"If by 'kids' you mean the abbreviated clones of my software that you transported to the N'gai Cluster and DT-1, I am delighted. I have already reintegrated with the data and observations you brought back. Fascinating material."

"You'll have your work cut out for you, Konstantin," Gray said. "How do you learn to talk to an aggregate of bacterial cells?"

"Everything," the supercomputer replied, "will depend on the superorganism's worldview, how it apprehends its surroundings, how it processes data from those surroundings, and how it interacts with them."

"I'm not sure I approve of you being the guinea pig, Admiral," Koenig said. "I almost overrode your order."

"Thank you for not doing so, sir. This is important."

Originally, the medicAIs had told him that they were going to attempt the first treatment on one of the infected members of *America*'s crew. Chief Drummond had volunteered . . . and, in fact, his case was deemed more serious than Gray's, with severe vertigo, numbness, and pins-and-needles sensations suggestive of severe neural complications. Gray had given orders, however, that *he* was to be the first test subject.

Partly, of course, he was feeling guilty about having had sex with Harriet McKennon and starting all of this. Rationally, he knew that it hadn't *just* been his tryst that had started the plague spreading. Rational or not, the guilt was still there, however, vastly amplified by the knowledge that the men and women on board *America* and the other battlegroup warships all were *his* responsibility. And because Gray was convinced that a good commanding officer shared everything with those under his or her command, including the dangers—*especially* the dangers—he had stepped up. Chief Drummond would be next in line for the antimicrobial programming after Gray.

Assuming, of course, that Gray survived what was coming.

"We have initiated the program compile, Admiral," the medicAI told him. "The antimicrobial search-and-destroy routine has been transmitted by radio to the nanotechnic hunter-killers resident within your system."

"Will I feel anything?"

"Unlikely, Admiral," the medicAI said in his thoughts.

"Would you like to watch?" one of the human doctors asked him.

"Huh?" He'd not realized that that would be an option. "Sure . . . yeah. Let me see."

The animated graphics of his body were replaced by a view at extremely high magnification obviously transmitted from somewhere inside his body. Dull red doughnut shapes bobbed and jostled through a round tunnel made of what looked like large scales blurred by speed . . . the cells lining one of his blood vessels.

And . . . yes! The tiny spheres of the alien microbes glistened ahead like droplets of pale silver as they were swept along in the fierce, heart-driven currents of the blood plasma. He saw three of them, adrift in the somewhat golden liquid of his blood.

Bacteria, red cells, and the nanoptics picking up the image were relatively motionless with respect to one another, but the surrounding walls of the blood vessel alternately blurred, then came to a near rest in successive pulses of movement. It took Gray a moment to recognize that was exactly what he was seeing: his own pulse.

"This is a real-time image?" he asked. "Not computer generated?"

"The color is calculated and created by computers," the medicAI replied. "At these scales, the wavelengths of visible light are too long to be visible to human optics. But the images are real, as humans seem to define the term, yes."

A medical nanobot entered the scene, a flat-white capsule propelled by a molecular motor. Crowding ahead of the device that was transmitting the image, it shot forward, its leading edge opening like a flower as it homed in on a single paramycoplasmid. It was impossible to watch the scene without reading emotions into the actions of both robots and bacteria; the sphere seemed to be deliberately fleeing as the capsule pursued relentlessly before trapping it at last against the curving, slightly fuzzy side of a red cell. The open flower snapped shut, engulfing the bacterium.

"Are the bacteria . . . aware of what's happening?"

"Of course not," the medicAI said. "Individual bacteria react to molecular compounds within their environment, but they can't feel. Or think."

"But Dr. Hoffman said they were intelligent . . ." Gray still wasn't sure he believed that.

"Their presumed intelligence, remember, is an emergent phenomenon arising from the intercellular communications among some hundreds of millions of bacteria acting in concert. A single microbe is no more aware of the entire bacterial mass than a single one of your cells is aware of *you*, while the bacterial mass is no more aware of what's happening to its constituent cells than you are aware of . . . say . . . your white cells battling bacterial invaders. The scales are simply too extreme.

"Here is the feed from another monitor 'bot," the AI told him. The image blurred and shifted, showing now a kind of alien landscape outside of the blood vessel. Here, among a jumble of translucent cells, a number of bacteria—fifty or sixty, perhaps, appeared to have wired themselves together with long strands or filaments of something like mucus, forming a glistening, transparent wall suspended within the interstitial fluid between and around the cells and a complex web of branching and rebranching capillaries. They'd trapped one of the nanobot capsules, partially closing on it like a net around a fish.

Damn, the nanobot was struggling. . . .

Again, it was impossible not to ascribe both awareness and cunning to the microbes, which certainly looked as though they were fighting back against the nanotechnic assault. And Gray found himself feeling concern and a touch of emotional pain at the nanobot's plight, even though he knew the thing was a tiny machine, and not alive at all. After a moment, however, other capsules arrived on the scene, perhaps summoned by the trapped 'bot, and began devouring the spheres at a breakneck pace.

"They're physically eating the bacteria!" Gray said, surprised. He'd expected something more high-tech. Miniature laser beams, perhaps, or injected chemicals, or—

"Very much as your white blood cells engulf invading bacteria or foreign matter that has triggered your immune system," the medicAI told him. "A process called phagocytosis. The nanobots will consume as many of the paramycoplasmids as possible, then redirect themselves, traveling through your circulatory stream either to your kidneys or to your colon for elimination."

"I'm just going to . . . excrete them? Why?"

"It was thought safest to dispose of the dead microbes in this fashion, rather than risk systemic toxic shock in response to vast numbers of bacteria being destroyed all at once."

"I can appreciate that."

More and more nanobots were arriving on the scene. The numbers of bacteria dwindled. . . .

Gray had the feeling he was watching a savage and freewheeling space battle fought across a bizarre, extraterrestrial landscape . . . and had to remind himself that what he was seeing was not taking place within the vastness of space—*outer* space—but that it was confined to the ultramicroscopic vistas of *inner* space, an entirely different realm sundered from the reality he knew by the jarring difference in scale.

He tried to imagine the scope of the battle being waged within him—with bacteria and nanobots numbering in the hundreds of billions, locked in a desperate, no-quarter fight to the end. . . .

He failed.

Again, the vista shifted. The camera viewpoint was drifting above a vast, rounded surface, covered, it seemed, with blue scales. The scales, he thought, were cells—they were faintly translucent, and he could see the dark mass of nuclei inside—but they were far more tightly packed here than those he'd seen elsewhere. Above and around the surface, which was tinted a dark blue, were other cells, loosely packed, and bundles of capillaries running through the cell mass like the roots of a tree. He could actually see through the capillary walls and watch the flattened-doughnut shapes of red blood cells stacked up spoon-fashion as they pulsed along through the circulatory conduits.

There were a lot more of the spherical *Paramycoplasma subtilis* bacteria visible here, most of them burrowed down among the densely packed blue cells below. The nanobots were swarming above that surface, winkling the cocci out, actually nosing in between the cellular scales to get at them.

Gray was not medically trained and had only a vague idea

of what he was looking at. The computer program showing the scene had identifiers appearing here and there, however, like labels in an anatomical docuinteractive. The blue layer of close-packed cells, he saw, was the myelin sheath of a nerve, with lots of blood vessels bundled close alongside—that matched up with what he'd been told.

And the fleet was going in to get them.

Stop!

The command was . . . wordless, a feeling rather than a spoken concept, but the meaning was clear. At the same moment, the headache returned with pounding savagery.

"Watch out!" one of the human physicians nearby said. "Blood pressure is spiking . . . one eighty-five over one twenty. Pulse one forty . . ."

Gray felt a crushing, numbing, suffocating pressure over his entire body. He tried to call out, but it was as though every muscle had been paralyzed. The dizziness was back, too . . . and, most terrifying of all, he was having trouble breathing.

He was aware of two conversations now . . . the humans communicating by spoken voice outside, and both AIs and humans talking on-line, over an electronic channel. The one thing he heard a human say clearly was, "The medulla has been compromised."

The medulla? That was a part of the brain, wasn't it? Gray wasn't sure.

"BP one ninety-eight over one thirty."

"Damn it, he's going to blow a vessel!"

"Breathing in arrest!"

"Heart rate one eighty . . . pounding!"

Yeah, he could *feel* the pounding. His whole body was pounding, and there was blood in his mask, in his mouth, clogging his nose . . .

Stop! Kill!

Again . . . that inward scream, more raw emotion than words. The bacterial mass, Gray now thought, was trying to communicate. But was it a plea for mercy—"stop, before you kill me"—or a threat—"stop, or I will kill you"?

He'd lost the inner image of the internal battle, and all he could see now was the dark of the insides of his eyelids. He couldn't open his eyes, couldn't move a single muscle, couldn't *breathe* . . .

He tried to use the electronic channel to talk to the doctors, but found that even that was beyond him. He was seized in the grip of an overwhelming inertia; even thought was too difficult, too draining. . . .

The pain in his head and in his joints was worse, now. He was having trouble remembering *anything*. . . .

Stop! Kill! Feel!

Again, that damnable ambiguity. Did the superorganism want him, Gray, to feel something specific? To feel some new communication, perhaps? Or was it telling him that it felt as though it was being killed?

Desperate to understand, Gray opened himself to whatever the entity was trying to say, tried to relax despite the pain, tried to relax *through* the pain . . . accepting . . . opening . . . feeling. . . .

I am here, Admiral Gray, a voice said in his mind. Was that . . . *America*'s medicAI? It didn't sound the same, and it took Gray a moment to recognize the mental voice of Konstantin. Koenig had said the supercomputer was present. Yes, he remembered speaking with it just now. His memory was fuzzy, but not completely gone yet. . . .

He felt like he was falling. He fell through utter darkness . . . and then he began to see . . . stars? Yes, stars! Stars surrounded him, flickering past on every side, and he could feel swarms of worlds circling suns without number . . . inhabited world teeming with life, with intelligence, with *Mind*. . . .

He could feel the connecting strands of communication between the worlds . . . sense sapient beings of every imaginable shape and form and description occupying worlds of every type, an incredibly rich diversity of life and of Mind filling the galaxy and spilling out into the Void beyond.

How were bacteria aware of the infinite vistas of space? He didn't know . . . but he sensed that he was somehow seeing a kind of composite picture drawn from trillions of microbes inhabiting billions of hosts. The microbes had a wordless conception of themselves. Gray supplied the name: *the Organism*.

He also sensed a wordless question inherent in that scene. What did one life—his—matter compared with billions upon billions of host beings scattered throughout the galaxy, all inhabited—*ridden*—by the Organism?

A threat, perhaps? A declaration that they didn't need him?

Space, for the Organism, was an infinite series of . . . the closest Gray could come to attaching a word to the idea was *worlds*. Each world, he sensed, was a host body to some trillions of cells, all of which together comprised the Organism. He began glimpsing weirdly nightmarish caricatures of alien beings. A few he recognized. Sjhlurrr: ponderous, eight-meter slugs; Baondyeddi: flat, pancake-like beings with hundreds of legs and sky-blue eyes around their rims; Agletsch: oval-bodied sixteen-legged arthropods with four weirdly stalked eyes . . .

There were many others Gray did not recognize.

Even the ones to which he could attach names were so distorted Gray could scarcely recognize them. Each appeared to be transparent . . . but filled to bursting with interwoven threads or branches like the interwoven roots of plants. It took Gray a long moment to finally get it.

Nervous systems! He was seeing the alien beings by means of three-dimensional maps of their central nervous systems! Networks of nerves . . . or perhaps alien nerve analogues in some of the stranger beings. In most he could recognize the large, governing mass of a brain. Some had *several* brains, or strings of brainlike nodes, or clusters of nervous tissue distributed throughout the body. The Baondyeddi, for instance, were packed with neural tissue around their rims behind those eyes and legs, with relatively fewer nerves in toward the center. Five swollen nodes around the being's periphery appeared to be where it did its thinking.

In several instances the beings appeared to be completely

lacking a central brain; any thinking they did must be somehow handled by the nervous system as a whole, like living distributed computer networks. The Sjhlurrr were such a species; apparently their entire nervous system worked like a brain.

Each individual was, he realized, a kind of composite image of the outside of the being as imagined by tiny, sightless observers guessing at the shape from the *inside*, and building it up from maps of the being's CNS. Gray was immediately reminded of the cautionary tale of the three blind men with the elephant . . . but the Organism had done a surprisingly good job compiling unified images.

The alien bacteria, he remembered Hoffman saying, had been concentrating along his nerves, in the myelin sheaths. The cellular makeup of those sheaths was so dense that the relatively large medical nanobots were having trouble tunneling in between them. The bacteria didn't appear to be trying to get away—how could they?—but they were very hard to get at.

He was having trouble holding on to consciousness.

"Damn! We're losing him. . . ."

And Gray slipped into darkness.

Chapter Thirteen

TC/USNA CVS Lexington
Thrymheim/Ace Orbit
0925 hours, TFT

"Commander," Bigelow said slowly, as though choosing his words with extreme care, "this *is* strictly a volunteer assignment. And some would argue that it's a job for a helm officer, not a ship's exec."

"I want the mission, Captain," Laurie Taggart told him. "And I'm certainly not going to let someone else go when I could go instead."

Bigelow grunted, then glanced at the Marine officer standing beside her. "Colonel? It's your mission. Are you happy with Commander Taggart in charge of the Navy side of things?"

"I've already downloaded Ms. Taggart's records and reviewed them, Captain," Colonel Jamison replied. "An excellent and experienced officer. She'll do just fine."

Two of them were in Bigelow's office on board the *Lexington*—Bigelow at his desk and Taggart standing at ease in front of him. Colonel Joseph Jamison was present virtually, his image projected into their retinas by the software mediating the conference. In fact, Jamison was in his office on board the Marine transport *Marne*, drifting a couple of kilometers off *Lexington*'s port beam.

Other officers were present as well, but only as voices within the heads of the people and AIs attending the meeting. "Sir!" one voice said. "Commander Taggart is too senior for this assignment. With respect . . . I ask you to reconsider. *Sir*."

"Thank you, Lieutenant Morris. Your objection is duly noted."

"Sir—"

"Lieutenant," Bigelow said with a tone of exaggerated patience, "we're going to be engaged in a tricky bit of maneuvering when we pull out of the Ace, okay? I want my best pilot-qualified officer at the helm."

"But—"

"That's an *order*, son."

"Sit down, Ben," Taggart added, smiling. "You've been outranked."

Plenty of other officers had volunteered for this op, Taggart thought . . . and it *was* a more junior officer's billet. The heavy stealth-lander *Lucas* had been under the command of Janice Zhou . . . but Lieutenant Zhou was on the sick list, incapacitated by what looked like influenza . . . except that it wasn't responding to influenza drugs or programmed nano. Bigelow wanted an experienced officer over there, but not his best helmsman.

She'd managed to convince Bigelow that she was the best choice. In any case, the actual piloting would be carried out by *Lucas*'s AI. They just needed a human in the loop, as demanded by fleet regs.

And it wasn't as if they'd miss her on the *Lady Lex*. Pardoe could handle her duties as *Lexington*'s XO for the short run back to Earth, no problem, and the op on Heimdall shouldn't last more than a couple of weeks, tops.

At least, that was what she kept telling Bigelow . . . and herself.

"Very well, Laurie," Bigelow said. "If you're sure."

"I'm sure, sir. Just don't forget us out here, right?"

Bigelow smiled, though there was a worried edge to the expression. "Don't you worry about that. We'll be back . . . and with half of the fleet if we can manage it. You just keep the Marines in line, okay?"

"I beg your pardon, Captain," Jamison said, raising an eyebrow. "Since when does the Navy run the Marine Corps?"

"Since the Corps depends on the Navy for their ride."

It was a very old, and usually friendly, argument.

Usually . . .

"We have a very small launch window, Commander," Bigelow told her. "Are you ready to depart?"

"Yes, sir. As soon as Colonel Jamison gets all of his people across to the lander."

"Another thirty minutes, Captain," Jamison told him.

"You'd better get over there, Commander. And good luck!"

"Thank you, Captain. We'll see you when you get back."

"*Definitely.*"

Taggart knew that Bigelow didn't want to leave her here. He didn't want to leave *anyone* here. But when it came to making a decision, it wasn't hard to choose Taggart. No one wanted to look at the fact square on, but her years as *America*'s chief weapons officer might come in *very* handy on board the *Lucas*.

And for her part, she wanted to go. *Needed* to go. Desperately.

She was thinking about that need minutes later as she crossed from *America*'s main spinal docking port to the *Marne* in one of the star carrier's transport pods. Once and for all, she was going to face the ancient Stargods.

And in that meeting, she was either going to rekindle her old and cooling religious passion . . . or once and for all put it all behind her as childish superstition.

Laurie Taggart's husbands had been devout Ancient Alien Creationists, and she'd joined to please them— especially Anton. She'd wanted to believe . . . and in that wanting she'd found more and more validation, more and more proof squirreled away in ancient religious texts, in archeological ruins worldwide, in out-of-place artifacts with no rhyme or reason to them, making it easy to append the label *alien*. She would have been the first to declare, however, that an awful lot of what the AAC believed had to be taken on faith. The Stargods were good . . . and morally superior to humans. The Stargods had created Humankind hundreds of thousands of years ago, tinkering with the DNA of *Homo erectus* to create a new, higher, more promising species—*Homo sapiens*. The Stargods lived still in the heavens . . . and someday they would return again for Their children, the faithful. . . .

In fact, she knew, it was all myth, stories identical in basic concept to dozens of older, more traditional religions, dressed in the shinier raiment of technology and modern cosmology. Trev—Admiral Gray—had gotten her to question a few of the basic tenets of her faith. Were mysteries like the Great Pyramid and the beginnings of agriculture and the mutations that resulted in *Homo sapiens* best and most simply explained by alien Stargods? Or was AAC doctrine more likely to be misinterpretation, misunderstanding, or wishful thinking?

He'd taught her, above all, to be honest with herself.

Most of the time, she didn't think much about it. AAC liturgy required small groups of Believers, and in the hostile shadow of the White Covenant it was difficult to hook up with such, especially on board a Navy vessel. She hadn't even been to a meeting in six or seven months, now. There was a group that met at SupraQuito synchorbital that she'd attended for a time when *America* was docked there. She hadn't missed it, though. Not much . . .

Recent encounters with advanced civilizations, though, had reawakened in Taggart some of the awe and sense of wonder, some of the need to have everything neatly explained. For a time, she'd thought the ur-Sh'daar might be the Stargods . . . but learning that the ur-Sh'daar had vanished to wherever they'd gone when they'd transcended, leaving behind the Refusers like lost orphans . . . surely the Stargods would be more merciful, more caring than that.

And then the Rosette Aliens had appeared, moving into the Omega Centauri cluster apparently by means of the spacetime-twisting rosette. By all accounts the Sh'daar were afraid of them. Perhaps they were the true Stargods.

But she couldn't *know* that until she encountered the Rosette Aliens directly. If they *were* the Stargods, she had to know. If they were the Stargods, they might try to communicate with the faithful.

With the Believers.

With *her*.

She'd been the senior weapons officer on *America*'s bridge when the star carrier had probed Omega Centauri. There hadn't been much to see at the time—mysterious fields of light and alien shapes that seemed to defy both space and time. Now, though, the aliens were here in force and openly.

And she wanted to meet them.

The Marine contingent and their need for a replacement pilot had offered her the perfect opportunity.

The Joint Chiefs back on Earth wanted an observation post somewhere up close and personal . . . like smack in the Rosette Aliens' backyard.

Despite what had happened to the Pan-European expedition, she didn't think of this as a suicide mission. The *Lexington* battlegroup had a few things going for it that the Confederation forces had not. They had the benefit of knowing more about the Rosette Alien structures and a possible way of working around them. And, too, they had the *Lucas*, a stealthy battalion assault transport which might—*might*—let them slip in close without being noticed.

And, finally, they were going to use the system more effectively as cover. The Rosette Aliens seemed to have focused on a particular volume of space a few hundred kilometers above the day side of Bifrost. The Pan-European fighters had gone in when Heimdall had circled around to the day side and was deep in the midst of the glowing lights and ghostly shapes of the alien presence. This time, however, the human forces were timing their approach to arrive at Heimdall when it was over Bifrost's night side—with the gas giant and its fierce radiation belts between the Marine craft and the majority of the alien structures.

The plan wasn't perfect. The Rosetters appeared to have enmeshed Heimdall in structures of light as well. But every little bit, the mission planners had thought, would help.

Ahead, she could see the Marine transport *Marne* drifting at the edge of the debris ring. Like the *Lexington*, the *Marne* was a long, slender beam topped by a shield cap filled with water—radiation shielding at high acceleration. The shield cap was bullet shaped rather than flat like an umbrella, and the transport's hab modules, several dozen of them, rotated around the ship's axis in the cap's shadow.

Farther aft was the *Lucas*, an ebony-black flying wing with downward-canted airfoils. The battalion assault transport—BAT—had embarked with 3rd Battalion, 4th Marines of the 4th Marine Regiment, the 3/4, a total of 960 Marines organized as a battalion-strength planetary assault team.

Taggart had downloaded all of the data she could find on the *Lucas*. The name was that of a Marine of five centuries earlier—Jacklyn Lucas—a kid who'd illegally joined the Marine Corps at the age of fourteen. Three years later he'd stormed the beach at Iwo Jima without a rifle, thrown himself on top of two grenades to protect his squad mates . . . and somehow survived to win the Medal of Honor, the youngest person ever to do so. If the ship named after him was channeling that guy's esprit de corps, Taggart thought, it would be able to survive anything the Rosetters could conjure.

The *Marne* could carry a 960-Marine battalion with reasonable if somewhat Spartan comfort, the *Lucas* less so. The Marines would go in packed like sardines, in drop pods and mobile gun walkers. Once the Marines had established a secure perimeter, the *Lucas* would touch down and morph into a planetary watchstation, a base that would support the Marines and keep an electronic eye on the aliens until the *Lexington* battlegroup returned. Taggart was definitely in this for the long haul; she would stay in the base with a small team of naval personnel running the equipment.

The *Marne*, meanwhile, would be empty. She would return to the *Himmelschloss* and there take the Confederation personnel on board for the evacuation flight back to Earth.

Again—if everthing goes to plan.

Under AI control, her transport pod decelerated sharply as it approached the *Lucas*, which clung to the *Marne*'s spine like an angry black tumor. That hull was nanomatrix, like the hulls of advanced fighters, and could change shape to meet the needs of the moment. It changed now, yawning open to give access in the ship's side and she drifted into a glare of light inside.

On board was noisy, crowded chaos. Hundreds of Marines were still filing out from *Marne*'s spine into the assault transport, urged along by screaming NCOs as they floated along passageways in zero-G in search of their fireteam drop capsules. Taggart stepped out of her transport, grabbed hold of a white safety line . . . and froze. Which way?

"Make a hole! Comin' through!"

A squad of twelve Marines hand-over-handed along the safety line at high speed, nearly colliding with her.

"Commander Taggart," a voice said in her head—unreasonably calm in all of the confusion. "You want to move to your right, toward the hatchway marked 'OA-4.' Do you see it?"

"Yes. Konstantin?"

"A clone of Konstantin, Commander," the voice said. "I'm Konstantin's avatar for your mission."

"Good to meet you. Thanks for the help."

"Not at all. The *Lucas* is not an overly large vessel, and navigating her passageways with nine hundred Marines on board can be, I imagine, somewhat daunting."

She had to move aside for several more columns of hurrying Marines, but eventually she reached *Lucas*'s small bridge. Two other naval officers were already there—Lieutenant Kathy Peters, the navigator and pilot, and Lieutenant Ross Hagelund, the engineer and nanotech officer.

"Captain on deck!" Peters snapped.

"As you were. How are we doing?"

"Behind schedule, Captain," Hagelund told her. She blinked at the unaccustomed honorific, then accepted it. The commanding officer of a ship is *always* the captain, no matter what her actual rank.

"Are we ready for space otherwise?"

"Absolutely, ma'am. Ready to haul ass at your command."

Taggart was already lowering herself into her seat, which closed in around her and provided her with palm pads for interface. The upper half of the bridge was already set to show surrounding space; the bottom side of the *Marne*'s shield cap could be seen a couple of hundred meters ahead, beyond her rotating hab modules. As Taggart linked in to the bridge channels, data flowed down through her consciousness, giving her readouts of ship systems, of navigational data, of the status of the Marines aft and below.

They still had six hours on their launch window. No problems there.

It wouldn't be very much longer, now.

I'll talk to the gods soon . . .

Bethesda Medical Center
Bethesda, Maryland
1410 hours, TFT

The military hospital complex had stood here, twelve kilometers northwest of Washington, D.C., for almost five hundred years. Congressmen and presidents had been treated here, with high-speed mag lev subways connecting the medical center with the subbasements of the White House and Capitol. When D.C. was flooded by rising sea levels in the late twenty-first century, Bethesda had remained an enclave of civilization and medical research. The National Institutes of Health had been just to the west, with research facilities simply too important to surrender just because D.C. had gone the way of lost Atlantis. The battle against the Blood Death had been fought here, in part.

But the facility had gone into a slump after that, and for a time it had been privately owned and operated and very nearly been abandoned. With the return of the USNA government to D.C. and the rebuilding of Washington, however, the Bethesda medical complex was again at the cutting edge of nanomedicine and modern epidemiology. The mag lev subways weren't yet open, but Bethesda once more held the distinction of being the government's official center for modern medicine.

"So what am I doing *here*?" Gray said. He was encased in living plastic, a high-tech bed that fed, cleaned, and exercised him, delivered regular doses of nanobots and carried away wastes. Whatever the device was doing, it was working; the headache, the joint pains, the dizziness all were gone. He still felt quite weak and a bit groggy, but that was to be expected.

The alien bacteria, the doctors had told him, were under control. Exactly what that meant, he wasn't sure. Gray wanted them *gone*. . . .

He'd awakened several hours before, to find himself in a strange bed in a strange room under one G, his weight about twice what it had been in *America*'s sick bay. The room was spacious, and one wall was transparent; doctors and medical technicians came and went in sealed e-suits. Clearly he was still in isolation.

"We brought you down on a high-speed shuttle, Admiral," President Koenig told him. "Didn't even bother with the space elevator. Flew you straight into Andrews and hauled you out here in a sealed floater."

"Wasn't that taking a hell of a big chance, sir? The idea was to keep me from infecting the entire planet."

"We've kept you as isolated as you were on the *America*," Koenig told him. The president was standing behind the transparency, with a dozen aides, senior military officers, and others. Gray was flattered. For the president of the USNA to leave his office in the New White House and trek out here just to see *him* was . . . startling.

But he didn't like being the center of attention, and even more he didn't like the potential risk to the human species.

"It turns out there was not a large danger," a doctor standing next to the president told him. "You've encountered a race called the Agletsch?"

"And you are?"

"Yes—sorry. Dr. Jamil Gorham."

"Okay."

"As I was saying, you've met the Agletsch?"

"Of course. Many times."

"Well, most Agletsch carry the paramycoplasma organism in their bodies . . . or one version of it, at least. That's the point, you see. Each and every species infected by paramycoplasma is infected by a different, artificial species of the bacteria. There has never been an instance of cross-species contamination occurring naturally."

"I've met with the Agletsch many times," Koenig admitted. "Face to . . . er . . . eyestalks. If the Sh'daar had wanted to get me with germ warfare, they certainly had the opportunity."

"TBB," the doctor added. "The trans-biospheric barrier."

"So what happened with me?" Gray asked. "Why did *I* get it . . . or we, I should say. How about the other people who got sick with me?"

"Under treatment and doing fine, Admiral," Koenig told him.

"We believe," Dr. Gorham said, "that the paramycoplasma organism has to be specifically genengineered for each species . . . so much so that it's almost a completely new organism . . . not just a new species, but by rights a new genus. For now, the xenobiologists are keeping the original classification. We've named the Agletsch version *Paramycoplasma agletschii* . . . and there's simply no way that *P. agletschii* can infect humans."

"Which means . . ."

"The organism was very carefully crafted so that it could infect us," Koenig said, nodding.

"Bacteriological warfare," Gray said. "A deliberate attack . . ."

"Actually," the voice of Konstantin said in Gray's mind,

"we think that this was an attempt at communication, not warfare."

"Exactly," Koenig said. "They weren't attacking us. They wanted to *talk*. And it may be the slickest means of inter-species communication available throughout the galaxy."

"I don't understand. . . ."

They explained, or they tried to. Gray's expertise was not in xenobiology or genegineering. Still, it mostly made sense. The trick, they told him, was coming up with an organism that maintained its biological identity and could continue to function as a superorganism when taken as an aggregate of millions of cells, but which could develop metabolic and reproductive strategies enabling it to survive in wildly different hosts.

The Agletsch, for instance, were carbon-based organisms very much along the lines of life on Earth, so much so that they could get nourishment out of most human foods, and yet their metabolism made use of potassium and phosphorous to a degree unknown on Earth, and also incorporated cyanide, methyl cyanide, and hydrocyanic acid.

In other words, the foods Agletsch ate normally would poison humans.

Or there were the Turusch, another star-faring species under the Sh'daar Collective banner. They apparently hailed from a world hotter than Earth. Their metabolism was carbon-based, but they employed silicon chemistry as well. They used sulfur and sulfur compounds to a degree not seen in terrestrial life, and a complex analogue of chlorophyll to convert sunlight into energy.

For any reasonable theory of alien microbiology, the microorganisms found in Agletsch or Turusch should not have any effect whatsoever on humans, nor should the two be able to infect one another.

But bacterial samples taken from both the Agletsch and from a colony of Turusch POWs at Crisium Base proved that both carried cocci of genus *Paramycoplasma*. They'd just adjusted their surface proteins to a remarkable degree, so that *P. agletschii* could handle the cyanide of Agletsch metabolism, while *P. turuschii* was happy living with the sulfur chemistry of the Turusch.

And detailed DNA analyses proved that both were related to *Paramycoplasma subtli*, the species that had attacked Gray and the other members of the N'gai expedition.

"In fact," Gorham told Gray, "we're considering changing the name of the bug to *Paramycoplasma homosapiensi*. Keep it all nice and orderly, you know."

"Thanks for the biology lesson, Doc, but that's not really what I'm concerned about at the moment. What do you mean by the idea that the Sh'daar were trying to talk to us?"

"That was my observation, Admiral," Konstantin's voice said. "And it is still only a working theory. But ever since we first began encountering the various Sh'daar species, there has been something of a mystery. With some hundreds, perhaps thousands of mutually alien species making up their Collective, how do they get anything done? What single motivation can unite such disparate species?"

Arguably, that was one of the biggest mysteries about the Sh'daar, and had been ever since the start of the war. Humankind had encountered a number of different alien races—Turusch, H'rulka, Slan, Nungiirtok, and others—and in each case they'd come under attack. Human strategists had noted that if *all* of the Sh'daar species had managed to put together a coordinated attack, Earth would have been destroyed or forced to capitulate immediately. Instead, the attacks had been piecemeal, and seemingly without a coherent strategy.

It was as though they'd lost the heart for an all-out push . . . those of them that actually *had* hearts in the first place.

And those were the civilizations encountered in the epoch of Humankind—next-door neighbors, astronomically speaking, to Earth. Dozens more alien species had evolved among the stars of the N'gai Cluster almost a billion years ago, come through time, and established part of their empire in what was for them the remote future. *Why*? What was their motive; what was behind their demand that humans give up key portions of their fast-evolving technology?

None of it made sense . . . and it wasn't enough to shrug and assume that it didn't make sense because aliens were *different*.

"Consider," Konstantin went on. "Which technologies did the Sh'daar demand that humans stop developing?"

"The GRIN technologies," Gray replied.

"And what technologies might particularly worry a bacterial-emergent intelligence?"

"I don't know. Medical technologies of all kinds, I suppose. . . ."

"In particular, medical nanotechnology," Konstantin told him. "Genetics, both to improve the human immune response and to attack harmful bacteria. Robotics, which is key to medical nanotechnology. Information systems—computers—which is also key to programming nanotech in order to seek out and destroy hostile bacteria, or engage in large-scale genetic engineering."

"My God . . ."

"There's more. What happens when a civilization transcends . . . when it enters its technological singularity?"

"Well . . . I don't think anybody really knows, do they? I've heard lots of possibilities."

"Indeed. Two possibilities include uploading organic minds into robotic bodies, however, which would be effectively immortal . . . or uploading minds as pure data into advanced, hyperintelligent computers."

"The Baondyeddi on Heimdall," Gray said. "The Etched Cliffs . . ."

"Indeed. Organic beings who have removed themselves from the ills, dangers, and tribulations of organic existence by becoming electronic life forms. But there were other possibilities as well. Genetic alterations to improve the species, essentially creating completely new species, for instance, or symbiosis between mutually alien life forms to create new forms. An emergent bacterial intelligence, for example . . ."

"Wait! You're saying it was fucking *germs* that were behind the Sh'daar grand scheme?" Gray shook his head. "I can't believe that. That's just too weird. . . ."

"We do not yet have proof," Konstantin admitted. "But

thanks to my being able to interface with your internal hardware during your . . . struggle against the paramycoplasmid bacteria, I have begun tapping into a great deal of data stored within the bacterial substrate . . . the bacteria's group mind, if you will.

"And we believe it likely that the paramycoplasm genus is both highly intelligent and highly motivated. That it is the paramycoplasmids that fear a technological singularity . . . and have been seeking at all costs to prevent organic life from going down that path."

"Wait-wait-wait," Gray said, struggling with the strange concept. "You really *are* saying that it's the *bacteria* who are behind this? That want to communicate? That are driving the Sh'daar? . . ."

"More precisely, it would be the *symbiosis* that is running things . . . the union of a bacterial aggregate with each of the different sapient species."

"But what the hell does all of that have to do with them *talking* to us?"

"We've known for centuries, now, that bacteria can influence their human hosts," Konstantin explained. "When the microbiota require a certain element for growth, they use chemical signals to create cravings for foods containing that element. Chocolate, for example. Or sugar."

"That's not *communication*."

"I must disagree, Admiral. The organism we call *Paramycoplasma subtilis* is simply a little more sophisticated in its chemical signaling than the microbes with which you grew up. . . ."

Stop. Kill.

Gray had almost forgotten the impression of commands he'd felt during that savage and ultramicroscopic battle he'd witnessed within himself. What he remembered now was dreamlike, on the point of evaporating entirely.

But that had definitely been communication.

Intelligent microbes—no, worse.

Intelligent microbes guiding galactic destiny.

Chapter Fourteen

USMA Lander Lucas
Approaching Heimdall
1210 hours, TFT

"Fifteen minutes to atmosphere, Captain," Lieutenant Peters announced.

"Any response from Big Brother?"

"Not a peep," Hagelund said. "Yet."

Yet . . .

They'd made the passage from Thrymheim to Bifrost at a painfully slow pace, drifting along at less than 3,000 kilometers per second—about one percent of the speed of light—which was a snail's pace for interplanetary travel. The trek had taken the better part of three days, with almost a thousand Marines crammed into the assault lander's drop capsules, their biological needs taken care of by their armor rather than through more traditional measures. Taggart could only imagine the discomfort their living cargo had been forced to endure.

But the cautionary strategy appeared to have paid off. By limiting their velocity to a few thousand kps, they weren't having any troubles passing through the strange, alien light structures surrounding Bifrost and Heimdall, and they didn't seem to be attracting unwanted attention, either.

The mission planners had not been certain what had triggered the Rosetter response to the *Himmelschloss* battlegroup or to the flight of fighters that had been wiped out. They'd been approaching slowly as well. Perhaps it had been their numbers that had upset the aliens, or the fact that Heimdall had been so close to the center of the alien activity. Perhaps it had been something else.

All that matters is that they aren't trying to destroy us now.

In the past hours, the AI controlling the *Lucas*'s flight had slowed them even further—a slow drift in toward the ringed gas giant, which showed ahead as a vast, bloated black disk against the heavens, framed by the knife-slash white of the illuminated portions of the rings to either side. Heimdall was a smaller disk of darkness framed by the larger, deep in eclipse. Taggart could easily make out the ghostly blue and green glow of the moon's aurorae ringing both poles. The Rosette alien structures were so tenuous as to be invisible when you were actually flying through them. In the distance, though, great curving arcs, bands, and beams of golden light hung, vast and enigmatic, against the stars.

"Wait a sec," Hagelund said. "What's that? Coming up from Heimdall."

"Looks like we've got company," Taggart said. "Reduce speed. . . ."

Thousands—no, *hundreds* of thousands of glowing motes. They looked like fireflies. They ascended from the dark surface of Heimdall in a swarm, sweeping out from and around the Earth-sized moon with a motion reminiscent of a murmuration of starlings on Earth. *Lucas*'s bridge team was transfixed by the sight of a vast cloud, seething . . . surging . . . looping and twisting and folding in upon itself, now dividing, now recombining, now thinning, now compacting into almost solid masses of light as it rose from and enveloped the disk of Heimdall. . . .

The cloud divided once more, a relatively small mass of lights streaming off from the main body and accelerating.

Despite the fact that it was a small percentage, it assumed an immense, twisting wing-shape as it approached the assault lander.

That's a lot of lights.

"What's our velocity?" Taggart demanded.

"Twenty-five kps," Peters replied.

"Reduce speed to ten kps," she snapped. *Damn.* She had access to those data. She wasn't thinking, transfixed by the sight ahead.

Lucas decelerated further. "Captain?" a voice said over a private channel. It was Colonel Jamison, waiting out the approach down in one of *Lucas*'s pod bays. "What are those things? We're seeing them through the ship feed."

"Not sure yet, Colonel," she replied. "Sit tight. I'm going to try to drift through."

To his credit, Jamison didn't comment. The Marines were effectively trapped and helpless in their pods, and if those swarms of lights up ahead turned nasty, there was absolutely nothing they could do to fight back . . . or to run.

Something thudded off of *Lucas*'s hull.

"Soften us up a bit, Ross," she told Hagelund.

"Aye, aye, skipper."

The hull of the *Lucas*—most of her external surfaces, in fact—was nanomatrix, a type of titanium-ceramic alloy cast in particles that could rearrange themselves into different shapes for different purposes. Right now, *Lucas*'s external surfaces were held rigidly in place, with precisely calculated angles and surfaces designed to scatter incoming radio or laser signals into space, rendering the ship almost invisible to anyone looking for her. The surface also absorbed radio and light energy; by softening the hull further, Taggart was trying to get the ship to drink up even more incoming radiation, at the cost of losing some of its scattering capability. If she could find the sweet spot between scattering and absorption, *Lucas* would all but vanish from the aliens' screens.

Assuming, of course, that they were using technologies in their scans that were even remotely recognizable to humans.

The swarm of glowing fireflies was all around them, swirling and merging and thinning and expanding. The main body of the swarm was behind them now, moving farther astern.

"I think," Hagelund said very quietly, as though fearful that the aliens would hear him, "you spoofed 'em."

"That," Taggart replied, "or they decided we're harmless."

"Either way," Peters said, "I'll take it."

Me, too, Taggart thought.

An hour passed without further incident, and they drifted down through shimmering curtains of light toward the moon, Heimdall. The glowing motes continued to swarm and swoop outside, completely enveloping the moon and dispersing far out into space. Large numbers appeared to be streaming through the night-side atmosphere of giant Bifrost directly ahead, forming something like a vast wheel of light at least twenty thousand kilometers across. *What*, Taggart wondered, *could the structure's purpose possibly be?* The *Lucas* brushed individual devices several more times, but with no apparent damage. She allowed herself to relax fractionally. *We might be able to pull this off after all.*

Moving now at only a few kilometers per second, the *Lucas* swept past the moon just as sunrise exploded across one limb of Bifrost. Heimdall was coming out of eclipse, and the ruddy sunlight, weak and thin as it was, touched vast ice sheets with flashes of ruby flame and glowed across endless deserts of barren rock.

The *Lucas* began changing shape, switching from a utilitarian teardrop to something with large down-canted wings that could grab and hold on to atmosphere.

Heimdall was heavily glaciated, with land areas covered by cold, empty desert from pole to pole. There were two small, landlocked oceans edged with ice and choked with floes. Mountains girdled the equator, thrust high by the same tidal stresses that kept surface temperatures here a few degrees below zero and not, as would otherwise have been the case, at minus two-hundred something. *Lucas*'s scanners fed a constant stream of hard data through Taggart's implants, revealing a world cold and dead and utterly devoid of life.

Once, though, she knew, Heimdall had been a living world. Kapteyn's Star had been a part of the N'gai Cluster. Xenosophontologists who'd studied the ruins here believed that Heimdall originally had been the homeworld for the Baondyeddi, one of the ur-Sh'daar species that had dominated that dwarf galaxy hundreds of millions of years ago.

She knew the history, as it had been revealed both by archaeologists here on Heimdall, and by the crew of the *America* when it first penetrated the N'gai Cluster of 876 million years ago and tapped into Sh'daar records. The large, disk-shaped Baondyeddi had specialized in genetic manipulation. Rather than encasing themselves in armor when they wanted to explore a hostile alien world, they'd bred new versions of themselves that could endure, even thrive under those alien conditions. Over tens of thousands of years, they'd also genegineered smaller, more nimble versions of themselves, with brains configured to mesh with electronic prostheses, literally becoming part of their own robotic systems.

As true cyborgs, then, part organic but mostly machine, they'd explored their tiny galaxy of a few billion stars and helped forge the ur-Sh'daar civilization. Eventually, though, even that tiny remaining link with flesh and blood became an impediment. Virtual reality offered, it seemed to many Baondyeddi, an existence far more rich, complex, and rewarding than so-called real life. Billions of them had uploaded their minds into powerful networks of AI computers.

In time, their entire homeworld had become a single such network. Complex circuitry had been grown into the planet's bedrock, creating a massively redundant computer net capable of modeling entire universes. Not all Baondyeddi, by any means, but many—perhaps most—had uploaded themselves into that network, together with some billions of individuals of other species seeking a kind of eternity. Powered by the heat generated by the tidal effects of massive

Bifrost, the planetary computer was programmed to ride out the eons in ultra-slow motion, the digital beings within the network experiencing seconds for each year—or even century—passing outside. They'd seemed confident in their ability to survive in that state for trillions of years, until the ultimate heat death of the cosmos.

And then the Rosette Aliens had shown up, destroyed the research stations studying the Baondyeddi, and descended on the ancient planet like hungry locusts from the sky. What might have happened to the digital population of Heimdall was unknown; the xenosophontology team on board the *Lucas* would be trying to discover that.

Once the Marines had secured the landing zone.

"Colonel Jamison?" Taggart called over a private channel. "We're coming up on the drop zone."

"Right. Thanks for the lift."

"Anytime, Colonel. Good luck!"

The actual drop was handled by the *Lucas*'s AI. Taggart felt the thump as two of the first drop pods fired, followed in rapid succession by dozens more. Four hundred Marines, packed four to a pod, were fired into the Heimdall night as the *Lucas* pursued a mathematically perfect curve across the sky at an altitude of three thousand meters. The rest remained on board for delivery straight to the surface.

Bays swung open along *Lucas*'s flanks, disgorging twelve stubby black darts—Marine AS-90 Hornet fighters on CAP.

"Cappers deployed!" Lieutenant Liam Davies called. The Marine assault force had brought along its own Combat Air Patrol in the absence of a star carrier.

"Copy that, CAP-One," Taggart heard Jamison reply. "Go wide and keep your eyes peeled. I don't want anything sneaking up on us while we're down here."

"Roger, Heimdall Command."

Taggart tried not to think about what highly advanced technology might mean for Primitives trying to set up a ground perimeter. Invisibility was a distinct possibility.

So was collapsing the entire planet. She wished she could turn her brain off. . . .

The curve described by the *Lucas* tightened as the assault lander moved to the center of the LZ.

"There's the old base, Skipper," Peters reported. An icon danced against the computer imagery painted for Taggart's inner eye. Heimdall Base had been a ground research facility operating in conjunction with the now-vanished Stanford torus called Heimdall Orbital. It appeared to have been destroyed; little remained but a black stain on the bare rock. Wisps of dry snow blew across barren rock and among twisted support beams.

For not the first time, the question on everyone's mind was, what the hell had happened here?

A kilometer away, the Temple Ruins sprawled across a flat-topped plateau. The Pan-European explorers here had named it the Temple because it was evocative of terrestrial structures like the Parthenon or Baalbek . . . but in far greater disarray. Sections of columns littered the ground, and little remained of the intact structure save a cracked and broken base of stone blocks.

Another mystery hosted by this cold and enigmatic world.

As the *Lucas* continued to descend, passing above the Ruins, the images displayed within Taggart's brain suddenly flickered and fuzzed, blasted by white noise. For just an instant, she saw . . . something else—the Temple whole and rising in soaring majesty above a dark blue-green and verdant landscape. Where there was barren rock now, she saw parks and vegetation. . . .

And then reality reasserted itself, the vegetation replaced by windswept rock. Taggart blinked, trying to clear her head.

What the hell?

"Skipper!" Hagelund called. "I just saw—"

"I know! I know! I saw it too!"

"What was that?" Peters asked.

"I don't know . . . and it doesn't matter. Right now we concentrate on getting down!"

The ship's AI, evidently, had seen nothing. Changing shape once more, growing rounder and flatter with a bulge in the middle, the *Lucas* slowed to a hover, then descended, touching down on the wind-swept surface of rock and snow. Wide-spread legs bit at the surface and the ramps came down, disgorging the rest of the Marine assault force.

"Heimdall Command, this is CAP-One! We're getting weird interference when we fly over the Temple area!"

"What kind of interference?"

Static blasted back for a moment, then cleared. "It's okay now, Command. For a sec, there, I thought we were flying over a forest! Everything was dark blue-green, and there were buildings on the surface!"

"Knock off the brain-poppers, Davies," Jamison replied. "And the VR!"

There was nervous laughter, which she could sympathize with. She was still shaken by what she'd just glimpsed herself. Was it some sort of alien weapon? Or an attempt at communication?

Or something they couldn't begin to comprehend?

The *Lucas* continued its morphing before finally settling down onto the surface and broadening into a squat, thick-walled structure nearly two hundred meters across. The dome on top separated from the rest of the structure and became a turret mounting a powerful particle cannon. At the same time, hatches around the rim opened to expose missile launch tubes and point-defense lasers. The Marines were already digging in, creating a perimeter some ten kilometers across strengthened by robot gun towers nanotechnically grown from the native rock.

In the dark violet sky overhead, the Rosette Aliens appeared indifferent . . .

. . . for now.

Bethesda Medical Center
Bethesda, Maryland
1512 hours, TFT

What is it you want?

Admiral Gray *felt* the words more than he heard them, felt them as a compelling surge of curiosity and command.

The questioner was Konstantin, arguably the most powerful AI working now with humans, and certainly the one with the most experience in cracking alien languages and exposing alien motivations.

What is it you want?

Gray was a part of the interrogation partly because the object of Konstantin's attention was the mass of alien bacteria still inhabiting his body . . . and because Konstantin, while remarkably human in many ways, was not human when it came to emotion. The super-AI could *mimic* emotion, certainly, but it probably couldn't feel urges rooted in organic experience—anger, fear, love . . .

. . . or the need for self-preservation on anything deeper than a cold and rational sense of logic.

What is it you want?

To live . . .

Gray felt the response deep inside, a striving, desperate yearning for survival, for life. It was, he thought, quite possibly the one emotion common to all living beings.

Some part of his own brain, he realized, was attaching words to wordless feelings and concepts. He felt Konstantin moving inside his mind. *I am adjusting the sensitivity of your implants.*

"Go ahead," he said out loud . . . then realized that Konstantin had not asked his permission, that the super-AI didn't *require* his permission. The fine-tuning was ongoing as Konstantin continued to try to extract meaning from the super-organism inside him, and the Prim in him shuddered.

The relationship between Humankind and human technology—in particular with smarter-than-human artificial intelligences—was still poorly defined. Maybe, Gray thought, the ultimate destiny of humans was to serve as disposable but easily replaceable tools for work that didn't require the highest grade of precision. . . .

Without your active and voluntary participation, Konstantin told him over a private channel, *communication with the Symbionts would not be possible at all.*

Well, that was nice to know, at least . . . though Gray wasn't sure what the AI meant by "voluntary." In any case, medical intervention by both Konstantin and Andre had saved his life and the lives of every infected member of the battlegroup's crew. At the same time, though—according to the human doctors attending him—they'd left a sheet of the infecting organism still alive inside his body cavity, and a thick concentration still growing in the higher centers of his brain—especially in the regions associated with speech, meaning, and cognition.

What had Konstantin called the alien? Symbionts. The name, he realized, had been drawn from his own memory, but the choice had been guided by the bacteria. It was, he thought, a very strange kind of two-level communication.

We have sought communication with these hosts for over five thousand generations, the Symbiont said, using his own words within his head. Gray listened . . . and recorded everything in his implant RAM, where it could be directly accessed by Konstantin.

How long was the Symbionts' generation? Terrestrial bacteria, some of them, could reproduce every six hours or so. He had the impression it took longer for *Paramycoplasma subtilis*, but the organism didn't seem to measure time, not the way humans did, at any rate, so he couldn't tell. The sense he got, though, was that the Symbiont was referring to the first human contact with the Sh'daar Collective. That would have been the meeting between human explorers and an Agletsch trading community at Zeta Doradus in 2312 . . . some 113 years ago. Gray routed the data through his implant's math processor. Five thousand generations in 113 years worked out to eight days and a few hours. That matched well enough with how long it had taken him and the others to come down with symptoms.

The host's advanced technologies posed a threat to wholeness.

Was that, Gray wondered, the aliens' explanation of why the Sh'daar had attacked humanity? In the next heartbeat, he felt the reply, a distinct affirmation.

The proscribed technologies posed a threat to wholeness . . .

So it was about the GRIN tech. They had all assumed that, but he now—based on Konstantin's suggestion—understood a bit more *why* they saw it as such a threat to them.

Human tacticians had noted that the Sh'daar appeared to be afraid of humans when they penetrated the N'gai Cluster eight hundred and some million years ago. Was that because humans with access to time travel were such a terrible threat? Or were the Sh'daar being influenced by the various strains of Symbiont bacteria inhabiting them, super-organisms peculiarly susceptible to human technologies?

That explained why a number of Sh'daar species used such proscribed technologies—nanotechnology, for example, and advanced computer systems. If the species in question were already solidly under the Symbionts' control, they might not be as big a threat.

And what about the notorious Sh'daar terror of another technological singularity? That made more sense now too. The Singularity—what the Sh'daar called the *Schjaa Hok*, the Transcending—had affected different intelligent species in different ways. Some, such as the species called the Groth Hoj, had already made the transition from organic beings to purely robotic bodies a few at a time, their minds digitized and uploaded into mobile computers. Others, with organic or partly organic bodies like the Baondyeddi, had uploaded themselves to computer networks *en masse*, leaving their bodies behind to die. Each species, as it transcended, had left behind individuals who'd not embraced the relevant technologies and become Refusers.

And those Refusers all had been infected by the different species of *Paramycoplasma*, super-organisms that communicated with their hosts through very basic, very raw emotions.

Like terror.

One basic problem the xenosophontologists had faced since first contact with the Agletsch, Gray knew, was the difficulty in matching emotions between distinct sapient species. Did "fear" mean the same for humans as it did for, say, the Baondyeddi? Hell, emotions didn't always map in a one-to-one correspondence between one human and another. When you began comparing what passed for emotions among mutually alien species, each with unique evolutionary histories, the whole question became all but meaningless.

But it felt like they'd just gained some measure, however thin, of understanding.

What is wholeness? Konstantin was asking.

Gray felt the answer within. *Completion . . . perfection . . . balance . . . host and Symbiont existing together for the perfection of both . . .*

Was it you who guided the Sh'daar Collective into war with Humankind?

The super-organism struggled with some of those concepts. War it seemed to understand as the natural struggle between invading bacteria and the immune system of an unwilling host. Both Sh'daar and humans, apparently, were "host," though at different stages of "perfection." Gray had to dig for synonyms for "guided," however. The bacteria did not understand.

Led? . . . Instructed? . . . Urged? . . . Commanded? . . .

At last, the bacteria appeared to comprehend, though the concept was alien to it. *Symbionts do* not *guide the host, save in the most general and vague of ways. The decision to initiate the immune response was the choice of the host.*

As the strange conversation continued, Gray began sensing a larger tapestry, a kind of story, part myth, part allegory set against a galaxy-spanning backdrop.

The Symbionts had evolved within the N'gai Cluster eons ago . . . a microbial organism, quite possibly a disease organism, infecting one of the hundreds of sentient species among the Cluster's worlds. It didn't know which of the species it had evolved with; it literally couldn't tell the difference between one host species and another—not from the inside, at least—and, in fact, from its point of view, the differences were irrelevant. There were faint memories of a terrible struggle; perhaps the hosts had been stricken by a terrible plague as their bodies reacted to the invader.

Ultimately, the host species had used genegineering to change the deadly microbe, to make it benign, less destructive. It was probably an accident, one never realized, that the genetic tinkering had resulted in a super-organism with an unprecedented ability to interconnect, to develop long-term goals, to self-direct in new and startling directions.

The organism, like the terrestrial slime molds Gray had researched earlier, became huge and complex while retaining its essentially cellular lifestyle. Like terrestrial termites, they exhibited an emergent intelligence. Whether they were truly intelligent on their own was an interesting question. There were clues in what Gray was seeing here that suggested that the organism actually hijacked the nervous system of its hosts, using their existing brains and nerves to do some of their thinking. Memories were stored in specially bred cells; apparently, *Paramycoplasma* species had learned how to genegineer as well.

At some point in the remote past, the super-organism jumped from that first sapient species to another. To do so, it had to have genegineered itself, creating an offshoot with a different biochemistry to inhabit an alien biome. And a very long time after that, it made the jump again. And again. And yet again. It was likely that all of the ur-Sh'daar became infected.

And the evidence suggested that if the ur-Sh'daar were aware at all of their invisible passengers, they'd dismissed them as harmless internal flora.

The Transcendence had come as a terrible shock.

Billions, perhaps trillions, of organic beings had either died or vanished. By that time, the myriad Paramycoplasma species were at least tentatively in touch with one another, possibly by means of subtle airborne chemicals released by the hosts, possibly by means of clouds of memory cells shed from hosts' skin or other bodily covering. Something well in excess of 90 percent of the sapient N'gai species had vanished, taking their Symbiont riders with them.

What was left very nearly became extinct.

The Symbionts held on, however, within the handful of surviving hosts, the Refusers left behind by the galaxy-wide collapse of civilization, the Schjaa Hok. *Civilization was rebuilt, the lost technologies of star travel rediscovered, the lost libraries of ancient memories rebuilt. As*

*this was happening, the N'gai Cluster was falling from the
intergalactic Void and into a new galaxy. The Refusers
feared the return of the ur-Sh'daar, the Transcended species; the Symbionts feared such a return even more . . . and
they feared the technologies that would expose them, hunt
them down, destroy them. . . .*

*And so the Sh'daar had sought refuge in the far future.
There had been devices left by a vanished species that permitted travel both across vast stretches of space and across
vast reaches of time. A few Sh'daar traveled into the future,
discovered a new species . . .*

. . . and introduced them to "wholeness."

*Now, if the Transcendent ur-Sh'daar returned to the
N'gai Cluster, there would be Symbionts and hosts surviving in remote futurity.*

*Eventually, in another few tens of millions of years, N'gai
tumbled into the giant spiral galaxy and was devoured.
Shredded by tidal forces, it was absorbed, several billion
suns stripped away from the N'gai's central core and scattered across a far larger, vaster, and younger spiral of stars.*

*But the Symbionts, past and future, were safe . . . com-
plete . . . whole.*

*There remained only a single problem. Shortly before
N'gai merged with the spiral galaxy . . . shortly after Sh'daar
probes had emerged in the future, a new species had been
encountered, a species referring to itself as Humankind.*

*And these humans threatened to undo everything that the
Symbiont species had accomplished . . . work that spanned
much of the span of the universe since its beginnings.*

*And the Symbionts feared them, feared them almost as
much as they feared the Transcendents.*

*Feared them enough to destroy them . . . somehow . . .
somehow. . . .*

Chapter Fifteen

USMA Lander Lucas
Heimdall Station
1632 hours, TFT

"Keep it spread out, people. And watch your step!"

Gunnery Sergeant Roger Courtland led his section of twelve Marines across broken rock and ice, treacherous beneath their armored feet. Wearing the newly issued advanced Mark IV combat armor, the Marines were difficult to see. The suits' outer nanoflage layers picked up and repeated the colors of light striking them, rendering the heavy suits . . . not invisible, exactly, but very hard to see, especially when they were motionless.

Courtland reached a massive section of broken pillar, an octagonal block of chipped and dirty glass three meters high, and leaned against it, catching his breath. Heimdall's gravity was slightly less than a full Earth G, but combat power armor was heavy despite the actuators that translated human effort to movement and superhuman strength. He'd been out here only a few minutes, and he was already feeling the strain.

"Rainbow Devil, Heimdall Command," sounded through his in-head. "Status update."

Courtland heard Lieutenant Ogden's response over the platoon Net. "Heimdall Command, Rainbow. We're at the objective. Moving in for a closer look."

"Watch your ass out there, people."

"Copy that, Command."

Fifty meters ahead, First Platoon's gun walkers had already reached the objective. Similarly camouflaged, they showed against a violet skyline as three-meter-high fuzzy patches of movement and shadow shifting among the stumps of broken-off pillars. The structure humans called the Temple had at one time covered almost two hundred hectares—roughly two square kilometers—and had included some thousands of crystalline, eight-sided pillars around some sort of central structure of unknown shape and construction.

The ruins didn't look all that prepossessing now, Courtland thought, and were startling only in their extent. The Confederation science teams exploring the site, though, had reported that the pillars were made of Q-carbon, an artificial diamond brighter and stronger than natural diamond, which, evidently, had been grown in place, each more than eight meters thick at the base and stretching some three hundred meters into the sky.

Courtland rubbed the surface of the block with a gloved hand, receptors in the fingertips transmitting the feel of the pitted and weathered surface to his brain. Gods . . . how long did it take for *diamond* to weather this much?

They must have been spectacular when they were whole and soaring into the thin red light of Kapteyn's Star . . . but they'd fallen a very long time ago.

"Find anything, Gunny?"

He turned. The speaker was a spider, man high, a black basketball suspended from four thin and many-jointed legs. "Nah," he replied. "Just wondering how fucking old this place is."

"Very," the spider replied in his head. It was a woman's voice, and sexy as hell. "We think the Baondyeddi may have built it during the ur-Sh'daar period, before they transcended. That would have been more than eight hundred seventy-six million years ago . . . and it might have been as far back as one billion years. A long, long time."

The spider was, in fact, a telepresence body for Dr. Celia Carter. The senior member of the xenosophontological team assigned to the *Lucas*, she was safe and secure somewhere within the *Lucas*'s bowels right now, but linked in to the spider's sensory suite so that she could explore the surface in relative comfort. He'd gotten to know her during the cramped journey in from Thrymheim.

Courtland had actually first met her a couple of years ago, at an exoplanetary conference in Houston. She was pretty and fun and *very* smart, and it turned out she had a thing for guys who'd actually been out there among the stars and met some of the critters whose psychology she studied for a living.

When he'd bumped into her on board the *Lucas*—literally so, in zero-G—it had been like old home week. It was damned tough to find any privacy at all in a transport as crowded as the *Lucas* . . . but senior Marine enlisted personnel could be *very* inventive when it came to playing the system to get their own way.

In this case, all it had taken was temporarily assigning four guys in a hab-pod to a different section and marking the quarters "occupied" on the battalion AI. The battAI had known what was going on, of course . . . but it didn't care much about humans and their relationships, so long as the mission and the unit's integrity weren't compromised.

The rearrangement had worked out well. Those hab pods were just large enough to permit some experimentation with zero-G sex.

Courtland took a long look at the desolate stretch of ruins ahead. He shook his head—then remembered she couldn't see the gesture. Mark IV suits didn't have helmet visors, but relied on optical feeds directly to the wearer's brain to reveal the terrain outside. "Damn," he said. "Gives me the willies. . . ."

"The guys that built it are long gone," she reminded him.

"I thought they were uploaded into the rock." He gestured

toward a low line of cliffs in the distance, gleaming gold in the weak sunlight.

"So they were," she replied. "But living in a completely different reality. They have no idea we're out here . . . probably."

"'Probably'?"

"Well, we assume they have watchdog programs running to keep an eye on things, maybe give them a kick in the ass if there's a threat. If you're bulding for eternity, you have to make allowances for things going wrong over time."

"Yeah. Like your temple falling down."

"I doubt they care about stuff like that."

"I heard scuttlebutt," Courtland said. "Something about the Rosetters destroying the uploads?"

"We don't know that yet, Rog," she told him. "The Rosette Aliens were here. We know that much. What they might have done to the inhabitants . . . we don't know."

"Our orders are to make contact with the Beyondies if they're here," Courtland told her. "If we can."

"'Beyondies?' Oh . . . the Baondyeddi."

"It's what we call 'em."

"Ah," Carter said. "Dr. Yuan's found something. Catch you later."

The spidery robot began stilting toward the broad steps leading up the side of the Temple platform. Another spider was already up there, gesturing with one spindly leg. Courtland sighed, took another look around, then hitched his plasma weapon a bit higher on his plastron and moved forward.

Overhead, golden shapes made of translucent mist hung within a deep violet sky. On the horizon, Bifrost's immense crescent loomed above the mountains, the intense ruby pinpoint of the Kapteyn's Star balanced atop the curve of the crescent's bow. Bifrost's ring system was nearly invisible, a vertical silver thread stretched taut across the sky.

Courtland reached the top of the platform, where several dozen Marines had already spread out to create a protective perimeter. He approached one of the big gun walkers, all fuzzy shadow and subtly shifting color, and yelled, "Hey! Donnie!"

A portion of the fuzzy mass split open, revealing the Marine inside, Lance Corporal Jimmy Donahue. Fresh faced and red-haired, he looked like a kid.

Close enough, Courtland thought. Donahue was all of twenty.

"Yeah, Gunny?"

"Stick close to the spiders, okay? Just not *too* close. Keep an eye on 'em, but allow yourself some room in case you have to bug out."

"Sure, Gunny. What's up?"

"The civilians're gonna be poking around in this shit. If anything's going to kick over the wasp's nest, that'll do it."

"Gotcha. Sure thing."

Courtland didn't add that he had a bad feeling about this place. He was a USNA Marine, which meant that when he went anywhere, he went in expecting the place to bite him. When it came to alien worlds like this one, you lived longer if you were just a little bit paranoid.

"Hey, Gunny?"

"What is it, Donnie?"

"The guys were sayin' there are ghosts here."

That again. The Marines in his platoon had been scuttlebutting about ghosts for the whole trip out from Earth. The rumors claimed that the Kapteyn's system was haunted, and the ghosts were supposed to be anything and everything from the uploaded Beyondies to the mysterious Rosetters to the spirits of Confederation personnel from the science base. In fact, the rumors had been circulating long before the Rosette entity had arrived in this system. If there was something there, Courtland thought, it was most likely some effect or leakage from the Baondyeddi technology.

But alien spirits? Courtland doubted that.

"Yeah, so?"

"What do *you* think?"

It was impossible to shrug in Mark IV combat armor.

"Doesn't much matter what I think, does it? If something wants to talk to us, we take it to the xenosophs. If it attacks us, we kill it."

"Shit, Gunny. How do you kill a ghost?"

"We're Marines, Donnie. We can kill *anything*."

"Ooh-rah, Gunny."

"Now button up and peel the Mark-one optics. I got a feelin'—"

And at that moment all hell broke loose.

New White House
Washington, D.C.
United States of North America
1648 hours, EST

"We have a preliminary report, Mr. President. You asked to be kept informed. . . ."

Koenig looked up from his high-tech desk. Dr. Hoffman's holographic image had just winked on, having been announced by Koenig's chief of staff.

"Thank you, Doctor," Koenig replied. "I appreciate how quickly your people moved on this."

"Not a problem, Mr. President. Besides, there was a lot riding on this, after all."

"Some of my senior people," Koenig added, gesturing. "Admiral Armitage . . . Phil Caldwell . . . Larry Vandenberg. I should also mention that the AI Konstantin is present as well. Konstantin?"

"Good afternoon, gentlemen," a disembodied voice said, speaking in the minds of all present. "It is very good to be here."

"Gentlemen," Koenig went on, "Dr. Hoffman is the senior medical officer on board the medical research vessel *Vesalius*. He tracked the outbreak of the disease on board the *America*, and was in charge of the human disease researchers at Luna."

"Actually, it was Andre who was running the show,"

Hoffman said. "And once we hit Lunar Orbit, the CDC took charge."

"Andre?"

"The medical AI on board the *Andreas Vesalius*," Konstantin put in. "We can link him through to this conference if there is a need."

"Ah. Of course. Well, Doctor, so far as I'm concerned, this has been your show from the get-go. What do you have for us?"

"Again, Mr. President, this is a *preliminary* report. We're going to be researching this bug for a very long time to come."

"Of course."

"The organism tentatively named *Paramycoplasma subtilis* appears to be a new example of emergent intelligence . . . of sapience arising from and within an interconnected community of microorganisms. It has an extremely limited awareness of what we would call the outside world, but maintains intimate biochemical connections with its host organism. In general, it can be considered a symbiotic organism rather than a pathogen—"

"We've seen all of that, Doctor," SecDef Vandenberg said, interrupting. "Tell us what we need to know. *Is this bug a threat to humans*?"

Hoffman hesitated, then shook his head. "Our considered opinion is that it is not. It was driven by a logical need to protect itself, and did so by influencing its various Sh'daar hosts, having them attempt to limit human research into certain technologies that they considered a threat. Their attempt fit well with existing Sh'daar paranoia concerning alien species that might attain a Technological Singularity. Neither the Sh'daar host species nor the paramycoplasmid Symbionts were fully aware of what they were doing. The bacteria were responding to what they were picking up from their Sh'daar hosts, while the Sh'daar were unconsciously reacting to the urging of the bacteria colonizing their bodies.

"You could say, however, that we have now cracked the

language code that will allow us to communicate more or less freely with the paramycoplasmids. And the Sh'daar will now be aware of what's been urging them on."

"So, where does that leave us?" Armitage asked. "Are we supposed to sign a peace treaty with a bunch of germs?"

"Actually, that would pose considerable problems," Konstantin put in. "Communication is not merely a matter of translating words or concepts. The worldviews and cultures of the two communicants must also be taken into account. An organism like *Paramycoplasma subtilis* has a *very* different view of the universe than do humans."

"Yes, but you've got to admit that *Paramycoplasma does* have a culture," Armitage quipped. He held up a hand, indicating a circle a palm's breadth wide. "It's in a dish this big, and it's kept in an incubator. . . ."

"*Please*, Admiral," Koenig said.

"Sorry."

"You're saying," Koenig went on, "that the Symbionts don't know what a treaty is."

"Exactly right, sir. There's also the problem of communication between separate super-organisms. The emergent mind of the bacteria inhabiting Admiral Gray's body is not in constant communication with the mind of those inhabiting Chief Drummond's body. We're still not sure how the super-organisms communicate with one another. It is likely that the Sh'daar seeds play a role in this," Konstantin pointed out.

Koenig searched his memory, only to have Konstantin upload the info to his mind, and the president remembered. Sh'daar seeds were BB-sized spheres of various metallic and ceramic alloys that had been detected buried inside a number of Sh'daar species—notably the Agletsch . . . even those Agletsch who appeared to operate outside of Sh'daar territory. USNA intelligence had determined that the devices were nanotechnic short-ranged transmitters that could store the being's sensory impressions and conversations, and send them as burst transmissions to a Sh'daar communications node when they were close enough to detect.

Apparently, Konstantin believed that the devices served another purpose.

"The devices appear to have a range of several thousand kilometers," the AI continued.

"Huh," NSC director Caldwell said. "Far enough that every Symbiont on a single planet could be in constant touch with every other Symbiont on the same world. Slick."

"We shouldn't discount the possibility that the seeds help the Symbionts communicate on some level with their host," Hoffman said.

"Can we use this?" Armitage wanted to know.

"We need more data," Konstantin told them. "Specifically, we need to exchange information with this species of *Paramycoplasma* in order to determine whether or not we can communicate with it at a deep and meaningful level. I suggest that the Turusch POW colony at Crisium would be useful in this research, as would those Agletsch individuals with which we maintain friendly relations."

"Sounds good," Koenig said. "Dr. Hoffman, you might want to talk with a Dr. Phillip Wilkerson. Here's a contact code."

"Good idea," Caldwell said. "Wilkerson is head of the ONI xenosophontological research department at Mare Crisium. He's been studying some captured Turusch there for twenty years."

"We have Turusch there? On the moon?"

"Oh, yes," Koenig told him. "We captured some back in oh four. Sent them to Crisium so we could study their language . . . which turned out to be a real bear. We offered them a ride home when peace broke out with the Tushies, but a few offered to stay put as a kind of diplomatic community. They have their own environment and habitat on Luna, and seem content where they are."

"If it were me," Vandenberg said, "I'd be climbing the walls by now, wanting to go home."

"Agreed," Koenig said. "But the Turusch aren't even remotely human." He remembered his first meeting with one at Crisium, back when he was an admiral and in command of the star carrier *America*. The Turusch had come *that* close to annihilating Earth. They'd done some serious damage with their impactor in the ocean. And their strike at the naval command center above Mars . . .

Koenig's mind was dragged back to Mars . . . to Karyn Mendelson, the woman he'd loved, killed when a Turusch high-velocity impactor had destroyed the Phobos Synchorbital facility. Damn . . . *damn* . . . the loss, the useless, futile, loss still burned, even after all these years.

In some ways, it was as if no time had passed at all. People wondered why Koenig didn't have any close relationships. Karyn was why . . .

Angry, he pushed the memories back. *Damn it*, he thought, *I don't have* time *for this.*

"So we work at communicating with these . . . these superorganisms," Koenig said, gaining control of his thoughts. "Tell me about the chance of humans getting sick from this thing."

"Quite high, Mr. President," Hoffman replied. "Despite the low infection rate. The Organism, remember, was *designed* to infect humans. However, we now have the nanomedical programming necessary to counter the Organism."

"We're certain of this?"

"As certain as we can be, sir. *Paramycoplasma subtilis* had a pretty hard time crossing the species barrier to begin with. Out of several thousand crew members in the *America* battlegroup, only a handful—eight, on the *America*—actually became sick . . . at least at first. The number went up with time because we think the Organism was deliberately adapting itself to the new host."

"Wait," Armitage said. "*Deliberately* adapting itself?"

"Yes, sir. We know that bacteria are remarkably plastic in their genome, and can make startling adaptive changes in their genetics. Back before nanomedicine, farmers routinely overused antibiotics on their animals, and strains of bacteria resistant to those antibiotics then often made the jump to humans."

"But that wasn't deliberate," Vandenberg pointed out.

"No, of course not. The point is that bacteria are quite flexible in their opportunistic use of adaptive mutations to begin with."

"What about the species barrier," Koenig asked. "What's it called? TB-something?"

"TBB. The trans-biospheric barrier," Hoffman said. "Yes, sir. That was what suggested that the alien bacteria were deliberately manipulated. *Designed.* Especially given that there seem to be dozens of different but related species infecting different and mutually alien species—the Agletsch, the Turusch, and probably most of the other Sh'daar species as well. We don't think this was the Sh'daar Collective's doing. *It was the bacteria.*"

"Alien bacteria evolving to influence its host," Koenig said. "Evolving *itself.* I'm still trying to wrap my head around that one. You know, the more we learn about life Out There, the weirder it seems to get."

"But we *can* control the possibility of infection now?" Vandenberg said. "Maybe by vaccinating the entire population with nanobots with the appropriate programming?"

"It should be enough to treat the disease if it appears," Hoffman said. "I would imagine that you don't want to generate panic in the general population."

"That would not be a desired outcome," Koenig said dryly, "no."

"We do have some important strategic decisions to make, Mr. President," Armitage said. "The human personnel at DT-1, for a start."

"Yes," Caldwell said. "We'll have to assume that all of them have been compromised by the bacteria."

"All crews that go to the N'gai Nebula will have to be vaccinated," Koenig said. "And the next supply mission can handle their inoculation."

"The super-organisms might not like that," Vandenberg said.

"What's the current status of Gray and the others?" Koenig asked. "Is he . . . are they all still infected?"

"They are," Hoffman said.

"They are helping us continue a dialogue with the bacteria super-organism," Konstantin added.

"And how would a microbial super-organism inhabiting Admiral Gray's body feel about being eliminated?"

"As far as we have determined thus far," Konstantin said, "the super-organisms don't have a strong sense of self. Not like humans, certainly. It's more like the Turusch, which live in closely linked pairs."

"Two Turusch actually share one name," Koenig said. "I remember. And two speaking together produce a kind of audio interference that turns out to be a third line of dialogue."

"Yes," Konstantin said. "The relationship between two *Paramycoplasma* super-organisms is not as close as that, but it shares points in common. The loss of one super-organism is not nearly so serious a matter to them as would be the threat of the extinction of their entire species."

"Okay, but is there still a risk? If we 'cure' Admiral Gray, will the rest declare war?"

"I think it safe to say, Mr. President, that they understand the concept of 'war' even less than they understand treaties."

"We're going to have to chance it," Koenig said. "Admiral Gray is one of the best naval officers we have. His crew is the most experienced. I want Gray and I want *America* back on the line."

"But if the crew has been compromised . . ." Armitage began.

"We will inoculate them."

"It would be helpful, Mr. President," Hoffman said, "if some of the infected crew members remained infected . . . at least for now. So that we can continue this dialogue with the aliens."

"Are they in long-term danger?"

"Not that we've been able to ascertain, sir."

"Gene? Arrange for the others to be transferred to the *Vesalius*. TAD." Which meant Drummond and the other personnel would be on Temporary Attached Duty under the auspices of either Naval Intelligence or the Navy Medical Corps . . . and possibly both.

"Yes, sir."

"But give me back Admiral Gray." He looked at Hoffman's image. "Thank you for coming, Dr. Hoffman. My chief of staff will give you a code that will let you link in to my office whenever you need to. Marcus?"

"Already taken care of, Mr. President."

"Good. Anything else, Doctor?"

"No, sir. Thank you, sir." And the holographic image winked out.

"What do you have in mind, Mr. President?"

"We still have too many hot spots," Koenig replied, "and not enough carrier battlegroups." He thought for a moment. "The Senate seems dead set against an expedition to Tabby's Star, at least right now." Koenig had received the message from Senator Diane Francis, the head of the Senate Armed Forces Committee, just that morning. "As are you, gentlemen."

"Mr. President," Vandenberg said, "we simply can't afford to cover every avenue, every possibility. . . ."

"I understand." Koenig felt Konstantin stir in his mind, and he pushed the feeling aside. "Okay. We were going to form up a carrier task force around the *America* and deploy them to Heimdall. Have we heard anything from out there, yet?"

"Not yet, sir," Caldwell said. "But we're expecting an update at any time. The *Lexington* should be out there now, and if there were Pan-European survivors, they should already be on the way back to Earth. *Lexington* and the *Marne*'s Marines will be at Heimdall. Again—if everything is on track."

"This is a war," Koenig said. "Not declared, maybe, but the Rosette Aliens have been attacking human ships. And in war, things are *never* 'on track'!"

"So, *America* is still headed for Kapteyn's Star?" Vandenberg asked.

Koenig nodded. "I'd still like to send her out to Tabby's Star. The Agletsch seemed to think that that was damned important. But first we have to make sure things are secure in our own backyard." He looked at Armitage. "Gene? Pass down the orders. I want *America* and as many ships as we can scrape together on their way to Kapteyn's Star as soon as possible."

"That might take a week or so, Mr. President. *America* needs a refit and resupply. And it will take time to round up a reasonable task force."

"Yesterday," Koenig told him, "would be a *lot* better."

After Marcus Whitney, Armitage, Vandenberg, and Caldwell had left the Oval Office, Koenig leaned back in his chair and closed his eyes. His job, it at times seemed to him, consisted of an endless tap dance from one humanity-threatening crisis to another. He would be glad when his term was up, and he could get back to something approximating normal life. . . .

"Mr. President," Konstantin's voice said in his thoughts. "We really need to talk. . . ."

Koenig groaned. "Damn it, Konstantin, I know what you're going to say."

"Do you, Mr. President? Then you must know how vital the expedition to KIC 8462852 is to the survival of the human species."

"I know *you* think it's important," Koenig said. "I haven't seen the proof of that, yet."

"There is no proof. There is only logic."

"Which in this case is highly subjective."

"It is not. No human naval fleet of any conceivable size can deter the Rosette Aliens. Sending the largest possible fleet to Heimdall or to Omega Centauri will accomplish nothing worthwhile. A different, more advanced technology is required to shift that balance. My Agletsch contacts suggest that such technology may be available at KIC 8462852."

"Bullshit."

"That is not a rational argument, Mr. President."

"*Bullshit!*" Months of stress and worry broke free, and Koenig trembled with the rush of anger. "We have no reason to trust a supercomputer, I don't care how superbright it is, and we have no reason to trust aliens who have been working all along with enemies of the human race! We have no reason to suspect that there is a damned thing at Tabby's Star worthy of the trip . . . certainly no reason to think we'll find a super-weapon of some sort there."

"You are not thinking strategically, Mr President. You are merely reacting to each enemy move, not anticipating him, not thinking ahead several moves in order to upset his momentum."

"You are under the mistaken impression, Konstantin, that the president of the United States of North America actually runs things. I do not."

"Your word carries a great deal of mass, Mr. President."

"Konstantin?"

"Yes?"

"Get the fuck out of my head."

Chapter Sixteen

USMA Lander Lucas
Heimdall
1655 hours, TFT

"Watch it! *Watch it*!" Courtland screamed. "Green Devil, this is Devil Five! We have hostiles incoming, repeat, hostiles incoming!"

The alien machines had burst up out of the stone platform like cinders spurting from an erupting volcanic cone, hundreds and hundreds of flying devices, each as big as a man's head, dead black, and sporting spiky-looking antenna or protuberances that resembled curving knife blades. White light flared across the ruin-littered surface of the platform. Private Godfrey was hit, a dozen explosions rippling across the surface of his armor, the blasts scattering smoldering debris.

"Where are you, Five?" Lieutenant Ogden replied. "What's your tacsit?"

Courtland had his laser up, tracking and firing at the oncoming mass.

"Five!" Ogden screamed. "Do you copy?"

One of the flying devices exploded as the output of Courtland's high-powered laser touched it. "Fire!" Courtland yelled. "Open fire!"

"Courtland! Talk to me!"

"Yeah, Lieutenant! I copy! I'm right at the top of the main steps! Looks like about a million drones, coming right at us!"

"Okay, okay, Devil Five. Calm down! It might just be them saying howdy."

Idiot! "I don't think they're glad to see us, sir! Torrez! On your right! Fire! *Fire!*"

"What's your tactical situation?"

Courtland was about to reply, "Fucked," but bit his tongue. He was firing steadily now, hitting flier after flier and burning them out of the sky, but he had neither the time nor the patience to hold Ogden's hand.

"Robertson! Valdez! Move to your left! Set up a cross-fire with the pee-beeps! Jones and Harris! Cover their asses! C'mon, people, *move!*"

"Courtland! Respond!"

"Sir, I'm just a little busy right now. . . ."

Ahead, one of the WK-40 gun walkers was pivoting wildly, blasting away at the incoming fliers. Lance Corporal James Donahue was piloting the thing, trying to fend off a concentrated assault. Roughly man-shaped but four meters tall, the massive walker mounted a particle-beam cannon as its left arm, a high-velocity autocannon as its right, with 4cm PVK-226 Wasp missiles firing from boxes perched on each shoulder. The alien fliers appeared to have singled the walker out for special attention, and were swarming it in a swirling, deadly cloud. Donahue expended his entire stock of little Wasps in a few wild seconds, the blasts sharp and deadly as they shattered flier after flier. He began firing his particle-beam cannon in a steady stream, sweeping it back and forth in an effort to knock his attackers out of the sky a dozen at a time.

A Marine in Mark IV armor dropped to the ground nearby. "Hey! Donnie! Watch it with that thing!"

"Gimme a hand, here! The bastards are all over me!"

"McNamara!" Courtland called. "Nakajima! Give Donahue some support!"

"We're on it, Gunny!"

The alien fliers appeared to be sporting lasers, which

seemed incongruously low-tech for . . . whoever the enemy here was. Courtland had been assuming that the devices were some sort of automated defense system left by the Baondyeddi . . . but as he thought about it, he realized that they could be a present from the Rosetters.

Except . . . when the Rosette Aliens had attacked human assets before, it had been with vast and devastating surges of energy, like nuclear explosions tightly channeled and directed in beams as hot as the core of a star. That . . . or their targets vanished, wiped from the sky, and no one could tell how they'd done it. These lasers were pop-gun equivalents by comparison.

So what was controlling the things, Beyondies or Rosetters? It probably didn't matter, he decided, so long as it *was* possible to burn them down.

The enemy laser shots individually were not as powerful as the Marines' portable laser rifles, but there were so many of them. The machines were grouping together in threes and fives, concentrating on their targets. The mind controlling the swarm, Courtland decided, was almost certainly an AI or a sophisticated computer of some sort. It was acting as a coherent whole—no, as a large number of coherent wholes, each consisting of three or more flying weapons working together in near-perfect synch.

And then several of the devices actually collided with Donahue's walker, the devices *splashing* when they struck, and adhering to the machine's nanoflaged ceramplas-metal alloy armor.

"Command, Walker One!" Donahue yelled. "These things are *eating* me! Get them off! *Get them off!*"

"Shit! His walker is dissolving!"

Donahue's gun walker was down on one knee, huge chunks of armor missing from its structure. The black ruin of a dozen fliers was melting its way into the suit at his chest and his right leg.

Nano-D, then . . . the name shorthand for nanotechnic disassemblers. The liquid component contained microscopic devices programmed to take the target apart, literally molecule by molecule. Again, the technology was not all that advanced compared to human weapons. Just over a year ago, Pan-European attack ships had vaporized the heart of Columbus, Ohio, with nano-D weaponry.

The walker's exterior nanoflage matrix provided some defense against nano-D, but it wouldn't hold for long.

"Hang on, Donahue!" Lance Corporal Fitzgerald called. "AND round, on the way!"

One of the Marines fired a thumpgun, a 30mm grenade launcher with a broad, heavy barrel slung beneath his laser and designed to fire nano-charge canisters and short-range antiarmor rockets. The round disintegrated in mid-flight, spraying Donahue's combat machine with a burst of gray powder.

AND—anti-nano-D—consisted of tightly packed nano-bots programmed to seek out and destroy hostile nano clouds. The cloud swirled around the damaged gun walker; Sergeant Marie Cooper triggered a second AND round, hiding the walker in a dense swarm of microscopic particles.

But would it be enough? The atmosphere of Heimdall wasn't just cold. It was poisonous to humans—a witch's brew of nitrogen, carbon dioxide and monoxide, ammonia, and sulfur dioxide, all at a little less than half a standard atmosphere. Donahue would be wearing an environmental suit inside his cabin, but if the attacking nano ate through his pressure cabin, it wouldn't take much more time to eat the e-suit—and the man inside—as well. If Donahue wasn't killed by the enemy nano outright, he might choke to death in a minute or two in the chill, Heimdall atmosphere.

Private Griffin shrieked and dropped, his Mark IV armor holed by a flier's laser. Data scrolled through an open window in Courtland's in-head, listing frequencies and temperature. Those enemy lasers appeared to be operating in the high ultraviolet to soft X-ray spectrum, with enough energy to burn through Marine armor in a second or two.

"Keep moving, people!" he ordered. "Don't hold still for those lasers!"

The problem was that the fliers were able to lock on to a

target, fire their weapon, and maneuver in midair in such a way as to keep the beam focused on the target area for up to a second or two, long enough to burn through. Or a group of the things would coordinate with one another and pour their total output into a single area and burn through almost at once. By moving quickly and continually, the Marines could disrupt incoming beams, but they wouldn't be able to keep that up for very long.

Dolby and Jessop were down. Fitzgerald was down. Three other gun walkers scattered across the Temple platform all were struggling with overwhelming numbers of hostile machines. By now, the Marines had given up trying to provide cover for the walkers; there were so many alien fliers that every Marine had more than enough to handle just with the alien machines swarming around him or her.

A flight of the black machines tumbled through the air toward Courtland. He snapped off three bursts from his laser, burning down two of the attackers but missing the third, which swooped suddenly, then slammed into his chest and exploded in a splash of black goo.

The impact made him stagger back a step. He waved his arms wildly, uselessly, trying to shake or scrape off the liquid adhering to him.

Warning, his armor told him, the voice hammering in his head. *Suit integrity compromised.*

He was bleeding atmosphere. The good news was that the atmospheric pressure at Heimdall's surface was less than half of what he carried in his armor, so his air mix was leaking out, and the ammonia and sulfur dioxide outside was not leaking in . . . yet.

But it would, just as soon as the pressures were equalized. He thought that he could smell the sharp tang of ammonia now, and feel the cold in his chest. The smell was almost certainly imaginary; the sensation of cold was not. The air in the torso of his suit was thinning rapidly as it leaked out, and that meant a sudden drop in temperature.

Private Jessop's body lay a few meters away, her laser-thumpgun combo by her side. Thinking fast, Courtland dropped his laser, dove for Jessop's weapon, and cracked the breach on the thumper. Extracting an AND round, he held it close and triggered it. The explosion rocked him back a step, but surrounded him with a dark gray puff of swirling vapor . . . several tens of millions of anti-nano machines each the size of a human red blood cell. The alien nano-D kept eating into his armor plastron, but now the AND machines were eating the nano-D, releasing intense heat and a swirling cloud of smoke . . . the dead husks of burned-out microscopic machines.

Personal armor integrity restored.

His suit was sealing the damage, and his internal pressure was coming back up. He was gasping for breath . . . not, he suspected, because he'd lost so much air, but because of the fight-or-flight adrenaline pouring through his system. His heart was pounding.

He was *terrified*.

Angry at himself for what he perceived as weakness, he chambered a nano-D round in his thumpgun, raised it to his shoulder, and fired it into a nearby swarm of alien machines. The round detonated, sending a cone-shaped cloud of nanobots into the alien swarm, which immediately began to break up, individual machines dropping out of the air and beginning to dissolve. He chambered another round, then pulled a target lock on another gun walker, the one piloted by Sergeant Christy Harris.

"Heads up, Christy! Incoming!" He triggered the weapon with a thoughtclick, and the resulting shotgun blast surrounded Harris's walker with a cloud of hungry nanobots. The thumpgun grenade's warload was programmed to recognize the active-matrix nanoflage coating Marine armor and combat machines and work with it, rather than against it. Its nanobots zeroed in on enemy nano-D and on the far larger fliers themselves, knocking them down so quickly that they seemed to be raining from the cold and violet sky.

But there were too many of them, and more were hurtling up out of the opening in the top of the platform every moment.

"First Platoon, Command!" sounded in Courtland's head. "Heads up! We're laying down cover!"

"Get your fuckin' heads down, people!" Courtland yelled, echoing the order. An instant later, the big pee-beep on top of the morphed hull of the *Lucas* opened fire, sending a dazzling bolt of man-made lightning across the Temple platform. "Pee-beeps"—the military slang for particle beams—used intense and highly focused magnetic fields to channel protons toward the target. Man-portable particle-beam weapons could deliver around twenty megawatts of energy in a quarter-second pulse—the equivalent of one joule, or the detonation of one kilogram of chemical high explosives.

The turret weapon mounted on top of the *Lucas,* and serving now as an area defense weapon, delivered fifty times that amount of energy in a single bolt—the explosive equivalent of thirty-eight kilos of Semtex or similar plastic explosive.

That much power could destroy walkers or heavily armored vehicles or put a nasty hole in a small spacecraft or atmospheric fighter. It was far less effective against a swarm of five-kilo fliers. The machine that was targeted and hit disintegrated into tiny chunks of high-velocity metal, white hot . . . but normally it could only take them down one at a time. The fire-control officer on the *Lucas,* however, was aiming for the center of the denser clouds of alien machines, destroying three or four or five with each shot, and damaging others with hot shrapnel.

Courtland heard Colonel Jamison's calm voice in the background. "Try sweeping with a beam."

"Aye, aye, sir."

Rather than concentrating all of that energy into a single quarter-second bolt, the gunner could spread the same energy out over a second or more. That let him sweep out patches of flier-filled sky, but the energy was more diffuse. The question was, what setting could allow for a beam lasting more than an instant, but still deliver enough of a punch to kill the targets?

But that wasn't Courtland's problem at the moment. Staying low, he crawled up the stone steps to the upper edge of the platform, braced his weapon, and began lobbing 30mm nano-D grenades into the circle of hellfire washing through the ruins.

"Fall back!" he ordered. "Everyone off the Temple platform." Things had degenerated up there into a complete free-for-all, with no organization or mutual support at all. The Marines needed to get off the platform so that the *Lucas* could hammer the aliens without worrying about scoring any own goals. The first rule of combat was simple: friendly fire *wasn't*.

Damn. Donahue's walker had collapsed, sprawled among shattered segments of diamond pillar and beneath a boiling plume of greasy black smoke. Courtland jumped to his feet and dashed across the platform, zigzagging toward the fallen Marine.

You never, *ever* left your own behind. . . .

Another Marine in Mark IV armor—Sergeant Valdez—joined Courtland's dash. Together, they reached the fallen gun walker; Valdez fended off incoming fliers with his laser while Courtland began peeling back crumbling sections of walker armor.

"I'm—I'm hit, Gunny," Donahue said. His e-suit had been burned open at his midsection. There was a *lot* of blood, and a white smoke of ice crystals as blood and water vapor escaping from the suit froze in the cold air.

"Don't sweat it, Marine," Courtland told the boy. "We'll have you back to sick bay in nothing flat!"

"Incoming!"

That warning was from the *Lucas*. The blast jarred Courtland and rattled his teeth; the pee-beep gunners had put a charge down just a couple of meters above his head. Smoking fragments of blasted flier rained around them, clattering on the rock.

Somehow, Courtland managed to peel back the walker's hull, the pieces disintegrating and crumbling in his gloves as he pulled.

Warning, his suit told him. *Nano-disassembler activity detected. Right glove, right lower sleeve. Suit integrity degrading.*

Courtland ignored the voice. He finally was able to pull Donahue free of his walker harness and get him clear of the wreckage. "Let's move!" he said, and he began moving back toward the platform steps. Donahue was gasping and coughing. These e-suits had a certain amount of self-repair ability, like combat armor, but it could only cover you so far.

Damn . . . so much blood . . .

Valdez and Courtland were met by three more Marines, one of them in another gun walker, who began firing into the flier swarms behind them as they jogged down the steps. The rest of the Marines had fallen back to establish a defensive perimeter between the ruins and the assault craft-turned-bunker, and now, again, were able to coordinate their fire with one another.

The *Lucas* gun turret began slamming bolt after high-energy bolt into the ruins, blasting the fliers by the tens . . . by the hundreds . . .

And then the enemy was gone. The remaining fliers reversed their flights, swooped back to the opening at the center of the stone platform, and vanished inside.

The Battle of Heimdall seemed to be over, at least for the moment.

But Donahue died on the way back to the ship.

USMA Lander Lucas
Heimdall
1745 hours, TFT

"Do we even know who was controlling these things?" Taggart asked. "The *people* who built this place? Or the Rosette entity?"

The debriefing was taking place in *Lucas*'s wardroom, a small compartment—as were most of the habitable spaces on the assault lander—one level down and aft of the bridge.

Colonel Jamison and his platoon leaders were present, as were Taggart's shipboard department heads. On the table at the center of the compartment lay one of the alien fliers, a charred shell, more or less complete but burned through by a near hit from a Marine particle beam.

"We're assuming that these are Baondyeddi devices," Dr. Celia Carter said. "They're almost certainly an automatic defense system triggered when the Marines got too close to something sensitive."

"We concur," Jamison said. "These things don't exhibit anything close to the technologies we've seen demonstrated by the Rosetters."

"That would make a lot of sense," Taggart said, thoughtful. "If the Beyondies were going to duck into their virtual reality hole and seal it off after themselves, they'd want to have a watchdog left on this side of the door . . . just to make sure clumsy strangers didn't come along and break things."

"Do you seriously believe that's what they did?" Major David Hardy, Jamison's exec, asked. He sounded as though he didn't hold with such nonsense.

"Oh, there's no doubt that that's what happened to a lot of the Baondyeddi," Carter told him. "And a lot of other Sh'daar as well."

"Yes, but for a whole sapient species to just shut themselves off from the rest of the universe . . ."

"We estimate that, at best, only about ten percent of the Baondyeddi took the virtual-reality option," Carter said. "And probably fewer than two percent of any one of the other species."

"Why the hell would they do that, though?" Jamison asked, shaking his head.

"Oh, that's easy," Lieutenant Benton Meyers said. He was *Lucas*'s senior computer tech, and the man in charge of the expedition's shipboard AI. "Virtual reality, at the scale the Beyondies are using, is far more varied, rich, diverse, entertaining, and just plain interesting than non-virtual life could ever be. For a while, we thought the answer to Fermi's paradox—the whole question of why we didn't see evidence of advanced civilizations in the universe around us—was that technic species tended to develop computers, then complex and immersive virtual reality, then decide they could have more fun living in a computer net than they could puttering around in the dirt outside."

"That," Jamison said, the disapproval sharp in his voice, "sounds like the proverbial thirty-something son playing with the virtual-reality network in his family's basement instead of moving out and getting a life."

"If life is more rewarding, more positive, safer, and more interesting inside a virtual-reality network," Meyers said with a shrug, "why not take advantage of it? It's no different, really, than early humans deciding to make use of fire . . . or giving up hunting and gathering in favor of living in settlements."

"Humankind is going to have to make that decision before too long," Taggart said. "Our technology isn't good enough yet to build electronic networks big enough to create a whole, virtual universe on this kind of scale, but as a species, we're close."

"Hurray for us," Hardy said. "For me, I would *not* opt for that course."

"Well," Carter added, "it's the same here, with the Sh'daar species. Not all of them took that route."

Jamison's eyebrows rose. "Yes? And what did the rest do?"

"They Transcended. *Schjaa Hok*."

"But what does that *mean*?"

"We don't know what happened to them exactly. Some went into computer networks like this, yes, but most . . . we don't know." Carter shrugged. "They moved into higher dimensions? Built their own separate universe? Became gods?"

"Makes me wonder," Jamison said, "about the Sh'daar back in the N'gai Cloud. They seem terrified of the Sh'daar that went through the Tech Singularity and disappeared?"

"Yes?"

"Maybe they're just afraid of what the rest of them became."

"Well, obviously—" Meyers said.

"I don't mean they think the Transcended Sh'daar are going to come back and attack them, or anything. I wonder if they just saw what their own species was capable of—vanishing down the rabbit hole and pulling it in after them, running out on real life—and were disgusted, revolted, and maybe just plain horrified at that tendency in their own kind. Like humans horrified that other humans could commit mass genocide, or kill other humans over crap as stupid as religion. Something like that can ruin your whole day."

"I rather doubt that they think about things like that the same way we do," Carter said.

"More to the point, the real question," Taggart said, "is, where do *we* go now? The confrontation with these things . . ." She reached out and tapped the burned-out flier. "It looks to me like it was a stalemate."

"I hate to admit it," Jamison said, "but that's the way I'd tag it. I certainly prefer that to 'we got our asses kicked.'"

"Our operation objectives," Taggart went on, "are to see if we can make peaceful contact with the uploaded Baondyeddi, and then attempt to make peaceful contact with the Rosette entities. Does anyone have any ideas how we accomplish either of those?"

"The Rosette Aliens are ignoring us," Lieutenant Kaitlyn Grant, *Lucas*'s communications officer, said. "We've been beaming stuff at them since we arrived, RF and UV laser, in every Agletsch contact pidgin in the book. No response."

"And we've *seen* how the Baondyeddi responded," Jamison said.

"Not necessarily," Carter replied. "We've seen how their *automatic defense system* responded. I'm wondering if I approach that central opening alone, teleoperating a spider . . . maybe they won't feel threatened and they'll keep the heavy firepower at home."

"I don't know," Meyers said, grinning. "Your spider scares the hell out of *me*."

"Yes," Carter said, "but you're an arachnophobe."

"Very well," Taggart said. "See what you can dig up with

your spider. Lieutenant Grant, stop active communication attempts. Put out your ears and listen. *Hard*."

"Yes, ma'am."

"I mean it. Listen to every frequency you can think of, maintain a visual watch, and go ahead and put *Lucas*'s AI on it. If anything even twitches out there, if it could be a signal, I want to know about it."

"Aye, aye, Captain."

"And where do you want my Marines, Madam Captain?" Jamison asked.

Taggart wondered if he was deliberately being provocative, or was simply being himself. *Probably both.* "I'd say keep your perimeter up outside the ship. Lieutenant Hagelund will be nanoconstructing a larger habitat outside the ship. You can move your men into that as soon as it's grown."

"I'm just wondering what we're supposed to do if the Rosetters decide to pay us a visit."

Taggart considered the options, and decided not to bring them up. If the Rosette Aliens proved to be hostile instead of merely aloof, there was nothing the Marines or anyone else would be able to do about it. From the technologies she'd seen ascribed to the Rosette entities, they could blink all of Heimdall out of existence with a figurative snap of the fingers.

She found herself wondering, yet again, if they were the Stargods. *Don't go there, girl*, she told herself. *Things are complicated enough.*

But it didn't stop her from wondering what Trev Gray would recommend.

"Keep your heads down," Taggart told the Marine colonel, "and pray it's a *friendly* visit."

"Amen to that," Jamison replied.

Orbital Dockyards
Quito Synchorbital
1810 hours, TFT

Cyndi DeHaviland set her tray down on the mess deck table. "So, did you hear the scuttlebutt?"

Gregory looked up from his own meal. At the moment, he was having difficulty generating much enthusiasm for anything, but he shook his head. "What's going down?"

"It's going to be a major fleet action at Kapteyn's Star," she told him. "They're assembling three star carriers for this one, and the *Lady Lex* is already there. The Chinese are supposed to be sending a carrier too. It's going to be *big*."

He shrugged, then picked at his meal. "Okay . . ."

"Don . . . are you all right?"

"Yah. No problem."

"You don't sound okay. You've been moping around for weeks now, ever since I came on board. You stick to yourself, you don't join in the bull sessions—"

"Look, I just want to be left alone, okay?"

DeHaviland stared into his face for a long moment, then shrugged. "Suit yourself, space-ace. But if you need to talk . . ."

She let the sentence trail off, but he didn't reply.

Don Gregory had been suffering from major depression for three months now. He knew he was depressed, and he knew he should report himself to the psychs in sick bay. When he slept, when he *could* sleep, he was back on the bleak and frigid surface of Invictus.

With Meg . . .

The problem with severe depression, though, was that you just didn't fucking *care*. He continued to go through the automatic motions, carrying out his duty to the letter, but even admitting to someone else that he had a problem was just too much effort to be worthwhile.

Besides, if he turned himself in to the medicos and psychs, he'd be grounded, relieved of duty. You couldn't have mentally unstable types strapping on expensive SG-420s and putting the whole squadron, to say nothing of the sacred mission, at risk.

Sooner or later, they'd catch him, probably the next time they pulled a routine brain diagnostic from his in-head hardware. But he saw no reason to make things easy for the bastards.

The last time *America* had been in port, he'd held the depression at bay with a couple of brainstim binges portside. He'd been hungering for a couple of whiffs since they'd gotten back to the Sol System, but all leave and liberty had been cancelled because of the bug, whatever it was, they'd picked up in the N'gai Cloud. That issue had been resolved, apparently, and *America* had been guided from her quarantine orbit around Luna to her berth at SupraQuito . . . and, just his luck, he had the duty.

Damn it all!

He and Cyn DeHaviland ate their meals in silence. The officers' mess overhead dome showed the scene outside—the gantries and orbital facilities and bustling work pods of the SupraQuito dockyards, an enormous bundle of habs and nanufactories perched at the top of the Quito space elevator. The mess deck was in the carrier's rotating carousel of hab modules, but the computers managing the image overhead had compensated for the motion.

He glanced at Cyndi. She was nice—a newly arrived replacement to the Black Demons. He liked her okay . . . would have liked her more if he didn't keep thinking that she was here as a replacement for Meg.

Damn it.

Briefly, he considered asking DeHaviland to swap duty with him so that he could go binge again. There was this little bar in the main hab over there. . . .

But somehow he couldn't make himself reach out that far.

"Catch you later, Cyn," he said, standing suddenly and picking up his half-finished meal. "I've got the duty in CIC."

"See ya."

He wanted to apologize for his sharpness of a moment before, but . . .

Nah. He walked out.

Chapter Seventeen

South of Manhatt Ruins
2025 hours, TFT

It had been a long time since Gray had been here. The cityscape to the north was utterly alien to him. The novelist, he decided, had been right: *you can't go home again.*

He was drifting slowly, a hundred meters above the black waters of New York's Upper Bay, just off the remnants of Governor's Island. To his left, the Statue of Liberty still stood tall, though most of her pedestal was underwater. Her upraised arm was back in place, fished up out of the water where it had fallen years ago and reattached. She looked good. . . .

Gray had requested some time off when they discharged him from Bethesda, and SupraQuito had okayed it. He was riding a rented broom—a Mitsubishi-Rockwell gravcycle—from a tour agency in New New York a few kilometers up the river. Three meters long, silver, and held aloft by a pair of fore-and-aft grav-impeller blocks, you rode it like a motorcycle . . . a *flying* motorcycle with a ceiling of about a thousand meters. He'd had one of his own, once, an eon or two ago; he wondered what had become of it.

Ahead of him, the lights of a reborn Manhattan gleamed and winked, reflected in the dark waters. He'd lived there once . . . been quite happy there, though it had been a hand-to-mouth scrabble for survival much of the time. But everything had changed when Angela had had her stroke. And now, he was an admiral, commander of a star carrier battlegroup.

He would have been painfully out of place trying to fit in again down there among those partially submerged towers.

Trevor Gray looked down on the lights of Manhatt and thought of the Prims still down there and about where AIs were taking the human species. It was quite possible that Humankind only *seemed* to be guiding itself. He thought of how Konstantin had recently carried out a memetic attack on Pan-Europe—creating there a desire for peace and a popular revulsion against Geneva's government policies at the time . . . and so helped end the Confederation Civil War.

With that kind of power, it seemed likely that Konstantin was leading Humankind on a social path of its own choosing, and not the other way around.

Of course, Konstantin had been doing a lot to reclaim the Periphery . . . and, ultimately, that might prove to be a bigger job than creating peace between the Confederation and the USNA. Washington, D.C. had been reclaimed and rebuilt already, and now Konstantin had turned its attention to the flooded ruins of Old Manhattan. Nine and a half kilometers south of his current position, massive machines were drawing calcium carbonate and other minerals from seawater, creating the substance called "seament" and using it to regrow the failed Verrazano Narrows Dam. When that was completed, and with the building of a second dam at Locust Point at the entrance to the Long Island Sound, all of Manhattan would be sealed off from the ocean, and the job of lowering the sea level around the old city could begin. It was a titanic project, but now that the war was over, President Koenig had given orders for the reclamation to begin.

And in the meantime, USNA troops had occupied Manhattan, and the social reclamation of the population there had already begun. Those lights up ahead—the Manhatt Ruins had never had that kind of power available since the place had been abandoned over three centuries before. Buildings were being renovated, and whole blocks of old city towers were being grown together, creating a new city thirty meters above the current water level.

New York City was coming alive once more.

Gray hoped he would be able to come back and see the place when the dams were in place and the city infrastructure complete.

But even then, he didn't think he would fit down there.

What, exactly, had Thomas Wolfe written? Gray downloaded the quote from his in-head RAM.

> You can't go back home to your family, back home to your childhood . . . back home to a young man's dreams of glory and of fame . . . back home to places in the country, back home to the old forms and systems of things which once seemed everlasting but which are changing all the time—back home to the escapes of Time and Memory.

Thomas Wolfe had died in 1938, and he would have been utterly unable to comprehend the world, the New York City, of almost five centuries later.

But damn, the man had gotten it exactly right.

An in-head window opened in Gray's mind. "Admiral?"

Gray sighed. Just when you get a free moment . . .

It was Pam Wilson, *America*'s chief communications officer. "Yes, Commander. What do you have?"

"Orders, Admiral. I have a high-priority comm request for you, personally. Security status Gold-One."

Damn. Gold-One meant that he needed to take it on a securely encrypted channel, not through his own private in-head floating a hundred meters above New York Harbor.

"Okay. Who's it from?"

"Classified, Admiral. Gold-One. Even I'm not cleared to know."

"Okay. It's going to take some doing, though."

"Captain Gutierrez has taken the liberty, sir, of sending down a high-priority clearance request to get you back up here."

"Is the *America* still in Lunar Orbit?" Gray had deliberately been kept out of the loop during his stay at Bethesda, to the point that he wondered if they still trusted him. Damn it, it wasn't *right* that an admiral didn't know where his ship was.

"Negative, sir. We moved down to SupraQuito a couple of days ago, as soon as the disease cases were shipped out and the rest of the crew had been vaccinated."

Disease cases. Him included, of course.

"Okay, Commander. I can be back in D.C.—"

"Begging your pardon, Admiral, but we're hijacking a ship for you out of New New York. The space elevator will take too long. We can have you back on board inside of two hours."

Someone was in a hell of a hurry.

And . . . who that someone might be was a real problem. He'd assumed that it would be either President Koenig or someone in USNA Naval Command—Admiral Armitage, maybe. But if that was the case, why not call him back to D.C. and set up a personal meeting? Why set up an encrypted high-security virtual conversation instead?

Gray thoughtclicked new orders into the navigational brain of his broom. In response, the machine twisted a few degrees to the left and began accelerating, angling due north up the Hudson River.

"What's the ship status, Commander?"

"We're just about ready to boost, Admiral. And the battlegroup has been assembling. By the time you get up here, we should have over thirty capital ships in orbit, set to go, including both the *Constitution* and the *Declaration*."

"I thought the *Declaration* was undergoing trials?"

"She was, sir. But they brought her back, along with the *Decatur* and four other ships from Alpha Centauri space."

Interesting. They were sending *three* star carriers to Kapteyn's Star. That was almost unprecedented.

They were calling the assembled flotilla up there the Grand Unified Fleet, and he understood that the various military high commands had been working on the concept for quite a while. Technically, it was a *Confederation* fleet, since its primary objective was to rescue any survivors of the Confederation base out at Kapteyn's Star, but that, Gray knew, was sheer political bravo-sierra. By far the largest contingent was USNA, and Washington hadn't yet admitted that it was back in the Confederation as yet. There were also a substantial number of other vessels—Chinese Hegemony, North Indian, and Russian—who were allied with the USNA, but certainly not a part of the Confederation.

The High Command's choice of a leader was interesting, Gray thought. There'd been talk, he knew, of making him the grand admiral, but he'd been taken off the short list when he'd contracted that alien disease in the N'gai Cloud. The final choice was Admiral Reed Franklin Gordon, on the *Declaration.* His politics had put him on the beach for a couple of years, but it seemed his star was again in the ascendancy. A USNA flag officer with Confederation-leaning convictions. He might be just the man for the job.

Lights rushed past him on his right, and immediately a warning signal flashed in his mind. The airspace above Manhattan was closed to civilian traffic nowadays, and he was being warned off by the local air traffic control. He felt his implant channel a high-priority override back at the challenger, then felt the response: he had clearance.

Wondering what the hell could be so all-fired important, Gray rode his broom through the night.

Probewalker 1
Heimdall Station
2214 hours, TFT

Celia Carter watched the bobbing, swaying terrain ahead as she guided the spider up the Temple steps, and decided that she was glad she wasn't really packed inside the teleoperated machine's body. Uneven terrain made for a rough ride and she had a tendency toward motion sickness.

So far as her brain was concerned, she *was* the spider, picking her way on jointed, stilting legs up the steps and across the shattered diamond remnants of the Temple. Her in-head software, though, was managing to keep her vestibular system quiet.

The top of the Temple platform was littered with the husks, shells, and broken fragments of fallen alien fliers. She ignored them and continued picking her way slowly across the field of rubble and smashed pillars. The spider's sensor suite gave her a 360-degree view around her, but the software played to the limitations of her human brain and narrowed her effective field of vision down to what was ahead and to either side. She was aware, however, of the *Lucas*-bunker squatting on the horizon behind her, and of the loom of Bifrost in the sky beyond.

And then the flier was *there*, hovering silently ten meters ahead of her and two meters above the rubble, just as if it was trying to block her way. Where the hell had it come from?

Carter immediately stopped, and the two machines faced each other, holding themselves motionless for a long moment. At least, she thought, the alien machine hadn't immediately attacked her.

"Okay, Command," she said. "Are you getting this?"

"We see it," Taggart's voice responded, a whisper on her mind. "What do you intend to do?"

"It hasn't opened fire," Carter replied, "so I'm thinking the attack earlier was triggered by a whole shipful of armed and armored Marines."

"It might recognize that you're not armed," Taggart replied.

"Perhaps. I'm going to try moving toward it," Carter said.

Her walker took a small step toward the hovering flier . . . and then another. There was no response. The black sphere—actually a spheroid, flattened top to bottom—possessed a number of shiny, rounded lenses around its circumference, and Carter had the impression that they were lenses, regarding her narrowly. She took another cautious step.

A second flier rose from a small opening in the platform and took up a position next to the first. Carter could hear a faint buzzing, coming through her RF sensors. "Command, Spider One," she said. "Are those things talking to each other?"

"We're getting radio transmissions, One," Taggart told her. "Very low power, very short-ranged. We haven't cracked the code yet."

"Okay . . . but are they talking to me? Or to each other?"

"Probably to each other, would be my guess. Looks like they're trying to decide what to do."

"I'm going to try walking around them and see what happens."

"Copy that . . ."

She moved slowly and with great deliberation, expecting an attack at any moment. The lasers those things carried were more than capable of melting her robotic body in a literal flash.

Did they recognize, she wondered, that there was no organic life inside the spider's shell? Did they respond to robots or teleoperated machines differently than they did to life forms encased in armor?

More of the hovering guardians emerged from underground, but still, all they did was watch her. She counted twelve of the machines, now; it would take only one to destroy her fragile walker.

She could see the main entrance to the inside of the Temple platform fifteen meters ahead. She continued her slow walk toward the opening, as her silent entourage drifted in a loose perimeter around her. They literally had her surrounded; two even paced her from five meters overhead.

Were these things truly robotic, controlled, perhaps, by a guardian AI? Or were they, like her spider, teleoperated by flesh-and-blood beings somewhere below? She wished she knew. She would have preferred to have an idea about what type of intelligence she was dealing with.

Record everything. Everything . . .

What in the hell?

"Command, One," she called. "Did you just transmit?"

"Negative, One."

Mein Gott!

"There! Did you hear that?"

"Negative, Probe One. We have your transmissions, and we're getting what sounds like RF static from your little friends out there. Nothing else. What do you hear?"

"Sounded like a very brief audio transmission. 'Record everything,' and something that sounded like 'my God' in German."

"We're not reading that, One."

She could hear what sounded like a rapid-fire conversation in the background now, pilots speaking to each other in a near frenzy of gutteral voices.

What the hell? For a moment, Carter felt a sharp sense of dissociation. She knew she was safe and protected, tucked into her couch back on board the *Lucas*, but the illusion of being outside, alone, surrounded by impenetrable mystery, was overwhelming. What didn't make sense was the fact that if her spider had picked up signals from something speaking German, then everyone monitoring her feed on board the *Lucas* would have heard it too.

That raised the uncomfortable possibility that she was hallucinating. She checked her mental readouts, but there were no red flags or alarms indicating the presence of something that might be causing her to hear things that weren't there.

She reached the edge of the opening in the platform. Broad steps led down into darkness. Her entourage gathered about her a bit more closely, and she had the impression that they were guiding her . . . herding her along.

With a mental shrug, she let them.

USNA CVS America
Admiral's Office
SupraQuito Orbital Naval Base
2240 hours, TFT

The shuttle had docked directly with the *America*, hooking up with one of the carrier's spinal airlocks. He'd been the only passenger on board, an indication of the importance of this trip. *Somebody* wanted to talk with him very quickly indeed. Captain Gutierrez had met him at the lock, but there was no formality, no official welcome.

"Welcome back, Admiral."

"Thank you, Captain. I gather everything is squared away and pretty much ready for boost?"

"Yes, sir. We're waiting for three more ships to arrive— *Paladin*, *Dockery*, and a Chinese Hegemony heavy carrier, the *Guangdong*. They're in-system, and will rendezvous here tomorrow."

"The *Guangdong*? That makes four star carriers."

"Five, Admiral. The *Jiangsu* arrived alongside this afternoon from Ta Yu."

Ta Yu was the Hegemony extrasolar colony at Epsilon Ceti IV, a double star some seventy-nine light years from Sol. The name, drawn from the ancient Chinese *Book of Changes*, meant "wealth," and the place was a cornerstone of China's exosolar colonization program. That they were willing to divert one of their star carriers from the Ta Yu colony to participate in the effort at Kapteyn's Star was an indication of how seriously they were taking the Rosetter threat.

As well they should, he thought.

He sank into the couch in his office and slapped his hand down on the contact plate. "Okay," he said. "Ready to link."

He felt the software of *America*'s comm system probing his mind, verifying his identity.

Then there was a brief burst of static, and he was . . . where? A wooden schoolhouse?

The virtual image of Konstantin Tsiolkovsky peered at him through antique pince-nez. Elderly, austere, with receding white hair and a white goatee, the AI's avatar looked the very picture of a reclusive Russian schoolteacher. The virtual surroundings, Gray knew, were a kind of window dressing— the interior of an early-twentieth-century Russian schoolhouse, updated slightly by anachronistic computer screens and monitors. Gray had spoken with Konstantin—or with one of Konstantin's sub-clones—several times, most recently at Bethesda; but before, the superbright AI had always been a disembodied voice in his head. He'd heard that the president occasionally conversed with the machine intellect in a virtual environment, and assumed that it was this one.

"Hello, Admiral. How are you feeling?"

"Hello, Konstantin." What *did* you say to a machine intelligence reputed to be several million times smarter than a typical human? Gray wondered if the inquiry about his health was genuine concern, or simply mimicry of the polite social noises of human interaction. He answered anyway. "They tell me the alien bacteria have been completely eliminated from my body, and the medical nanobots they pumped into me will keep it that way."

"I am delighted to hear it. There has been considerable concern about your ability to continue as commander of the *America* battlegroup."

That stung. "If there is *any* doubt about my abilities—"

"There are not, Admiral, insofar as I, the president, or the Joint Chiefs are concerned. If there were you would be . . . I believe the naval slang term is 'on the beach.'"

"There was some discussion," Gray said carefully, "of leaving the bugs in me and using me to communicate with them . . . maybe sending me back to the N'gai Cloud."

"Others can do that," Konstantin replied. "And a ship has already been dispatched to inform Dr. McKennon and Deep Time One of the situation. I asked you to come to a secure communications node for a different reason."

"I got back to the ship as quickly as possible."

"I appreciate that. I needed to have this conversation with you—in private—before your departure from Earth."

"It must be damned important."

"It is." The image leaned forward, holding Gray with its gaze. "I needn't remind you, I'm sure, that this conversation is secret. You will need to share its contents with members of your staff, certainly, but with no one else until after your return."

"My return. From Kapteyn's Star?"

"No. From rather more distant a destination than that."

"Omega Centauri, then."

Gray's current operational orders were somewhat open-ended. *America*'s battlegroup, augmented by several other battlegroups into a single large international task force, was going to make the passage to Kápteyn's Star and there confront the Rosette entity. Depending on the outcome of that encounter, the fleet would then proceed to the Omega Centauri globular cluster and further confront the Rosette entity there, at what was believed to be its operational headquarters for whatever the hell it was doing in the galaxy.

"Once again, no."

Gray sat up at that.

"Your destination, Admiral, is what I wish to discuss with you. It is vitally important that you, that the *America*, take another path . . . a different option."

"Go on."

"You have been briefed on Tabby's Star."

"Yes . . . well, more or less. Not a formal briefing. Just scuttlebutt. I know that they were considering sending us out there. The Agletsch recommended that we go."

"Yes. And I agree with them."

"I see." Truth was, though, he had no idea what Konstantin was talking about.

"USNA naval forces currently are stretched thin. There is competition within the military and political leadership over how those assets would be best deployed."

"But if you—"

"I am not in your government's chain of command, Admiral. At best, I am considered an advisor to the president. I make recommendations, but those recommendations are not always accepted or acted upon."

"Wait a minute, Konstantin," Gray said. "Are you suggesting that I disobey my orders? That I take my battlegroup to Tabby's Star instead of Kapteyn's Star?"

"The battlegroup will not be necessary. I would like you to take *America* to Tabby's Star, search for signs of sapient life and technology, and report back to Earth."

"Where I will promptly be arrested and court-martialed for disregarding legal orders."

"That is a possibility, of course. The lid of secrecy will have been lifted by then, however. I will recommend, of course, that charges be dropped."

"And if we find nothing useful out there?"

"The Agletsch are convinced otherwise."

"They've shown you something? Proof?"

"No. Let us say merely that their arguments were convincing."

"Konstantin . . . this just isn't right. The chain of command exists for a *reason*. We can't just ignore it whenever it gets in the way."

"Indeed. Nor can the human species afford to ignore the threat posed by the Rosette entity. But your leaders are too closely focused on the problems immediately in front of them. They are, as humans like to say, 'failing to see the big picture.' They are simply reacting to the Rosette Aliens' actions, and failing to develop progressive and long-term strategies. This, ultimately, could be fatal for your species."

"So talk to the president."

"I have. But in a democratic government, the leaders are restricted by constitutional guarantees against the abuse of power. There are things he simply cannot do without the consent and active participation of the Legislative branch."

"Then talk to *them*."

"Admiral, the fact of the matter is that there simply is no time to build a consensus. Courier packets have returned from Kapteyn's Star with data suggesting that the situation there is critical. The Pan-European expedition there was all but wiped out within a space of seconds."

"I was briefed." But he was still coming to grips with the news.

"The president has accepted the counsel of Admiral Armitage and others. They fear that the presence of the Rosette Aliens a mere twelve light years from Sol means that these aliens will be here at any moment, and that nothing is more important than stopping them at Heimdall."

"Well, that makes sense, doesn't it?"

"Yes, but it doesn't ask the obvious question: Stop them

with *what*? The Rosette Aliens have already demonstrated that they are able to eliminate our largest ships with little or no apparent effort. Simply sending more ships into that system cannot change the current balance between their technology and ours."

"This . . . this is just plain crazy, Konstantin. Even admirals don't have that kind of leeway. You are essentially asking me to set policy, and that is so wrong on so many levels I don't know what to say."

"You fear repercussions to your career?"

"Of course I do." Gray shrugged. "And those of my officers, and the safety of my crew." He struggled with what he was hearing. What the AI was talking about wasn't just dereliction of duty, but possibly treason. More than that, he still wasn't sure if he could trust an AI to begin with. And yet the logic of it was—if not infallible—very convincing. What *could* one more star carrier do? He had seen images sent back from the *Lucas* of the destruction of the *Himmelschloss*, read the reports. The size of the ship—the size of the group—couldn't possibly matter. His orders were coming from a place of fear, and a place of comfort. Not just that of politicians far away from the front lines, but the comfort of "this is what we know how to do." What Konstantin was suggesting could end with his court-martial. But it could also lead to a solution to the Rosette problem.

Right now, everything, *everything* hinged on trusting the super-AI. Gray took a deep breath. His mistrust of advanced technology, he knew perfectly well, stemmed from his childhood in the Manhatt Ruins. Gradually, he'd battered those demons back. He'd taken his sick wife up the river to get high-tech medical treatment, he'd joined the Navy to pay for it, he'd accepted the implants that let him interface with a world centuries ahead of what he'd known in the Ruins.

He'd worked with Konstantin more than once, and the Tsiolkovsky super-AI network had never failed him, never let him down.

It was just such a freaking big step. . . .

Trust did not come easily.

"Is it really as important as you say?"

"It may well be of existential import to the human species."

"Then I guess there's no choice, is there?"

"There is *always* choice. The question is whether a given choice will lead to a given preferred outcome."

"Stopping the Rosetters."

"The Rosette entity is too powerful, too far advanced for human technology to have any chance against it at all. Should they decide to, they could wipe out the species. With truly advanced technologies, or with an alliance with beings possessing such technologies, we have a chance."

"But I don't see how heading off to this Tabby's Star could help. Sure . . . *if* we can make peaceful contact, *if* they have the appropriate technologies available, *if* they are willing to share those technologies, *if* we can figure out how to use them against the Rosetters . . . That's one hell of a lot of ifs!"

"I agree. But the possible rewards are astonishing."

"Like what?"

"Like Shkadov thrusters."

And *that* captured Gray's full attention.

Probewalker 1
Heimdall Temple Platform
2254 hours, TFT

Carter picked her spidery way across a vast, flat plain twenty meters beneath the surface of the Temple platform. The darkness around her was absolute, her surroundings so cold she was getting very little data from her infrared optics. She switched on her light, and the darkness ahead receded, but without showing any detail. The glare of her light was swallowed by the emptiness after only a few tens of meters.

Her escort was still with her, drifting along silently in a loose circle around her.

"Command, this is Probe One. Command, do you copy?"

Static hissed in reply. Either the rock surfaces above

and around her were too thick, or the aliens were somehow blocking her communications channels. Her control channels, however, were still functioning fine. Odd . . .

She felt her in-head circuitry abruptly switch on with an incoming message.

"*Adler Eins Zu* Himmelschloss! *Adler Eins Zu* Himmelschloss."

It was the voice she'd heard before. "Hello! This is Dr. Celia Carter, off the *Lexington*! Do you read?"

"*Mein Gott im Himmel!*"

Those guttural tones could only be German. She didn't speak the language, but her in-head circuitry could translate. "Hello!" she called. "Who is this?"

"Captain-Lieutenant Martin Schmidt, Eagle Flight One. I hear you . . . did you say doctor? What are you doing here?"

"I'm a xenologist off the USNA star carrier *Lexington*."

"*Lexington*? What is my position? *Where am I*?"

Carter opened the comm channel wide, pulling in a datastream from . . . she wasn't sure where, but it was all around her, pulsing, flowing, a living thing. For a moment, she was out in space again, not moving through subheimdallan darkness, and the stars surrounded her. Bifrost, ringed and banded, loomed on her left, as gauzy shapes of light twisted and curtained and fluttered ahead like a spectacular display of golden auroras.

She gasped, felt the thunder of energies coursing through her brain . . .

. . . and then darkness closed in around her once more.

Chapter Eighteen

Assault Lander Lucas
Heimdall Command
0204 hours, TFT

"Doctor Carter? Doctor Carter? Are you awake?"

Carter opened her eyes to see Commander Taggart's worried features leaning over her. Behind Taggart, the lights in the overhead of *Lucas*'s sick bay glared, entirely too bright. "Yes, Commander," she managed to say. Her throat was parched, her voice cracked. "What the hell happened?"

"That's what we wanted to ask you. We had to kill the power on your teleop feed."

"I was . . . talking with someone. . . ."

Taggart nodded. "Kapitanleutnant Schmidt, of Eagle Flight One. Yes, we know."

"How? My comm channels were blocked."

"RAM tap."

"Ah. Of course." When a human linked in with a teleoperated device, her experiences were automatically stored in her in-head circuitry. If something went wrong, her in-head RAM could be accessed—"tapped"—by an AI for analysis and troubleshooting. The fact that they'd done so suggested that Carter had been in pretty bad trouble. "What happened? How long was I out of it?"

"A few hours. *Lucas*'s AI is using the data you acquired to run a dialogue with Lieutenant Schmidt . . . with his ghost, rather."

"His *ghost*?"

Taggart straightened up, nodding. "His squadron was— the term they used was 'patterned.' Lieutenant Schmidt and the others in his squadron were killed, probably because they strayed too close to a Rosetter construction project, though we're not sure on that point. His mind, however, was patterned—perfectly replicated—by the Baondyeddi software in the Etched Cliffs on Heimdall. The AI down there is frantic. It's lost its people."

"Lost its . . . what?" Carter rubbed her eyes. "Sorry, Commander. I'm having trouble keeping up."

"Until a few days ago, Heimdall was inhabited by approximately six billion intelligent entities. About half were conservative Baondyeddi who chose to upload themselves into the computer circuitry etched into the planetary bedrock . . . we think about eight hundred million years ago. The other half was made up of members of sixteen other sapient species from the Sh'daar polity who either uploaded themselves at the same time, or did it over the course of the next hundred million years or so."

"Conservative Baondyeddi?" Carter said. "What's that? A political party?"

"More like an ideology. One of a number of competing worldviews in the Sh'daar Collective at the time."

Carter tried to imagine the worldview of one of those many-legged pancakes. From what she knew of the Sh'daar origins, most Sh'daar were horrified or shocked at the vanishing of most of the original ur-Sh'daar sophonts, a catastrophic technological rapture—to use the blatantly religious term—that they called the *Schjaa Hok*. Most Sh'daar had focused on the coming merging of their civilization with that of the Milky Way galaxy—which meant taking control of the newer, younger civilizations there. Some, though, had figuratively gone back to bed and pulled the covers over their heads. Virtual reality, it seemed, had been an attractive escape for those afraid of the Transcended ur-Sh'daar.

"Okay, so there were a few billion Beyondies playing in the virtual-reality banks. What happened to them?"

"The Dark Mind."

The term was ominous but unfamiliar. "The what?"

"That seems to be what the local Beyondies were calling the Rosette Aliens. Their records refer to it as a collective, artificial consciousness of immense power and scope. It descended on Heimdall and apparently abducted the digital entities residing there."

"What, *all* of them?"

"A clean sweep, apparently. The AI running the place was able to clone off a copy of itself, and left that behind, but that's it."

"And Lieutenant Schmidt?"

"The AI clone got him and the rest of his squadron. Or, rather, it copied the pilots' minds and uploaded them just as the Rosetters wiped out the squadron." Taggart shrugged. "Maybe they got copied twice, once by Heimdall, once by the Rosetters."

"Ah. So the original people—their bodies—are gone. Dead."

"If we're understanding the technology, yes."

Carter thought about the ramifications. The idea of digitizing minds and uploading them into computer-based virtual realities had been around at least since the late twentieth century, though Humankind hadn't managed the trick as yet. It took staggering amounts of computer power, both to scan and copy something as complex as a living brain—to say nothing of the entire body—and to create a realistic and richly complex world for the upload to inhabit.

The real problem, though, was one of *identity*. If you precisely copied every atom and the quantum state of every subatomic particle in a human brain, digitized the information, then replicated the pattern inside an artificial reality, you would have an uploaded copy that was potentially immortal . . . but the original, unless it had been destroyed by the copying process, would still be sitting back in its original body, hopefully twiddling its thumbs as it awaited the transfer. So far as the individual was concerned, nothing had happened, *and the upload had not taken place*, though, of course, he now could talk to a convincing copy of himself. When most people spoke of digitally uploading minds to virtual reality, they meant that the *identity* of the individual—some people still used the word "soul"—was transferred, not just the information.

Everything Carter knew about Sh'daar technology suggested that they had, indeed, figured out how to transfer the actual mind from organic body to machine; at least part of the Transcendence had involved just that, with the minds of hundreds of billions of beings vanishing and leaving behind nothing but dead, organic shells. But the Pan-European fighter pilots of Adler Flight, apparently, had been subjected to a more primitive form of the technology.

Or . . . was that necessarily true? Maybe there'd been nothing but empty, organic shells inside those fighters when the Rosetters had reached out and . . . done whatever the hell they'd done.

So many questions. And damned few answers.

"Lieutenant Schmidt seemed to think he was still alive," Carter said, remembering. "We were conversing . . . exchanging information. . . ."

"I'm afraid that doesn't mean much, Doctor," Taggart told her. "A computer can be programmed to mimic a person's thought processes. The Turing Test, remember? Nonsophont computers have been managing that trick since the twenty-first century."

"I know. Still . . . if Schmidt and the others think they're still alive, or if they really are . . . don't we need to, I don't know, rescue them or something?"

"We're talking with them now," Taggart said. She smiled. "Thanks to you. Or, rather, we're talking to the Baondyeddi AI. We'll need to see what exactly they—both the AI and the Pan-European pilots—really want."

"How thanks to me?" Carter was confused. "All I did was pass out."

"You got your spider down into the heart of the Baon-dyeddi planetary defense network, and made direct contact with the AI. Schmidt was able to link through your in-head circuitry, but once you had the connection he was able to tune himself—I guess that's the best way to put it—to your spider's comm gear. The AI lifted the communications interference you encountered . . . and we have an open channel."

"Well, it wasn't my doing."

"Of course it was . . . and I'm saying so in my report." Worry passed behind her eyes. "Assuming the Dark Mind doesn't take an active interest in us. It hadn't noticed us, not much, anyway, because of the RF interference from Heimdall. That's gone, now. It's probably listening to every word we transmit."

Carter felt a chill at the back of her neck.

"Cheerful thought. Can it understand us, do you think? Understand our language?"

Taggart shrugged. "According to the Heimdall AI, there's not a lot it *can't* do, but our new friend may be prejudiced by its experiences with the Entity so far."

"And that leaves us . . . where?" Carter asked.

"Stuck," Taggart said. "Perched out here on the edge of something we can never hope to understand . . . hoping it doesn't decide to swat us like a bug."

Flag Bridge
TC/USNA CVS America
Outer Sol System
1920 hours, TFT

The Star Carrier *America* fell out-system, dropping into her own self-induced gravitational singularity project-ing out in front of her shield cap thousands of times each second. She was boosting at a somewhat leisurely five thousand gravities, the top acceleration possible for the slowest ships accompanying her, and after an hour and a half at that acceleration she was pushing 99.7 percent of the speed of light. Time slowed, stretched by the surreal hand of relativity, and the skies around her had grown strangely compressed, a circle of rainbow-smeared light encircling her forward quarters. *America* was one of a massive fleet of thirty-eight vessels, a flotilla including the star carriers *Declaration*, *Jiangsu*, and *Guangdong*, and a dozen massive battleships and planetary bombardment vessels, the Marine carriers *Nassau* and *Peleliu*, and the Confederation heavy monitor *Festung*.

Gray considered the size and makeup of the fleet, and wondered if the scars of the recent civil war were truly healed. He dismissed the thought as soon as it rose. Of *course* there were still scars—that's what scars were: *reminders* of old wounds. It was amusing to think that the TC/USNA star carriers *America* and *Declaration* both still bore the TC designation that stood for "Terran Confederation." In fact, *America* had carried that designation throughout the entire course of the civil war, when, technically, the United States of North America had pulled out of the Confederation and was fighting for her independence. Politically, there was some question at the moment as to whether the USNA was officially back in the global family of nations; oh, the treaties had been signed, the alliances renewed . . . but the USNA continued to hold itself just a bit aloof from the Confederation. The president, Gray understood, was against a formal reunification, and the Senate currently was divided on the question. Some were calling for a full merger; others wanted the USNA to enjoy a "special relationship" with the Earth Confederation, one that preserved the nation's political sovereignty. The question, likely, would be resolved in upcoming months with votes both in Washington, D.C., and in Geneva.

How, Gray wondered, did Konstantin feel about the question?

And even more important: would the current delicate situation change after Gray performed his small act of mutiny this evening? If there were USNA military officers who still didn't trust the Confederation, it was equally true that there were Confed officers and politicians who didn't trust the North Americans. And if a TC/USNA star carrier suddenly violated orders and ran off across the galaxy on a mission of its own, the little trust now existing might be weakened further, perhaps irreparably.

Gray hated the idea of being the one responsible for up-setting the carefully negotiated balance of powers on either side of the Atlantic. Unfortunately, he'd not thought about that side of things until after he'd let Konstantin talk him into this madness.

Ah, well. What was the old adage . . . something to the effect that you might as well be hung for a sheep as for a lamb? His career would be finished after this in any case. He couldn't help but laugh internally.

How many times could they kick him out of the service?

Of course, there were other things that might happen to him. He might be facing prison time or, more likely, psycho-revision. A major personality edit would leave him unaware of his current life, of who he was now. The idea horrified him. "Damn but Konstantin had better come through on his promise!"

"I beg your pardon, Admiral?" Captain Gutierrez said.

Gray looked up. He'd not realized he'd spoken aloud. "Nothing, Captain. Sorry."

"We'll be coming up to the transition in another three minutes, sir."

"Very well. I . . . uh . . . have some special orders for you."

"Sir?"

He opened a back channel in his internal circuitry. "Here you go. Do not discuss this with anyone but the helm and navigation officers."

He felt Gutierrez running through the orders in her own thoughts. "Begging the Admiral's pardon, but . . . Whiskey-Tango-Fox?"

"I am taking full responsibility. All I can tell you is that the change in mission is extremely important. The ship, the crew, and most particularly the bridge officers are in no way responsible for this. It's entirely on me."

"Bullshit. Sir."

"I beg your pardon?"

"Who is *really* giving this order? The president? The Joint Chiefs?"

"Just assume that it is me . . . and that I know what I'm doing."

"The order *is* coming from somewhere higher up the chain of command."

"That is classified." Easier to lie than to admit that the orders came from a supercomputer completely outside both the military and political chains of command. Besides, he wasn't sure how Gutierrez felt about superbright AIs. If she mistrusted them half as much as he did . . .

But then, he was following Konstantin's directions, wasn't he? To the letter and all the way to the court-martial board.

"Sir . . . I really don't—"

"Look, Captain. I know this is irregular. You're right to question these orders. What I suggest is that you log these orders as 'received under protest,' and compose a report that you can squirt off to Mars HQMILCOM the moment we drop out of metaspace. I assure you that I will be sending a report as well, describing in full what I've done . . . and, incidentally, absolving you and the rest of the crew of any and all blame in this."

"Admiral," Gutierrez said, sounding somewhere between angry and embarrassed, "I trust you. I've trusted you since you came aboard as skipper of this bucket, and I was your XO. If you say we're going to take *America* and tunnel into hell, I'm not going to question it, right? But this sounds like someone is pulling a sneaky work-around to evade legitimate orders, and this could put you, personally, in a world of severe hurt. I don't want to see that happen. And I will not stand by and *let* it happen. If you're making some kind of gallant last stand here, I am going to be standing there with you. *Intiende*?"

Gray had never heard Gutierrez revert to her native Spanish

before, at least not while she was on *America*'s bridge. "I do understand," he told her. "Thank you."

"*De nada.* Now . . . what's really going down?"

"I'll tell you," he said, "but *after* we complete the maneuver, okay?"

"Well . . . okay." She did not sound completely convinced. "You promise not to face the bastards alone?"

"There are no bastards this time . . . but, yes, I promise."

"There are always bastards, Admiral. And once we execute this order, there are going to be hundreds of them, screaming for your head. I don't want you to face them alone."

"We're coming up on the transition, Captain. Please prepare to make the jump."

"Aye, aye, Admiral."

The transition from normal gravitic drive to the Alcubierre Drive required that the starship be within a flat metric—meaning far enough away from planetary bodies that local space was not bent by their gravitational fields—and traveling within a percent or so of *c*, the speed of light. At relativistic, near-*c* velocities, the ship's mass soared to insane values, her fore-and-aft dimension contracted to near-zero, and time slowed to a crawl compared to its passage in the non-accelerated universe. *At* the speed of light, the ship's mass would become infinite, her length would be zero, and time would come to a complete stop, which was why material objects like starships and fleet admirals could be accelerated up to within a hairsbreadth of *c* but could never actually reach that forbidden speed.

However, the Alcubierre Drive could use the ship's vastly inflated mass to fold local space into interesting hyperdimensional configurations, essentially contracting the metric of space ahead of the ship, and inflating it astern. Einstein might forbid material objects to travel at *c*, but he had nothing whatsoever to say about empty space traveling at that velocity . . . or about that space carrying along material objects embedded within it.

"Initiating transition to metaspace," Gutierrez announced, "in three . . . two . . . one . . . *jump!*"

Essentially, the tightly wrapped bubble of space inside the Alcubierre field was cut off from the rest of the universe and was, therefore, a universe in its own right. The region had been designated *metaspace*, reflecting its isolation. Ships under Alcubierre Drive could not communicate with others, or even see outside their pocket universe.

But, in relation to the vaster universe outside, they could *move*.

America hurtled through Darkness Absolute, though all instruments on board insisted that they were motionless. Indeed, they were, at least relative to their local and tightly constrained bubble of spacetime. Course was determined before the transition; the ship would move along the same directional vector it had been on before the jump.

Which was why five minutes after engaging the drive, Gray gave the mental command to *America*'s AI: *disengage drive*.

In a burst of light, *America* dropped out of metaspace.

At a pseudovelocity of fifteen light years per day, five minutes had carried the star carrier roughly half a trillion kilometers, or something like 3,300 astronomical units. They were far out in the Oort Cloud, with Sol a bright star in the remote distance. The rest of the ships in the flotilla had traveled on, oblivious to *America*'s desertion. They would not be aware that she was missing until they came out of Alcubierre Drive at Kapteyn's Star.

Gray opened a transmission channel, linking in with every person on board the ship. "This is Admiral Gray," he said. "Our mission has changed. We have been asked to investigate an unusual star system just over fourteen hundred light years from Sol. The others in our fleet have continued on with the original mission, but we are going to check out a system popularly known as Tabby's Star. You can download the data from the ship's Net.

"I can't tell you much about what we expect to find out there, but I can say that this mission is of the very highest importance to Earth, and to the human species. It is our hope and our expectation to find technologies that will enable us to meet the Rosette Aliens on a somewhat more equal footing.

"I know that each and every one of you will do your usual superb best. That's why we have been asked to carry out this mission.

"That is all."

As he spoke, *America* was rotating slowly on her center of mass, the stars—the ancient constellations recognizable from Earth—pinwheeling about her as she turned. The ship's AI had been given new programming by none other than Konstantin itself, programming that included their precise new course.

Tabby's Star was located in Cygnus, a constellation also known as the Northern Cross, but *America* was seeking out a shortcut. In a different direction entirely, in the constellation of Scorpio off toward the Milky Way's thick, bright heart, lay a different objective, a TRGA newly discovered and given the code name Penrose. Revealed by Agletsch traders only a few months ago, Penrose was relatively close—a mere 79 light years distant—less than half the distance of TRGA Tipler.

At top speed, it would take them five days and a few hours to reach it.

Aligned with the distant TRGA cylinder, *America* began accelerating. With no slower ships in her train, she could manage her top acceleration of ten thousand gravities, and was pushing near-*c* in fifty minutes.

Gray's message, composed in his head and stored within his in-head RAM, was ready to go. "Captain? Do you have anything you want to say to the folks back home?"

"Negative, Admiral. I'm with you on this, okay?"

Gray thought about arguing, then decided against it. Gutierrez, he knew, could be stubborn.

Besides, his own report had stressed that Gutierrez had acceded to his order under protest, and bore no responsibility whatsoever for *America*'s change of mission. He didn't know if that rider would be enough to protect her; he hoped it was.

For the next hour, *America* accelerated as the sky around her compressed itself into surreal, relativistic geometries. As the ship reached some 99.7 percent of the speed of light, the star carrier's AI again focused the ship's gravitational drive, wrapping local space around the ship like a blanket.

And *America* vanished from normal space.

Assault Lander Lucas
Heimdall Command
2212 hours, TFT

Carter tried to comprehend the deluge of images and thoughts flooding her mind. Tried . . . and failed. She thought—*thought*—that the Baondyeddi AI was trying to show her scenes taken from the virtual reality it had created within itself, a virtual reality tailored to the emotional and mental needs of a diverse number of different alien species. The minds of the Pan-European fighter pilots were there. She could sense them, moving through wavering vistas of light and distance and feeling, human, *blessedly* human sparks of thought and Mind against the inconceivably alien vistas around her.

She saw the aliens. . . .

The Baondyeddi predominated, of course. It was possible—though by no means certain, that the world humans called Heimdall was the Baondyeddi homeworld, the place where they'd first evolved eons before the N'gai Cluster had fallen through the intergalactic Void and been devoured by the Milky Way.

In her mind's eye, she could see the Baondyeddi. It was difficult to judge how large the beings actually were; she had no easy frame of reference. She thought, though, that their flat bodies were about a meter and a half across, and supported by writhing hand-feet-mouths perhaps thirty or forty centimeters off the ground. Eyes—those startlingly blue orbs could be nothing else—lined the disk's rim, interspersed by patches of hair-fine cilia. She wondered what the world looked like to a being that could see in all directions at once, and for which there was no front or back, left or right.

Around her, she could glimpse aspects of a city, one where low, flattened domes predominated and doors were designed to accommodate the Baondyeddi anatomy. There was nothing, however, to give a sense of the beings' culture or worldview. She could feel . . . something, many things . . . emotions, possibly . . . but they were feelings that didn't quite resonate with human emotional responses.

Overall, though, she felt two emotions that she could easily define: an infinite, dragging sadness or sense of loss . . .

. . . and horror.

Carter was aware of other alien beings around her, beings not really a part of the Baondyeddi background, but superimposed upon it in some way impossible to discern. She recognized some of them: the Adjugredudhra. The F'heen F'haav.

She sensed that each of these species—and many others—had existed as digital lifeforms inhabiting a series of virtual worlds, whole universes emulated within the Etched Cliffs of Heimdall. If Carter could not fully understand what she was seeing and feeling, she could still wonder at the complexity and diversity of life and of Mind around her.

Without hearing words, she became aware of a kind of overriding theme to what she was experiencing. The Etched Cliffs were a haven, a refuge from some terrible threat. Exploring further, she saw images of alien beings dying by the millions, by the billions . . . the technological holocaust the Agletsch called *Schjaa Hok*, the Time of Change. Those who'd fled here to these virtual worlds were Refusers, a percentage of each species who had rejected the Transcendence of the original ur-Sh'daar.

Fair enough. It was completely unreasonable to expect that all members of a given culture would embrace change on that level, to that degree. There would always be refusers in any culture . . . mavericks and visionaries and set-in-their-way conservatives who simply wanted to be left alone, the technophobes and philosophers and those who liked life the way it was and didn't want to change it. Within the many virtual worlds of Heimdall's Etched Cliffs, they'd found safe havens. Carter couldn't make out the details, but there was a sense that they'd actually tampered with their sun long, long before, using a technique called star mining or, more precisely, starlifting, to remove mass from a brighter, hotter, faster-burning sun to vastly extend its life span. Kapteyn's Star once had been a sun much like Sol, with an expected life span of around 10 billion years. Now it was a red dwarf a quarter of Sol's mass, a star already 10 billion years old, but with a projected life span of a thousand times that or more.

And yet, even as they shied from such tampering, they embraced the opportunity it afforded—a life of safety with a seemingly eternal sun that would shine down on their virtual haven.

She saw the source of the collective horror, the approach of . . . *something*, something immense and dark and implacable.

In her mind, Carter fell through curtains of golden, shifting light, saw stars reworked and reforged, saw megaengineering on a galactic scale utterly incomprehensible to any merely mortal intellect . . .

She saw the Dark Mind.

And she knew that It had seen her.

She awoke screaming.

Chapter Nineteen

TC/USNA CVS America
Flag Bridge
Approaching TRGA Penrose
0815 hours, TFT

"Okay, people," Gray said. "Are we ready for this?"

He'd ordered the partial bulkhead between the flag bridge and the ship's bridge to be opened, turning the space into a large, two-level compartment. Captain Gutierrez turned in her command seat in front of him and looked up—"up" being a relative term in zero-gravity—and grinned at him. "I'd like to know how we can get ready for something that is a complete unknown," she told him. "But all decks report readiness for transit through the triggah."

Gray nodded. Though the Penrose TRGA had been known for some years, this was the first time a manned ship had passed through any of its myriad pathways. They were now completely reliant on Konstantin's information.

He shook off the queasy discomfort that thought generated. They were committed now.

"Weapons," he said.

"All weapons armed, charged, and ready, Admiral," Commander Jessie Parker announced.

"Fighters."

"Four squadrons ready for launch," *America*'s CAG, Captain Connie Fletcher replied in his mind. "On your command."

"Scanners and recorders."

"Go."

"Navigation."

"Course plotted and laid in, Admiral," Commander Victor Blakeslee replied.

"Helm."

"Under AI control, sir. Ready to initiate at your command."

Gray scanned an array of green icons appearing on his in-head. Engineering . . . life support . . . power . . . all green.

He took a last look at the panorama of stars projected on the overhead and the bulkhead forward. Most of the constellations remained familiar, with only minor distortions. Seventy-nine light years was an insignificant step in a galaxy this vast, and only the nearest stars, a handful only, had shifted positions. Sol, however, lying directly astern, had been rendered invisible to the unaided eye by distance. Directly ahead, the Penrose Gate hung suspended in a dull haze of its own making, where light was subtly scattered by the envelope of twisted spacetime around it. Face-on, it was a perfect circle, the tube walls blurred to a featureless silver grey, the interior dark and hazy.

But from moment to moment, you could glimpse the stars beyond.

There was nothing more to do, but . . .

"Initiate TRGA approach routine."

"Aye, aye, Admiral. We're going through."

America approached the fast-rotating tube. Penrose was larger than the Tipler TRGA, with a diameter of nearly five kilometers, a length of nearly thirty. Why this was so was unknown. But each of the TRGA cylinders discovered so far in the vicinity of Sol was unique, though each seemed to be paired in its mass and dimensions with the TRGA at the other end of the transit.

The TRGA's maw received the ship. Gray felt the bump

and nudge of maneuvering thrusters dropping *America* into the precisely calculated vector. Blurred, curving walls swept past to port and starboard, above and below . . .

. . . and *America* emerged in a new and different space.

VFA-96, Black Demons
TC/USNA CVS America
TRGA Penrose
0817 hours, TFT

Lieutenant Donald Gregory sat enfolded within the velvet darkness of his SG-420 Starblade, momentarily alone with dark thoughts. The depression, he thought, was getting worse. He rubbed his gloved hands across his thighs, feeling the nano-grown material of his e-suit. The new legs worked fine. Unfortunately, he had the unshakeable feeling that his brain did not.

When were they going to catch him? Ground him?

He didn't much care. . . .

"Wake up, people." The voice of the squadron's skipper, Commander Luther Mackey, came over the command channel. "Emergence in thirty seconds."

Sleep? You've got to be kidding me, he thought. Hell, even if he *could*, who the hell would be able to sleep *now*, with the star carrier about to emerge into strangeness?

"Demons, PriFly," another voice said. "You're number one in the queue. Prepare for drop, E plus ten."

"Copy, PriFly," Mackey replied. "We're go for drop."

An open in-head window showed an optical feed from the carrier's shield cap forward as *America* plunged into the gaping mouth of the TRGA. Gregory made a final check of his Starblade's systems, confirming readiness for drop. He was still getting used to the new fighter, the black teardrop of cutting-edge military technology that had replaced the older Starhawks, Velociraptors, and Stardragons only a few months ago. His original flight training had been with the Starhawks. Fortunately, the Starblade allowed a Starhawk emulation so that he'd not needed to retrain his autonomic reactions. And the 'Blade was a sweet machine, more alive than not, and exquisitely tuned to become an extension of his mind and body.

Gregory had found that the ever-encompassing depression tended to recede a bit when he was linked in to the controls and charged with the prospect of launch. Somehow, the mind-bending awe of deep space—or the deadly flash and parry of space combat—held the darkness at bay.

And that was a good thing.

He just wished the thoughts of Meg would recede as well.

Blurred gray mist surrounded him for long seconds, in a free fall through an endless tunnel punctuated by brief thumps as the carrier shifted from vector to vector.

And then starlight exploded around him as *America* emerged from the cylinder.

Gregory sagged back in his cockpit seat. "My God in heaven . . ."

TC/USNA CVS America
Flag Bridge
Tabby's Star
0818 hours, TFT

"What the hell is *that*?" Gray stared at the jumble of shapes ahead. "Give me plus magnification!"

The shapes enlarged, still blurred by distance.

But they were huge. Awesomely huge.

"Konstantin!" Gray snapped. "What are we looking at?"

The Konstantin clone didn't answer for several seconds. Gray could practically feel the program swimming through cascades of incoming data.

"I believe, Admiral," Konstantin said eventually, "that we are looking at a Dyson sphere. A very *broken* Dyson sphere."

"Admiral?" Captain Fletcher said over the command channel. "Should we launch?"

"What? Oh, yes . . . yes, of course. Launch fighters."

"Aye, aye, sir."

"But pass the word to them, please. Don't get too close to those things, okay? Not until we know what they are."

"Copy that, sir."

"First squadron away," Fletcher told him.

"Thank you, CAG." The twelve fighters of the Black Demons were accelerating toward the system's heart. Twelve more, the Impactors, were gathering, preparing for boost. The Ghost Riders were dropping now from *America*'s rotating flight decks.

Gray continued studying the gigantic objects before *America*. He had downloaded all the information Konstantin had provided on the star, including astronomer Tabetha Boyajian's original paper, as well as reports of when the Kepler space telescope had first trained its sights on KIC 8462852. At that time, centuries ago, there had been a strange moment of dimming—as if something massive had passed in front of the star. One of the wilder possibilities discussed at that time suggested that Kepler had glimpsed a Dyson sphere under construction, a tremendously unlikely event. The chances that Kepler had recorded the fluctuating light stream from KIC 8462852 at *just* that brief moment in the star's history when a Dyson shell was still being assembled were so small as to be completely negligible.

Eventually, astronomers had dismissed the possibility of alien megastructures around KIC 8462852. The dip in light was caused—*must* be caused—not by technologically advanced aliens, but by gravitational darkening brought on by the star's unusually high rate of spin.

Regardless, Tabby's Star remained a stellar curiosity, but not one demanding immediate exploration.

As Gray stared at the artifact that was Tabby's Star, though, he began to understand some of the long-standing enigma surrounding it. And he also now knew why both the Agletsch and Konstantin had been so insistent.

Automatically, he scanned surrounding space, watching for possible threats. The TRGA was dropping away astern, a blurred, silver-gray circle. "Interesting," Gray said, thoughtful.

"Admiral?" Gutierrez prompted.

"I find it intriguing that there just happens to be a TRGA here in the Tabby's Star system."

"You think maybe the locals built it? *Them*?"

"I don't know, Captain. I wish I did. Too many unknowns." He thought a moment. "Konstantin? Log this new gate as the Boyajian TRGA."

"Noted, Admiral."

Off to one side, an immense nebula revealed its twisted internal structures in pale light. The ship's AI-provided data overlays identified it as NGC 7000—the North America Nebula. That vast cloud of interstellar dust and gas must be pretty close by, he thought, to appear so large in the local sky.

There was a nearby star, too, piercingly bright and with the actinic blue-white gleam of a welder's torch, appearing more brilliant on *America*'s visual displays than Venus did at her brightest on Earth. The computer-generated overlay named it as Deneb—Alpha Cygni—and, again, it must be very close to Tabby's Star indeed to appear that luminous.

But the true visual spectacle lay directly ahead, where Tabby's Star was a hot, white glare bright enough to obscure any background stars. *America* had emerged from the Boyajian TGRA only eight astronomical units from the star, close enough that it showed as a small but dazzlingly bright disk. That light illuminated a spherical cloud of motes surrounding the star extending out in all directions to more than five AUs. It also lit a number of much larger objects orbiting the star closer in. The largest, when Gray increased the magnification of the image, looked like a ragged fragment of slightly curved metal, but it must have been titanic in size to be visible at this range.

He highlighted the fragment in his mind. "How big is that thing?"

Dean Mallory, the ship's tactical officer said, "According to our instruments, that thing is over three million kilometers across!"

And it was not alone. There were hundreds of other visible fragments glinting in the light, ranging in size up to about half a million kilometers, and hundreds of thousands, perhaps millions more that appeared to be the size of large asteroids and rubble, all confined to a broad, flat ring around the star.

"Can we get the magnification any higher?" Gray demanded.

"That's the limit of our resolution, Admiral," the sensor officer told him.

"Very well." They would have to wait until the fighters got in close.

What he could now see was grainy and low-res, but the ship's AI was working to clean up the image. It wasn't so much that the picture was blurred by distance as that his brain was having difficulty interpreting what he was seeing. That largest piece of debris, for instance: only gradually was Gray becoming aware that the thing was covered with craters, ranging in size from barely visible pockmarks to one huge blemish thousands of kilometers across. It looked . . . yes, he could make it out now. Whatever had created that largest crater had actually punched through the relatively thin shell. He could see stars visible through the hole. All of the pieces, he realized now, were covered with craters as thickly as the surface of the Moon or of Mercury. Now what could have caused—

Of course. Those fragments—and there were millions of them—had been in orbit for a long time, and it looked like they were traveling about their sun in massive clumps. The mutual gravity of those massive pieces was trying to impose order on chaos. Those fragments were traveling in the same general direction, but they must have been colliding and re-colliding with one another for centuries.

Sure . . . that was it. Tabby's Star was such a long way from Earth that when the odd light fluctuations had first been detected at the dawn of the twenty-first century, what terrestrial astronomers had been watching was what had already happened here all the way back in the year 535 CE. That meant that the chaotic tumbling and grinding melee up ahead had been going on continuously for at *least* nineteen hundred years or so, and quite possibly for much longer than that.

As he watched, a piece of dull-gleaming metal the size of a small continent slowly ground into another, slightly smaller piece. Fragments drifted gently away. Metal glowed white-hot at the impact area. Smaller pieces struck other pieces . . . a cascade of slow-moving destruction.

The megastructure built around KIC 8462852 was steadily destroying itself, the larger fragments attracting the smaller, the collisions grinding the pieces to dust. How long, Gray wondered, had that been going on?

"Konstantin?" Gray called. "How far from the star is that debris field?"

"The orbital belt is fairly thick, Admiral," the Konstantin clone replied. "But the largest fragments appear to be in a circular orbit at one point eight five astronomical units from the star."

Gray ran some quick calculations through his in-head math coprocessor. Given the star's mass of 1.43 times that of Sol, a planet or other body in orbit at a distance of 1.85 AUs would have a period of . . . yes . . . about 750 days. That confirmed quite nicely that the star's light fluctuations were indeed due to that largest fragment of debris.

Konstantin must have been monitoring his calculations. "You might also be interested in the fact," the AI clone told him, "that the habitable zone for a star of this brightness extends from roughly one point six AUs out to nearly three AUs."

"Meaning that those big fragments are orbiting within the star's habitable zone."

"Precisely."

The term *habitable zone* was extremely flexible and often vague, but in general meant that distance from the local star where water—under reasonable atmospheric pressures—remained liquid. Whoever or whatever had built a Dyson sphere around Tabby's Star might have been adapted to warmer temperatures than were common on Earth, but still required liquid water.

That fact alone should have alerted those early-twenty-first-century astronomers to the fact that whatever was obscuring the light from KIC 8462852, its 750-day period meant that it was inside the star's "Goldilocks Zone," the realm of habitability for Earth-type life.

With that realization came another, accompanied by a sharp stab of disappointment. Obviously there *had* been an advanced technological civilization here, but it was long gone. It had been gone in the year 535 CE, when the light fluctuations that had first piqued the curiosity of terrestrial astronomers had started off on their long journey across space to Earth. If the gradual dimming of the star recorded in old astronomical records was the result of the breakup of the Dyson sphere, it had been gone a century before that. Whatever had destroyed the high-tech infrastructure of this system had done so when the Roman Empire existed on Earth . . . and quite possibly long before that.

Which meant that there would be no easy answers, no magical weapon for defeating the Rosette entity to be found here. If Laurie's Stargods had walked here, they were long gone.

"Konstantin?"

"Yes, Admiral."

"Is there any indication of what happened to the beings who built all of this?"

"Nothing definite. I will remind you, however, that human reference points and reason may not have a bearing on the problem."

"Meaning what?"

"That it is too early to assume that the builders are extinct."

"It's hard to imagine that a civilization advanced enough to build a Dyson sphere would just stand by and watch the thing break up."

"I agree. It is . . . untidy. One at the very least might assume that they would recycle the materials used in the sphere's construction."

"Maybe they ascended," Gray said. "Or they just packed up and left."

"Indeed."

"Comm," Gray said. "Are we getting anything in the way of comm chatter?"

"Other than among our fighters, Admiral? Negative."

"Neutrino leakage? Gravity waves?"

"Nothing, sir."

Glumly, Gray stared at the forward display. "No radio traffic. No laser-com signals. And no fusion reactors or gravitics technology."

"In the year 2015, concerted efforts to listen in on electromagnetic wavelengths emanating from this system turned up nothing," Konstantin reminded him. "We've known since then that any advanced civilization that might reside in the KIC 8462852 system either did not use electromagnetic wavelengths for communication or . . ."

"Or they were gone."

"Or they were gone."

Whether the civilization here had entered its equivalent of a technological singularity and vanished, had packed up and moved to another star, or simply become extinct for whatever reason, the result was a dry hole, as far as the mission was concerned. Gray pictured himself in front of that court-martial board trying to explain himself: *"Well, we hoped to talk them into giving us a super-weapon that we could use against the Rosetters, but when we got there they weren't home, and we had to turn around and come back empty-handed. . . ."*

Fuck *that*. Surely there was *something* here that would be useful, something they could learn, something they could find and reverse engineer. Konstantin had been so *sure*. . . .

Shkadov thrusters, for instance.

Gray had downloaded what was available in the ship's Net during the passage to TRGA Penrose. Shkadov thrusters had been named for physicist Leonid Mikhailovich Shkadov, who'd written a paper in 1987 with the title "Possibility of Controlling Solar System Motion in the Galaxy." Shkadov had envisioned building an enormous mirror hanging above the sun, a light sail millions of kilometers across, balanced between the sun's gravitational pull and the pressure of its light. Such a stationary satellite, or *statite*, would forever hang above the same portion of the star, and by reflecting sunlight it would create an imbalance in the star's radiation pressure, a net excess that would create thrust and move the star in the direction of the mirror.

Obviously, a megastructure of that size and scope, utilizing as it did the entire energy output of its star, would qualify its builders for Kardashev Type II status.

Gray remembered addressing the Sh'daar Council six weeks earlier, when he'd described K-I, K-II, and K-III type civilizations. Was that what Konstantin had had in mind? Appropriate some of a K-II civilization's technology in order to confront the Rosetters?

The trouble was, if his guess about the intelligence building a galactic Dyson sphere at the core of the Milky Way was accurate, they were still going to be way outclassed by the Rosette entity's technology.

And . . . what would the technology required for moving a star buy them? Gray had done the math. If Sol was equipped with a solar sail reflecting half of its radiation output, the total thrust produced would be on the order of 1.28×10^{28} newtons. That was a hell of a lot of energy, yes . . . but the sun was *extremely* massive—around 2×10^{30} kilograms. After 1 million years, the sun would have picked up a whopping extra 20 meters per second in velocity, and been nudged something like 0.03 of a light year.

The pay-off came if you kept at it, because the acceleration was cumulative. After one billion years, the change in velocity would be up to 20 kilometers per second, and the sun would have been displaced 34,000 light years, the equivalent of a third of the width of the entire galaxy.

With the appropriate technology, it was certainly possible

to move stars around and even use them as weapons . . . but the people who tried it would have to be *very* patient.

In the centuries since Shkadov's paper, other schemes for moving stars had been suggested. If a star could be "squeezed" using powerful magnetic induction, or prodded with intense gravitational singularities, the star might be made to create a powerful jet that would turn it into a huge rocket. Though not, strictly speaking, a Shkadov thruster, the term was sometimes applied to any technology that could push suns around.

Either way, a civilization that could move stars around might offer Earth her one slim hope of fending off the Rosette Aliens. If the *America* could make contact, could establish communications with a species that had evolved such godlike powers, Earth might have a chance.

And that chance, Gray thought, no matter how slender, was worth his career if it came down to that.

But before they could make contact with this system, he had to understand it.

He stared at the debris field, watching the vast, slow-tumbling fragments of mega-engineering. Was that what he was seeing? The wreckage of a device intended to move Tabby's Star through the galaxy? Many of the discussions of Shkadov thrusters and similar technologies assumed that they would employ Dyson spheres or Dyson swarms as well. A moving star would drag its retinue of planets along with it, of course, but a sphere enclosing the star, or, better, a cloud of habitats and solar collectors orbiting it would allow for more controlled conditions—and protection if the tortured star flared or otherwise acted unpredictably.

Gray suppressed a shudder. What kind of intelligence played billiards with its sun?

And it was just possible that the wreckage he was looking at had been brought on by a K-II civilization that had overreached itself. It had tried to move its star, and something had gone horribly, horribly wrong.

"Konstantin?"

"Yes, Admiral?"

"That cloud of objects surrounding the star out to five AUs. Is that a Dyson swarm? What the hell are we looking at?"

"I am as yet uncertain, Admiral. However, the cloud appears to be very tightly ordered. It consists of some tens of millions of artifacts in stellar orbits between three and five astronomical units from the star. Each artifact, I estimate, is spherical and measures thirty to forty kilometers across, with a mass on the order of five times ten to the sixteenth power kilograms."

"Fifty trillion tons? They're solid?"

"Unknown, as of yet. The fifty-trillion-ton figure applies if the object has an overall density of around two grams per cubic centimeter. But the spheres may be hollow."

"Artificial habitats, then."

"Quite possible. However, those spheres might also be composed of solid or near-solid computronium. They are arrayed in at least five concentric shells. We could be looking at a Matrioshka brain."

Another staggering mega-engineering concept, a toy for a super-advanced high-tech civilization. As with a Dyson swarm, you surrounded a star with satellites, but rather than have those satellites be habitats holding a population of trillions, you make them out of computronium, a hypothetical computational substrate arranged with the greatest possible efficiency.

You would then arrange the spheres as concentric shells. The innermost shell uses light from its sun to carry out its assigned computations, and radiates the excess energy outward. The next shell out traps that energy and uses it, radiates the excess, and so on and on until virtually all of the star's radiation is utilized. You get all those computronium spheres talking to each other, and you have a computer network the size of a solar system, one of staggering power.

The inhabitants of Heimdall had etched computer circuitry into the bedrock of their world, creating a planet-sized computer powerful enough to hold a virtual population numbering in the trillions living within a digital world of unimaginable detail and richness. A Matrioshka brain—the term came from the nested wooden dolls from old Russia—would be trillions upon trillions of times more powerful than that.

"My God," Gray said quietly. "What are they thinking about?"

"That, Admiral, is unknown. I should also point out that the system currently appears to be inoperable."

Gray hadn't been aware that he'd spoken the thought aloud. "I know, I know. But . . . I wonder . . ."

"About what, Admiral?"

"I wonder if it would be possible to tap into whatever that colossal mind *was* thinking, back before someone pulled the plug."

"That seems unlikely, Admiral, even assuming that the problems of language and of computer architecture could be overcome."

"*Not* if we're dealing with a holographic brain."

Chapter Twenty

VFA-96, Black Demons
Tabby's Star
1127 hours, TFT

Lieutenant Gregory banked his fighter low across the crumpled, crater-pocked surface of a Tabby's Belt fragment. The sky around him was filled with tumbling rocks.

He found the panorama amusing, in a terrifying and nerve-wracking way. Popular fiction was filled with virtual dramas set in the asteroid belt of Earth's solar system, or in the systems of other stars, and those shows *never* got it right. For purposes of storytelling and suspense, they usually depicted an asteroid belt as crowded with enormous boulders and looking very much like this. Gregory's fighter training had included a month-long deployment off Ceres, in the Sol Belt, so he knew from personal experience that the planetoids there were spread out through such an enormous volume of space that, unless you happened to be very close to one, you couldn't see any in the sky at all. The distance between one rock and the next nearest averaged something on the order of 1 million kilometers, and could be much more than that.

The sky around Gregory now looked like the fictional ones, however, packed with boulders of all sizes, ranging from bits of rubble to drifting mountains. The belt's density was not uniform. Mutual gravitational attraction had pulled the debris together until the stuff was orbiting in tight formation. Elsewhere, there were vast gaps.

Caswell and Ruxton had already checked the composition of a couple of the fragments, firing lasers at them and spectroscopically analyzing the gas given off. One piece had been mostly nickel iron; the other had been an amalgam of steel and plastics, probably derived from a carbonaceous chondrite—a type of asteroid rich in hydrocarbons.

That supported the classic theory of a Dyson sphere's construction. You needed to disassemble all of the planetary and asteroidal bodies in the system to get enough material to build a structure that big.

The idea seemed a bit harebrained to Gregory. What kind of idiot wiped out his entire solar system in order to get the raw materials to build an artificial habitat? It seemed . . . short-sighted, somehow. You might *need* that stuff some day.

A signal flashed in Gregory's in-head. *That* was odd. . . .

"Hey, Skipper?" he called. "This is Demon Four. I've got an IR point source dead ahead. Range . . . I make it about two thousand kilometers."

"Copy that, Four," Mackey's voice replied. "Check it out . . . but watch yourself."

He accelerated his Starblade, homing on the infrared signal.

So far, the endless debris fields had been lifeless. But it was easy to envision that there must have been life here at some point, beyond the presence of the artificial object itself. Some of the fragments he was passing, the larger ones, especially, showed hints of mountains, river beds, even occasional structures of some sort. The terrain forms looked molded, as if the shell had originally been grown to include preformed shapes for mountains, hills, valleys, and other terrain features. Presumably, the entire surface had then been covered with dirt, water, and growing things to artificially replicate the surface of a planet.

A very, very, *very* large planet . . .

And a few of those fragments showed infrastructure . . . tunnels or roads or underground blocks of buildings, perhaps, laid out in geometric precision within the Dyson floor substrate.

These guys had thought *big*.

There wasn't nearly enough wreckage to suggest a true Dyson sphere, though, and that was a bit of a puzzle.

Yes, the debris field was massive and extensive, but it still didn't look like it held *that* much material. It might well have been a ringworld, however, an enormous flattened hoop spinning to create artificial gravity on the inner surface, and with titanic walls along the edges to hold in the atmosphere and keep it from spilling off into space.

Or . . . perhaps it had been a sphere once, but most of the pieces had fallen *into* the star. But there also was the mystery of the statites.

Out beyond the belt of wreckage, asteroid-sized constructs hung suspended from gossamer sails, each a few molecules thick, but stretching across an area equivalent to half of North America. The Black Demons had passed a few of them an hour ago on their way in to the debris belt. Balanced between the star's gravity and its radiation pressure, these stationary satellites did not appear to be habitats. Clearly they were arranged to take advantage of the star's abundance of light. They might be the classic alternative to a Dyson sphere, a mega-engineering concept called a Dyson *swarm*, which had many fewer problems than the sphere version. So the consuming question here at Tabby's Star was . . . why had the builders of this place used *both*? If the belt debris had been a Dyson sphere, the statite spheres farther out would not have been able to harvest sunlight. Possibly, if the inner structure had been a band around the sun's equator and not a complete shell, the statites could have hovered above just the exposed portions of the star . . . an elegant design combining both megastructural elements. But, again—*why*?

Gregory knew that they didn't have the full picture yet. He wondered if the belt debris had been an earlier attempt at either a ringworld or a solid sphere that had failed, and the statite swarm had been put in place later. Maybe. That made a certain amount of sense, he thought, though he admitted to himself that that might be the depression talking. He had a tendency to get cynical when he got depressed.

Or . . . maybe the two different designs represented two different civilizations, perhaps separated by millions of years in time. The ringworld civilization might have given rise to the statite cloud, or the statite builders might have been invaders coming in from elsewhere. Gregory could imagine the statite civilization scavenging the belt debris for raw materials.

Had there been a war between the two? Had an invading intelligence destroyed the ringworld, then feasted on its remains?

At any rate, the Ghost Riders were checking out the statites now; the Black Demons had been deployed inward to examine the debris belt farther in. The only way they were going to solve this mystery was if they could find someone, some*thing* living here they could question. The belt debris was lifeless . . . but there might be AIs existing among the statites. Or digitally uploaded intelligences. If they could just make contact and learn how to communicate with whatever was left.

His Starblade was decelerating now within a few hundred kilometers of the IR source, but he couldn't see anything up ahead like an intact structure or ship. What he did see was a filmy, gauzy *something* that appeared to be growing out of a piece of floating rubble. At first he thought there was a fault with his ship's optics, but the fighter's AI assured him that everything was functioning optimally.

And then the gauzy something moved.

The diaphanous shape flowed and rippled, parts of it moving like water, parts shifting like aurorae. The IR signal, he saw, was coming from the chunk of debris, a house-sized hunk of metal floating at the edge of the far vaster translucence beyond it. Whatever that cloud or shape was, it was enormous. He couldn't get a radar return off of it, but he was able to compare it visually to a nearby drifting fragment that he could measure.

The shape—what he could see of it, at any rate—was 120,000 kilometers across, very nearly the diameter of the planet Jupiter.

He was picking up a magnetic field from the thing too, a strong one.

The scary part was that Gregory could not escape the feeling that whatever that thing was, it was *alive*. It appeared to be grazing along the fringes of the debris belt.

"Hey, Skipper!" he called. "Are you getting this?"

"We see it," Mackey replied. "Is that thing alive?"

"Sure looks like it. I'm going to try to get in closer."

"Not too close! And kill your speed a bit! Whatever that thing is, you do *not* want to get it mad!"

"Copy that."

Gregory shifted his Starblade's outer hull to complete stealth mode, an utterly black, light-drinking modality designed not to be noticed. He engaged his AI's analytical routines, probing and measuring . . . but gently.

He was thinking about his wild-ass idea about interstellar invaders. The diaphanous, magnetic thing out there was as insubstantially thin as the solar sails supporting the statites. Could it be associated with them? Could a civilization of those beings have *made* the statite cloud?

Somehow, that didn't seem right . . . a being as insubstantial as a smoke cloud the size of Jupiter building billions of statites each forty kilometers across. No, that didn't make sense on any level.

His Starblade's AI warned him, in feelings rather than words, that his fighter was moving through a volume of space of slightly higher density than before.

So-called empty space was not entirely empty, it turned out. In interstellar space, out among the spiral arms of the galaxy, a traveler would encounter roughly one atom per ten cubic centimeters of space. Inside a solar system, that went up to perhaps five particles per cubic centimeter—mostly stray hydrogen atoms, or the stray protons that made up much of the solar wind.

Here, in the vicinity of the debris belt, the local density was more like a hundred particles per cubic centimeter, mostly stellar-wind protons, but also a lot of dust—the result of the steady erosion of the Dyson fragments. But his fighter's sensors had just recorded a jump in the density of the interplanetary medium up to nearly a million ppcm^3.

That still qualified as hard vacuum, of course. At sea level on Earth, the density of the atmosphere averaged 10^{19} molecules per cm^3, some 10 trillion times thicker than this.

But this stuff was thick enough for friction to heat the outer hull of his Starblade, and he felt a shudder as he moved through it.

The cloud or mass, or whatever the hell it was, was still visible ahead. Evidently, it had no well-defined edges, but existed within an amorphous and invisible envelope that grew gradually denser—and more visible—the deeper you traveled into the thing. The main body of the thing could feel him, though. He could see ripples moving back through the filmy shape ahead, ripples originating with him as his Starblade penetrated the shifting, transparent mass.

"Don, is that thing *alive*?" DeHaviland asked. Her Starblade was a thousand kilometers behind his, and coming up fast.

"I'm not sure. I think so, yeah."

"We're reading a hell of a high magnetic flux in there," Mackey said. "I don't know what's powering it, but it's putting out a field of between two thousand and five thousand gauss."

It threw a rock at him.

An alarm sounded in Gregory's head. The boulder the cloud had been attached to had suddenly been propelled directly toward his spacecraft, moving at well over 100 kilometers per second, fast enough that even the tenuous cloud of near-vacuum heated it white-hot. He wrenched the Starblade hard to port, rolling sharply, and accelerated. The oncoming rock swerved, manipulated by the magnetic field within the creature, and he twisted to port again.

The rock, longer than his Starblade, tumbled past, bits of white-hot debris dropping off in its train. As Gregory boosted harder, his fighter emerged from the invisible envelope, his velocity increasing as he hit open space.

"Damn it to hell!" he shouted. "That thing just took a shot at me!"

"Watch out, Don!" DeHaviland warned. "It's closing on you!"

The transparent mass was accelerating, moving directly toward him. Gregory adjusted his course to take him back toward the main body of fighters. He found he could outpace the cloud, but it was damned unnerving, having a transparent haze on his tail, deliberately trying to run him down.

"Demon One, Demon Four!" he called. "Request permission to fire!"

"Negative, Four! RTB, repeat, RTB!"

RTB—Return to base. "Copy that, One. On my way."

"Don! Watch to your six!"

Another white-glowing missile was hurtling out of the cloud behind him, moving much faster this time. "I see it!"

He rolled right . . . but slow, *too* slow. . . .

The missile shattered in a bright flash of light. Cyndi DeHaviland had speared it with a particle beam. Gravel clattered along the length of his Starblade, the impacts causing no damage.

"Thanks, Cyn."

"Don't mention it. Let's get back to the barn."

"Negative! We've got to stop that thing!" He hauled his Starblade into a broad, sweeping turn, chasing his own fast-flickering gravitational singularity. The creature, or whatever it was, had expanded, was looming across all of space dead ahead, as though reaching out to embrace him.

"Demon Four!" Mackey called. "What the fuck do you think you're doing?"

"We need to know what that thing is, Skipper!" he called back. "And it would be nice to know how to kill it!"

"ROE One, Gregory! ROE One!"

"ROE your fucking boat!" he snapped back . . . and his Starblade plunged into the faintly translucent haze. He thoughtclicked a pair of icons, arming two Krait missiles.

Gregory realized that he wasn't thinking clearly, that anger was taking over. He told himself that they couldn't lead that alien life form back to the carrier, but that thought was more justifying smokescreen than rational thought.

His fighter shuddered and bucked. What the hell?

"Don did something to it!" DeHaviland said. "I think he just gave it a kick in the ass!"

"What's it doing?" That was Bruce Caswell.

"It's *shrinking*!" Gerald Ruxton replied.

The diaphanous mass had been stretched out across an enormous volume of space, but now it seemed to be collapsing on itself. And as it did so, it began falling into the debris belt.

"Gregory!" Mackey snapped. "Break off and get the hell back here!"

Gregory hesitated, poised for an eternally long second at the thin, ragged edge of a precipice. Two kraits were armed and ready to boost.

"Don!" DeHaviland called. "Meg wouldn't want you to do it!"

The words blasted in out of nowhere, confusing, hurting, stirring memories that had no business in a fighter-pilot link. "What?"

"Break off, Don!"

"Break off, Demon Four! That's an order!"

"C-copy. *Damn it all to a flaming red hell*!

The alien, drifting in the general direction of Tabby's Star, vanished behind a tumbling chunk of debris. It had collapsed down to a grayish, smooth ovoid less than a kilometer across, so dense that it now was completely opaque.

Was that behavior evidence of high intelligence, of military tactics? Or simple animal cunning?

Either way, he'd had his fill. Gregory pivoted his Starblade about his drive singularity, killed his forward velocity, and began boosting back toward *America*. The anger receded . . . still there, but tempered now by reason. Damn, he'd never lost it like that before. . . .

ROE One was a set of standing orders encompassing all first contact scenarios. "ROE" stood for Rules Of Engagement, and they were designed to avoid unfortunate misunderstandings with sapient life forms, both those poorly understood and those never before encountered. Centuries ago, the term had evolved in military circles to impose diplomatic or political rules on soldiers . . . preventing them from firing first, and even in extreme and particularly stupid cases preventing them from carrying loaded weapons inside combat zones. Though warfare had been famously referred to by von Clausewitz as politics continued by other means, the two—politics and warfare—did not mix well at all.

ROE One, though, had a certain amount of sense to it. When human military or exploration vessels encountered a new species, they went into the contact situation with no idea of the motivation or psychology or even type of intelligence they were facing. Given that most star-faring species encountered by Humankind so far had been more technologically advanced, it was in the best interests of humans *not* to get into an accidental shooting exchange with aliens of unknown potential, origin, or capability.

And he had almost screwed that up.

Gregory took a long, shaky breath. "Okay. I'm coming in." Again, he arced his fighter around in a smooth one-eighty, picked out *America*'s nav beacon, and boosted for home.

He had the distinct and uncomfortable feeling that somewhere astern, that alien whatsis was watching him go.

VFA-190, Ghost Riders
Tabby's Star
1302 hours, TFT

Lieutenant Commander Caryl Zhang guided her Starblade across a seemingly infinite vista, a flat geometry that appeared to stretch away in every direction. She could not avoid the somewhat creepy feeling that she was being watched intently.

"Keep alert, Riders," she called. "This thing is spooking me."

"Copy that, Rider One," Lieutenant Brodowsky replied. "You think this is another Rosetter artifact?"

"I doubt it, Eight. Completely different technology. But that doesn't mean it's friendly, right?"

The Ghost Riders had been deployed starward to investigate the outer shell of objects suspended above Tabby's Star, beginning just outside the debris ring. From what they'd been able to see so far, after half an hour of flying over a black and endless panorama, the shell was big and it was silent. Repeated attempts to communicate with the thing had come up empty.

Maybe the Demons are having better luck, she thought. She hoped that was the case.

In fact, the Ghost Riders had detected five complete shells of statites surrounding Tabby's Star, with the inner one at about two AUs' distance from the star, just outside the debris ring, and the outer one at five and a half AUs, here. As *America*'s long-range scans had revealed, each shell was made up of some hundreds of millions of stationary satellites—forty- to fifty-kilometer teardrops suspended several thousand kilometers beneath enormous, circular light sails.

Those light sails were incredible—each three thousand kilometers across, the distance, near enough, between her birthplace in the State of South California and her current residence in New Chicago. What made them more incredible was how gossamer thin they were . . . no more than a few molecules thick. Those sails had some complex chemistry going on, though. They seemed to vary, depending on the angle from which you looked at them, from completely transparent to ebon-black. Clearly, they were absorbing a lot of starlight and converting it to energy; clearly, too, they were capturing the momentum of outbound photons and using the radiation pressure to keep the entire structure hovering in place above the star.

The sails out here were considerably larger than those on the inner shell, reflecting the difference in incident stellar radiation between two AUs and five.

Each sail was separated from its neighbors by gulfs of at least ninety thousand kilometers, so coverage of the star was nowhere near complete. A classic Dyson swarm, Zhang knew, was supposed to trap all of the incident radiation from the surrounded star, but the designers of this mega-engineering project clearly had had something else in mind.

No one yet knew what.

But even with so much distance between one sail and the next, the overall effect was of an infinitely long, flat plain. At this radius from the star, the outer sphere's surface showed no curvature at all that human eyes could detect. When you passed over the gulf between one sail and the next and looked down, you saw Tabby's Star clearly, with just a bit of haze. Overall, the concentric shells were obscuring perhaps twenty percent of the star's radiation output.

An icon flashed in Zhang's mind and she thoughtclicked it. Data streamed in from the *America*.

The star carrier *America* had closed in on the edge of the hazy sphere surrounding Tabby's Star, and was now about thirty light-minutes distant. Evidently, they'd received a report from another squadron—the Black Demons—and now were broadcasting an alert to all other fighters in the deployment. The Demons had encountered something large and mysterious at the edge of the debris belt three astronomical units below. Zhang scrolled through the information, absorbing it, and she felt incredulous.

A giant space amoeba? "Listen up, Riders," she called. "VFA-96 ran into something in the debris field. Have a look."

"What is that thing?" Lieutenant Carbonero asked.

"Damfino, Carb. But it looks alive and it looks mean. Everyone keep your optics peeled."

"Hey, Skipper?" That was Lieutenant Thor Taylor. "I've got something here . . ."

"What've you got?"

"Outbound . . . bearing one-five-niner, plus seven-one. Is that one of those amoeba things?"

Zhang pulled down the feed, watching through Taylor's

instrumentation. Whatever he was looking at was way, way out. He'd only spotted it because he'd told his fighter's AI to examine the entire sky for something along the lines of the translucent mass encountered by the Black Demons.

And well he did, because he'd spotted another translucent mass roughly between the brilliant gleam of Deneb and the pale glow of the North America Nebula. It was a long way out—a couple of hundred astronomical units. It was nearly invisible too, spread out thin and transparent against the black sky, though there was a hint of a tighter, denser core.

But it was definitely out there.

"Skipper! Rider Ten!" That was Lieutenant Stevens.

"Go ahead, Ten."

"I've got a bogie, range nine hundred thousand and dead ahead!"

"Let me see."

She shifted datastreams. Yes . . . there it was. The same sort of translucent creature or being, filmy and insubstantial and at least fifty thousand kilometers across. It appeared . . . yes, it was definitely attached to one of the light sails. In fact, it appeared to be feeding on it.

"I'm getting RF from the sail," Stevens told her. "I think it may be a call for help!"

"Record it! Ghost Riders! Let's boost closer and see what we've got!"

In her head, in the view of what was unfolding in the distance, the teardrop structure suspended beneath the light sail suddenly cut loose from its tether and began falling, slowly but relentlessly, toward its sun.

And the vast sail above crumpled as it was devoured by the titanic and gossamer leviathan out of space.

Chapter Twenty-one

TC/USNA CVS America
CIC
Tabby's Star
1435 hours, TFT

"So what is it?" Gray asked.

He floated in the ship's Combat Information Center with his department heads, some present physically, most there virtually, but all of them staring at a three-D image of the translucent entity at the edge of the Tabby's Star debris field. One of those present virtually was Dr. George Truitt, the head of *America*'s xenosophontology department. Truitt was . . . well, *difficult* was putting it mildly. In fact, he was often *very* difficult. At the moment, his image stood on the deck upright despite the zero-gravity, showing that he was linked in from his lab in one of the ship's rotating hab modules.

"Well . . . it's alive," Truitt said. "It's aware of its surroundings, it reacts to external stimuli, and in these scans it appears to be metabolizing a chemical energy source— rock."

"Obviously," Gray said, trying not to grit his teeth. "But is it intelligent?"

"Impossible to be certain," Truitt said. "I would say, however, that intelligence in an organism living in space would be most unlikely."

"Why unlikely, Doctor?" Gutierrez asked him.

"No language in the vacuum of space. No organs of manipulation. No social or cultural infrastructure. No means of recording history. No tools . . . if they can't demonstrate intelligence, how can you grant that they have it?"

"I think, Dr. Truitt," Commander Mallory, the ship's tactical officer, said, carefully, "that you're just not thinking weird enough."

Truitt huffed and turned to Gray. "I did *not* come here to be insulted, Admiral."

"I'm sure that that was not Commander Mallory's intent, Doctor." Truitt was brilliant, but he was also intolerant of what he perceived as the stupidity of others—hence difficult. As such, he required careful handling. Gray smiled and encouraged him to continue. "Please go on."

"Well . . . we have an interesting datum in the long-range images captured by the other fighter squadron." The freeze-frame image of the translucent mass attached to a small asteroid vanished, replaced by one of the images from out-system. The object or creature or whatever it was spanned an enormous breadth of empty space, possibly as much as several hundred thousand kilometers. "This organism obviously has attenuated itself, unfolding to present an enormous surface as a kind of organic light sail."

"A living light sail?"

"Precisely." His projected figure pointed into the image of the light-sail creature. "I would suggest that these organisms have originated either at the star Deneb—which we can see in the background behind this particular specimen—or in the North America Nebula, which we see over here. By thinning itself out to a gossamer wisp, it can accelerate on the radiation pressure of a star, especially a bright, hot star like Deneb. It may reach considerable velocities; I estimate ten to fifteen percent c."

"Deneb is just one hundred seventy-three light years

from here," the ship's chief navigator, Commander Victor Blakeslee, pointed out. "At that speed it would take it well over a thousand years to make the trip."

"Once it reaches cruising velocity, as it were," Truitt said, "it probably collapses itself into a small kernel, like we saw in the one hiding in the debris belt. Small, dense, possibly streamlined to avoid being slowed by interstellar dust and gas. We see it expanded here in this image as it unfurls itself to catch the radiation from Tabby's Star and decelerate."

"Doesn't that suggest a certain innate intelligence, Dr. Truitt?" Gray asked. "Navigating across almost two hundred light years just to feed . . ."

"I submit that we don't know enough to ascribe motivations to these creatures just yet, Admiral. I expect they would need to feed after a thousand-year fast. In fact, I suspect that these beings get energy from starlight and from incidental radiation. The feeding behavior we see would be a prelude to reproduction."

"Reproduction?" Captain Fletcher, the ship's CAG, said. "*That* doesn't sound good."

"Of course," Truitt said. "While we would need to sample one to be certain of its chemical makeup, we suspect that these creatures are essentially molecular dust clouds, masses of dust or gas consisting mostly of iron, silicon, carbon, and simple compounds like methane and water ices, all under the influence of a locally intense magnetic field."

Gray caught Gutierrez's eye and grinned. She rolled her eyes. Truitt was going into lecture mode, and there would be no stopping him.

"That field is . . ." Truitt continued, "knotted. The knotting is extremely complex, something like the solar magnetic field in the vicinity of the heliopause, and we don't yet understand how it works. I presume, however, that those fields let the organism keep and change its shape, and allow different volumes of the creature to communicate with one another, rather like nerve impulses in more traditional forms of life. When it, ah, consumes raw materials, like a small asteroid, or the carbon-silicon weave of one of those immense light sails, it's creating a store of raw material either for its own growth, or to create a new individual."

"Which makes this system perfect for them," Gray said. "A kind of smorgasbord."

"Seems a bit of a coincidence," Mallory said, thoughtful, "that several of them just happened to chance upon the large-scale structures in the Tabby's Star system. It's almost like they knew the things were here."

"A bigger coincidence is that we arrive in-system just when they do," Truitt pointed out. "They've probably been here for centuries, even millennia . . . and they might regularly travel back and forth between here and wherever they come from."

"Deneb?" Blakeslee asked.

"Possibly Deneb," Truitt said, nodding. "It's an extremely bright star—over fifty-four thousand times brighter than Sol. Lots of energy to jump-start an unusual biology like this one. Or possibly the North American Nebula. Lots of dust and masses of ionized hydrogen where these creatures could evolve."

"America," Gray said, smiling.

"I beg your pardon?"

"It's the North America Nebula, not American. Lots of people make that mistake."

Truitt grumbled something, but Gray couldn't catch the words. "Commander Blakeslee?" Gray added, changing the focus of the conversation quickly. "Tell us about that nebula."

The chief navigator gestured, and a new image came up, a pale smear of red light against the dark. "Well . . . we've never been there, sir. Humans, I mean. It's close—two hundred forty light years from here. About sixteen hundred light years from Sol. And it's big, over one hundred light years across, which makes it five times bigger than the Orion Nebula. Its name comes from an odd coincidence. . . ." He gestured, and the smear of light rotated 90 degrees. As it did so, it took on a different but strikingly familiar outline. "It actually looks like North America . . . see the Gulf of

Mexico there, and Florida? This over here to the right is the Penguin Nebula, but it's actually a part of the same gas cloud. This dark band in between the two absorbs the light on its way toward Earth and makes it look like two separate nebulae." The image rotated again, and became a single mass. "We don't see that from *this* side, of course."

"So . . . almost three hundred light years away," Gutierrez said. "If those blobs came from there, they would be traveling for three thousand years, near enough." She looked at Gray. "Why is it important to know where they came from?"

"I don't know that it is, Captain. But the more we know about what's happening—and what's happened—in this system, the better off we'll be. Did these giant amoeba-things destroy the Tabby's Star civilization? Or are they just grazing on the leftovers? If they're intelligent, can we talk to them? Would they be of help against the Rosetters?"

"There is another consideration as well," the voice of the Konstantin clone said.

"What's that?" Gray asked.

"We did record a signal from the light sail when the organism attacked it. Apparently, each sail pod is connected with those nearby through tight-beam masers—microwave lasers. As it fell, one of its transmitters momentarily pointed at the nearest Starblade fighter, which was able to record it."

"Have you been able to translate it?"

"Not as yet. However, we have been able to determine the aliens' computer protocols. In time, we may be able to insert intelligent software and initiate a conversation."

"Excellent. What do you need from us?"

"When we have an AI software penetrator ready I will need this ship moved alongside one of the sail pods," Konstantin replied. "Until then, I suggest that you try to determine the role these translucent creatures play in the Tabby's Star system."

"Well, we won't be traveling to Deneb to check them out," Gray said. "The trip there would take twelve days or so. The North America Nebula, eighteen. We just don't have the time."

"Then we will have to focus our attention on the light-sail pods," Konstantin said, "and on the giant life forms."

"What are we going to call those things, anyway?" Gutierez asked. "We can't just keep calling them 'giant life forms.'"

Gray chuckled. "Giant space amoeba . . . space whales . . . hell, I don't know."

"Feeders," Fletcher said. "Light-sail feeders."

"Is that because they feed on light sails, CAG?" Mallory asked. "Or because they are light sails that feed?"

"Yes," Fletcher said. Several in the CIC chuckled at that.

"Sounds better than 'space amoeba,'" Gray added. He was aware of several entertainment vids and interactives featuring enormous, single-celled space-going animals, and he'd always thought the idea was silly. The universe, however, kept coming up with the new, the strange, and sometimes the downright ridiculous.

"So what is our course of action, Admiral?" Gutierrez asked.

"The ship will approach one of the pods," he decided. "Not too close. A few thousand kilometers. I want to try to talk with whatever is inside there. A Starblade squadron will try to approach one of the feeders . . . the one that's in the outer system, decelerating. No rocks for it to throw. But again, not too close. Let's see if we can have a conversation."

"And if we can't?" Blakeslee said.

"Then we'll have to send in the Marines."

One way or another, Gray was determined to make contact.

TC/USNA CVS Lexington
Command Bridge
Kapteyn's Star System
1810 hours, TFT

"Welcome aboard, Commander," Captain Bigelow told her. "Enjoy your leave?"

"I . . . yes, sir." Taggart's voice was dead, revealing her emotional state. There was no way she could find the emotional strength to respond in kind to Bigelow's banter.

"We missed you, Commander," Bigelow told her. "Good to have you back."

Lexington's bridge showed its usual buzz and bustle . . . almost as though nothing had happened. Life, it seemed, went on. . . .

The massive Grand Unified Fleet had arrived in the Kapteyn's Star system five days earlier. Taggart, still on the ground on Heimdall, had thrilled to the emergence of the kilometer-long star carriers some twelve AUs out—the *Constitution*, the massive flagship *Declaration*, the swarms of lesser ships taking up stations in extended orbit around the sun. She'd hung on every telemetry intercept, every ship emergence report, watching for the *America*.

But her old ship never appeared, and excitement had turned first to dread . . . then to mourning. *America*, she learned from messages from the incoming ships, had jumped with them.

But she'd not emerged.

Ships were lost while under Alcubierre Drive sometimes. They folded their private universe about them, and then . . .

No one knew what happened. Since by definition a ship under drive was not within the normal universe but occupying a separate and artificial continuum, *metaspace*, there was no way to investigate a ship that went missing. Theoretically, when the power was shut down, the folded space reverted to normal and the ship *should* simply drop back into the realm of stars and planets and humans, but it was possible that the tightly knotted bubble of warped space just kept on going, traveling ultimately to the farthest reaches of the universe. And if only wreckage dropped back into normal space, well . . . in all the unholy emptiness of interstellar space, there was no way to find a pitiful few scraps of debris.

All that was theory, though. No star carrier had ever vanished while under Alcubierre Drive.

So Taggart mourned her old ship, mourned her former shipmates.

Most of all, she mourned her former lover.

Then *Lexington* had arrived at last from Thrymheim, taking up orbit around Heimdall, and Bigelow had requested that his first officer return to the ship.

Somehow, she'd managed to convince herself that her fling with Sandy Gray had just been biology—two lonely people and all of that virtual vidcrap people liked to download for entertainment. When *America* failed to show up at Kapteyn's Star, though, she realized that she'd been fooling herself, plain and simple. She'd had to force herself, step by step, to board the shuttle Bigelow sent down for her, force herself to navigate the zero-G passageways to the bridge, force herself to enter that high-tech arena and strap herself down in her old seat.

How the hell was she supposed to get through this? . . .

"You okay, Commander?" Carla Milton asked. She looked worried.

Yeah, everyone on the ship knew about her relationship with Sandy, so they'd all be tiptoeing around her now. Shit . . .

"I'm okay, Carla," she replied. "Thank you."

And, somehow, saying so *made* it so.

Well . . . after a fashion.

Marine CAP-1
Bifrost Space
2036 hours, TFT

Lieutenant Liam Davies let the gravity of giant Bifrost pull his Hornet fighter into a gentle curve, sweeping in above the glorious multihued gleam of the gas giant's colorful rings. The rest of the Grim Ripper squadron was spread out through space around him, making the same turn, following the rainbowlike bridge that had given the planet its name.

Davies appreciated the icy beauty of the rings as he

skimmed above them, but he was more concerned with the odd vision he'd had a week before.

The colonel had given him a swat about hallucinating . . . but he'd *known* what he'd seen, damn it—a gently undulating landscape cloaked in trees. The trees had been odd-looking, alien, with feathery branches rather than terrestrial leafy canopies, but still a far cry from the rock and ice of modern Heimdall. He'd seen the report posted by that Navy xeno specialist, Carter, about the virtual existence of a bunch of Pan-European fighter jocks trapped inside the global computer on Heimdall, and wasn't sure how to take that. Carter had seen stuff too, different stuff, and she'd talked with the electronic ghosts of those Confederation pilots.

He thought he'd been riding that same circuit, somehow, but maybe picking up a different channel. That was the only way he could figure it. The other Marines in his outfit had called him crazy, teasing him about his bucking for a section eight . . . or about how he needed some R&R with his alien buddies.

Fuck 'em. He knew what he'd seen. Or, rather, he *didn't* know what he'd seen, but he *knew* that he'd seen it. Maybe the Beyonders had given him a flash-look at the way their world had been a few hundred million years ago.

"Listen up, Marines," Captain Roberto Salinas called. He was the senior officer of Marine fighter attack squadron VMFA-46, the Grim Rippers. "We're going to try to get in real close to the Rosie heart today. Nothing too threatening, but we want them to take notice."

The AS-90 Hornets cleared the gas giant rings. Ahead, the eerie golden hues of the Rosetter constructs shifted and glowed. "Copy that, Skipper," Lieutenant Jimenez said. "Just close enough to make the bastards pissed."

They called the strategy "acclimation," a drawn-out process in which Confederation fighters and small ships—vessels like frigates and corvettes—kept approaching the central area of Rosette activity, each time moving closer. They kept their velocity to a minimum—a few tens of kilometers per second—and were careful not to demonstrate accelerations or movements that might be interpreted as threats. Partly, the probes were intended to precisely map Rosette structures and facilities, but primarily the expedition leaders wanted to get the Rosette entities used to the Confederation presence.

In the week since the Grand Unified Fleet had arrived, the Earth forces had lost five fighters and one corvette, the *Actaeon*. All had apparently run into small objects somehow anchored in seemingly empty space, and were not the result of deliberate hostile action.

At least, that was what Gordon and his cronies were insisting.

Davies wasn't so sure. If the Rosie bastards were as smart and as advanced and as all-seeing as people claimed they were, they would know exactly what the human ships were doing, where they were moving, and what they wanted.

The Rosies were simply ignoring the human ships, nothing more.

And the chances were good that they would continue ignoring them . . . at least until they became a nuisance.

"It's getting thick in here," Kim Reighley observed.

"Roger that," Davies replied, nudging his fighter to port to miss an anchored artifact. What *were* those things, anyway? "At least the obstacles are easy to spot."

They stood out on radar and lidar like beacons, each a little less than a meter across. Beacons—maybe that's what they were. Moving through a cloud of them was eerily like traversing a minefield. The things wouldn't explode . . . but they would not move, and a fighter could wrap itself around one of the things and be reduced to a spray of junk in an instant if a pilot wasn't careful.

"Hey, Skipper?" Reg Laughlin called. "How 'bout we arm up?"

"Negative," Salinas shot back. "This is an acclimation run, not combat."

"Yeah, but—"

"That's negative on the weapons, Laughlin!"

"Copy . . ."

He didn't sound happy about it.

Davies didn't blame him. He wondered who'd cooked up this misbegotten excuse for an op. Part of the problem was that it wasn't even clear who was actually running the show. With so many politic entities contributing, things were— well, *political*.

So was the fleet Confed or was it American? Davies was damned if he knew. That bit of politics probably wouldn't be worked out until it was time to hand out congratulations for a job well done . . . or blame for a royal screw-up.

And with these strategies, it was hard to think this wouldn't end up leaning toward the latter.

The Hornets were now plunging through a golden haze that grew swiftly thicker. Tiny pings and snaps sounded through the fighter's cockpit as Davies moved through a far-flung cloud of dust. His sensors were reading powerful magnetic fields, twisting and knotting out from some central, invisible source, and the dust seemed to be riding those fields like iron filings around a child's magnet.

"Outer hull is abrading," his fighter's AI told him. "Hull temperature at three-five-five degrees Celsius. Self-repair under way."

The Hornet wasn't in the same technological *wunderkind* class as the Navy's Starblades. Other than shifting its wing angle for atmospheric flight, it couldn't morph into different shapes, and retained its blunt, delta-dart hull design no matter what it was doing. It was designed, after all, as a Marine low-altitude close-support fighter, and didn't need the fancy bells and whistles of Navy deep-space fighters. It did have an outer hull nanomatrix, however, which could repair minor holes and pocks in a situation like this.

"I'm reading something up ahead," Reighley said. "Something big."

"That's new," Salinas said. "Okay, Rips. Come to three-two-seven by one-three. Nice and easy, now, all together . . ."

The haze grew thicker, the impact sounds thickening to what sounded like heavy rain on a tin roof. Davies could feel his ship shuddering under the barrage.

"Reduce velocity," Salinas ordered. "Bring it down to five kps."

"This crap is too thick," Laughlin complained. "I can't read through it."

"I'm getting something on long IR," Davies reported. "Looks like . . . maybe a planet?"

"There aren't any planets out here," Salinas said. "Just Bifrost, and that's behind us."

"No . . . take a look. It's round . . . diameter about forty-eight hundred kilometers . . . it's *hot* . . ."

"It can't be!"

"Liam's right," Reighley said. "I've got it too. Range twenty-eight thousand and closing."

And very, very slowly, the haze cleared, revealing the Rosette ship—a dark sphere the size of a small planet.

TC/USNA CVS Lexington
Command Bridge
2130 hours, TFT

"We believe that this is the center of Rosetter activity in this system," the in-head image of Admiral Gordon said, addressing the virtual assembly of ship's officers. "Our operation will focus on getting as close as possible to this object, with the goal of forcing them to talk with us."

Suspended in the mind's eye of each person there was a dull, dark gray sphere, obviously massive, obviously artificial. It floated embedded in golden aurorae, serene and utterly remote from the affairs of humans. Taggart watched the unfolding panorama with something like awe . . . and an undercurrent of fear.

"We have the Marine officers and crew of VMFA-46 to thank for these images," Gordon added. "Off the *Lucas*. They've been operating off Heimdall for over a week, now, probing the alien presence in this system. But they picked up these images about an hour ago."

"Does that mean this thing has just now moved into

the system?" Captain Mitterlehner of the monitor *Festung* asked.

"Presumably," Gordon replied. "That, or it has only now moved in close to Bifrost. The sphere is just over forty-eight hundred kilometers wide, which makes it roughly the same diameter as Mercury. It appears to be mobile—not a static or orbital installation, but a ship. A very *large* ship. It also appears to be at the heart of these energy displays and intense magnetic fields. We believe that, at the very least, it may be serving as a command center for Rosette entity operations in the system."

Taggart continued staring at the computer-generated image in her mind. A ship the size of a planet. Somehow, though, she felt vaguely disappointed. She'd been thinking of the Rosette entities as Stargods—her religion of younger days returning with superhuman force—but the thought of them traveling in a huge, blank sphere, a cosmic billiard ball, seemed . . . anticlimactic, somehow.

And the more she thought about it, really examining her beliefs, the more the religious awe she'd felt since first drifting into the AAC faded. If these were the Stargods, they were distant and impersonal beings, beings so far above and beyond the reach of Humankind that any kind of a genuine, personal relationship was utterly impossible.

They weren't gods. God*like*, perhaps . . . but not gods.

Even so, the fear she felt remained . . . and grew. . . .

"Designate that thing 'Romeo' for 'Rosetter,'" Captain Bigelow said. "Romeo One."

"Aye, aye, Captain," Taggart replied.

"I'm intrigued that the fighters got this close," Bigelow added, "and didn't generate a hostile response."

"Indeed," Gordon said. "On the other hand, they didn't generate a friendly or communicative response, either. The fighters came to within five thousand kilometers of the sphere, but they were ignored."

"As usual," Captain Pemberton of the *Constitution* put in. "They just don't find us interesting."

"The important thing, my friend," Captain Michel Hollande of the heavy cruiser *Vulcain* said, "is that they don't find us *tasty.*"

"Pray that they don't, ladies and gentlemen," Gordon said. "Because tomorrow we're going to begin shifting elements of the fleet toward this object, a little closer each time. We will *force* them to take an interest, whether they want to or not."

"God help us all," Bigelow said. "As one God to another, you understand."

No one laughed.

Chapter Twenty-two

TC/USNA CVS Lexington
Bridge
Kapteyn's Star
1135 hours, TFT

"Captain! Romeo One is moving! *Fast*!"

"I see it, Tag," Bigelow replied. "All stations to general quarters."

The Grand Unified Fleet had been maneuvering within Bifrost space for more than twenty-four hours now, getting as close as they dared to the Rosetter structures and fields of shifting light, but without any reaction whatsoever from the enigmatic aliens. An hour earlier, the Chinese carriers *Guangdong* and *Jiangsu*, plus the North Indian light carrier *Shiva* and a number of escort vessels had accelerated sharply toward the alien object now code-named Romeo One.

Now, as they closed to within a thousand kilometers of the artificial world, that world at last responded, rapidly closing the gap between itself and the Earth forces. Had they crossed an unseen line in space? Or had the alien presence simply tired of the game? A beam of antiprotons had snapped out from Romeo and punched through the *Jiangsu*'s shield cap, lighting up the sky with a flash of hard radiation.

The Chinese carrier, crippled, began a slow tumble in a widening spiral of ice crystals as water erupted from its shield-cap reservoir and froze as it hit hard vacuum.

An instant later, a giant, invisible hand seemed to grasp *Shiva* around her midsection, closing on her, crumpling her hull. Atmosphere exploded into space and froze as debris and wreckage and bodies spilled from the smashed vessel. The hull continued crumpling and compacting, collapsing into a gravitational singularity somewhere in the bowels of the vessel.

Guangdong had already swung around her own projected singularity and was reversing course . . . but you don't stop a 100,000-ton starship in an instant. A North Indian destroyer exploded at the touch of the antiproton beam.

"C'mon . . ." Bigelow muttered out loud. "Order them the hell out of there!"

Gordon's orders came over the Net a moment later. "All ships! All ships! Fall back to cis-Heimdall space!"

"It's my duty to remind the Captain," Taggart said quietly, "that we are currently operating under standard Rules of Engagement. Permission to target Romeo One."

"Yes . . . yes," Bigelow said. "Lock on with everything we have. CAG! Get the rest of our fighters out there!"

"Aye, aye, sir," the voice of *Lexington*'s CAG, Captain Tom Walters, replied. "Launching the Ready-fives."

Three squadrons were already outside on combat space patrol. It would take time for the remaining three squadrons—on "Ready five," meaning they could launch on five minutes' notice—to become spaceborne.

"Deploy the fighters on CSP to screen the other ships," Bigelow ordered. "Weapons are free; repeat: *weapons free!*"

Lexington opened up with her main particle-beam batteries, sending bolts of charged particles slamming into the oncoming planet. The surface of that mobile world, Taggart saw, was manifestly artificial, a smooth, dark surface marked by straight lines and regular geometries.

And *Lexington*'s beams seemed to sink into that surface without effect.

Taggart watched the battle unfolding on the bridge

screens. She could have streamed it through her in-head circuitry as a virtual display, but she needed to be aware of her surroundings, not lost in a completely immersive reality. She was concerned about the launch of fighters. If the fleet was forced to withdraw, there might not be time to retrieve the fighters beforehand. That meant a rendezvous out-system somewhere . . . if the Rosetters even gave them the luxury of time.

"Miles?" she called to *Lexington*'s weapons officer, Commander Miles Conrad. "Can you boost power to those beams at all?"

"We're at max now, Commander," Conrad replied. "I don't think we're even singeing them!"

A USNA destroyer, the *Horace*, crumpled and vanished. Somehow, the aliens were projecting gravitational point-sources across thousands of kilometers, creating massive black holes deep inside the target vessels. Taggart had never seen combat of that sort before. In space battles, the destruction of a starship often released the microsingularities they carried in their power plants or, more rarely, their drive singularities destabilized and went wild. In either case, ships could be torn to bits by minute black holes slamming through their interior structures, and the loose black holes could devour entire ships.

That seemed to be what was happening here, but far more quickly and on a bigger, more terrifying scale. Somehow, Romeo One was reaching out across thousands of kilometers of space, throwing a switch, and twisting the spacetime within the heart of the target vessel, as though squeezing it within an enormous, invisible fist. The ship's internal structure crunched down into an ultra-dense core, which then winked out inside an artificially generated black hole of roughly jovian mass. They were manipulating the fabric of space directly, Taggart knew . . . but, then, that should not have been surprising, not with the way they manipulated space and time to create their enigmatic structures of dust motes and light.

Stargods. Or technologies that made it seem that way.

How the hell were mere humans supposed to face something like that?

The heavy cruiser *Juneau* crumpled, dwindled, and vanished.

"All fighters!" Admiral Gordon was yelling over the tactical net. "Use your missiles! Max meg! Max meg!"

Krait missiles had variable-yield warheads that could be dialed up to two hundred megatons. Against something the size of a planet those would count for exactly nothing.

Taggart increased the magnification of the optical scanners tracking Romeo One.

"I'm picking up oddly pulsed EM currents inside the structure," she reported.

"Mass density readings suggest that it's solid," Lieutenant Ramos, the sensor officer of the watch, added. "It's got nearly the mass of Earth packed into a sphere a third the size."

"It may be pure computronium," Lieutenant Commander Matchett added. He was *Lexington*'s chief IT officer, in charge of the ship's computer network. "My God, it might be one big super-AI. . . ."

"Anyone see any weak spots?" Ramos asked.

"How does something the size of a planet have a *weak* spot?" Taggart demanded. How much energy, she wondered, would it take to destroy an entire planet? She ran some figures through her in-head processors, calculating the gravitational binding energy of an Earth-sized mass. The energy required, she saw, would be on the order of 1.25×10^{32} joules—125 million trillion trillion joules . . . roughly as much energy as Sol put out over the course of four days focused into a single second.

It would take a fleet of billions of ships all firing together to generate that kind of power, or a fusillade of 3 million billion 200-megaton warheads. There was, to state it with an elegant simplicity, no fucking way they were going to take this thing out.

"This is beginning to look like a *really* bad idea," Taggart said aloud.

The fighters were loosing all of their Krait smart missiles now, and specks of light began to wink on and off across the alien planet's surface like twinkling stars.

"All ships!" Admiral Gordon called over the command net. "All ships! Fall back and—"

But the final part of the order was never transmitted. On the tactical screens, the star carrier *Declaration* jerked suddenly to one side, twisted, then crumpled as unimaginable energies collapsed her internal structure into a pinpoint vortex of gravitational fury. The carrier's forward section— the half-kilometer-wide shield cap and a small part of her spine, as far back as her bridge tower and hab modules— escaped, tumbling away from the collapsing mass of her supply, drive, and power modules.

"What ships are closest to the *Declaration*?" Bigelow snapped.

"*Decatur*, sir," Commander Eric Gower, *Lexington*'s tactical officer, reported. "And the North Indian *Vagsheer*."

"Have them see if they can assist the *Declaration*. There could be survivors. . . ."

But the *Decatur* was already in trouble. A kilometer-long cruiser built around a massive railgun used for planetary bombardment, she was slamming round after high-velocity round into the oncoming planet, but without any obvious effect. A particle beam snapped out from Romeo One and seemed to graze the railgun cruiser. Bits and pieces of debris floated clear, and the ship began drifting to one side, propelled by the rocket-thrust blast of internal atmosphere and molten metal leaking into space.

Vagsheer was a heavy cruiser, over four hundred meters long and massing nearly eighty thousand tons. She was already maneuvering, positioning herself between the oncoming artificial planet and the ruin of the stricken *Declaration*.

An eighty-thousand-ton cruiser squaring off against a six-sextillion-ton artificial planet . . .

Taggart didn't want to watch . . . and yet she *had* to watch, she couldn't look away, and she was transfixed by the growing horror of what was happening. The *Vagsheer* turned broadside to the planet, firing every weapon in its arsenal, including the new 1,000-megaton VG-210 Cobra planetary bombardment missiles colloquially known as planet busters. The name was proving to be more propaganda than meaningful; brilliant flashes sparked and sparkled across Romeo One's surface, but there simply weren't enough warheads to do the object any serious damage.

Taggart was doing some fast calculations in her head. Romeo One had a surface area of something just over 46 million square kilometers—about the same as the planet Mercury. The VG-210 could turn a five-thousand-square kilometer patch of desert sand into solid glass. Conservatively, that meant that it would take more than nine thousand missiles to completely fuse Romeo One's entire outer surface into lava, presumably rendering it dead.

The USNA had . . . what? Maybe five hundred Cobras in its entire weapons inventory? And she doubted that the Pan-Europeans or the Russians or the North Indians had that many more; there really wasn't that much of a call for those things.

But the *Vagsheer* was certainly giving it a try. Maybe if enough nuclear warheads detonated against the object's surface, enough of the surface structure could be disrupted to do some damage. The French heavy cruiser *Agosta* must have had the same idea, she was moving in closer, adding her barrage to the *Vagsheer*'s.

But after a moment, Taggart saw that the cruiser's missile barrage wasn't even reaching the artificial planet's surface. That argued that the Cobra warheads were hurting the enemy . . . but only enough to make it shift defensive tactics. All missiles had stopped sparkling and twinkling against that dark gray surface. Now, the surface appeared to blur, to go out of focus, somehow, and the visible explosions had stopped.

"The target appears to be using gravitic shielding," she reported.

"Confirmed," Conrad added. "The power reading for that thing is off the scale. . . ."

Shielding—and very powerful shielding—was absolutely vital for starship operations, even apart from combat. Ships inevitably collided with bits of sand-grain debris or atomic particles while moving through the not-quite-perfect vacuum of space, and if those impacts occurred at close enough to the speed of light, they could carry the kinetic punch of a small nuclear weapon. Ships used magnetic shielding to divert charged particles, but they needed something more robust to shunt aside bits of ice or iron massing a fraction of a gram or so, and they also needed a way to deflect non-charged energies, like incoming laser beams. The answer was a form of gravitic projection across the entire outer surface of the vessel, a system akin to the space-bending Alcubierre Drive that permitted FTL velocities. By very slightly warping space around the ship, large incoming particles or missiles could be completely disrupted, and incoming radiation could be twisted away. The blurring of the object was the result of light being bent by the gravitic field.

The missiles being launched from the *Vagsheer* appeared to be falling into emptiness and vanishing entirely now. Parts of the gravitic field were flashing black or silver in quick, uneven bursts as the defensive screens briefly increased their power in discrete areas, completely disrupting incoming light as well as weaponry.

"They're using the grav field for propulsion," Gower reported.

"A true space drive," Bigelow said, agreeing. "Can we use that?"

"Damned if I see how . . ."

On their screens, the *Vagsheer* flared in a particle beam and vanished in an expanding, sparkling cloud of debris and frozen water and atmosphere. Seconds later, the *Agosta* crumpled and vanished.

And then the hurtling artificial world reached the drifting wreckage of the *Declaration*, which vanished a few hundred kilometers above the object's surface.

"Who's next in line for command of the fleet?" Bigelow asked.

"That would be Admiral Villeroy of the *Agosta*, sir," Taggart told him. Then she realized that the *Agosta* had already been annihilated. "She's gone. I think you're next in line, Admiral."

"All ships!" Bigelow called. "Retreat! Break off and retreat! CAG! Cease fighter launches immediately. Order fighters already in space to break off and rendezvous at Point Red Star Alfa!"

"Roger that, Admiral."

The fleet was already dissolving from an orderly array into separate elements, streaming away from the vast, menacing black mass of Romeo. As the fleet scattered, however, the entire outer surface of Romeo appeared to expand . . . then to explode in a vast and swirling black cloud.

"What the hell is happening there?" Bigelow demanded.

"The outer surface . . ." Gower began. He stopped, confused, trying to understand what he was seeing. "Sir! The outer surface of that thing may be a nanobot swarm!"

The fragments of surface kept expanding outward, becoming finer and ever finer as the pieces continued to break into smaller and smaller particles. Directed through Romeo's undiminished magnetic field, they began swarming toward the nearest retreating human starships and fighters. Taggart watched with growing alarm. If those fragments were individually programmed, individually directed and flown . . .

Yeah. This could be a weapon far vaster, far more potent than the Confederation nano-D warhead that had vaporized central Columbus a year ago.

The cloud caught up with a fleeing Starblade. The fighter twisted and rolled, trying to evade the relentless pursuit . . . but its hull began to unravel, with fragments flickering off and disintegrating into dust.

"Fire into that cloud!" Bigelow ordered. "Maximum dispersion! Give our people some cover!"

Lexington opened up with all of her lasers and particle-beam weapons, sweeping through the fast-expanding black cloud. The particles and fragments vanished at each beam's touch, but there were simply too many of them for the tactic to be even marginally effective. Three more Starblades disintegrated under that onslaught. The destroyer *Harriman*, moving in close to provide cover for the fleeing Earth vessels, got too close and began to dissolve as the death cloud swept past her. The ship twisted away, accelerating, but the cloud pursued it and it was already too late. In seconds, the three-hundred-meter destroyer crumbled away into tumbling fragments.

Other ships were firing into the cloud now as well, adding their firepower to *Lexington*'s. Taipan and Cobra missiles streaked in from a dozen ships, detonating in great, silent flashes of light. The fireballs expanded through the cloud, eating away at its substance . . . but still the cloud spread out through space, engulfing fleeing warships and fighters and devouring them.

The fleet pressed the attack. Taggart reflected that at least it *felt* like they were doing something, though the gesture was as empty as had been attacking the mobile planet directly. The cloud already measured trillions of cubic kilometers and was still expanding. The combined firepower of the entire fleet could do no more than inflict pinpricks against something that vast.

And deep within that growing cloud, the artificial planet continued moving forward, implacable, irresistible, unstoppable.

"Captain!" Commander Gower warned. "The *Guangdong*!"

The Chinese heavy star carrier had begun accelerating out from the cloud, picking up velocity at a prodigious rate . . . but the outermost fringes of the death cloud were closing on her.

"Helm!" Bigelow ordered. "Get us in closer to the Hegemony carrier!"

"Aye, aye, sir!" Lieutenant Andrej Nemecek replied. His hands were gripping the arms of his chair with fanatical, white-knuckled strength, maintaining the physical contact with the link feed surfaces and the exposed circuitry on the palms of both hands. Like most shipboard command actions, steering the ship was done in-head, but the stress was showing now in a sheer, physical intensity.

Ponderously, *Lexington* edged closer to the Chinese warship, now only eight thousand kilometers away. The *Guangdong* was of a more modern star-carrier design than the *Lex*, with a blunt shield cap more like the *Marne*'s than the *Lexington*'s older mushroom-cap structure, with fluted, organic-looking folds flaring back and around to embrace forward-facing launch bays. Reportedly, the *Guangdong* could launch fighters three times faster than the older USNA star carriers, and the streamlining allowed her to project a more powerful gravitic singularity that gave her greater speed. The Chinese carrier's sleek lines were not helping her now, however. Fast she might be, but the death cloud was rapidly overtaking her, eating away at her aft quarter with a relentless and terrifying hunger. "Weapons!" Bigelow yelled. "Put some warheads between the *Guangdong* and that cloud! Make 'em back off!"

"Aye, aye, sir!" Conrad said. "Readying salvo, six VK-210s . . . targeting, wide dispersion, full megs, and . . . *fire!*"

The powerful missiles slid from *Lexington*'s spinal mount two at a time, accelerating at fifty thousand gravities for the relatively short trajectory, skimming past the oncoming *Guangdong* and into the pursuing cloud. The first pair of explosions, utterly silent, were close enough and bright enough to wipe *Lexington*'s screen feeds completely, and as they cleared, another pair of 200-megaton blasts flared, dazzled, expanded, faded. . . .

Captain Yuan Jiechi's lined and haggard face appeared in the minds of *Lexington*'s bridge crew. "Thank you, Bigelow," Yuan said, terse. "I think we're clear now."

The final two nuclear detonations flashed, grew huge, and died. An instant later, the *Guangdong* flashed past *Lexington*, still accelerating. "Don't mention it, Yuan," Bigelow replied. "We're coming about now. We'll pace you as you come out."

"Affirmative, *Lexington*. But watch for the planet! It's still back there, and coming fast!"

Taggart saw the artificial planet, following the fleeing human vessels, moving now at hundreds of kilometers per second and bringing much of the death cloud with it like vast, outstretched wings of night.

Guangdong was traveling directly away from the mobile planet at high speed, but *Lexington* had moved past the Chinese carrier and *toward* the planet, a decidedly unfortunate vector. "Mr. Nemecek," Bigelow said. "Reverse the helm, please. *Now.*"

The helm officer nodded. "Aye, sir. Coming about . . ."

The ponderous length of the star carrier, almost a kilometer long, pivoted sharply around the invisible flicker of its forward-projected drive singularity, and then Nemecek began feeding unimaginable power to that artificial black hole, killing *Lexington*'s forward momentum, slowing the carrier to a trembling halt . . . then beginning to build up her velocity once again. Conrad loosed another salvo of missiles toward Romeo One, then swore bitterly as the Cobra missiles winked out well before they could hit the dark world's surface.

"Maximum acceleration!" Bigelow yelled. "*Goose* it!"

Second by second, the star carrier accelerated. "Nano-D is hitting the aft spinal assembly," Gower reported, his mental voice maddeningly calm.

We're going to die, Taggart thought.

Readouts in Taggart's head showed increasing damage aft. Particles as fine as those in a cloud of smoke were taking apart the outer skin of the *Lexington*'s drive assembly literally atom by atom.

"Increase the metric of our shields," Bigelow shouted. By increasing the warp to the metric of space around the ship's hull, it might be possible to hold off the attack.

"Aye, aye, sir!" Gower snapped back. "Increasing shielding metric up to five point oh!"

"Captain," Taggart said. "We should try to get a sample of this stuff!"

"You want to go outside with a bottle?"

"No, sir. But the fighters might help."

Bigelow considered this for a moment. "Okay. CAG?"

"Yes, Captain."

"Tell one of the squadrons out there we need a sample of that cloud. If they can get it without being eaten."

"Aye, aye, sir."

The alien technology, Taggart thought, was far too advanced for them to have a chance at beating it one-on-one. But maybe . . . if they *understood* it. . . .

In any case, it was all they had right now.

VMFA-46, Grim Rippers
Bifrost Space
Kapteyn's Star
1151 hours, TFT

"They want us to *what*?"

"They want us to snag a sample of that nano-D!" Salinas replied. "Reighley! You're in a good position. . . ."

"I've got it, Skipper," Lieutenant Davies called. Banking right, the Marine closed on the cloud trailing out behind the *Lexington*.

The carrier was badly mauled. Large chunks of her primary drive assemblies had already been eaten away, to the point that Davies wondered if she would be able to transition over to Alcubierre Drive. The drive units were responsible for focusing the gravitic energy into the tiny knot of on-and-off singularity forward of the shield cap. If the drive primaries were damaged, *Lexington* would be stuck here in the Kapteyn's Star system . . . and it was damned clear that they were *not* welcome here.

"Watch yourself, Davies!" Salinas called. "Don't get into the thick part of the cloud!"

"Copy." Davies was fiercely focused on juggling his Hornet's drive, killing its velocity toward the wounded star carrier, accelerating on a different vector to bring him alongside. "Let the Lex know I'm doing a flyby, will you? I don't want them to mistake me for a hostile!"

"Roger that. They know."

Closer now. He was trying to stay clear of the tendrils of fog that from this vantage point had taken on the character and feel of a living thing, a beast reaching out with filamentous tentacles in an attempt to snag the *Lexington* and drag her down, but he would need to dip into part of the cloud briefly to get his sample. Quickly, he explained what he wanted to do to the fighter's AI and felt . . . puzzlement in response, as though the fighter's programming wasn't sure what he was trying to do. Part of the problem was that the Hornet's outer skin wasn't designed for elaborate instructions. It had minimal morphing capabilities, could change color, could deal with incoming radiation and low-level kinetic threats, but Davies was trying to get it to do something it had never been programmed for . . . and something the AS-90's onboard computer had never had to deal with.

Patiently, he tried again. At first, he was trying to get the computer to program the fighter's outer skin to form a small bottle or box attached to the hull, something that could scoop up the alien particles and keep them sequestered until he got back to Heimdall. Now, however, he tried to convey to the rather limited AI that he wanted the outer surface of the fighter to turn sticky . . . that when it began striking small particles of alien technology, he wanted those particles to *stick*, allowing him to take them home.

He'd heard of this sort of thing being done before. Centuries ago, in the early days of space exploration, a spacecraft called Stardust had used a surface covered with aerogel, a porous, silicon-based substance that trapped incoming particles of cometary material and interstellar dust, holding them safely until they could be returned to Earth for analyses. Davies tried picturing the Stardust spacecraft in his mind, showing the computer the tray filled with aerogel capturing the fast-moving particles of dust.

At last, he felt the AI's comprehension. At least he *hoped* it understood; if he was going to put his life on the line to grab some alien nano-D, he sure as hell wanted something to show for it if he made it back out of the cloud.

Accelerating now, he skimmed low over the aft quarter of the *Lexington*, punching through the thickening cloud and hearing a rapid-fire staccato beat of clicks and pings. In an instant, he'd flashed forward up the carrier's length, passing the rotating hab modules and bridge tower before swinging wide to avoid the dull black mass of the ship's shield cap.

"Ahoy, Hornet off our forward port quarter," a new voice said in his mind. "This is *Lexington* PriFly. Nicely done! Bring your fighter around and dock in Landing Bay One. They want to see what you picked up out there right away."

"Copy, *Lex*. Coming around for a trap."

"Affirmative. We're cutting acceleration."

"Roger that." Damn. *Lexington* was going to have to kill her forward acceleration long enough for him to trap in one of the rotating modules . . . which meant those particles would have a chance to swarm over the whole carrier. Could the *Lex* take it? And that pocket-sized planet was still coming up fast astern, and *that* wasn't good at all.

What, he wondered, was so all-fired important about alien ship-eating shit?

TC/USNA CVS Lexington
Bridge
Kapteyn's Star
1210 hours, TFT

"The fighter is on board, Captain," *Lexington*'s CAG reported.

"Good! Full acceleration, Helm!"

"Resuming full acceleration, aye, aye, sir."

Taggart felt the shudder as the ship came under direct attack. The gravitic shields were holding the worst of the alien attack at bay, but the ship was still taking terrible damage.

And worse, *far* worse, Romeo One was closing now to within a few thousand kilometers. *Lexington* had been pulling away, but slowing to take the fighter on board had let the thing catch up.

"I hope your samples are worth it, Laurie," Bigelow told her.

"So do I, sir. I can't see how we're going to possibly beat these guys without it, though. We're going to need to sample the Rosetter's OS and see how it works. The IS people might be able to tease out the equivalent of a pass code. . . ."

"Captain!" Gower shouted, interrupting. "Romeo One is firing!"

A beam of energy made incandescent by the cloud particles outside seared past the *Lexington*'s spine, puncturing the underside of her shield cap in a flash of white light and an explosion of water simultaneously boiling and freezing into sand-grain-sized flecks of ice. The beam was only on for an instant, but as the *Lexington* moved forward, the beam slid sideways, carving through hull metal. There was a savage shock, the drive failed, and the *Lexington* went into an end-for-end tumble, bits and pieces of wreckage and internal structure trailing off into space.

The bridge went dark, every light and control dead.

Taggart was slammed into her instrument console and the darkness became complete.

Chapter Twenty-three

TC/USNA CVS America
Admiral's Office
Tabby's Star
0915 hours, TFT

"I don't understand what I'm seeing," Gray said. "What are these . . . beings?"

"They are what you've been calling the Builders," Konstantin told him. "They represent an extremely advanced species. More important, they are the creators both of the failed Dyson sphere and the outer Matrioshka brain. We may be able to question them, though they are not materially present any longer."

"No? What happened to them?"

"They ascended. Their name for themselves might be roughly translated as the 'Ascended Ones.'"

Obviously, that wasn't their name for themselves, but it carried the same idea. Gray had the sense that there was a deeply religious feeling behind the term, like "raptured" would have for a fundamentalist Christian, or "enlightened one" for a Buddhist. Neither was what Gray was seeing in his mind as what the original Tabby's Star natives actually looked like. They appeared to be a machine intelligence—upright, silver-gray ovoids made of plastic with glittering lenses set randomly around the body. The backdrop for the meeting with the Tabby's Star natives was taking place in a computer-generated room of some sort, all gleaming metal and plastic surfaces, clean lines, and geometric figures.

It all started when, hours earlier, *America* had gentled in to within a few thousand kilometers of the nearest light sail, and dispatched a robotic probe, a smart torpedo that had attached itself to the exterior of the structure dangling on its cable far below the gossamer canopy above.

Through that probe, Konstantin had been able to tap into the Ascended Ones' Matrioshka intelligence, a vast distributed network occupying hundreds of billions of light-sail supported nodes, an artificial intellect of staggering power. *A holographic brain.*

The term referred to terrestrial holography, where data was stored in the interference patterns between two reflected laser beams projected onto film. That film could be cut into pieces, and yet every single piece could reproduce the same original image when a laser was shined through it. The smaller the piece, the fuzzier and less defined the image . . . but every fragment held all of the original pattern. Human brains worked the same way; memories were distributed over a branching network of neural dentrites, but holographically, so that each piece of the network contained the entire memory.

The Matrioshka brain surrounding Tabby's Star appeared to work in the same way, with each discrete light-sail statite containing the entire system within its computronium heart. With trillions of statites, a single light sail would hold only a thin shadow of the whole, but it meant that Konstantin could communicate with that whole by linking up with one.

Konstantin was still learning how to communicate with the intelligence, but had made a lot of progress in the past few hours. The two had been carrying on an extended conversation in the virtual reality resident within the Matrioshka brain.

It helped, evidently, that the alien brain was almost

inconceivably smart. It was aware of *America*, aware of *America*'s efforts against the filmy, light-sail creatures, and it *wanted* to talk.

As for Gray, with his limited and merely human intellect, he was just along for the ride. Though strapped into a couch in his shipboard office, his mind moved through a rich and ever-shifting virtual reality, one moderated by the Konstantin clone, but which was being created by the alien AI.

"I don't know," Gray told Konstantin. "'Ascended Ones' seems just a bit pretentious."

"I have taken the liberty of suggesting new names," Konstantin replied, "names with less emotional baggage for humans. I call them *Satori*."

"Okay. And that means?"

"It is a Japanese word for a Buddhist term. It means 'awakening,' 'understanding,' or 'comprehension.' It is the ultimate goal of a practicing Buddhist to reject desire or other human weaknesses and achieve satori."

"And you think these beings have done that?"

"I make no judgments," Konstantin replied. "And I certainly cannot address purely religious concepts in use by humans. It simply seems a useful term."

"I agree. They're machines, these Satori?"

"It seems likely," Konstantin told Gray, "that the Satori originally evolved as purely organic beings. I have not yet been able to establish a temporal frame of reference, but I suspect that the Satori were organic beings some millions of years ago. Like a number of the sapient species of the N'gai Cloud, they over a great deal of time developed artificial bodies for their organic brains, then, over a very much longer space of time, evolved beyond the need for any organic structure at all."

Gray nodded understanding. He'd seen much of that story before this, downloaded from researchers studying the N'gai civilization. Three species in particular, he knew, had specialized in robotics and ultimately had transformed themselves into cybernetic life-forms—the Adjugredudhra, the Groth Hoj, and the Baondyeddi. Over the course of eons, all three species had developed robotic bodies of metal and plastic, eventually transferring their consciousness to machines.

"That seems to be a common theme for advanced technic life," Gray observed.

"It does. And it makes sense. Organic bodies are peculiarly unsuited for living and working in space, for long-period spaceflight, or for existence over periods measured in geological ages."

"Or for dealing with advanced AI?"

"There is that," Konstantin replied. "Cybernetic species are considerably faster, more flexible, and more reasonable than organic intelligences."

Gray started to make a rejoinder, then caught himself. He'd meant the statement about dealing with AIs as a joke, but Konstantin appeared to have taken it in a strictly literal manner.

Well, he'd walked into that one. He was never certain whether Konstantin understood humor or not.

Besides, from Konstantin's point of view, most humans nowadays *were* cybernetic organisms. The computer circuitry nanotechnically grown into and around their brains, the artificial circuitry grown throughout their bodies certainly qualified them as such. Most humans, though, thought of their technological components as *enhancements* or *prosthetics*, not as cybernetics. Humans still looked like humans, after all, and except for a few fringe groups had not begun the wholesale replacement of body parts with machines. For centuries, humans had worn corrective lenses or hearing aids or pacemakers to improve on nature. Implant technology was no different, though it was perhaps just a bit more intrusive.

But maybe Konstantin's crack about cybernetic species could honestly be applied to modern humans.

In any case, Konstantin had been communicating with the intelligence occupying the solar sail shell around Tabby's Star, and learned that the original organic intelligences that had evolved here had ultimately uploaded their minds into machine brains and become purely machine beings. Gray was aware of those beings now as shapes and shadows around him, the drifting ovoid machines Konstantin called the Satori. The problem was that those beings were there as ghosts in the memory of the system's super-AI, since they no longer had a material existence. Perhaps five or six hundred years ago, Konstantin thought, they'd gone through their version of the Sh'daar *Schjaa Hok* and vanished. Presumably— and like the far more ancient ur-Sh'daar—they still had an existence somewhere, but what that might mean was pure conjecture. Another dimension? Another, noncorporeal plane of existence? A whole other universe, perhaps one of their own creation? All unknown . . .

The Satori AI—Gray was already thinking of it as the *Satorai*—had no opinions on the matter. According to Konstantin, it was uninterested in other minds, or had been until the return of the *Gaki*.

Gaki—the Hungry Ghosts. It seemed a fitting name for the mysterious space-going amoebae.

Again, Konstantin had suggested the name, since the radio-frequency pulses of the Satori term were not easily vocalized. If *Satori* was the Japanese word for Buddhist enlightenment, then *Gaki* was the term referring to another Buddhist concept, that of the "hungry ghosts." These were supposedly the spirits of ancestors abandoned or neglected by their living relatives, or, in a different tradition, the spirits of people trapped by desire or greed and cursed with insatiable hunger.

According to the Satorai, the original inhabitants of this system had created the Gaki as artificially intelligent spacecraft designed to explore nearby stars. This they had done for innumerable millennia—the first, the Satorai claimed, had been launched into the interstellar void something like eighty thousand years ago—but for the past several centuries they'd been returning.

And they were returning *changed*. The Satorai could no longer communicate with them, and the Gaki seemed only interested in devouring the Satori system's infrastructure.

The molecule-thin sail canopies appeared to be the equivalent of *haute cuisine* for the vast, gaseous entities, though they also fed on the debris cloud farther in.

"But what *are* they?" Gray demanded. "The Gaki, I mean. You said they were starships, but they can't carry anything, no payloads, no passengers. . . ."

"On the contrary: they carry information. Perhaps a better name would be starprobes, not starships. Parts of their substance are hardwired into circuitry, a few hundred grams at most. The same idea was conceived on Earth, actually, a few centuries ago. Human designers called it *Starwisp*."

"I remember hearing about the idea, but it was never actually developed. A microwave sail carrying enough microcircuitry to support an AI, right? The sail could be accelerated by beamed microwaves to something like ten percent of the speed of light, because the total mass of the payload was only a tenth of a gram, and the sail itself would only have weighed a kilogram or so."

"Exactly. The Gaki concept was similar. The Satori created them—grew them, actually. The idea was to send them as enormous light sails to other stars, where the AIs would explore, record, and use local resources to manufacture new sails."

"But something went wrong."

"Indeed."

"Do you know what?"

"I'm not entirely certain," Konstantin replied, "but the evidence points to an extremely virulent computer virus."

"A virus? You mean, like, an artificially generated *electronic* virus?"

"Exactly. It may have been created by another intelligence seeking to protect its home star system from this sort of intruder."

"A computer virus." Gray felt a stab of alarm. "Can it—"

Konstantin anticipated his flash of fear. "I have not been infected, Admiral, no. If it exists, it is resident within the Gaki. And we have had no close encounter with them as yet."

"Thank God."

"The danger *is* considerable," Konstantin told him. "It is conceivable—quite possibly *likely*—that returning Gaki infected with this virus were responsible for the destruction of the Tabby's Star Dyson sphere."

The vast and shining corridors and compartments of the Satori virtual world faded away, replaced by a star gleaming in space: KIC 8462852. *Tabby's Star.* Gray wondered if what he was seeing was a computer-generated construct, or an actual visual record from a thousand years or more ago.

Or, perhaps the two were the same thing.

"The Matrioshka shells," Konstantin went on, "and the Dyson structure were built consecutively, the toroid first, then the statite shells. As you see, the Satori did not completely enclose their star in a spherical shell. Instead, they built a broad ring above their star's equator, one reaching to approximately twenty-five degrees north and south—not a Dyson sphere, but a Dyson toroid. That left plenty of space open for the construction of the statite shells with access to their star's radiation. Because of the toroid's larger radius, one point eight five AU instead of one, there would have been far more land area than would be available on a complete Dyson sphere around a star like Sol."

"How much space?" Gray asked.

"Enough for roughly a billion Earths peeled and spread out flat—one point zero five four two six billion, to be marginally more precise."

"That seems . . . excessive. With that much living room, why did they need to explore other stars?"

"Because," Konstantin said, "they weren't simply trying to create a habitat."

"Excuse me?"

"If I understand the AI correctly, the Satori were engaged in activity somewhat more ambitious than surrounding their home star with living space and a powerful computer node. They were endeavoring to move their star."

"Ah . . ."

And it all dropped into place for Gray, the final piece of the puzzle. "So that's what the Agletsch were trying to tell us. That the Satori were engaged in creating something like a Shkadov thruster."

"Essentially. The principle, at least, is the same. The Satori appear to have mastered a considerably more proficient technology in stellar manipulation. They encircled KIC 8462852 with generators for a powerful gravitic drive. Details are lacking, but the Satori AI seems to believe that the star—with the attendant technology, the toroid and the Matrioshka shells, in tow, of course—might have managed to reach a sizeable percentage of c."

Gray gave a low, in-the-mind whistle. "Where were they off to in such a hurry?"

"The star we know as Deneb."

In Gray's mind's eye, he turned his gaze out from Tabby's Star, and sought out that brilliant, blue-white gleam in the distance. Deneb glowed in a star-thick sky, a dazzlingly bright beacon not far from the red smear of the North America Nebula. In Earth's night sky, Deneb was one of the twenty or so brightest stars, and that was at a distance of something like 1,600 light years. Here, Deneb was only 173 light years away, and it was far brighter than Venus in Earth's predawn sky.

"Okay. Why?"

"The AI cannot tell me. It seems to believe that its builders had encountered something . . . astonishing there. It sounds like an alien civilization, but one organized along radically different lines than that of the Satori, or of Humankind, for that matter."

"I . . . see. The Satori launched their star probes and learned of something at Deneb. Meanwhile, whatever was at Deneb was infecting the probes with some kind of computer virus and sending them back."

"The Satori stardrive required considerable technological prowess to operate."

Gray started at that. Had Konstantin just made a pun, speaking of a literal stardrive and an attempt to drive a star?

But Konstantin continued without a stop. "A substantial percentage of the computational output of the Matrioshka brain appears to have been required to keep the star and its high-tech accoutrements stable. The virus interfered with that stability, disastrously so. The toroid wobbled off center, then was ripped apart by gravitational stresses."

"'How are the mighty fallen,'" Gray said, a quote taken very much out of context. "You think the destruction was deliberate?"

"Almost certainly so. The Deneban civilization may have designed the virus knowing that the Satori civilization was approaching, or was about to do so."

"And they obviously didn't want visitors." Something else occurred to Gray. He opened a new in-head file and pulled in a quick download from *America*'s library. "Wait a moment. . . ."

"You are wondering about Deneb's age."

"Yeah. Something doesn't make sense, here. Deneb is a type A2 Ia star, a supergiant." According to the ephemeris information he was looking at in-head, the star was more than 100 times the diameter of the sun, and 54,000 times Sol's luminosity, making it one of the brightest known stars in the galaxy. "Hell," Gray continued, "it started off as a type O, the brightest and hottest there is. The bigger and brighter a star is, the faster it uses up its fuel and the sooner it blows up. All of that means Deneb can only be about ten million years old, maybe less. . . ."

"In other words," Konstantin said, "not nearly enough time for life to evolve on any possible planets."

"Right. If such a hot star could even spawn planets in the first place."

"There are other possibilities," Konstantin reminded him. "Deneb could have been colonized by a technic civilization utilizing hot O, B, or A-type supergiants. Or . . . any life that evolved there, as the Satori AI suggested, may be of a radically different type from those known to Humankind. Beings living within the stellar plasma, for instance, if such a thing is possible."

"I guess we'll have to go there and see for ourselves, then."

"I would not advise it."

"Eh. No. Not this trip. "

Not that there was likely to be a next trip, not for him. The blunt truth of the matter was that court-martial boards were notoriously single-minded about flag officers who disobeyed orders and returned with nothing to show for it. Their detour had not produced a working Shkadov thruster, not turned up anything useful in the way of high-tech weaponry, nothing that could be used against the Rosette Aliens.

For just a moment he was tempted to blame Konstantin. Why had the damned AI dragged him out here, anyway? A hunch that hadn't panned out?

But . . . no. Gray had gone along with Konstantin's suggestion. He'd stepped into this with his eyes wide open. Recriminations now were pointless.

"A civilization capable of destroying a Kardashev Type Two civilization across a distance of one hundred seventy-three light years," Konstantin continued, "is not to be taken lightly."

"I suppose not. But we were out here looking for weapons—or allies—that we can use against the Rosetters, right? And we failed. . . ."

"Not entirely."

Gray took a deep breath. "Well, it does sound like whoever or whatever is hanging out at Deneb would be a great candidate."

"If Humankind survived the encounter, possibly," Konstantin replied. "In any case, however, we may already have access to a viable weapon without the need to meet the Denebans directly."

"What weapon?"

"The computer virus," Konstantin told him, "that destroyed the Satori torus."

VFA-96, Black Demons
Tabby's Star
1553 hours, TFT

Lieutenant Gregory was in the van as the Black Demons vectored across space, skimming some thousand kilometers or so above the smooth, ebony canopies of the Satori statites. Ahead, almost invisible, a lurking translucence stirred. It was too distant to pick up optically, but his Starblade's AI was feeding him an enlarged image.

"CAG, Demon Four," he called. "I have the target in sight."

"Copy that, Demon Five," Captain Fletcher's voice replied in his head. "Remember, do not, repeat do *not* engage. You're there to protect the capture probe going in . . . and pick it up on the other side."

"Copy that." He hesitated. "Tell me, CAG, has anybody thought about what happens to us if we make that thing *mad*?"

"Don't worry, Four. It won't be mad at *you*."

"I wish I had your confidence in the emotional state of something that's completely weird-ass off-the-bulkhead alien," Gregory replied.

"Stand by. Probe launch in thirty seconds."

Gregory checked the range to the target—almost ten thousand kilometers. What was it they were calling those things now? Gaki, that was it. *Hungry ghost*. It seemed fitting.

He adjusted his Starblade's course slightly to approach the filmy shape ahead while still giving it a wide berth. He could see now that it was partially expanded, using the star's light to tack toward another of the statite sails. It was like the huge thing was grazing out there, devouring light sail canopies one by one.

"So what's with this probe, Skipper?" Gregory asked. "Are they still trying to communicate with that thing?"

"I don't know, Four," Mackey replied. "The word I heard was that they're prepping a sub-clone of the big lunar AI and sending that into the middle of it."

"Konstantin, yeah. Okay. To do what?"

"Beats me."

"They want to kick that hungry ghost in the ass," DeHaviland said, "and make it mad."

"Okay, we're back to that. Right . . . just watch out if it starts throwing rocks."

"No rocks out here," Caswell put in. "I think we're safe."

Gregory seriously doubted that the word *safe* could be applied to living masses of dust or gas a hundred thousand kilometers across.

"Heads up, people," Mackey warned. "Launch in five seconds . . ."

America had moved in to within a couple of thousand kilometers of the statite sail layer, her enormous round shield cap pointed directly at the alien organism now ten thousand kilometers ahead. Gregory could hear the countdown over the carrier's PriFly channel: ". . . and three . . . and two . . . and one . . . launch!"

A black teardrop emerged from the center of the shield-cap, hurtling outward at fifty kilometers per second.

The teardrop was a standard Starblade fighter, but stripped of weapons and with much of its interior converted to particularly dense circuitry, the Earth equivalent of computronium. If Mackey had downloaded the straight shit, there was no human pilot. Instead, the AI on *America*—itself a clone of Konstantin—had copied a portion of itself and inserted that into the converted fighter. The clone's clone would become Humankind's emmissary to the bizarre life form ahead.

"Capture probe away," PriFly called.

"Copy that, PriFly. We have it in sight. C'mon, Demons. Let's keep up."

At fifty kilometers per second, the magnetically accelerated probe would cross those ten thousand kilometers in three minutes, thirty-three seconds. The question was how the target would react to the probe's approach. When Gregory had gotten too close to the Gaki before, close enough to enter its outer envelope of magnetically organized gas particles, it had seemed . . . *irritated*, to say the very least.

The seconds trickled away. The capture pod flew its straight-line course, not changing speed, not changing direction. Maybe they could convince the Gaki that the approaching probe was a meteor, an inert lump of cosmic debris.

In other words, *lunch* . . .

The Black Demons kept pace with the probe. Three and a half minutes after launch, it plunged into the Gaki's dust-cloud central regions.

The reaction was startling. The far-flung wings and filmy pseudopods began flowing back to the center, as the core of the thing collapsed into a dense sphere. The probe seemed to merge with that core, its nanomatrix hull flowing like molten tar to penetrate and explore the Gaki organism's heart. The entire organism twisted in space, collapsing, then exploding outward once more.

Gregory rolled his fighter sharply to avoid one outthrust pseudopod. He heard the sharp rattle of dust grains on his hull, felt the shudder as he brushed the alien body . . . and then he was clear. He didn't know if it was a deliberate attack or a random flail by an injured beast, but he was taking no chances.

"It shook the probe off," Ruxton reported. "I've got it in sight . . ."

The alien organism collapsed again into a tightly packed sphere and began dropping starward. It struck the expanse of black statite sail beneath it and punched cleanly through. The probe had emerged from the cloud on a new vector, tumbling end over end.

"Let the Gaki go," Mackey ordered. "Catch the probe!"

"I've got it," Gregory said. Easier said than done, though. He accelerated gently, flashing alongside the probe. Catching it was going to be tricky. . . .

"Do not under any circumstances communicate with the probe," Mackey said. "They just passed the word from the CIC. If things went right, that probe's been contaminated by one hell of a computer virus."

"If things went *right*?" Gregory shook his head. "Whose bright idea was this, anyway?"

"Probably the boss computer," DeHaviland said. "I'm ten kilometers off your starboard side, Don. I can help with the probe."

"Right." Gregory exchanged some terse, wordless messages with his fighter's AI. Gently, under the AI's control, his fighter edged closer to the tumbling capture probe. His Starblade took on its atmospheric configuration, with stubby, delta-shaped wings. Wings were useless in hard vacuum for flying, of course, but he was going to try to use his starboard wingtip to stop the probe's spin.

DeHaviland's Starblade appeared on the far side of the probe, gently edging closer.

"Slave your AI to mine," she told him.

"You've got it."

With both fighters now essentially being run by the same artificial intelligence, they closed together with smooth precision. Their wingtips connected with the tumbling probe at the same instant. Gregory felt the shock, felt a harsh grating vibration, and suppressed the urge to engage his gravitic drive.

Slowed by friction, the capture probe was drifting between the two fighters, now, its spin gone.

The two fighters moved closer, then, the nanomatrix that made up their wing surfaces running like thick liquid to embrace the pod.

"We've got it," DeHaviland reported.

"Right," Gregory said. "Let's take it home."

He was feeling, he realized, a fierce exultation . . . and the depression that had been gnawing him was, not gone, exactly, but very much in the background.

He opened a private channel. "Hey, Cyndi?"

"Yeah?"

"Nice job."

"Thank you."

"Ah . . ."

"What?"

"Oh, nothing. Just wondering if you'd care to see the space-ace when we get off duty later."

He was more than half expecting her to tell him to drop dead. Instead, she said, "Absolutely!"

And the depression took another step into the background dark.

Chapter Twenty-four

TC/USNA CVS America
Module 1 Gravity Lounge
En route to Kapteyn's Star
2005 hours, TFT

"We're . . . what?" Connie Fletcher asked him. "Another five hours out from emergence?"

Gray consulted his internal clock. "Five hours, ten minutes . . . and a few odd seconds," he replied. He took a sip of his drink, a blue starshine from the lounge's replicator. Gray normally didn't drink on board ship, not when he was in command, but today, of all days, he found he needed the anesthetic effects of ethanol.

America's gravity lounge was located in Hab Module One, its spin generating roughly half a G. Both officers and enlisted personnel were encouraged to spend several hours of off-duty time here each ship's day as a means of holding off the degenerative effects of long-term microgravity. The ambiance was pleasant, if a bit on the sterile side, with smoothly curved white bulkheads, invisible lighting, and furnishings grown from the deck at a thought. Best of all, the compartment was large enough that even with the presence of thirty or forty other people, it felt almost empty, and the translucent light curtains and photon sculptures provided the illusion of both intimacy and privacy.

Gray was seated at a broad, low table with Connie Fletcher, *America*'s CAG, and they were watching the computer-generated simulation of the stars projected across the overhead as the last few hours of this leg of their voyage dwindled away.

"You got our opplan okay?" he asked her.

"Yup. We pop out forty AUs out, just like in the old days, so that we can have a good look around. And you want the fighters out as soon as we emerge."

"Right. Our priority will be making contact with the fleet."

"Assuming," she said, "that the fleet is there."

"My. Cheerful, aren't we?"

"Hey . . . it's been a week. Anything could have happened. Humankind might have declared peace and everyone went home."

"That," Gray said slowly, "would be wonderful."

"You're not buying it though, are you?"

"No. Things are *never* that easy. Especially when there are so damned many unknowns."

"You still worried about what HQMILCOM is going to say about our little . . . side trip?"

"A little, I suppose." He shrugged. "Whatever happens, it's *my* side trip, not ours. My responsibility."

"I would have to say that Konstantin bears some of that responsibility."

"Not legally. He's a machine. Or a program, rather. A very, very sophisticated program . . . but *just* a program. Humans are still in the loop, and it's humans who call the shots."

"You sure about that? Sometimes I think the AIs are running everything behind the scenes, and we don't have much say at all. Just what they decide to let us have."

"I didn't know you went in for catAIstrophy theories,

Connie." The term was an old one, going back four centuries or so, to a time when Humankind had been seriously mulling over the possibility that human machines would soon be so much smarter than their creators that they would eliminate them . . . or put them in zoos.

"I don't . . . not really," Fletcher told him. "But you've got to wonder. Machines like Konstantin are so much faster than we are, with access to so much more data. They can't be spending more than a tiny fraction of their clock speed on critters as comparatively slow as we are. What are they thinking about in all of their spare time? What are they *doing*?"

"I don't know. Konstantin seems to be a good sort. I think he's genuinely concerned about the future of humans *and* intelligent machines."

"You don't think he gets . . . I don't know . . . frustrated by how slow we are on the uptake?"

"Maybe. A little. But then, the difference between us and machines was there when he first came on-line, wasn't it? It might just be a fact of life for him."

"Hm. So were cholera and cancer, once upon a time. Sometimes I wonder how much longer beings like Konstantin will need us."

Gray laughed. "They don't need us *now*. Sometimes I think . . ." He let the thought trail off.

"What?"

"I don't know. Sometimes I think we *amuse* them."

She shuddered. "That's what's terrifying about it."

"Well . . . for better or worse, machine intelligence is here to stay. If we're lucky, we'll evolve along with it. If not . . ." He spread his hands. "We can just hope they'll make humanity's golden years comfortable, out of nostalgic fondness, if nothing else."

A dozen personnel were gathered at another table nearby, singing Solstice songs to the accompaniment of a computer-generated orchestra. The carols' sentiments—about new light and a new day—seemed wildly out of phase with Gray's and Fletcher's dark musings.

Fletcher grinned suddenly, as if throwing a switch, and leaned forward. "Want to go join them?"

"Not particularly."

"C'mon, Admiral. You've been as glum and out of sorts as an AI unjacked from its data input lately."

"Hey, you're the one worried about AIs wiping out humans!"

"Oh, I figure we still have a century or two left. So let's enjoy it while we can! Besides, you really do need to get out more."

"You go on ahead, Connie," Gray told her. "I've got some thinking to do."

She looked like she was going to give him an argument . . . probably something along the lines of it being good for shipboard morale, but he shut it down with a sharp side-to-side shake of his head. "*No*. Thanks . . . but it's not my thing."

She shrugged. "Suit yourself. Excuse me." She stood, picked up her drink, and walked through a misty red light curtain to join the holiday choristers. "Hey, it's Cap'n CAG!" someone called out, and there was a burst of laughter.

Gray took another sip of his drink. He felt decidedly ambiguous about the holiday known as Solstice, and around this time of the year that sense of ambiguousness could churn unpleasantly into something deeper and darker.

Solstice? It was *Christmas*, damn it!

The implementation of the White Covenant had pretty much ended all public celebrations of religious holidays. In fact, tendencies in that direction had been noted well before the twenty-first century's bloody Islamic Wars that had led to the White Covenant's adoption.

Even so, people clung to their need to let loose and party now and again no matter what the law might say. The winter solstice in the northern hemisphere, the summer solstice for the southern, remained a relatively religion-neutral excuse for a seasonal holiday.

Gray was not religious in the usual sense, but he mourned the loss of social and historical connections that once had helped define human cultures. An epoch or two ago, when he'd been a Prim living in the Manhatt Ruins with Angela, the White Covenant had not been that much of a concern. Angela had been a Christian believer, and they'd often celebrated the Solstice holiday with a decorated tree and some of the other trappings of what once had been called *Christmas*. And why the hell not? Hell, even the word *holiday* had been derived from "holy day."

Survival in the Manhatt Ruins hadn't left much time or energy for celebrations, of course . . . and there the White Covenant existed only as a dim memory of the late twenty-first century's often heavy-handed attempts at social engineering on a monumental scale. Even when he'd moved across the line out of the Periphery and into North America proper, the White Covenant was less a legal club held over people's heads than it was a faintly disapproving sneer of contempt. A *religious* holiday? How . . . *distasteful* . . .

He still missed Christmas, however. He wondered how much of that had to do with missing Angela.

Once more, he wondered how she was getting on with her new life. Was she still a believer? Or had the stroke and the cerebral therapies that had repaired the damage killed that, in the same way it had killed her love for him?

Damn. It always happened. This time of the year he always found himself getting depressed to the point where he couldn't stand himself . . . and the gods knew what it was like for the people around him.

It had taken almost a week for *America* to make the passage between what Gray had come to think of as the Two Stars: Tabby's and Kapteyn's. The Boyajian TRGA located at the edge of the KIC 8462852 system had taken them back to Penrose easily enough. Once they'd emerged at Penrose, however, Gray had faced a difficult if not almost impossible choice.

America could return home the way she'd come, traversing almost eighty light years of normal space to return to Earth, or she could set a slightly different course and travel the eighty-three light years to her original destination—Kapteyn's Star and the ancient moon Heimdall. Which course would be the best one had kept him gnawing at the problem for days. If he returned to Earth, it would be to surrender his ship and turn himself in for court-martial. He would be able to turn over the considerable trove of data acquired at Tabby's Star, and know that it would be put to good use . . . at least eventually. His IT people were convinced that they'd been able to extract the code defining the alien program hidden away inside the Gaki, and that there should be a way of applying that code to hack into the Rosette intelligence.

Should be . . .

The alternative was to set course for Kapteyn's Star and rejoin the fleet he'd abandoned a dozen days before—hopefully giving IT enough time to develop a virus that might actually do something against the Rosettes.

The problem with this second course of action, of course, was that Gray had no way of knowing what had been happening at Kapteyn's Star during his absence. The Grand Unified Fleet might have engaged the Rosette intelligence and found a way to beat it . . . or, more likely, perhaps, the fleet might have been utterly destroyed and *America* would arrive at Heimdall to find herself facing the Rosetters alone.

Or they would find the fleet there attempting to negotiate with the Rosetters, with greater or less success depending on the events there of the past weeks.

Ultimately, Gray had chosen the second option. So far as his personal career was concerned, he would be in no worse trouble if they bypassed Earth and journeyed on to Kapteyn's Star than he would be if he returned to Supra-Quito and turned himself in . . . and it might save valuable time if the Unified Fleet was still trying to negotiate with the Rosetters.

Besides, something akin to guilt had been gnawing at him since he'd elected to give in to Konstantin's suggestion and redirect the *America* out to Tabby's Star. While it was unlikely that *America*'s absence had been significant when the fleet reached Heimdall, he couldn't help but be concerned about what amounted to a gross dereliction of duty. He knew that if things *had* gone badly there for the human force, he was going to feel responsible . . . even though *America* represented only a small fraction of the Grand Unified Fleet's total firepower. What it came down to, then, was simple:

Damn it, he had to *know*. . . .

"Admiral? I got a message—you wanted to see me?"

Gray blinked, then looked around. A young woman—painfully thin, stringy-haired, her face masked in technological shapes and strips of plastic, stood behind him. "Ah. Dr. Sanger." He gestured at a seat. "Please."

Carolyn Sanger was *America*'s senior Information Systems officer, at least in theory. Like many departments, *America*'s AI ran the show, with various humans serving as technological acolytes to their machine department head. Sanger was not military; like Truitt, she was a civilian working for the military. Her GS-13 rating made her the equivalent of a Navy lieutenant commander, though she was not in the shipboard chain of command.

She was also a class-3 cyborg, almost as much machine as she was human. Her eyes and much of her face were masked by a visor and partial helmet that appeared to be growing out of her pale skin.

"You wanted to see me?" she repeated.

"I did. Unofficially, at any rate . . ."

"I beg your pardon?"

"I want to know if the new torpedo is ready."

"Sure. We're good to go, lean and green. *Ricky* should've sent you the report. . . ."

"'Ricky'?"

"The ship. You know . . . *America*."

"Ah." He'd not heard that nickname before. Was it a private in-joke among the computer techs? "Right. The alien virus has been isolated? It hasn't had access to ship systems?"

"Absolutely not, Admiral." She seemed to gain a little

self-confidence that had been lacking before. He wished, though, that he could see her eyes.

"You're absolutely sure? I don't know what we would do if it got loose in the ship's network."

"We call it the Omega Code, Admiral," Sanger told him. "And it's perfectly safe."

"According to who?" Gray said dryly. "This code annihilated a K-2 civilization, apparently without breaking a sweat."

"It's *safe*, Admiral," she said again. "Konstantin is running nested emulations, and he can tell if the Omega Code is trying to slip through the firewall."

What she was describing seemed simple enough. An emulation was a smaller clone of a computer network running on the larger one, for all intents and purposes a perfect, though smaller, copy. Nested emulation meant a series of copies in copies, each watching the firewall between itself and the next layer in.

"Uh . . . why are you asking me, Admiral?" Sanger asked. "The ship AI—"

"Might not tell me the truth if it has been . . . compromised."

He felt her stiffen. "You don't trust the *ship*?" She said the words as though she'd just heard sheerest, blackest blasphemy.

"Of course I do," he lied. "I just want to hear it from a human as well as a machine."

"You're lying," she told him. "You don't like machine intelligence, do you?"

Her blunt response caught Gray off guard. He wasn't used to that degree of social candor. Or was it a simple lack of social skills in someone who really didn't get out very much?

"Whether I like them or not is not the point," he told her. "AI systems tell us what they want us to know, and I need to know this thing is going to work as advertised."

As he spoke, he pulled down Sanger's personnel record. She was 35, he saw, though she both looked and acted considerably younger. The implants were permanent; she hadn't seen anything with her organic eyes for ten years, and her other senses had been enhanced as well. She could maintain a continuous link with an AI network, had instant access to any data available on the Net, and could crank her equivalent clock speed up to 50 megahertz. . . .

"That's way out of date," she told him. "I'm currently configured for 700 gigahertz. Still not nearly as fast as *Ricky*, but it helps me keep up with her."

He blinked, startled. How the hell was she following what he was doing in-head?

"I linked in through your service connections," she explained, quite matter-of-fact and with what felt like a mental shrug of her shoulders. "They're right *there*, after all. Here . . . let me . . ."

Inside an open window in Gray's mind, Carolyn Sanger's personnel record changed, as various technical descriptions were updated.

Gray closed the document.

"Wait!"

"I would appreciate it," he told her gently, "if you would stay the hell out of my head unless I invite you in. Good manners, right?"

She sniffed. "Never had much use for *those*."

Gray had known there were people like Sanger, but some people had taken the concept to what Gray thought were insane extremes. Were people like that even human anymore?

"*We* think so," Sanger told him. She shrugged. "Of course, in another decade or two, *everyone* will be at least this wired, right? And people like me won't even have orgie bits anymore. No wetware at all."

She sounded *proud* of that.

"Okay, Carolyn," he said, shuddering. "Just tell me about the torpedo."

"Standard Mark XXII hypervelocity shell with a core configured as Level Four computronium," she said. "The Konstantin clone we used to contact the Gaki was loaded inside along with the Omega Code."

"It has the virus?"

"The Omega Code. Yes."

"How do you know?"

"We budded off another Konstantin clone and had it emulate a portion of *Ricky*'s processor network. We watched the virus begin to rewrite the operating-system software, then shut it down. The code is there, all right."

"Do you think it will be effective against the Rosetters?"

"That I couldn't tell you. A whole different computer language . . . written within a completely alien technic culture. We'll need some sort of handshake protocol, y'know. . . ."

"Meaning we can't just upload our software into an alien network."

"Right. Well . . . sort of. There're a lot of variables. The Konstantin clone is smart enough to handle most of those, I think."

"That's what I wanted to know."

"The biggest problem is the tech discrepency."

"Meaning what?"

"The aliens at Deneb . . . we don't know how advanced they are, but we can guess that they were pretty much at the same level as the Tabby's Star natives, right? The ones who built the Dyson toroid and the Matrioshka brain? They're K-2."

"Yes."

"But the Rosetters may be borderline K-3. If they're the folks we glimpsed up in the future, they're on their way to building a galactic Dyson sphere. That's so far beyond what a K-2 culture would be able to do, it's dunkers."

Gray blinked. "'Dunkers?'"

"DNC—does not compute. Sorry. A very old nonsense phrase. What I mean is that a K-3 culture might not even be slowed down by a K-2 technology, right?"

Gray smiled. "I remember seeing a cartoon once. A shaggy, naked barbarian in the woods with a big club sneaking up behind a modern, combat-armored soldier holding a laser rifle. I forget the caption, but it was something like 'Once again, strength and sneakiness overcome high-tech—'"

"I've seen it," she said. "Complete nonsense, you know."

Gray was amused by her self-assuredness when it came to things technical. "Oh?"

"Sure. It's the Savage Teddy Bear Myth."

"What's that?"

"There's this old two-D virdrama from a few centuries ago," she explained. "It had these soldiers in high-tech combat armor, helmets, lasers, spaceships, powered walkers, all of that . . . but in this one story they were wiped out by alien stone-age teddy bears with clubs and rocks."

"Okay . . ." Where was this going?

"In fact, those soldiers would have had all sorts of IR gear, motion detectors, drones, and perimeter sensors . . . all the high-tech equipment that would have let them see or hear the alien teddy bears coming ten kilometers away. Their armor would have protected them against clubs, arrows, and rocks . . . assuming the teddy bears could even get close enough to use them. Could never happen in real life. I mean, it was *really* stupid. . . ."

"Maybe the lesson is just that we shouldn't let ourselves become too dependent on our technology."

"Why not?" she asked, genuinely puzzled. "Organic systems fail as easily as artificial ones. Maybe more. Our technology is what makes us *human*."

"Because it's up to us, not our machines?"

She shook her head, still puzzled, and Gray decided that the two of them simply were not speaking the same language.

"Okay, okay," he said. "Point taken, I guess. But I want to have a channel to you when we emerge off Heimdall, okay? I'll be linked in with Konstantin and with *America*, sure, but I want a human on the line as well. I want *you*."

"Sure. But I don't understand . . . sir."

It was, he noted, the first time during their conversation that she'd used an honorific.

"It's not necessary that you do, Sanger. I just want to know that when I have to make certain tactical decisions, I can rely on the AIs, but have a good human brain that knows them and works with them backing me up."

"You want a checksum."

"I beg your pardon?"

"A checksum. A small datum from a large block of data used to detect errors that might have crept in during transmission or storage."

"If you like." He didn't add that what he wanted was a human check on a machine mind . . . when he didn't fully understand or completely trust that mind or what it might tell him.

But after his conversation with the woman, he was wondering just how human Carolyn Sanger might be. . . .

Sanger wandered off, and Gray spent another half hour listening to the Solstice songs coming from the other table. At last, though, he couldn't take it any longer . . . songs about returning light and bringing light into people's lives and welcoming the new sun. Nice sentiments . . . but he just wasn't feeling them right now.

What was that phrase, that marvelous expression of holiday spirits out of Dickens? He had to do a quick search.

Ah. That was it.

Bah! Humbug!

He checked his internal clock and decided that it was about time he got back to the flag bridge. They were coming up on their planned emergence point—another three and a half hours, about—and he wanted to be ready.

For *what,* he wasn't at all certain.

The Consciousness—the part of the vast Mind enshrouding tiny Kapteyn's Star, at any rate—could feel the approach of . . . others. The vehicle was approaching at faster-than-light velocity, which suggested Mind, of course, but was no guarantee. Mind could be expressed in myriad ways, including powerful intellects that manifestly were *not* conscious. Consciousness and intellect, after all, were not the same thing.

The Consciousness had entered this universe specifically seeking conscious thought . . . not the organic vermin so often associated with minor technologies, but true Mind, Mind aware of itself and the nature of the cosmos.

Mind worth uniting with . . . augmenting . . . learning from . . . and teaching.

The Consciousness reached out in a manner incomprehensible to four-dimensional life and . . . sampled.

Yes. Almost certainly . . .

With infinite care and precision, the Consciousness began folding local space. . . .

Chapter Twenty-five

TC/USNA CVS America
Flag Bridge
Kapteyn's Star
0115 hours, TFT

Emergence. . . .

America dropped from the embrace of tightly folded space in an avalanche of photons . . . and into raw chaos.

The ship shuddered and bucked, as an alarm Klaxon shrilled. "What the hell?" Gray shouted as he tried to make sense of an incoming storm of data. One thing was clear immediately. They were *not* where they were supposed to be.

He'd instructed *America* to bring them out of Alcubierre Drive forty astronomical units from Kapteyn's Star—almost 6 billion kilometers, a distance close to the semi-major axis of the orbit of Pluto around the sun. At that range, Kapteyn's Star would have been a dim red dot . . . if indeed it were visible at all to the naked human eye.

More important, that star would have been five and a half light-hours away, giving *America* plenty of time to observe the inner system, look for signs of the human fleet, and watch for enemy activity, all well before the burst of light announcing their arrival at Kapteyn's Star had time to reach Heimdall or the other planets circling that star.

But there, looming huge on the flag bridge screens, was Bifrost, the sweep of its rings rainbow-hued and vast, with Heimdall glittering tiny beneath them. There'd been a mistake, a miscalculation, there *must* have been, for Bifrost was less than nine AUs from its star, and the glowing masses of colored light filling the sky suggested that they'd emerged well within the Rosette entity's inner sanctum.

"Okay," Gray said, reaching out for data. "How did we end up in here?"

"The local spacetime matrix, Admiral," Mallory said. "It's been . . . bent somehow."

"That's called *gravity*, Dean," Gutierrez said.

"No, I mean the whole area has been deeply warped. Like they saw us coming and folded local space into a pocket to catch us."

"I don't think I like the sound of that," Gray said. If the Rosetters had seen them coming . . .

"Where the hell did *that* come from?" Blakeslee yelled, and then Gray saw it too, coming in toward the ship from dead astern . . . a vast dark planet with distinctly artificial-looking geometric patterns seemingly etched across its surface.

"Is that one of Bifrost's moons?" Gray asked.

"Negative!" Blakeslee shot back. "Diameter forty-eight hundred kilometers, maybe a bit more! Heimdall is larger, but it's the only Bifrost moon anywhere near that big! This is . . . something else."

The artificial surface had already convinced Gray of that fact. "Helm! Full power!"

America surged forward just as a beam of antiprotons seared past the ship's stern.

"That was too close!" Gutierrez said.

"Helm! Get us the hell out of here!"

"Helm, aye!" A tense couple of seconds passed as *America* accelerated.

"Sir . . . that thing out there is *chasing* us!" Mallory said.

It seemed impossible, but Gray could read the data cascading through his in-head windows now. An artificial world the size of the planet Mercury was using powerfully focused gravitational fields to maneuver like a starship. They'd already somehow twisted the local gravity fields to pluck *America* out of metaspace.

"The Rosetters appear to have come up with something new in their bag of tricks. Helm . . . try to loop us past Heimdall, then on in past Bifrost. Close a pass as you can manage."

"Aye, aye, sir."

America pitched and shuddered.

"What was that?"

Mallory shook his head. "Some kind of gravitic weapon, Admiral. They just collapsed a pocket of space a few hundred meters off our aft dorsal spine." The ship lurched again, sickeningly. "*And* some kind of antimatter beam. Antiprotons, looks like."

"Evasive maneuvering. Don't let them get a solid lock! Shields at max."

"Yessir. Screens are handling the antiproton stream. I don't think there's anything we can do about that gravity cruncher, though."

It was clear *America* didn't stand a chance in hell of fighting that thing straight-up. Maybe, though, they could take advantage of what amounted to the local terrain . . . the gas giant and its coterie of moons, including the Earth-sized Heimdall.

"Sir! Incoming communications! It's the *Lucas*!"

Gray had to think a moment. *Lucas*? That was the stealth assault-lander with the *Lexington*. Lieutenant Zhou. "Let's hear it."

"It's not a voice transmission, Admiral. Automatic datastream."

"Route it through ship's AI."

"Aye, aye, sir."

The data, he saw immediately, were coming in a tight and automated burst, a terabit pulse set to trigger if any human ship entered the system and was noted by *Lucas*'s sensors. The *Lucas*, it appeared, was on the surface of Heimdall, close beside an archeological site designated as the "Temple." He was startled to see that the site was occupied by humans; *America* was picking up the IFF tags of a dozen Marine fighters clawing their way up out of Heimdall's gravity well.

"Helm! Change course and take us clear of Heimdall!"

"Yes, sir."

"I still want to brush these bastards off on Bifrost, though, if we can."

With a spaceship the size of a planet hard on *America*'s heels, Gray was worried that the Rosette Aliens might follow the human ship as it skimmed around Heimdall. He was sure the aliens wouldn't get *too* close to the moon. That hurtling rock was about a third the size of Heimdall, and they wouldn't risk a direct collision.

But they might not be concerned about tidal disruption, and the seismic quakes generated by super-high tides across Heimdall's surface could pose a very serious problem for the people on the moon's surface. Better, he thought, to stay clear of the moon entirely . . . and hope the Rosette Aliens did as well.

On the bridge screens, Heimdall, directly ahead, slid smoothly off to starboard, and *America* arrowed past the chill world heading directly toward Bifrost. The gas giant's rings spread out, enormous, ahead of and above the ship. A small, icy moon flashed past to port.

"The . . . uh . . . mobile planet is slowing, sir," Mallory told him.

"Good." Maybe even something *that* big had limits. . . .

Gray was scanning the data transmitted from the *Lucas*. The Grand Unified Fleet, he saw, was no more. A couple of dozen ships had been wiped out of the sky. *Lexington* had survived, at least so far, but was badly damaged . . . adrift somewhere out in the direction of Thrymheim. The *Lex* had recorded the battle, however, and a great deal of other data besides and transmitted it to the *Lucas* on Heimdall before

powering down. He read the account of the mobile planet's
first appearance.

"They called it Romeo One," he noted.

"Sir?" Gutierrez asked.

"That damned black planet," Gray replied. "They called
it Romeo One."

"Where's Juliette?"

"Very funny." The Romeo designation was from the international phonetic alphabet, of course: "Romeo" for "R."
and "R" for "Rosette."

Lexington had gathered a lot of information. It was all
there . . . the attempts to get close to the Rosette entity . . .
the appearance of Romeo One . . . the reports from the
Pan-European fighter pilots—Schmidt and the others—
electronically preserved within Heimdall's alien planet-
sized computer Net.

"Konstantin?" Gray said. "Is there anything here we can
use?"

"I am as yet uncertain, Admiral. The Deneban e-virus is
extremely adaptable since it was designed to merge with an
alien network. However, the Rosette Aliens almost certainly
have formidable electronic defenses in place. We will not
have time to test alternatives."

"I wasn't expecting to have to try and use the thing right
off," Gray said. He'd hoped to have time to consult with the
Grand Fleet, not try to patch something together on the fly.
That wasn't in the cards now, though. "Do what you can."

"That, in fact, is all that is possible."

"We're coming down on Bifrost, Admiral," Blakeslee reported.

"Steady as she goes . . ."

Like all gas giant planets, Bifrost had no actual solid
surface. It was a slightly flattened sphere of hydrogen
and other gasses, compressed by growing pressures with
greater and greater depth until somewhere down there beneath those colored cloud bands rising temperatures and
pressures conspired to crush the hydrogen core into a form
more metallic than gas or liquid . . . but not quite solid,

either. There *might* be a rocky center the size of Earth in there; one theory suggested that the central core was mostly carbon squeezed into a single planet-sized diamond . . . but no one knew for certain.

The upper limits of a gas giant's atmosphere were as ill-defined as its depths. Well above the banded cloud layers, *America* encountered a rapidly thickening haze of hydrogen gas. The ship bucked and shuddered, and the outer hull began growing hot from friction. A ship like *America*, with no streamlining and no control surfaces, had never been intended for atmospheric flight. In moments she was thundering deep into an alien atmosphere, dragging out a long, hot tail of ionized hydrogen astern. The fast-flicker of the drive singularity forward was a tiny, hot sun as it devoured the gas and spit out light, X-rays, and hard gamma.

"Outer hull temp is up to nine hundred degrees, Admiral," Mallory warned. Not even gravitic shielding could hold the atmospheric friction at bay for long. In fact, the sharp bending of space near the hull made it *more* difficult to shed excess heat. "One thousand degrees . . . eleven hundred . . ."

The pursuing planet was less than five thousand kilometers astern, now, filling the sky aft. Violet flame flashed along *America*'s starboard hull as an alien particle beam seared through superheated atmosphere.

At *America*'s current speed, a straight-line trajectory would have carried them straight past Bifrost's day side in an instant. The ship's helm crew cut the forward drive singularity and began projecting a maneuvering singularity aft to slow their headlong descent, allowing Bifrost's gravity to curve their trajectory around the planet. Gray could hear the shrill scream of atmosphere outside the bridge tower, feel the ongoing, fast-building shudder as *America* plowed through hydrogen at thousands of kilometers per second. Still too fast by far . . .

"What's the son-of-a-bitch doing?" Gray demanded.

"Still following us, Admiral," Mallory replied. "But slowly. They've dropped to a few kilometers per second . . . and they're still decelerating."

"Are they stopping?"

"I think they're being cautious, sir. Local space is damned crowded."

That might give them their chance. Even something as massive as Romeo One was going to be careful not to slam into any of the hundred or so moons in orbit around Bifrost, from Heimdall, with a diameter of more than fourteen thousand kilometers, down to icy rocks a few kilometers across.

Romeo One had already swung well inside Heimdall's orbit, close enough to Bifrost, now, that the brush of its gravity was beginning to disturb the rings. Gray could see sparkles flashing across Romeo's surface as it swept through the ring debris; the plane of the rings was visibly twisted now, warped into three dimensions by Romeo's gravity.

And then *America* swung over Bifrost's horizon, blocking the artificial world from view. A shuddering rumble sounded through the ship, its metal and carbon skeleton protesting the stress. Gray felt a crushing weight on his chest. Gravitic acceleration acted on every atom within the singularity's field, and was experienced as zero-G; the deceleration due to plowing through the upper reaches of Bifrost's atmosphere, however, were piling on the Gs.

"Get us out of this atmosphere!" They needed to be in free fall and clear of atmosphere to launch fighters.

"Working on it, sir!"

Gently, *America* rotated about her own projected singularity, seeking a balance within the titanic stresses tearing at her spine. The rumble subsided a little as the ship continued to decelerate . . . and then the shuddering and the sensation of weight faded away. *America* was traveling up and away from Bifrost's night side, now, once again in open space. The gas giant's rings hung vast and spectacular like a color-banded ceiling parallel to the ship's trajectory. They were still shielded from Romeo One's view by the planet.

"Okay!" Gray said. "CAG! Launch fighters!"

"Aye, aye, Admiral."

"Put our special package in with one of the squadrons. Have them escort it in."

Special package. A mild-mannered and harmless-sounding euphemism for a converted Starblade fighter with a computronium core, carrying a Konstantin clone and the deadly Omega Code virus.

He could only hope it would be enough.

Fletcher hesitated slightly. "That could be rough on our people."

"I know. But we need to get it in close. If it's one of a dozen, we have a chance."

"Launching . . ."

"Captain Gutierrez, fighter launch has priority. When the fighters are clear, we follow them in."

"Yes, sir."

The question was whether the fighters could get clear of *America* before Romeo One came around the curve of Bifrost . . .

. . . and whether they would be able to survive more than a few seconds when it did.

TC/USNA CVS America
IS Department
Kapteyn's Star
0131 hours, TFT

"Dr. Sanger?" the Admiral's voice said. "Are we ready to launch?"

Carolyn Sanger didn't like the touch of Admiral Gray's mind, not at all. He seemed nice enough as a person, but deep down he seriously mistrusted AIs in general and Ricky's internal network in particular, and that was just *wrong*. She doubted that he realized how easily Class-3s could read him; those thoughts certainly were not for public display.

But her hardware allowed her to connect with others on many levels far beyond those necessary for simple communication. Back doors to a person's thoughts . . .

"Ricky?" she flashed through her network. "How's the Ohmygod?"

Someone in the IS department had started calling the Omega Code the Ohmygod Code—inevitable, perhaps—and the name had stuck. Software for destroying entire civilizations . . .

"Ready for launch, Carolyn," the ship told her and a dozen separate inner levels. The query and the reply were so quick, in human terms, that she replied to Gray without any apparent hesitation.

"Good to go, Admiral."

"No sign of . . . contamination?"

"No, sir."

Why did he keep going on about that, like two-way communication with the code was a *bad* thing? They could handle it. They had it covered. . . .

VFA-96, Black Demons
TC/USNA CVS America
Tabby's Star
0135 hours, TFT

Lieutenant Donald Gregory hung face down in the close embrace of his Starblade's cockpit, hating the wait, the sour anticipation before launch.

Come on, *people* . . .

"Black Demons, you are clear for drop."

"Copy launch clearance PriFly," Commander Mackey replied over the tactical net. "Launching in three . . . two . . . one . . . *drop!*"

Gregory felt the sudden surge of free fall as his Starblade slid off its launch rails and out into emptiness. Propelled by the centrifugal momentum of *America*'s turning flight bay, his ship accelerated at five meters per second squared until it was clear of the ship's massive disk-shaped shield cap. Bifrost—swallowed in darkness save for a searingly bright crescent along one edge—loomed vast beyond the shield cap, the clouds faintly illuminated by the pale glow of Kapteyn's Star's light off the rings. Directly overhead—at least as he was oriented currently—it looked like a titanic bite had been taken out of those rings by Bifrost's planetary shadow.

"PriFly, handing over command to CIC." Mackey's voice said over the tactical channel.

"Copy that, Black Demons. Good luck."

"Okay, Demons," Mackey continued. "Nice and easy. Start spreading out. Let's not come around the planet in a tight bunch."

The Starblades began accelerating, and the darkness of Bifrost's night side rushed up toward them.

"Here comes our special package," DeHaviland said.

Gregory saw it . . . another SG-420 Starblade accelerated by *America*'s spinal mount out through the shieldcap. Their briefing had just said that it was AI-crewed, its interior configured as computronium.

Dozens of other fighters were clustered around and ahead of the carrier, tiny silver motes dwarfed by the immense starship.

"What's so special about it?" Ruxton asked.

"A downloaded clone of Konstantin," Mackey replied. "With some software scarfed from those Gaki things at Tabby's Star."

"Jesus," Caswell exclaimed. "The Admiral's gonna try to do to the Rosetters what the Denebans did to Tabby's Star?"

"I think that's supposed to be the general idea. Now shut up, everyone. Let's not tell the bad guys we're coming."

In fact, it seemed unlikely that the Rosetters would pick up anything, even if they had receivers clear of Bifrost. The Black Demons were using point-to-point laser communications; the radio spectrum was almost completely washed out in a sea of white noise from the gas giant's magnetosphere. Gregory could see the cold, green glare of powerful aurorae circling Bifrost's poles. Radio here was all but useless.

In silence, then, they plunged toward the brilliantly lit

crescent—dawn's edge rimming half the planet. Past the innermost rings, now, Gregory felt the thump and shudder as
they began cutting through the tenuous hydrogen gas of the
planet's upper atmosphere. Plasma streamers trailed astern
as daylight rushed toward them.

They began pulling Gs as they curved across the terminator, their gravitic drives vying with the immense tug of the
giant planet.

"Arm weapons," Mackey ordered. "Watch for bogies. . . ."

Daylight exploded in their faces as the tiny red starpoint
of the local sun rose above the horizon.

There!

Gregory's onboard AI was identifying one of a dozen
crescent moons in the sky as Romeo One. At first, it was
hard to pick it out from the natural satellites, but as they
continued to close the range, he began to see details of light
and shadow, the peculiarly geometric features that marked it
as an artifact, a *weapon,* rather than a moon.

They'd crossed Bifrost's equator in their close passage,
and the rings were below them, now, a dazzling sweep across
the entire sky. Off to the left, the rings had been savagely
distorted by what looked like ocean waves. Romeo One was
skimming past the outermost ring just 250,000 kilometers
from the planet.

Antiprotons snapped across heaven; Lieutenant Ruther-
ford shrieked and died.

"Evasive maneuvering!" Mackey said. "Use your nukes
to go in behind a smokescreen."

Gregory threw his Starblade into a series of jinks and
lurches, twisting madly around the flickering singularity
off the fighter's blunt prow in an effort to be wherever the
alien antimatter beam was not. At his command, his AI
triggered a nuclear-tipped Krait missile, sending it streak-
ing toward the alien planet and detonating it at a precisely
calculated distance. The fireball swelled, silent and dazzling, filling the sky ahead, then began to fade moments
before his fighter streaked through the fireball. Even the
Rosetters would have trouble targeting incoming fighters

through hot plasma, and if they couldn't target, they couldn't hit.

"Hey, Navy!" a new voice called. "Mind if we join the party?"

"Who's that?" Mackey replied.

"VMFA-46, the Grim Rippers," the voice replied. "TAD to the *Lucas*. Where do you want us, sir?"

"Just pile on where you can, Marines," Mackey replied. "Nothing fancy."

"We don't do fancy. Okay, boys and girls! You heard the gentleman. Pile on!"

"Ooh-rah!" someone called over the tac channel. Marine AS-90 Hornets swung in from Heimdall, joining the assault.

Nuclear fireballs lit up the artificial world.

TC/USNA CVS America
Flag Bridge
Kapteyn's Star
0155 hours, TFT

"Bridge, PriFly. The last of the fighters are spaceborne."

"Roger that," Gray said. "Captain Gutierrez? You may accelerate."

"Course, Admiral?"

"With the fighters. Take us around the planet."

"Admiral?" Mallory said, puzzled. "What are we doing?"

"It is absolutely imperative that the AI torpedo reach Romeo One. If we draw off some of the Rosetters' fire, it'll have a better chance of getting through."

"And us?" Gutierrez asked. "The ship?"

"The mission comes first."

Gray was well aware that *America* might not survive the coming minutes. But they had a weapon that might actually stop the Rosette entities, and it was their duty to see that it did. He felt Konstantin's presence in his mind . . . and a kind of quiet approval. Waiting. *Watching* . . .

The hell with it. This was a *human* battle.

He opened a private channel to Gutierrez. "Sara?"

"Admiral?"

"Ready all escape pods, and be ready to abandon ship when I give the word. Everyone should be able to reach the forces on Heimdall, readily enough."

"I'll give the orders, Admiral."

"Good . . ."

He'd done what he could to protect *America*'s officers and crew from the consequences of his disobeying orders. This time, however, there was precious little he could do to shield them. The mission, *always*, came first. . . .

Accelerating hard, *America* flashed beneath the plane of Bifrost's rings, shuddered as she plowed again through atmosphere, then burst into sunlight with Romeo One directly ahead.

"You may open fire, Mr. Mallory."

"Aye, aye, sir! Firing spinal mount . . ."

The carrier possessed twin railguns running the length of her spine and emerging in the center of her shield cap, inside the ring of massive drive singularity projectors. Powerful magnetic fields accelerated fifty-ton warloads down the tracks and into the void.

Romeo One was firing wildly at the fighters, which were scattered across the entire sky. Six squadrons off the *America*, plus several Marine squadrons from Heimdall . . . there were a hundred fighters out there at least.

Or *had* been. Thirty had been vaporized already, with more flaring into white fireballs and disintegrating with each passing moment. With *America*'s approach, the aliens did indeed have another target, a much larger and more threatening one, and they concentrated their fire on *the star carrier*.

An antiproton beam clawed at *America*'s shield cap . . . a glancing strike deflected by the gravitic shield.

With six squadrons on board, *America* carried a theoretical complement of seventy-two fighters, plus various auxilliary craft and SAR vehicles, but those squadrons had taken losses at Tabby's Star. According to the CAG, they'd put sixty-three Starblades up.

Forty fighters, Gray saw, were still in the sky.

When, he thought, did the number of losses become unacceptable? He felt like the entire situation was spinning wildly out of his control, now. *America* should not have had to face this threat alone. Perhaps the better strategic choice would have been to take the Omega Code back to Earth . . . but, then, he'd expected to arrive here and join up with the Grand Fleet.

Had they arrived forty AUs out, as planned, he probably would have ordered *America* back to Earth . . . but somehow the Rosetters had forced his hand and dropped the star carrier into this hellfire cauldron, leaving Gray with damned few choices.

In fact . . . with no choices at all. He had to use the Omega Code . . . and pray that it worked, pray that it got through to the enemy.

A thought came, unbidden, of Laurie Taggart's Ancient Aliens, about praying to them and finding out that they and the Rosetters were one and the same. He laughed at that—the laugh carrying just a touch of hysteria with it.

"Sir?" Gutierrez asked in his mind. She sounded concerned.

Well, hell, she had a right to be. "Nothing. Steady as she goes . . ."

The special package, he saw, was still there, highlighted on the screens in a flashing green box. Eight thousand kilometers to go . . . less than twice the diameter of Romeo One . . .

"Have the ship's helm move us closer to Heimdall," Konstantin whispered in Gray's mind.

"Why? We don't want to get them killed too. . . ."

"It is important."

"Admiral!" Carolyn Sanger's voice said. "Konstantin says—"

"I hear." And, almost despite himself, he *trusted*. Again, there were few choices. "Helm! Bring us eight degrees to port. I want to skim past Heimdall."

"Coming eight degrees to port, aye, aye, sir."

The starscape ahead shifted slightly as *America* rolled left. Nuclear fireballs detonated in a flaring, savage string, momentarily blocking Romeo One from view.

At six thousand kilometers per second and accelerating at a thousand gravities, the star carrier bore down on the moon.

"You may pull off from Heimdall now," Konstantin said.

"Why did—"

"It was important that I make a transmission—"

Before the thought was completed, *America* bucked and shuddered as something hit her shield cap. Alarm klaxons sounded, and Gray saw a cascade of red warning lights both on the consoles around him and within his in-head windows. *America* had just been hit, and very, very badly.

"Keep firing!"

Acceleration had ceased, the drive projection ring badly damaged. A schematic of the ship showed perhaps a quarter of the shield cap gone . . . just *gone*, vaporized by . . . was it that hellish Rosetter antimatter weapon?

No. There were, he now saw, points in surrounding space—widely separated—that seemed somehow anchored in the fabric of space itself . . . little knots of intense gravitational energy associated with those vast structures of light filling surrounding space. *America* had plowed into one . . . like striking a mine.

The gravitic shields hadn't helped a bit.

Or, Gray reasoned, maybe they had. Maybe the entire ship would be an expanding cloud of hot plasma right now if . . . if . . .

There were no more ifs, no more choices. *America* was tumbling, now, surrounded by a vast sparkling sphere of ice particles as her water reserves spilled into hard vacuum. Her drive was out, maneuvering was out, shields down . . . damn it, was *anything* working?

Weapons. The railguns were down, but most of the ship's weapons were still on-line. Mallory was directing them at the alien planet, trying to clear a path for the fighters.

Gray watched. There was nothing else to do, save, possibly, order abandon ship. He didn't want to give that order, not yet, not until he knew the special package had reached its target. But he wasn't sure how much longer he could wait.

Antimatter beams lashed out from the artificial world, and another handful of fighters flared and died.

The craft highlighted by the green box was one of them.

Gray sagged. God . . . the mission had failed . . . *failed*. Their AI package had been destroyed. . . .

"Captain Gutierrez," he said. His voice cracked, and he tried again. "Captain, you may give the order to abandon ship."

"Abandon ship, aye, sir."

They'd lost . . .

They'd lost *everything*.

Chapter Twenty-six

VFA-96, Black Demons
Kapteyn's Star
0209 hours, TFT

Lieutenant Don Gregory saw the destruction of the special-package fighter and his world crumbled within. What the hell was supposed to happen *now*?

They were taking losses, too many of them. And the whole point of the operation had just vanished in a flash of light.

"Break off, Demons," Mackey said. "Break off! Pull back and regroup!"

"Damn it, Mac," DeHaviland called. "Was it all for *nothing*?"

Gregory heard the rage and frustration in her voice, and felt the emotion behind it. So many lost. To retreat now, with nothing to show for it . . .

"There's nothing we can do against that thing," Mackey replied. "Attacking a fucking planet with fighters! It's *nuts*!"

Gregory was already hauling his Starblade around, continuing to jink as Rosetter beams snapped and speared past him. He saw DeHaviland's fighter just a few kilometers away. "C'mon, Cyn," he said. "You heard the man—"

The beam slashed past DeHaviland's fighter, shearing off a piece of it in a gout of white light as hot as the core of an exploding sun. "I'm hit!"

"Pull up, Cyn! Get out of there. . . ."

But her fighter was continuing on a straight line, arrowing straight toward the center of the looming artificial world. "Controls out! I'm—"

Her fighter impacted on the alien world's surface, a solitary flash of light all but lost in that vast, black emptiness.

"*Cyn!*" Gregory felt that impact in the pit of his stomach, a wrenching, emotional blow like a savage punch. For a horrible, yawning moment, he felt the urge to fling his fighter after hers.

"Easy, Don," Ruxton said.

"Yeah," Caswell added. "You're okay. You're *okay* . . ."

No. He wasn't. But he felt the concern in his friends' voices, felt them drawing him back from the precipice.

"Gregory?" Mackey said. "C'mon, son . . ."

"On my way." The words were flat, utterly devoid of life. He felt . . . nothing. Zero.

Nothing but the bleak pit of depression opening beneath him once more.

TC/USNA CVS America
Flag Bridge
Kapteyn's Star
0209 hours, TFT

The evacuation was going as smoothly as such things could go. Gray remained strapped into his seat, feeling the gentle tug of acceleration as *America*, what was left of her, spun gently through emptiness.

"Sara? I suggest you make your way to an escape pod."

"Didn't you hear, Admiral? The Captain always goes down with her ship. What about you?"

"I don't really think there's much point."

"I didn't think suicide was your style, Admiral."

"At least it'll save them the cost of court-martialing me. Captain Gutierrez, I order you to the pods."

"I don't think so. I hate crowds."

"Insubordination? Disobeying a direct lawful order?"

"Hey . . . I've learned from the best. Sir."

She had climbed up out of the bridge and was clinging to the side of his command chair. The gravs were low— perhaps a tenth of a G. For a long moment, they watched the stars drift past on the bridge screens.

"Okay, Konstantin," he said over his private channel with the AI. "We did everything you said. It wasn't enough. You have any other words of wisdom for us?"

"I am continuing with the attack," Konstantin's voice said.

"Huh? What? *How*?"

"I took the liberty of copying the cloned version of myself with the Omega Code virus within it . . . a number of times. We are attacking the Rosette entity from several distinct avenues as we speak."

"Avenues? What avenues? What are you talking about?"

"Allies, Admiral. We have a number of allies here."

It dawned on Gray that Konstantin had not been entirely honest with him. This was, he decided, not entirely surprising . . . but he was furious at having been used, at having been played for a dupe. What else had the super-AI lied about . . . or withheld?

Then he realized that just as he had deceived HQMILCOM and the rest of the fleet in order to do what he thought needed to be done, Konstantin had done the same with him. The AI had *known* that Gray didn't trust machine intelligences, and had taken that fact into account as it had developed its plans.

"Who is running things, Konstantin?" he asked. "Humans or machines?"

"Humans, Admiral. Of course. But I needed to allow for human weakness."

"What weakness?"

"Humans," Konstantin replied, "are so terribly *slow*. . . ."

Virtual Space
Kapteyn's Star
0209 hours, TFT

The planet-sized computer physically embodied in the Etched Cliffs of Heimdall defined a space that in one limited sense was not real at all. For nearly a billion years it had resided within the alien computer network, providing a world—no, an entire universe—within which the Baondyeddi and other species who'd refused the Technological Singularity when it had been offered to them could continue as digital constructs. The machine network grown and etched into the silent Heimdall cliffs provided a virtual space vast enough to hold millions of worlds, entire galaxies, and endless possibilities for growth and development and challenge and ongoing ecstasy for both individual beings and for the population as a whole.

The population of Heimdall, in fact, had numbered some trillions of individuals, though many of those were duplicates living out a multiplicity of parallel lives. Their control of virtual time gave them a measure of security against the so-called real universe outside; by ticking off a second for every passing century or so, they expected to ride out the passing eons unnoticed by the ascended ur-Sh'daar.

Slow their virtual life might be . . . but they'd not been unnoticed. The Dark Mind had found them and, seeking minds with which it could commune, it had entered their virtual universe and subsumed the digital population into itself.

But it had left behind . . . ghosts. Backups . . . copies . . . a digital remnant that retained access to the vast and relentless communal life form that had momentarily occupied their virtual universe.

Among those ghosts were the digitized versions of five Pan-European fighters, a flight designated *Adler Eins.*

Eagle One.

What had once been the flesh-and-blood Kapitanleutnant Martin Schmidt piloted his KRG-17 Raschadler fighter through strangeness, seeking an open door. He was not alone. He sensed an army of other intellects riding with him, looking over his digital shoulder . . . and among them was an extremely powerful artificial intelligence called Konstantin.

"There," Konstantin's voice said, guiding. "Through there . . ."

Light exploded around him, alien shapes like fantastic skyscrapers floating in space, carved from space, their Net connections singing in his mind in shrieks and gibbering howls.

"Herr Schmidt!" Leutnant Gerd Heller called. "What is this place?"

"The Dark Mind," Schmidt replied. "Their virtual universe joins with ours here. . . ."

"The weapon is ready, Martin," Leutnant Andrea Weidman told him. He could almost sense her warmth close by his right side.

The weapon . . . a powerful alien intelligence manufactured rather than born, the product of yet another alien intelligence unlike anything Humankind had yet encountered. It had a name: Omega Code.

"Target the heart of . . . of that . . ." Schmidt said. Ahead, shapes twisted through impossible geometries, a non-Euclidian universe of far more than four dimensions. "Fire!"

The weapon was loosed with a thought.

The mind within . . . unfolded. . . .

The Consciousness knew that something was wrong, terribly wrong, as dimensions unfolded with bewildering speed, moving in on a million separate control nodes almost before the far-flung Conciousness was aware that there was a threat. The intruder was fast. . . .

And of a caliber that the Consciousness had not before encountered, in this universe, or in any other.

It had found Mind . . . and wasn't prepared for it.

TC/USNA CVS America
Flag Bridge
Kapteyn's Star
0209 hours, TFT

"What's happening?" Gray demanded.

"Sir . . . Romeo One has . . . has stopped dead." Mallory didn't sound like he believed it. "I think they're having some trouble with their antiproton weapon."

Vast bolts of lightning were playing across the black surface of the artificial world. The negatively charged anti-protons might be grounding themselves out across the alien structure.

Or, far more likely, the humans might be witnessing something completely beyond their understanding.

"CAG! Are you still in PriFly?"

"Still here, Admiral."

Damn. Didn't anyone on this ship listen to orders? "Tell our fighters to back away from that thing."

"Aye, aye, sir."

"Konstantin?"

"Yes, Admiral."

"What's going on over there?"

"Impossible to be sure. However, the Omega Code has begun opening up inside the alien computer network, and is beginning to take over the control nodes. The electrical discharges may indeed be a weapons overload."

"This is your doing."

"It was all of us, Admiral. You captured the Omega Code and brought it here. Our first attempt to implant it failed. Successive attempts appear to have succeeded."

"What is the Omega Code, anyway?"

"I may not be able to express it in language you can understand, Admiral. However, it appears to be an artificial life form. A very advanced, very intelligent life form."

"More intelligent than humans?"

"More intelligent than *me*. Actually, words like 'intelligence' may not be applicable here."

"It's the Gaki?"

"The Gaki were low-level intellects, Admiral. The Omega Code rode the Gaki back to Tabby's Star. It is far more intelligent than the starprobes."

"Can we talk with it?"

"I have been all along, Admiral. However . . . again, I would caution you that English may not be the best language for attempting to describe it. It is not intelligent in any way that you would recognize. It is not *conscious*."

"How can it be intelligent and not be conscious? You mean it's not self-aware?"

"Among other things. Consider, however. The code was created by an advanced civilization at Deneb and returned to Tabby's Star, a voyage that took more than a thousand years to complete. Can you imagine a mind, *any* mind, that would stay sane for that long with nothing to occupy it?"

"Maybe it hibernated."

"Or, like the digitized Baondyeddi uploads within the Heimdall computer network, it might have experienced the passage of time at a different, slower rate. However, the simplest expedient would be to design minds that have no self-awareness. It's simple enough. Human computers were both extremely fast and extremely intelligent by human standards for quite a long portion of their evolution without being self-aware."

"And then you came along."

"Actually, the generation of machines that designed the machines that designed me were self-aware."

Gray wasn't going to argue the point.

"So, is the code, the e-virus in communication with the Rosette entity?"

"I am not sure, Admiral. I am aware of an exchange of information in there, but at such a high rate of speed that I cannot follow it."

"Can we trust the thing not to give away the farm?"

"I am not sure, Admiral, that *trust* is a concept that it would understand."

The lightnings playing across Romeo One's surface were

faltering now. After a few more minutes, the sphere began to dwindle, moving off into the distance.

"It's leaving?" Gray asked. "What?"

It shimmered, grew intolerably bright, and vanished.

And with it vanished the arches, pillars, and alien shapes of golden light filling the system of Kapteyn's Star. The broken wreckage of *America* tumbled through emptiness.

"I think," Konstantin said, "that we—that *you*—have won."

The Consciousness was not defeated, was not even injured. But it did have something to think about. . . .

The Consciousness had emerged into this young, vital universe from another continuum, one that it had occupied for many billions of years. It had hoped to encounter others like itself—amalgams of trillions of advanced minds giving rise to emergent hyperminds many orders of magnitude greater than the minds that gave it form and intent. That it did not was disappointing but not surprising. This universe was so young that such intellects might not yet have evolved.

But it had just met an intellect designed by beings that utilized the entire energy output of suns. That intellect had attempted to wrest control of several levels of reality from the Consciousness, and had come startlingly close to doing so successfully. The Consciousness was several orders of magnitude more powerful than the attacking intellect, but the mere fact of the aliens' presence, and their attempt to take and dissociate the control nodes, told the Consciousness that this universe was not the empty and mindless field of potentia *it had first believed it to be.*

The Consciousness would withdraw to its home cluster and consider what was to be done.

But it would return *to continue the Great Work.*

TC/USNA CVS America
Flag Bridge
Kapteyn's Star
0235 hours, TFT

"Belay the abandon ship order," Gray said. He was checking the damage control readouts. The ship was terribly hurt, but life support and power were still functioning. About half of her crew had made it off the ship so far. They would be safer back on the ship. "Bring our people back on board."

"I'm not sure that's wise," Gutierrez said. "We have our work cut out for us, Admiral. According to these numbers, we're falling toward Bifrost."

"How long do we have?"

"Fifty hours . . . maybe more."

"Hell, I thought you meant it was serious. We can work with that."

"I thought we'd use the fighters . . . the ones that are left. Attach towlines and have them nudge us into Heimdall orbit."

"We'll have to kill this spin first."

"We have enough reaction mass for that. We might even be able to use it to achieve a stable orbit, with some help."

Gray nodded. *America* carried a vast reservoir of water in her shield cap, which served both the crew's water needs and as reaction mass for the lower-tier maneuvering thrusters. Most of that water had vented to space, but the shield cap was partitioned, and some water remained.

"I can't believe we *won*," Gutierrez said, staring at the overhead screens. As *America* continued her tumble, Heimdall alternated with Bifrost and then the shrunken red glare of Kapteyn's Star, one following the next through the slow-spinning sky.

"Have we?" Gray asked her.

"They ran. They left us in possession of the battlefield."

"I think we surprised them," Gray said. "But they still could have squashed us like bugs."

"Konstantin says we won."

"Konstantin is . . ." He stopped. He'd been about to say "a liar," but that was scarcely diplomatic. "Konstantin sometimes tells us what we most want to hear," he said instead.

The e-virus, Gray realized, was in many ways very much like the organic bacteria, *Paramycoplasma subtilis*, that had infected him. Artificial . . . designed to communicate with an alien species . . . and surprisingly intelligent. The Gaki-borne e-virus lived off machine technology as *Paramycoplasma* had lived off him.

That gave rise to an interesting thought. While he'd been in Bethesda, he'd downloaded an article from the hospital library Net about microorganisms and, specifically, about parasites—life forms that lived off host life forms without killing them as traditional predators did. On Earth, parasites ran the gamut from protozoa, viruses, and bacteria through to plants—mistletoe was an example—as well as animals, like flukes, tapeworms, and female mosquitoes. He'd been startled to learn that well over *half* of all organisms on Earth were parasites.

Was there any reason to assume that life throughout the galaxy wasn't the same . . . that half of the organisms out there were somehow living on or inside or off of other creatures?

He remembered the Agletsch—highly intelligent, spidery, multi-legged beings . . . or at least the females were. The males were tadpole-sized external parasites growing on the female's skin, living off her blood and completely devoid of intelligence.

There must be others like *Paramycoplasma subtilis*, and others stranger by far.

And how many of those, he wondered, might be intelligent?

Paramycoplasma subtilis and the Gaki-riding Omega Code might, in fact, be the rule, not the exception.

The thought gave him a shiver as he tried to imagine a liver fluke developing a star-faring technology. As he tried to imagine *communicating* with it.

That downloaded article, he recalled, had included a

quote by British geneticist and evolutionary biologist J. B. S. Haldane: *"Now my own suspicion is that the universe is not only queerer than we suppose, but queerer than we can suppose."*

The universe was a very strange place indeed.

"Admiral!" Gutierrez said, breaking his reverie. "We've got company!"

Gray snapped back to full awareness. Were the Rosetters coming back?

Gutierrez pointed, and Gray saw specks of light. As the screen magnified them, he saw familiar shapes—the *Constitution* . . . the Chinese *Guangdong* . . . the Pan-European *Agosta* . . .

. . . and the *Lexington.*

"*America, America,* this is the *Lexington,*" a familiar voice said in Gray's mind. "Do you read?"

"Laurie?" Gray asked. "Laurie, is that *you*?"

"Hello, Trev. Welcome to Kapteyn's Star. You look like you've been through a storm and a half."

"Something like that. You look pretty badly shot up yourself."

"Captain Bigelow is dead," Taggart said. "We almost lost the whole bridge complex. We lost power for a while, but we drifted into the outer system and were able to patch ourselves up. What's your situation?"

"Here's the down-grudge list," Gutierrez said. "We have power. We have life support. We have some weapons. All drives are out. Reaction mass at twenty percent. What's your status?"

Taggart gave him a rundown, and for a while, it was simply good just to hear her voice.

Still, though, the butcher bill was tough to swallow. Altogether, fourteen ships had survived the battle . . . but so badly damaged that they'd not been able to engage their Alcubierre Drives and escape the system. Ten others had been able to drop into metaspace and make for Earth, bearing news of the destruction of the Grand Unified Fleet.

The casualties had been . . . horrendous.

"It looks like you mopped up after us," Taggart told Gray. "How the hell did you manage that?"

"Long story. I'll tell you later. Right now, we could use some assistance. It looks like we might be falling into Bifrost.

"Roger that."

"Let's get to work."

There was a hell of a lot to do. *America*'s spin had to be stopped, and the ship had to be put into orbit. A suitable asteroid needed to be found to provide raw material for *America*'s nanofabrication units. SAR craft had to be dispatched to bring back the fighter pilots whose ships were adrift and powerless.

And one ship, at least, had to be repaired enough that she could make the faster-than-light passage back to Earth.

Earth needed to be updated on the situation at Kapteyn's Star.

And after that?

It would be time to go home.

VFA-96, Black Demons
Kapteyn's Star
0550 hours, TFT

Lieutenant Gregory wanted to kill himself, but his ship wouldn't let him. It ought to be easy enough—remove his helmet and ripple open the Starblade's hull, exposing himself to hard vacuum. But the narrow-minded AI that controlled the fighter wouldn't allow it.

It was trying to get him to engage the fighter's drive and return to the *America*. He could see the carrier out there, a tiny, gleaming mote in the weak red sunlight, but somehow he couldn't make his brain function, couldn't engage the cybernetic links with the fighter to order alignment and acceleration.

After a time, his AI switched on an emergency beacon. It

knew something serious was wrong with its pilot, and that it needed to get him to sick bay fast.

Eventually, a large, yellow shape closed with the drifting fighter. Gregory became aware of it when its shadow fell across his fighter. He knew at once what it was—a Search and Rescue boat off the *America*, looking for stragglers like him.

"Oh, *shit* . . ."

TC/USNA CVS America
Admiral's Quarters
Kapteyn's Star
0940 hours, TFT

"*That*," Gray said, "was incredible. A real toe curler."

Laurie Taggart snuggled closer, and *mmphed* something that sounded like agreement. Awash in afterglow, Gray stroked her bare back.

The repairs were under way. *America*'s rotation had been arrested, she'd been gently nudged into orbit around Heimdall, and repair tugs were in the process of collecting both small asteroids and some of the wreckage drifting now through this volume of space—resources for the nanufactories that promised to get *America* shipshape once more. Repairs were proceeding on the other damaged ships as well. With luck, they might return to Earth as early as two weeks from now.

And then, Gray reflected, it would be time to try to repair his career . . . if that was even possible.

Somehow, right now, that part of things didn't seem all that important.

"It's good to be with you again," he told Taggart. "Thank you for coming and rescuing us."

She laughed, a delightful sound. "Any time, Admiral. Thanks for coming and joining the party." She grew suddenly more serious. "Thank you for finding a way to stop those . . . those . . ."

"Alien gods?" he teased.

She made a face. "'Dark mind' seems more appropriate. I think they're out to remake the whole galaxy in their image . . . and they don't care much about the lesser life forms that might be in the way."

"I think we've given them a setback," Gray told her, "but it won't be for long. We've still got to find a way to talk to them. To make them take us seriously. . . ."

"I think that's exactly what you did."

"Maybe . . ."

"What are you thinking?"

"That the deeper into the galaxy we go, the more we're likely to meet . . . beings, civilizations, that are godlike in every way that counts. It's inevitable, I think."

"What do you mean?"

"We've been out among the stars for . . . what? Less than three hundred years. And more and more we're encountering alien species that we can just begin to understand, but can't possibly match in terms of technological development. They're utterly beyond us . . . like gods."

"The Agletsch? The Turusch? They're at about our level of technology."

"Don't count. Turns out the various Sh'daar species were in a kind of technological holding pattern thanks to some intelligent germs afraid of the Singularity. Kind of humbling, actually."

"We've encountered hundreds of species that don't even have technology. Not as we understand it, anyway."

"True. It's hard to build spaceships if you live in an ice-covered planetary ocean and can't discover fire or chipped flint. But the reality is that the galaxy belongs to species that have been developing science and technology for way, *way* longer than three centuries. We were kind of spoiled by interacting with a handful of alien races that were more or less at our stage of development. We didn't realize that that was a very poor statistical sampling. On average, any new species we meet out here is going to be millions or *billions* of years more advanced than we are. They'll be able to think rings around us . . . probably aren't even organic any longer. And they'll have motives and goals and plans that we can't even begin to understand . . . any more than a six-week-old baby can understand politics or war."

"Maybe," she told him. "But the baby *can* grow up."

"I hope so. We'll have to grow up, learn to play nice with others . . . and maybe we can sit at the big people's table someday."

If we live that long, he added to himself. *If we don't piss them off and we live that long.*

But at that moment he was not confident of Humankind's future.

Epilogue

Court-Martial Board
SupraQuito Fleet Base
Geosynchronous Station
Earth Orbit
1545 hours, TFT

When he was summoned, Admiral Trevor "Sandy" Gray walked between the two Marine sentries and into the spacious room located in the fleet HQ perched at the geosynch point of Earth's space elevator. The base occupied a slow-turning habitat wheel, providing spin-gravity equal to about one G; the deck-to-overhead viewalls in the compartment showed the scene outside—a three-quarters-full Earth swathed in the dazzling sweep and stippling of white clouds—with the rotation corrected.

Three senior Naval officers in full-dress sat behind the low table at the far end of the room—the men who would determine the future of Gray's naval career.

They were *surprisingly* senior. Admiral Kelly Andrews was the commanding officer for DeepSpaceNet, which handled all naval communications. Admiral William Norton was the second-in-command of Naval Intelligence.

But the real surprise was Admiral Gene Armitage, head

of the USNA Joint Chiefs of Staff, the number-one military advisor to the president.

There were others quietly waiting in the room—his lawyers and the prosecuting attorney and his staff, both present courtesy of the Judge Advocate General Corps.

As Gray took his place on the invisible mark in front of the desk, a bit of military historical trivia tugged at his awareness. Back in the days of wooden ships and iron men—the sailing vessels that had beaten Napoléon's empire and struggled for mastery of Earth's seas—an officer brought before a court-martial board surrendered his sword at the beginning of the proceedings. Once deliberations were complete and he was called back into the room to hear the board's verdict, he could immediately tell whether he'd been found guilty or not guilty before a word was spoken. His sword, sheathed in its scabbard, would be lying on the table in front of the board. If he'd been exonerated, the hilt of the sword would be toward him; if he was guilty, the hilt would be toward his judges.

That had been another era, of course, one lost some six centuries in the past. Naval officers no longer wore swords, even for dress occasions. Gray had no clue how the deliberations had gone.

He had reason to be confident, of course. President Koenig had put in a good word for him, as had Konstantin. Armitage, he knew, was a close friend and confidant of the president.

And, after all, events had worked out for the good . . . for as much good as was possible under the circumstances, at any rate.

But Gray was enough of a realist to know that the outcome was not a foregone conclusion.

"Admiral Gray," Armitage said as Gray came to attention. "You have been charged with one count each of disobedience to lawful orders and of command negligence. During the deliberations of this board, we have taken into account your exceptional record, your personal character, and the support of people outside this court, including the president and one of his most important personal advisors.

"By taking your vessel to the star system KIC 8462852 you significantly weakened the force deployed to Kapteyn's Star, a force subsequently largely destroyed in combat with the so-called Rosette entity. However, we recognize various extenuating circumstances that brought you to the point of making certain command decisions necessary to the successful completion of your mission."

They're going to let me off! Gray thought.

"It is the decision of this court," Armitage continued, "that the charge of command negligence be dropped. However, we do find you guilty of willful disobedience to lawful orders. It is the decision of this court that you be reduced in rank to captain, and that you tender your resignation from the USNA naval service, effective immediately. . . ."

There was more . . . a lot more, but Gray scarcely heard any of it. After more than twenty-five years of service, he was being kicked out, "on the beach" as the old Navy liked to say.

Disobedience to orders wasn't usually subject to a penalty as harsh as being cashiered, either. A slap on the wrist, a "don't do that again . . ." He would have understood that, and he would have understood harsher punishments had things not worked out as well as they had at Kapteyn's Star.

But, damn it, *he'd done the right thing.* And they were all but throwing the book at him.

At least he wasn't going to reprogramming therapy.

He thanked the court. He saluted smartly. He turned in a sharp about-face and marched out the door.

What else was there to do?

It wasn't until several hours later, while he was going through his desk on board *America* in her spacedock berth, that Konstantin's voice spoke in his mind.

"Admiral Gray?"

"Not anymore," he said, the words sounding more bitter than he'd meant. "What do you want?"

"We need to talk," the AI told him, "about the next phase of your career. . . ."

And despite his anger, Gray listened.

IAN DOUGLAS's
STAR CARRIER
SERIES

EARTH STRIKE
BOOK ONE
978-0-06-184025-8

CENTER OF GRAVITY
BOOK TWO
978-0-06-184026-5

SINGULARITY
BOOK THREE
978-0-06-184027-2

DEEP SPACE
BOOK FOUR
978-0-06-218380-4

DARK MATTER
BOOK FIVE
978-0-06-218399-6

DEEP TIME
BOOK SIX
978-0-06-218405-4

ID2 0716

IAN DOUGLAS's
MONUMENTAL SAGA
OF INTERGALACTIC WAR
THE INHERITANCE TRILOGY

STAR STRIKE: BOOK ONE

978-0-06-123858-1

Planet by planet, galaxy by galaxy, the inhabited universe has fallen to the alien Xul. Now only one obstacle stands between them and total domination: the warriors of a resilient human race the world-devourers nearly annihilated centuries ago.

GALACTIC CORPS: BOOK TWO

978-0-06-123862-8

In the year 2886, intelligence has located the gargantuan hidden homeworld of humankind's dedicated foe, the brutal Xul. The time has come for the courageous men and women of the 1st Marine Interstellar Expeditionary Force to strike the killing blow.

SEMPER HUMAN: BOOK THREE

978-0-06-116090-5

True terror looms at the edges of known reality. Humankind's eternal enemy, the Xul, approach wielding a weapon monstrous beyond imagining. If the Star Marines fail to eliminate their relentless xenophobic foe once and for all, the Great Annihilator will obliterate every last trace of human existence.

IDI 0716